Dead Sight

Also by Glenn Chandler

FICTION

The Sanctuary

The Tribe

Killer

Savage Tide

NON-FICTION

Burning Poison

GLENN CHANDLER

Dead Sight

Hodder & Stoughton

First published in Great Britain in 2004 by Hodder and Stoughton
A division of Hodder Headline

1 3 5 7 9 10 8 6 4 2

A CIP catalogue record for this title is available from the British Library

ISBN 0 340 82877 3

Typeset in Plantin Light by Palimpsest Book Production Limited,
Polmont, Stirlingshire

Printed and bound in Great Britain by
Clays Ltd, St Ives plc

Hodder Headline's policy is to use papers that are natural, renewable
and recyclable products and made from wood grown in sustainable forests.
The logging and manufacturing processes are expected to conform
to the environmental regulations of the country of origin.

Hodder and Stoughton Ltd
A division of Hodder Headline
338 Euston Road
London NW1 3BH

For Alan and Christopher

Contents

PART ONE
Death

I

Detective Inspector Steve Madden logged the call at 3.37 p.m. The time was irrelevant. The call probably was too, he thought. Brighton was full of clairvoyants who, every time there was a major crime, peered into their crystal balls or swung their pendulums over maps or did whatever else it was they did, and contacted the police with information regarding psychic visions of red barns and black cars and mossy ruins.

But Lavinia Roberts wasn't just any clairvoyant. She had once been the most famous psychic in Brighton. In her glory days, she had been 'Vina the Mystic', with her booth on the Palace Pier a shrine to the many stars and celebrities whose futures she had beheld. Lavinia Roberts was an original. With her long, dangling earrings, her gypsy head square and her long scarlet-painted fingernails, she played the part to perfection. Those days were long gone, however. It was Madden's perception that she hadn't been seen for almost a decade. He had entertained the thought occasionally that she might be dead.

She wasn't. She was on the other end of the phone. She had asked for him specifically. And she sounded drunk.

'Mr Madden, I'm so glad you were there to take my call,' she said.

Madden thought, rather cheekily, that she should have foreseen that.

'What can I do for you?' he asked.

'It's very difficult to explain over the telephone. I'm sure you understand. But it is about a crime. Perhaps more than one crime.'

Jasmine Carol glanced at him from her desk through the open

door of his office. She had taken the call first and had been prepared to deal with it. You just didn't put clairvoyants through to your superior. In her experience, unless you were desperate for a lead in a case, you took down the information and stuck it at the bottom of the pile. But as soon as she had spoken the name of Roberts, her superior had gestured to the phone and to his lips in a manner that suggested to her he might have gone momentarily mad.

'Which crime would this be?' Madden drew on his reserve of patience.

'Oh,' she said, 'It's not a crime that's happened yet. It's a crime that might happen.'

'I see. And where might this crime happen?'

'That's just it. I don't know. But when it does happen I'll know about it.'

'You'll know about it?'

His reserve of patience was beginning to run quickly dry.

'Yes, I'll know about it. Maybe I'm not making much sense but it is important, very important, and I think you ought to know about it too.'

Madden let out a great sigh. Jasmine smiled and tossed her head from side to side. He knew what she was thinking. That it served him right for taking the call.

'Miss Roberts, your information about this crime, can I ask you where you obtained it?'

'From a reading. And not just from that, but through the young man I gave a reading to. It's hard to explain over the phone. Perhaps I can come and see you?'

'I have a better idea, Miss Roberts. Why don't I come and see you?'

'That would be very nice,' she said.

'Where are you living now?'

'The top of Southover Street. Hanover. I haven't moved.'

He felt a sudden *frisson*. He had grown up just round the corner from Southover Street, and knew the house at the top of the hill where Lavinia Roberts had, and apparently still, lived.

'I'm over in Queen's Park. Just about ten minutes' walk away. I'll come over tonight if you like.'

'That would be wonderful.' She seemed almost ecstatic. 'That would be so wonderful. I do hope you don't think I'm wasting your time, Mr Madden.'

'Of course you're not wasting my time.'

Jasmine arched her eyebrows.

'I'll see you tonight. Shall we say eight o'clock?'

'Eight o'clock will be fine.'

Madden put the phone down. Jasmine looked down at her desk, pretended that the last five minutes hadn't happened, and that even if they had, she hadn't payed the slightest bit of attention. Madden called her into his office. She walked in blithely, as though she didn't have a clue regarding what he wanted to talk to her about. She was the only female Hindu officer on the Sussex force. They had worked together for over a year, and possessed a bond born of the fact that most of the time he treated her like any other member of the human race while most of the time she treated him like a detective inspector. The newer intakes of police officers, fresh from training college, had political correctness and human rights drilled into them as though they were training to become lecturers in Humanities instead of coppers. The old school, of which Madden had reluctantly to admit he was one, were a different breed. Jasmine hadn't always been lucky in her working relationships, but with Madden she had struck gold.

It perhaps had something to do with the fact that their relationship had occasionally drifted from the professional. Not recently. Some weeks had elapsed since she had last spent the night at his place, and neither had talked about it since, as was their unspoken rule. Sex between the ranks was not encouraged. But sex, as it always did, transcended rank and everything else that stood in its path.

'You wanted to see me, sir?' she asked casually.

'Yes, Sergeant Carol. Regarding that conversation—'

'What conversation?'

'The one I just had, every word of which you listened to, and is now carved on your memory.'

'Oh, *that* conversation.'

'It didn't happen. Okay?'

'What didn't happen? The conversation you just had or the one you didn't have?'

'You've got the message.'

She was an exercise in colour coordination. She normally was. Madden assumed that she spent most of her salary on clothes. Today was beige day. Beige jacket, beige trousers, white blouse that hinted of beige, beige shoes, all of which blended in with her coffee-and-milk complexion and perfectly white teeth to a point that was almost obscenely perfect. She was the only DS he knew who wouldn't look out of place on the front cover of a Sunday newspaper supplement with the words *cool chic* next to her.

'I just wouldn't want it to get around that I take clairvoyants seriously,' he explained. 'It might invite comments.'

'I never thought for one moment you took them seriously,' she said.

'This one's different,' he told her.

'How different?'

'We grew up in the same neighbourhood. Haven't seen her for ten years. To be honest, I wasn't even sure she was still alive.'

'Maybe she isn't. Maybe the call came from beyond the grave.'

'Do you see me laughing?'

'No sir.' She looked at him closely.

'Then I wouldn't wait for me to do so.'

'Sorry.' Jasmine sat down and crossed her legs. Clearly the conversation which had not taken place had now taken place after all, and she felt less constrained in talking about it. Besides, she was curious. 'I take it from your conversation she wants to talk to you about a crime that hasn't happened yet?'

'It would seem so.'

'I didn't know we worked on the *X Files*?'

'She was famous in her day.' Madden ignored her second jibe.

'Celebrities and politicians used to visit her on the pier. Having Vina the Mystic read your cards or look into her crystal ball had a kind of cachet to it. Bit like appearing on *The Morecambe and Wise Show*. I understand she even got invited to a Royal Garden Party and met the Queen.'

'Dare I ask – did you ever?' she inquired.

'No. Of course not.'

It was a lie, but he wasn't going to go into that now.

'Wonder why she asked for you specifically?'

'Puzzles me too. I didn't think she remembered me.'

'Well,' she said, 'I hope you'll tell me all about it tomorrow.'

'I might,' Madden informed her. 'Then again I might not. It depends how serious you can be.'

'Oh, I can be very serious.' She added, with her one of her sweet smiles, 'And discreet.'

She left his office. Madden went to the window and looked out. Over the red-brick roof tops of the houses he could just see the Channel, the sun reflected upon the water in a long belt of burning silver. Sometimes he checked himself for taking it for granted, his good fortune in being a detective inspector in that city by the sea. Brighton had its fair share of oddball and eccentric characters, of which Lavinia 'Vina the Mystic' Roberts was only one. It was a puzzle, unless she had a phenomenal memory, as to why she had singled him out.

What was less of a mystery, at least to him, was why he had taken her call. He wouldn't under any normal circumstances have intercepted such a conversation. Jasmine undoubtedly thought he was going soft. But Madden had good reason for wanting to see Lavinia Roberts again. And an hour out of his life that evening was hardly going to be an ordeal.

He would go back to that house at the top of Southover Street at eight o'clock and relive an episode from his boyhood that he had, until that afternoon, almost completely forgotten.

2

He had been twelve years old. Far too young in that pubescent state for hormones to be racing round his body at the speed which they would when he reached fourteen. He had grown up in the Hanover district of Brighton after his parents moved from the East End of London, his father to set up a tattooing business in the town. Hanover wasn't seaside or fish and chips or donkey rides. All that, of course, was only a walk or a bus ride away. Hanover was community, a tightly-knit area of small terraced Victorian houses in the north of the town, the main artery of which was Southover Street, a steep hill down which he had fond memories of riding in a box cart, and even sledging during the one real winter he could recall, when the snow swept up against the fronts of the houses in packed drifts and no vehicle could negotiate the tortuous climb.

Age twelve was not, however, without its stirrings. The seminal influence in that department was the regular sightings he would have of a girl more than twice his age who lived 'up the hill', a pretty girl with raven black hair and huge earrings that swung as she moved. A good time girl with a never-ending (it seemed) string of boyfriends, who was always standing around on the street corner with one of them, or riding around on and getting on and off motorbikes. What mesmerised that twelve-year-old were her knees and her long stockinged thighs, always amply and generously exposed beneath a short skirt. Her name was Lavinia Roberts.

For a time, their orbits never crossed. He was a kid, she was a young woman in her prime. In the local shops, he would blush if she so much as looked in his direction. But it was always those knees to which he was in thrall. It was rumoured that her mother was a witch and came from the highlands of Scotland. Then his own mother told him that she 'told fortunes' with a crystal ball and tarot cards. Madden wasn't sure when he learnt that Lavinia Roberts also 'told fortunes'. She was said to have 'the gift'. The girl who bewitched him for reasons he couldn't even understand had other powers he was equally incapable of fathoming.

Then one day a schoolfriend told him that Lavinia Roberts had looked into her crystal ball for him and told him that his mother was dying. Three weeks later she was dead.

Whether or not the prediction was a safe bet didn't matter. Madden found himself concocting a plan by which he could at last meet the girl who conjured up such delights in him. It wasn't so much a plan as a brave step. One night he simply knocked on her door and asked if he could have his fortune read. It worked. Lavinia Roberts invited him in.

To this day, Madden couldn't remember what she told him. He wasn't even sure why that ball of glass in front of her should hold information about his future. Twelve-year-olds rarely thought beyond the present anyway. What he was there for was to gaze at those legs. As she sat across the table from him, her hands caressing the crystal sphere, Madden stared downwards, his young heart thumping with the thrill of it all, his blood dashing round his body, his mouth watering with excitement.

And then it was all over. He walked out into the street. A chill wind was blowing up it and almost blew him over. Home was just around the corner, and so too, it seemed, was adolescence. It was one of the last times he saw Lavinia Roberts. He heard she had got married and moved away. Then, years later, she was living back in Brighton and working on the pier and calling herself 'Vina the Mystic'.

By that time Madden had married, and was living in the adjacent district of Queen's Park. His orbit and that of Lavinia Roberts had never crossed again.

Yet here he was, all those years on, standing at the top of Southover Street, about to knock on a door and remembering that formative day in his life. It was a strange feeling. The house was the same, but it was brighter than he remembered, white-washed and with red frames surrounding its bay-fronted window. Up a narrow side passage was a wooden gate that led into a tiny courtyard garden. There was no bell, just a brass lion's head that made a clattering din.

And suddenly, in the doorway, stood Lavinia Roberts.

The sight of her took Madden aback. She looked far older than he had imagined she would. She could only have been in her sixties, but her face was heavily lined and white as chalk. Her lipstick was ruby red and crudely applied. A tiny smudge of it had adhered to a few hairs above the corner of her mouth. Her hair was not so much white as a pale, sickly yellow. Between the forefinger and the middle finger of her right hand dangled a cigarette. But what struck Madden most were her clothes. They were twenty years too young for her, including the skirt which stopped well above her knees. Incredibly, those legs had retained their perfect shape. They were still the same legs that had stirred in him such a yearning when he was a boy. Older, more veiny, but still recognisable as those of the swinging sixties girl who had opened this same door to him nearly four decades ago.

'Miss Roberts?' he said.

It struck him that those were the exact words he had used as an awestruck youngster.

'Mr Madden, come in.'

Inside, Lavinia Roberts's house was like Aladdin's cave. Lamps were everywhere. A profusion of little objects, mementos, photographs cluttered up the ornate antique sideboard which filled up one entire side of the room. A huge rococo and gilt mirror hung above the fireplace. Some of these Victorian terraced houses had had their smaller front rooms knocked into one large room more suited for modern living, but Lavinia Roberts's remained unaltered.

Some things he didn't remember. Some things he did. It was strange how, after a period of over thirty years, tiny details of domestic geography still played with his memory, tugging at a thread here, a thread there. It was as though this room, or parts of it, had somehow been etched on his mind. Like the doorway through into what he knew was the back kitchen. It was there, he recalled, she kept a card table with a purple cloth pulled over it, the very table at which he had sat. The door was closed. Even so, it was as though this house at the top of Southover Street had been pickled in aspic, awaiting his return.

'I've been here before,' he said.

'I don't recall.' She looked at him quizzically.

So she hadn't remembered him. Why should she have? He was only a kid.

'I lived round the corner.'

'I think I remember you,' said Lavinia Roberts.

'I knocked on your door once to have my fortune told.'

She gave a throaty laugh.

'All the kids knocked on my door to have readings. At one time or another. It got around, I think. Have a seat.'

Madden sat down in an armchair that seemed to have been designed for a person half his size.

'Did it come true?' she asked him.

'Did what come true?'

'What I said. I must have said something.'

'I don't remember,' Madden confessed. 'I was twelve at the time.'

'Would you like a glass of sherry?'

It wasn't his favourite drink, but he had one because it seemed to fit with the occasion and the surroundings. Lavinia Roberts filled two large schooners to the brim. Her own overflowed as she drank from it. Her hand trembled.

He looked at her walls. They were festooned with photographs and press cuttings. Her glory days on the Palace Pier were well represented. There were pictures of her with pop stars and television celebrities and politicians. The most recent was at least fifteen years old. All were curled and faded.

'Why did you ask for me?' he inquired curiously.

'I'd read your name in the paper,' she said, guardedly. 'About that sad business.'

People he met referred to it in many ways. *That sad business* was just one of them. Whichever way it was referred to was painful. Some months had passed since his own son Jason had been brutally murdered. He had not yet got over it. He doubted that he ever would. But he had got on with his life as best he could. At least Jason's killer was behind bars and was likely to stay that way for a very long time. But it was the guilt that stayed with you. Madden had suffered his fair share of guilt – regret at not having known his son as well as he should. The circumstances were so painful that sometimes now he just shut them out of his mind. He wanted to remember Jason and yet he needed to forget him. He had not been the most perfect father, but then who was. *That sad business* hung over him sometimes like a shroud when he woke up in the morning. By the time he got to work, he would have cast it off. And then somebody would bring it up. Like now.

He changed the subject. He had learnt to do that.

'You said you had something to tell me?'

'I don't want you thinking I'm crazy.'

'I wouldn't be here if I thought that.'

'Most policemen would. Shortly after my marriage broke up, about twenty years ago, I offered my services in a murder case. I was regarded as a crank. Oh, they never tell you that to your face, but you can tell from the way they look at you. Times have changed now, of course.'

'In what way?'

'Well, people's minds are more open. You have this psychological profiling. What's that if it isn't looking into a crystal ball? Same thing, in my opinion.'

Madden couldn't quite see the connection. But he could see the direction she was going in.

'You got married?'

'Something I don't like to talk about. Just like there are things right now which you find painful to bring up.' She sat opposite him and briefly touched his knee. 'Yes, I married. One foolish stupid mistake I should have foreseen. At least I have a daughter from it.'

'Then it wasn't a stupid mistake.'

'If I could have had Natalie without the mistake of the marriage, I would have been happier.' Lavinia smiled. 'Oh, I'm Mrs Roberts now. Didn't want his name so I got rid of it. Call me Lavinia.'

She imitated the brushing off of a fly with the back of her hand. It was clear to Madden that even after twenty years the legacy of her marriage was pain and sorrow and distaste. He tried to imagine what kind of a love could still create anger after so long.

'You spoke about some crime?'

'This is where you'll think I'm mad.'

'Try me.'

'Well I gave a reading yesterday to a young man. And – well – it wasn't so much the reading, although that was part of it. I do *feel* things about people, you see, and I felt something very strongly about him. The best way I can describe it is by saying it was a feeling of great evil. And not just ordinary evil but *occult* evil.'

'Perhaps it was something to do with the clothes he wore.'

'I've had psychic gifts ever since I was a girl, Mr Madden. People's wardrobes don't distract me.'

He felt suitably chastised.

'Sorry. And please call me Steve.'

'That wasn't all I felt. I really did feel that this person was capable of murder. You know how there must be these serial killers out there who haven't killed anybody yet, but they're just waiting for the right moment. Well I felt this way about him. A serial killer in embryo I suppose is what I'm saying. Does that make sense?'

'You didn't get the impression he had actually killed anybody?'

'No. And if he had I'm sure I would have felt it. Murder is such a terrible act that it distorts the whole fabric of space around a person and I would feel it, like I have in the past. I've met a murderer.'

'Who was he?' Madden asked.

'Tony Mancini.'

Madden knew the name. Most older policemen in Brighton knew the name. Those who didn't certainly knew about the Brighton trunk murders. Although they had happened seventy years ago, they were still by far the most famous murders which had taken place in the town. Tony Mancini, a kitchen hand in a seaside café who had a criminal background, had battered his dancer girlfriend to death with a hammer and kept her rotting body in a trunk. Amazingly he had been found not guilty, but later he had confessed all to a Sunday newspaper. The second Brighton trunk murder remained unsolved to that day.

'You met Tony Mancini?' said Madden.

'Yes. When I was just a young girl. I didn't know he was Tony Mancini, of course, until afterwards, but I knew he had killed someone. He was a very wicked man.'

'Going back to this guy yesterday – who did you feel he might kill?'

'I didn't feel anything terribly strongly about that, but I did see a child. A very young child. I think it might be a child.'

'I don't suppose you can tell me what it was about him that gave you that – that feeling?'

'There was nothing about *him*. Nothing specific. You have to understand – I feel those things. As a psychic I'm very sensitive to anything spiritual in someone else, for instance if someone else has psychic abilities. And what I felt from this person was great evil. Great *spiritual* evil.'

'How did he contact you?'

'Through my advert. I still advertise in the *Evening Argus*. Though not as Vina the Mystic any more. She had her day, and a good day it was. Hated that word *mystic* but the customers liked it.'

Now, at least to her clients, she said, she was just plain Vina. She preferred it that way.

'I'm sure you understand, Lavinia, that there's very little I can do. Murders that have been committed are one thing, but murders that haven't – well, they're quite another.'

'I appreciate that.'

'But if you see him around again, around town or anything like that, or learn anything about him, let me know.'

'I will, but I've never seen him before.'

'Do you know where he lived? Where he came from? Was he local? A visitor?'

'I don't ask them anything about themselves. There's only what they volunteer. After all, if you're giving a true reading, you don't want to be influenced. But I did feel almost certainly he was local. And I got this feeling of authority, something like a military background. I saw marching, as though maybe he was a soldier or had been a soldier.'

'I'm not decrying your gift, Lavinia, but you'll know I'm sure that a soldier would convey certain mannerisms, a way of walking, an attitude. Subtle signs that you might pick up.'

'I know that,' she said. 'I also got the sense he was a leader of some kind. Perhaps a sergeant or a corporal. I saw him sending someone else into battle, ordering someone to fire and kill. I know that sounds a bit dramatic but I felt it quite strongly, this standing back while someone else did the killing.'

'A Gulf War veteran, perhaps?'

'I don't know.'

'Maybe if he was a soldier, that's what you saw. Him killing someone.'

'It wasn't in battle I saw him killing someone. What I *felt* was *evil.* I saw an evil murder for pleasure's sake. And this interest he had in the occult came over very strong. I feel uneasy now even thinking about it.'

She finished her sherry and poured herself another. Madden declined a second glass.

'Sorry I can't do more,' he said.

'Would you like a reading?' she asked.

'No thanks.'

'You were anxious enough all those years ago. What's changed?'

Madden didn't feel inclined to tell her the real reason for his visit 'all those' years ago.

'Nothing's changed,' he said.

'Have a reading while you're here. If you have any questions, ask them.'

Madden gave in. He wanted to look in that little back kitchen again, to be taken through the door. When you were scared of the future, you ran headlong into the past. And he was scared of the future. Scared that he would never get over Jason's death. Scared that he would. He wasn't sure which scenario worried him more.

She led the way, though she didn't need to. The card table was still there, just inside and to the right of the door with a little cane-back chair sandwiched between. She sat on it while Madden placed himself at the other side. There was a purple cloth stretched across the table, threadworn and frayed at the edges. Madden had no doubt it was the same one. The kitchen window looked out onto the little courtyard rear garden and an unpainted fence, a view that was equally and eerily familiar. It was as though a secret cupboard, full of forgotten objects, had been opened in his memory. The crystal ball was on a shelf just above the table. Next to it, incongruously, was a telephone which she unplugged.

'Don't want to be disturbed, do we?' she said.

She took a pack of tarot cards from the corner of the table. They were wrapped in a piece of scarlet silk. She opened the silk as though unveiling a gold bar.

'What date were you born?' she asked him.

Madden tried to resist feeling foolish. He'd always entertained the thought that this kind of thing was for suckers.

'Tenth of March,' he said.

'This card represents you. What we call the significator,' she said, plucking out the King of Swords and placing it on the table. 'Clairvoyants don't bother to do this any more, but I like to. My mother did it. So there you are. Shuffle the cards and divide the pack into three.'

Madden would never have made a croupier. He shuffled the cards as best he could. They were large and bulky. He divided them into three piles. Lavinia Roberts put the piles together and laid out a number of cards in a cross and four in a row.

'This is called the gypsy or Celtic spread,' she said.

It looked unpleasant. In fact, it looked positively grim. Madden began thinking he was right to have avoided this kind of nonsense. Right in the centre was the death card, with another card across it that depicted a despairing man on a bed with nine swords suspended over him. Above it was a picture of a man hanging by one foot. Elsewhere in the layout was a tower being hit by lightning.

'It looks very positive,' said Lavinia.

'I'm glad you think so.'

'The death card doesn't mean death. It means change, it means the end of one thing so that something else can begin. Crossed with the nine of swords, it means you've been through a great trial, but you will come out the other side. But you mustn't just think you'll get through it by being passive and just waiting for the pain to pass, you have to go out and physically fill your life with new things. That's what the hanged man is telling you: you're hanging around, you're waiting, you're in a state of suspension. You can't go on like that.'

She turned some more cards on to the cloth. Two showed golden cups. They looked like good cards. Madden wondered if these might be the bad guys.

'That's very interesting.' said Lavinia. 'I'm getting a lot here about new relationships. The two and the three of cups together is very strong. There's a reunion here, an old relationship that you thought was over but there are new, wonderful things to discover in it. An old friend perhaps. I see a woman who's been through torment, suffering a lot of problems, and you want to help her with them. Be very careful. Don't rush in. There's also a falling out, a man, I see an argument, quite a serious argument. A very serious difference of opinion. He's somebody you respect. Do you know who that might be?'

'I'm a detective. I often have differences of opinion.'

'I'm seeing a child. A young child. The child of a friend, or someone you know. The child needs to be careful, to be looked after.'

The last card she lay down was all he needed. It showed the Devil.

'This is you,' she said.

'Thanks.'

'It doesn't mean you're the Devil. This card tells me about all the guilt you've stored up inside yourself, all the negative feelings, that's what this means. You have to let go of them. You're judging yourself, and you're doing it too harshly. And you can't go on blaming yourself, Steve, you really can't. You have to get rid of all these terrible emotions. Whatever it is you're feeling about the past, you're not to blame. It's like you've chained yourself up too long. You have to break free of them.'

Madden felt he had heard enough.

'Do you have any questions?' she asked him.

'None that immediately spring to mind,' he said.

She gathered up the cards.

'I hope that helped you.'

'It was interesting,' Madden told her.

'Have another sherry.'

'No thanks. I'd really better get home.'

'There was another reason I asked for you,' Lavinia said. 'I get messages too. From the other side. Not often, just when there's something important one of them wants to say. And when he knew you were coming to see me, Jason spoke to me.'

'Lavinia, please, I don't want to hear any more.'

He sounded callous. He didn't mean to be. But she had opened a raw nerve. His son's death was too recent. Besides, he gave spiritualism as much credence as he gave tarot cards.

'Even if you don't believe, hear me out,' she begged him. 'Jason knew you were coming here. He wanted to tell me to let you know he forgives you and you must stop feeling guilty about his death. He loves you and doesn't want you to suffer any more.'

She rested her hand on his arm.

'I don't really know what to say.'

'He also said something about a red scarf. Look after the red scarf. Something like that.'

Madden felt as though a whole army had just trampled over his grave.

'Is a red scarf significant?' she asked.

'Yes. But how did you know about it?'

'I didn't.' She looked a little sheepish. 'I don't have these kind of messages very often, but when I do they're usually very strong and very important. Natalie says I should have developed my spiritualist powers more. Bit late for that. I'll be on the other side myself soon enough.'

'I should go,' said Madden.

As he went to the door, he did think of a question.

'The young guy you had such strong feelings about, what was his name?'

'He called himself David,' said Lavinia. 'But that wasn't his real name.'

'How do you know?'

'I'm a psychic. I know these things.' She shrugged dismissively.

'That's a lot to go on.'

'Take care of yourself,' she said, and pressed his cheeks between her hands. They were cold as ice.

Madden stepped out into Southover Street. Three boys were weaving their way effortlessly down the hill on rollerblades. The wheels made a loud grinding noise on the tarmac. The last time he had walked out of Lavinia Roberts's house he felt just as free. He could have skated down the hill then. This time he felt anything but free. Lavinia Roberts had been well meaning, he felt sure, but she had brought back too much, too soon. Perhaps it had been a mistake to go back. It usually was.

He went home. He had never got used to it, going back to an empty house where once there had been laughter. He kept Jason's bedroom door shut when he went out, but often opened it when he returned and sat on the bed. He did so this night. To have a son die was painful enough, but the fact that Jason had been murdered and might be alive had he been a more caring and better father was heartache beyond imagining. On the pillow – he kept the bed made – was Jason's red Arsenal football scarf. He lifted it, and caressed it with his fingers. It was the most poignant item of Jason's clothing he possessed. It took Madden back to the days when, as a father, he had felt no shame, no guilt. He remembered buying the scarf for Jason when the boy was ten, standing on the terrace with him and seeing it wrapped proudly round his neck, dangling down almost to his knees. It was far too long for him, of course, but that didn't matter. Nothing could be too long or too big or too grand for one's only son. The only things he hadn't given him were time and commitment and understanding, the things that would have truly united them in later life. You couldn't buy time like a scarf and wrap it round a neck. The pressures of his job had driven a gulf between them, a gulf in which Jason had grown up all too quickly and drifted away.

Madden wanted desperately to believe in the truth of what Lavinia Roberts had said. That Jason had forgiven him. But that was a problem. An almost insurmountable problem. Madden found believing in such things very hard. He dealt in evidence, hard, solid facts. Yet there was no way, he told himself, Lavinia Roberts could have known about that scarf.

No way that a detective's mind could fathom.

3

Madden had been embarrassed at first at the thought of joining a gym. There was the feeling that all the younger guys would look at you and size you up. He *had* let himself go and now he was trying to grab back, in as short a space of time as possible, what he had let slip away. But then you couldn't call the Leisure Club at the Brighton Marina a gym. It was, to the run down and the unfit and the crisis hit middle-aged, what places of holy pilgrimage were to the spiritually starved; a bright, modern, high-tech, state-of-the-art palace of health by the sea. You could swim in a half-Olympic-size heated pool which hosted Moonlight Sonata nights, when all the overhead lights were turned off and the moon and underwater lights bathed both body beautiful and un-beautiful. You could exercise while looking out to sea, or plant yourself at an aerobic station while watching TV with head-phones on, or have your body subjected to 3D silhouette technology which made you scream when you saw your arched back and protruding stomach in cold computer graphics, or simply sit in the cafeteria and pile all the calories back on. Madden had thought of getting himself a personal trainer. There was a girl called Jill he had his eye on, but that had more to do with the personal than the training, and a lot more to do with the middle-age crisis that had taken him there in the first place.

The embarrassment was gone now, of course. He was used to the routine of the workout now, and saw the same faces most times, and realised they, like him, were interested in nobody else but themselves. Now, powering away on the treadmill, he felt like one of the herd. All those little endorphins created in his brain made him feel good. He would walk out of there glowing.

During the summer he liked to swim in the sea, as his own father had done, but this was October. A body jaded by overwork and irregular meals cried out for heated pools and warmth and nurturing. On the way out, showered, towelled, dried and regenerated if not rejuvenated, he passed Jill. The personal fitness trainer smiled at him. He smiled back. She had the kind of body men must dream of when they're dying, he thought to himself. You didn't see many of them bouncing in and out of the icy water of the English Channel. Brighton was lively, but it wasn't California or Bondi Beach.

There was another reason he had joined the Leisure Centre – why were such hard, gruelling, sweat-inducing bodily exertions called leisure he wondered – at the Brighton Marina. It was to be near Clara, his ex-wife. She lived in the Marina Village now with a bald accountant called Clive who drove a BMW. If he was honest with himself, she was a big part of his reason for wanting to look after himself. The death of their son had brought them close together again. It seemed callous sometimes to think of it in that way, but it was one good thing which had come out of the nightmare. He wanted a new body for that relationship. Getting fit when you were pushing fifty was not a downhill sleigh-ride.

Clara was waiting for him at her art gallery and shop in the North Laine. The name was centuries old. Once there had been five Laines – West Laine, North Laine, Hilly Laine, Little Laine and East Laine. They were the names given to five great fields, now built over and part of the new city. The North Laine was the only one that survived in name. It was the trendiest part of town, a network of streets running due north and south and directly east and west. Avida Art was tucked up one of the latter, sandwiched between a café bar selling organic produce and an antiques emporium. It was bright, cheerful and accessible, the sort of gallery that sold pictures you wanted to put up in jazzy rooms and bright passageways.

'Hi,' he said, hoping he looked like the ex-husband who was leaner and fitter and altogether a different guy. 'How's it going?'

'*It* is going amazingly well, thank you,' Clara said breezily.

There was a time when his visit here would have generated a conversation so stilted as to be almost painful. He wondered how she did it. After twenty years of marriage, one of separation, four weeks of divorce and two years of remarriage to her passionless second husband, she looked much the same as she had always looked. She was still the same Clara he had married, for better or worse, even if it had turned out for worse. Her auburn hair and freckles still excited him wildly, and her figure was not much changed from her university days. A little more filled out around the middle, perhaps, but he was not one to complain.

'Thought we might drive out and have lunch at a pub in the country,' he said.

'Sorry. Can't take that amount of time away. There's a new veggie place opened just round the corner. I thought we might go there.'

'Veggie?'

'Don't look so horrified. I hear it's very good.'

'Not one of these rabbit food places, is it?'

'None of them are *rabbit food places* these days,' she chastised him gently.

'All right, mozzarella and roasted things in some Italian roll, then. Whatever happened to the good old greasy fry-up?'

'Try the motorway,' said Clara.

Stephanie came out from the back shop. Stephanie was round and short and mildly asthmatic and helped Clara run the gallery. She glanced at Madden and then turned away again, without a smile. Madden wondered if she disapproved of her employer meeting her ex-husband for lunch. Clara was, after all, a married woman again. But they were both adults.

'I'll be back in an hour,' Clara told her.

'Enjoy your lunch.'

Still no look.

'Am I persona non grata?' he asked her as they walked.

'It has nothing to do with her,' said Clara.

'How is the accountant from the black lagoon?'

'If you're going to persist in calling him that, then lunch is off. The joke's gone rather stale, Steve.'

'Sorry. I take it Stephanie wouldn't say anything to him? About us meeting?'

'Clive never comes to the gallery, never comes into Brighton. He says there's everything we can possibly want in the Marina Village.'

'You're joking.'

'No, I'm not. We have restaurants, bars, a supermarket, a car wash. What more could we want?'

'How about excitement?'

She frowned at him. He knew that puckered look between her eyebrows. Her 'frog' look of disapproval, he used to call it.

'We go up to London for that.'

'You also have a very nice leisure centre down at the Marina. I know because I joined it a few weeks ago.'

She stopped in her tracks.

'You joined *our* leisure centre?'

'Hang on, it's not *your* leisure centre. It belongs to anyone who wants to join.'

'But why did you join that one? I mean, there are lots of other leisure centres.'

'Why? Is Clive a member?'

Madden imagined that Clive entering a leisure centre, other than for a social drink, was probably less likely than a nun entering a brothel.

'Of course he isn't.'

'Then that makes it all right, then.'

They went into the restaurant and sat down at a table. It wasn't as bad as Madden feared. After working out, he felt like a steak, but had to settle for a vegetarian chimichanga. Clara had the same.

'The wine's organic,' Clara said, pouring.

'What does that mean? Someone's pissed in it?'

'Still the philistine.'

'Guess who I went up to visit a couple of days ago. Lavinia

Roberts. She used to be Vina the Mystic on Brighton Pier. She still lives up the top of the hill in Hanover, near where I grew up.'

'What did you go and see her for?'

'Just a bit of police business. Nothing important.'

'I didn't think you went out on police business that wasn't important?'

'She seemed to think she had a young man come to her for a tarot reading who was a serial killer.'

'That sounds serious,' said Clara.

'Trouble is, he hasn't killed anybody yet.'

It felt like old times. Meeting in town, casually chatting about some of the bizarre things that happened at work. The difference was she wouldn't be there waiting for him when he got home. She would be going home to await somebody else. It was not as difficult as it once had been, but it was still hard. If only he hadn't made so many mistakes. He could see it was his fault now. What had Lavinia said? *You can't go on blaming yourself.* He had been doing a lot of that, reflecting on his life, where he had gone wrong. It wasn't easy to stop blaming yourself when there was nobody else to whom you could attach it.

'She picked me to talk to because of what she'd read about the case in the paper.'

The case in the paper. Another euphemism. Like *that sad business.*

'What did it have to do with that?'

'I don't know. She's a psychic, she – said she had some message from Jason. You know how it is. Some people think they get messages from the other side.'

She stopped eating for a moment. When the subject of Jason came up, as it always did, their conversation automatically slipped into a different gear. This was not the usual way in which he came up however.

'I didn't think you believed in that kind of thing,' she said.

'I don't. Do you?'

'How long did we live together, Steve?'

'Twenty years.'

'And you still don't know what I believe in?'

'You might have changed. You might have been converted by Clive into living like a monastic Buddhist.'

She carried on eating again. She ignored the dig completely.

'I haven't. I suppose emotionally I want to believe in it, but intellectually I find it hard. Very hard.'

'Me too,' said Madden. 'She sounded so sincere, though.'

'She was giving you comfort. Us comfort. There's nothing wrong with that.'

'She saw a red scarf. Jason's red football scarf.'

'These people always see *something*, Steve.'

'How would she know about a red scarf?'

'Is that how she put it?'

'Yes.'

'*She* saw a red scarf. *You* saw Jason's red Arsenal football scarf.'

It was strange how, only seconds after talking about being comforted, they were rationalising it away.

'What was the message?' she asked.

'That I was to stop feeling guilty.'

'And have you?'

'No. And I don't see why I ever should, Clara. I was too preoccupied with my own problems to talk to him on a night in his life when he desperately wanted to talk to me. That was the last time I ever saw him. I know I can't have that night again, as dearly as I wish I could. I'll just have to live with it.'

'Steve, just talking to him might not have prevented his murder.'

'We'll never know that.'

'We'll never know a lot of things. Sometimes *I* was too busy to talk to Jason. It could just as easily have been me.'

'But it wasn't you.'

'Maybe,' said Clara perceptively, 'you need to believe that that message was real.'

'How can I? Jason's dead. I don't believe there's some hereafter where the dead hang around and pass messages back to the living. I'm a detective, I deal in material evidence. As you said, it's hard to grasp intellectually.'

'It obviously isn't hard for – what was her name?'

'Lavinia. Lavinia Roberts. Lavinia she liked to be called.'

'I sometimes envy people like that,' Clara said, thoughtfully. 'People who can believe – well, just believe. Without having to have material evidence.'

They ate in silence for a few moments, lost in their own thoughts.

'Clive bought a boat,' she said.

'Wonderful.'

'Thirty feet long.'

'Didn't know size mattered to you?'

'It's called the *Armadillo*.'

'That's an anteater, isn't it?'

'He wants us to go cruising on the Channel in it.'

'Very romantic. Doubtless stopping off at exotic Southsea and Portsmouth.'

'Isle of Wight actually.'

'Don't you ever miss us? What we had?' he asked.

She looked down into her glass of organic wine and made the contents gently swirl.

'I don't think of it any more,' she said.

'That wasn't the question I asked you.'

'Yes, I miss the good parts, I don't miss the bad parts, and you have to admit there were a lot of those.'

'There were a lot of good parts too.'

'I'm married again, Steve. We both burnt our bridges.'

'You burnt yours. Mine is still standing.'

'We shouldn't even be having this conversation.'

He felt like asking why she had met him for lunch in the first place but didn't. The truth was, they couldn't talk about Jason all the time. It hurt to do that and always led to bouts of self-incrimination, usually his. Talking about themselves lightened the mood. They used euphemisms of course. For the good parts, read sex. For the best parts, read sex, he thought. The worst parts had been those fuelled by tiredness, overwork, insecurity – his possessiveness, his jealousy, his crazy suspicions, the demons that drive love away. He had them under control now. For a long time, he had agonised over her, tortured himself with the thought of her sleeping with another man. Now he knew the truth, that she had moved from a highly sexed relationship into one which was devoid of it. Platonic almost. He could cope with Clive under those circumstances. Just. It still irked him that another man should now have access to the one person on the planet who had fulfilled his every need.

They finished lunch and he walked her back to the gallery. He wondered if he ought to kiss her. She anticipated his uncertainty.

'Well, see you around,' she said, opening the door in full view of Stephanie, demonstrating in her own sweet way that she had nothing to hide.

'Don't make it so rushed next time. Maybe when Clive has a business meeting that keeps him in London one night we could have dinner in a romantic little pub out on the Downs. Like we used to do.'

'That,' said Clara, 'was a very long time ago.'

'I know.'

'I want us to be friends,' she said.

'Okay. Friends is good enough for me.'

He wanted to say they owed it to Jason but he didn't. Jason had been devastated by their break-up but had taken his mother's side. He'd never blamed Jason for that. He would have done exactly the same in the boy's position. He liked to think that Jason would have wanted them to become friends again after his death, and even perhaps because of his death. It would make his death *mean* something.

'See you,' Clara said in her sing-song manner, and disappeared inside.

'Yes. See you.'

Their meetings and their lunches and their hastily snatched

coffees and drinks always ended that way. *See you* meant just that. Still, it was better than what he called his nightmare time. That period of his life was over, and he was grateful for it. To suffer the pangs of sexual jealousy to the extent that you sat outside your ex-wife's new house twisting the screws inside and making yourself sick and gorging on junk food wasn't the quickest way to a healthy body and mind. He had travelled some way since then. Not a long way, but far enough. He'd heard that the bodies of people under torture assimilated pain. He didn't know how true it was. But it was like that with him. The emotional trauma and psychological stress he had suffered over losing her seemed lessened now. The corners, once sharp and painful, were blunted. It was as though the poison in his veins – and sexual jealousy was just that, a debilitating, destructive, corrupting poison – had run to ground, done its stuff, cleared out.

Five days after he had been told of Jason's 'message' from beyond the grave someone stole a piece of his past that lay much further back, that was pleasurable, that afforded him great comfort, like all agreeable childhood memories did. Someone – it felt – had stolen a part of *him*.

'That clairvoyant you never had the conversation with, remember?' Jasmine nudged his memory, as though it needed nudging.

They had just come on duty and she had taken the call. He had never discussed that night with her. If he had, she might not have been so flippant.

'What of it?'

'The one who wanted to tell you about a crime that hadn't happened yet?'

'Lavinia Roberts is her name. What about her?'

'The crime has happened,' she said. 'Her daughter just found her. She's been murdered.'

4

There were people who found bodies and there were suspects. Sometimes the people who found the bodies were the suspects. Then there were relations. Relations were always suspects, and sometimes they were also the people who found the bodies.

And then there was Natalie Blance.

Madden first set eyes on her just as they were leaving the police station in John Street to head for Southover Street and the scene of the crime. It wasn't the prettiest building in Brighton. Police stations never were. A functional piece of seventies architecture, it served that function by being near the law courts. Natalie Blance was stepping out of a police car, accompanied by a sympathetic-looking woman police constable. She was in an obvious state of shock and distress. Madden knew that she was Natalie. He knew that she was Natalie because she looked the image of her mother.

In fact, Madden did the kind of double-take that made you question pretty well every law of the universe. It was not possible that Lavinia Roberts could have propagated such a perfect and captivating image of herself. And yet there she was, a young woman of about thirty, as slim as a wand, with a head of dark curls and large, saucer-shaped eyes that seemed to harbour the answers to secrets, and long, jet-black eyebrows. She was wearing jeans cut off above the knees and open-toed sandals. Madden would have recognised her from the knees alone. They were perfect copies of those that had driven him to knock on her mother's door many years before.

Madden walked up to her.

'I'm Detective Inspector Steve Madden,' he said. 'I knew your mother.'

'Did you?' she responded plaintively, as though a friend was all she sought at that time.

'A long time ago,' he qualified the remark.

'She's dead. I found her.' Natalie dissolved into tears.

'We're on our way up there now. This officer will make you comfortable, then we'll want to talk to you later.'

Natalie nodded. She understood. There was nothing so sobering as tragedy.

'I've got to phone my husband Richard,' she pleaded.

'That's not possible. I'm sorry. There's been a murder, and, well, there's a procedure we have to follow.'

She nodded again, as though she understood. And then she was gone, inside the police station. Madden climbed into the car with Jasmine for the short journey to Southover Street.

'Is there anything I should know?' Jasmine asked.

'Like what?'

'Like why we interview the suspect before viewing the crime scene?'

'Who said she was a suspect?'

'She found the body. She's the daughter. I spent two years in police training during which time we were told that most people are killed by someone within their own family. Or is there something I should know?'

'Drive on,' he said.

'You look like you saw a ghost.'

'Maybe I did. Maybe that's what I just *did* see.' Madden pulled his seat belt across and fastened it.

She gave him her don't-mess-me-around-or-I'll-make-life-difficult-for-us look and started driving.

'I'll tell you later,' he said.

'You'd better, Steve.'

'Is that a threat?'

'Have you met her before?'

'No.'

'You never told me what you discussed that night you went to see Lavinia Roberts.'

'You never asked me.'

'Was it important?'

'It wasn't then, but it may be now,' said Madden

It took them only a couple of minutes. Ever since finding the body of his own son, murder had ceased to be something Madden dealt with just as part of his job. He knew the pain, the agony, the terrible ripples it caused. Like the effects of a rock being thrown into a millpond. How had Lavinia put it? *Murder is such a terrible act that it distorts the whole fabric of space around a person.* Around the top of Southover Street, it had distorted and changed a neighbourhood. And shattered that precious memory of so long ago.

Along with the SOCOs they kitted up in the boots and one-piece suits that made them look and feel like space travellers but which were essential to avoid contamination of the crime scene. The back kitchen in which Natalie had found her mother was tiny, so there wasn't room for many at a time. While the medical examiner officially pronounced the victim dead and the SOCOs went about their job, Madden filled his time by talking to the police sergeant, Tony Collins, who had been first on the scene. Madden knew Collins. He was a passionate rugby player, fit as an ox, ran every marathon going and sailed in the Force regatta. Madden hated him. Nobody had the right to be so physically bloody fit. But then he was only twenty-five. Collins had been called to the scene and had found Natalie Blance wandering about looking dazed at the top of Southover Street with her mobile phone in her hand and in an obvious state of grief and shock. She had let herself in with her own key by the front door, as she always did, and discovered her mother dead in the kitchen. He was in no doubt that her anguish and distress were genuine. That was important. You couldn't understimate it. How a person behaved in the first seconds after discovering and reporting a crime was essential, family notwithstanding. If they were blowing up balloons and having a party, they were right up there at the top of the list of suspects. Even overt grief was inclined to make you suspicious. Madden was in a position to know. When he had discovered his son's body, not many streets away from where they were standing, he had left the crime scene and wept in the street. He had first-hand experience of bereavement and its immediate aftermath. He knew just how it toppled you, like a strong tree suddenly struck and felled by an axe.

It was time to step into the crime scene, following the same path as the SOCOs had through the small rear courtyard garden, now laid with duckboards to preserve any footprints, and by the door into the back kitchen. The Home Office pathologist, Dr Colleen Redman, was just coming out, clutching her notebook and pencil. She hadn't had to travel far. She had previously lived midway between London and Brighton but had now relocated to the latter, which meant Brighton murders were literally on her doorstep. Many knew her as Dr Colly, or simply Colly.

'Hi, m'duck,' she said in a cheery and unmistakable Nottinghamshire accident.

She didn't look like a Home Office pathologist, whatever they were supposed to look like, and Madden had met a few. Short, pudgy and sweet, with curly auburn hair and rosy freckles, she would have looked more at home running a craft shop and serving teas. She was a lesbian, which in Brighton and Hove was no big deal. She was also an out lesbian which was no big deal either. She shared a flat in Royal Crescent, a pretty exclusive address overlooking the sea, with her partner, a television producer called Rosy Porter, whose name appeared on the credits of a long-running TV drama about a woman pathologist who looked – and behaved – rather like Dr Colleen Redman, sexuality excluded. It was rumoured that the exploits of Colleen's television counterpart were based on her own experiences, but Colleen never saw the resemblance. In *Dead Men Tell*, her fictional counterpart, pathologist 'Sarah Mahoney', had affairs that never worked out, chased villains, fell off roofs, survived car crashes and exploding bombs, interfered in police investigations, was shot at regularly and occasionally had time in between to do the job she was paid for.

Nothing like that ever remotely happened to Colleen. It was

her job to work out how somebody died, when they died, and where they died. And then fill in the paperwork. It wasn't a dangerous job. Corpses didn't bite, only policemen, she'd once told Madden.

Straight away, Madden saw signs of a break-in. A tiny ivy-covered window next to the door had one of its panes smashed, and the glass lay on the inside on the kitchen surface. It wasn't up to him to tell the SOCOs their job but he knew right away that whoever had put their hand through that window pane had got ivy hairs on their sleeve. If that was basic crime-scene stuff however, the rest wasn't. In fact it was downright bizarre.

In the kitchen, where Madden had been only a few days before, Lavinia Roberts sat in her nightdress, slumped over her card table just in front of the door to the living room. Her tarot cards lay scattered about the table and she still had two in her left hand, the Page and the Knight of Wands. Three were laid out, in a row. They were Death, the Devil and the Magician. Her hair showed little trace of the nicotine yellow. Instead her curls were a mass of red blood. Where they had been parted by the blows, there were a few clear circular depressed fractures. Blood also lay in a pool, covering most of the cards. It had sprayed up onto the wall and dripped down the side of the chair and on to the floor. Madden noticed that the telephone receiver was off the hook. It lay on the floor under the table, streaked with blood, and someone had cut through the cable.

'Looks like she was doing a reading for someone,' said Jasmine.

'In her nightdress?'

Madden looked at the broken window from the inside. Whoever had smashed the glass had used a wire coat-hanger to slide the bolt along and gain entry. The coat-hanger lay on the floor, slightly bent for the purpose. Some of the shards of glass had been knocked on to the floor in the process. Broken glass travelled. It blew out and it blew back and Madden imagined that along with the ivy hairs some fragments had adhered to the killer's clothes.

What was really odd was that Lavinia had been facing the very door through which her assailant had entered.

'If she was sitting here doing a reading, she must have watched him break in. It doesn't make sense,' said Jasmine.

Jasmine looked at the three cards laid out on the table. Like most of the others, they had blood on them. Madden noted them too.

Death. The Devil. The Magician. In that order. Death showed a skeleton ploughing the ground with a scythe, the Devil depicted a horned and winged figure presiding over two cowed minions, while the Magician portrayed a flamboyant character with a wand standing at a table laid with the paraphernalia of his profession. Madden remembered Death and the Devil. Lavinia had dealt those for him.

'Appropriate,' said Jasmine.

'Probably don't mean what you think,' he said.

'You're an expert?'

'They're allegorical.'

'Of course. I'm forgetting. You've been here before.' She intoned her growing suspicion that he hadn't told her everything.

'I've been here twice,' he said. 'Once a very long time ago.'

They went upstairs. The Scene of Crime Team in their white oversuits and overshoes gave an air of unreality to a small terraced house, a feeling that normality had suddenly been invaded. Madden felt it more keenly than usual. He thought back to his visit. Lavinia Roberts pouring out the sherry, getting him to shuffle the cards. No hint then of the horror that was to come. Now, that life was reduced to forensic samples. Blood, brain, fingerprints, stomach contents, body temperature, fluids, DNA, fibres, photographs, bags and labels. He had seen it many times. The last moments of the victim's existence broken down into the component parts of an investigation.

He looked into her bedroom. The covers were pulled back. The light was on. She had, it seemed, been to bed that night. Why had she got up to do a reading? The one single most important component of any crime scene was the victim. More often than not, victims knew their killers. Sometimes victims even unwittingly attracted their killers. Madden wondered if this might be the case here. He tried not to take it personally, but in this case it was hard. Only a few nights ago, she had not only foretold his future but given him some unsolicited crumbs of comfort. The fact that he hadn't willingly received them was his problem, not hers. He could see that now. Now she had departed to that other world herself, if it existed.

They went back outside where Colleen was talking to the driver of the black van, or the CTS – Coroner's Transfer Service – as it was known. She came over when she saw them. She smiled at Jasmine and winked. Jasmine always appeared uncomfortable in Colleen Redman's presence, and on this occasion looked down at the pavement. Madden guessed why, but he saw no reason to complain. If anyone could fancy you, lesbian or straight, when you were kitted out head to foot at a crime scene, then that was flattery indeed.

Also, Jasmine had a thing about being called 'duck'.

'I would guess,' said Jasmine, 'that something like a hammer was used. I could tell from the shape of the fractures.'

'You want to do my job, duck, I'll do yours.' To Madden she said, 'Sweet, isn't she. But she's probably right. It's difficult to tell until the head's shaved but I estimate about a dozen injuries.'

Jasmine bristled. Neither did she like being called sweet.

'Any sign she resisted?' asked Madden.

'None at all. No defence marks on her hands. Seems she was just sitting there reading those tarot cards when somebody struck her.'

'Seems odd,' said Madden.

'Very odd.'

'Time of death?'

'We know,' Jasmine butted in, 'that it must have been the middle of the night because she got out of bed.'

'If you know, why are you asking me?' Colleen clucked. 'Time of death's an inexact science, but given the temperature of her body and the room, and that rigor's well set in and the fact she's in her nightdress at two o'clock in the afternoon, I'd say roughly about twelve hours. But like I always say, don't quote me on that. If a pathologist ever gives you the exact time of death, arrest her straight away because she did it.'

'Or him,' said Jasmine.

'If he's a bloke, yes.'

'Which means,' said Madden, 'that even on a conservative estimate she got up about two o'clock in the morning, or at least some time after she'd gone to bed, sat down to do a reading before, during or after someone broke in through the kitchen door, and just sat there while somebody killed her.'

Jasmine was remembering the cards clutched in her hand.

'Are we talking cadaveric spasm?' she asked.

'You might be, duck,' laughed Colleen. 'Nothing like a good cadaveric spasm.'

'I wish you would be helpful,' Jasmine told her straight out.

'It's an uncommon event. I'll consider it.'

'She used to be known as Vina the Mystic,' Madden intervened, changing the subject and putting Colleen in the picture. 'She had a booth on Brighton Pier for a long time. She was famous in her day.'

'Cor, is *that* who she was? I never knew,' said Colleen, open-mouthed. 'I went to see her once. When I was a girl. She was famous. I was with a crowd of friends and she told me all sorts of stuff about my relationships and who I was going to marry – got that wrong, didn't she. Never recognised her.'

'She changed,' said Madden. 'She had her day.'

'It happens,' said Colleen. 'You meet them in life and you meet them in death. Bet she didn't predict this, guys.'

'I'm not so sure,' Madden threw in.

'You see my TV counterpart last night?'

'Don't usually get time to watch TV.'

'She found a hand in a shark's stomach. Got shot at again. I keep saying to Rosy, pathologists don't get shot at, at least not once a week. But they never listen. Oh, and she fell in love with a policeman. That one won't work out, mark my words. Wish my life was as exciting. Well, better get this one back to the mortuary. Take it you guys have finished with her?'

'She's all yours,' said Madden.

Jasmine hated being called a guy as much as she disliked being called a duck. She also didn't like being kept in the dark. Madden had kept the lights off for too long and she was becoming aggravated.

'What did you mean, you're not so sure?' Jasmine asked him.

'About what?'

'When she said she betted Lavinia Roberts didn't predict this. You said you weren't so sure.'

'Just an idle speculation.'

'Well, let me make an idle speculation, Steve. One of the nice things about a partnership is the sharing. I get the very strange feeling there's a lot I don't know about. Do you want my theory?'

'I'd love your theory.'

'The break-in was staged. I can't believe she just sat there and watched it happen.'

'Neither can I. Unless it didn't happen like that. Lavinia told me something when I visited her a week ago that might have a bearing.'

Jasmine waited. He would have to put her straight eventually.

'In fact it was her main reason for contacting me. She said she gave a reading to a young guy that she had bad vibes about. Worse than that, she was convinced he was going to murder somebody. A serial killer in embryo is how she put it.'

Jasmine looked as nonplussed as he expected she would look.

'You never told me,' she said.

'I'm afraid I didn't take it too seriously. Would you?'

'I suppose not.' Then she asked him the question he hoped she wouldn't ask him. 'What did he look like?'

Madden shifted uneasily.

'I don't know, Jaz,' he confessed to her. 'I didn't ask her.'

'You didn't *ask*?'

'It's all very well having benefit of hindsight. What was I supposed to have done? Taken a description of the guy?

Circulated it? On the basis of what? A clairvoyant with too much sherry to drink who suddenly sees a murder that hasn't happened yet?'

'So what did you talk about?'

'This and that,' said Madden.

'How long were you with her?'

'About an hour.'

'And in that hour, you never asked her anything about this – mysterious sitter.'

'Are you interrogating me?'

'Yes.'

At least no one was pretending.

'So what *did* you talk about?' she repeated the question, folding her arms. He loved it. If he was a criminal, Jasmine Carol was the only officer on the force he'd willingly confess to.

'She gave me a card reading.'

Jasmine's eyes looked wide enough to envelop him.

'She gave *you* a card reading?'

'That's between us. If it gets out, I'll know where to find you.'

'And what was the reading? Or were the meanings of the cards too allegorical.'

'It was private.'

She turned serious. He was thankful.

'Do we know *anything* about this person? Did she drop any hints?'

'What are you thinking, Jaz? She saw her own murder? Or he came back and killed her because he somehow knew she'd seen deep into his soul? I don't believe in that stuff.'

'It may not matter what you believe in. Or me,' said Jasmine. 'The point is some people do. And some people believe in much crazier ideas. And some beliefs and delusions make people kill.'

Madden recalled his conversation with Lavinia Roberts. What he knew about her mysterious sitter was scarcely worth repeating.

'She got the feeling he was connected with the military. The army. She saw him standing back and sending someone else into battle. As though he was a corporal or something.'

'These were what? Just feelings?'

'Maybe not. A military guy gives off certain signals. A way of walking. Maybe it's nothing more than the haircut. But a clairvoyant picks up signals and uses them, maybe inadvertently. I can't believe Lavinia Roberts would have said that if he was a slouching layabout type with shoulder-length hair.'

'That's not a lot to go on.'

'She felt he was evil.'

'Great,' said Jasmine. 'We're looking for an ex-soldier with hate in his eyes. That could account for half the yobs on the south coast.'

'Not sure the British Army would want to hear you say that.'

'Maybe, but the super might want to hear *you* say it.' Jasmine glanced over his shoulder.

Madden spun round. Detective Chief Superintendent Ray Millington stepped out of a car which had just pulled up. Madden had never completely seen eye to eye with him. During the abortive investigation into his son's murder, Millington had, for a time, been more concerned with protecting the good name of the force than in finding Jason's killer. Madden had threatened to resign. It was only that action, he was convinced, that had forced Millington to take the steps which he had done – allowing Madden to search for the evidence which eventually led to the arrest of Jason's murderer and a conviction. Millington didn't like loose cannons in his force but for a while he had allowed Madden to become one, in spite of the fact that the resulting enquiry revealed the unsettling fact that one of his colleagues had arrested the wrong man who had later killed himself. That detective was still in denial and disgorging his bile on anyone who would listen, but as far as Madden and Millington were concerned, the brush was still stuck in the tar.

'Afternoon, sir,' said Madden.

A Methodist with a rather schoolmasterly gaze, Millington didn't mess about.

'You knew the victim, Steve?'

'These things get around.' He looked at Jasmine.

'They reach the ears of those entitled to know.'

'I didn't know her personally, sir. She was just somebody who lived here in my old neighbourhood. She called me out a few days ago with some information.'

'You know she used to be the most famous clairvoyant in Brighton?'

'I know, sir.'

'She helped me in a case once. Long time ago. Twenty years. Can't say she was very much help really, I got there without her in the end. But you have to show willing, don't you? What was the case she wanted to help you on?'

'It wasn't a case, sir.'

Millington looked a little put out.

'I see. When you said information, I naturally assumed—'

'It was about another matter entirely.'

'What matter?'

Madden stalled.

'Don't you think that *any* matter she asked you out about might be worth sharing, Steve?'

Madden shared it with him. Jasmine kept her mouth tightly shut as he recounted a tale of evil vibes, ex-soldiers and embryonic serial killers, but he was aware of her running her tongue along the backs of her pearly white teeth.

'I see,' Millington said at length. 'Rather strange. I never had one of them try and warn me of a crime in advance. Let's hope it doesn't set a trend.'

'What would you have done, sir?'

Madden had a good reason for asking.

'In the same circumstances as me?' he added.

'In the same circumstances? Probably filed it under fruitcake. Forgotten about it. After all, we've got enough crime to solve without ones that haven't happened yet.'

'This one's happened. Maybe it hasn't happened in the way that she predicted, but I don't think we can ignore the evidence.'

'Quite right. That's why I think you should put out a description of him. At least let's rule him out.'

As Millington walked back to his car, Madden said, 'I don't have a description of him, sir.'

Millington turned round on his heel, his face darkening.

'You *don't* have a description? I'm sorry, I thought you said you *interviewed* her?'

'I'm afraid I did what you would have done, sir. Filed it under fruitcake and forgot about it.'

He heard a suppressed chortle emanating from Jasmine. He wasn't sure that Millington didn't hear it.

'Your job is not to do what I would have done, it's to do the job *I* would have done *better*.' Millington put him in his place.

'Yes sir,' said Madden, with the appropriate air of penitence.

5

Madden had been looking forward to seeing Natalie Blance again. She was the perfect incarnation of her mother, almost too perfect. Wherever her father's genes had gone, they hadn't gone into her physical make-up. Maybe they had run deep inside, for he had yet to plumb the depths of this girl. He angled his chair slightly so he could look at her legs. She took a cup of weak tea, which she clasped between delicate white hands, but declined the milk. She was a vegan, right down to her sandals. Literally. Madden recognised the kind she was wearing. He had seen similar in a shop up the North Laine that specialised in vegetarian shoes. Such shops were very Brighton. So was the one she ran with her husband Richard, a New Age emporium and alternative therapy centre called Hubble Bubble. Madden had never been inside, but then he regarded himself as more of an old age kind of guy.

'I have to see Richard,' she insisted.

Richard was along the corridor in a separate interview room but she didn't know that.

'I'm afraid that's not possible,' Madden reiterated.

'Why is it not possible?'

'Because you're family. Next of kin.'

'You make us feel like criminals,' Natalie said, beating back a wave of emotion that came over her. Her voice cracked as she spoke. Her skin seemed anaemically white but she did not look unhealthy. Quite the reverse. A sheen of sweat on her bare arms defined small muscles. She wore a necklace of black beads around her neck, which she played with nervously. 'She was just sitting there when I walked in, covered in blood. I thought she was asleep at first, and then—'

She looked up at him, and at Jasmine, and ran her fingers over the black beads, and said, 'And then I saw her *head*!'

She was replaying the nightmare. Madden had done that himself. With Jason's death, where the mutilations had been both cruel and deliberate, he had played the tape over many times. Sometimes you felt it was on a loop. When you went to bed at night it was playing and when you woke up in the morning it was playing, and there was no off-button, not even a pause that you could control. If Natalie was faking or feigning, she was doing it well.

'Did you touch the phone in the kitchen, Natalie? Attempt to use it?'

She tossed her head from side to side in an exaggerated fashion. It was a clear 'no'.

'Were you close?' he asked.

'Very close,' she gave him a tearful assurance.

'That's a pretty necklace,' said Jasmine, relaxing her into what was going to be a necessarily unpleasant interview.

'Thank you,' said Natalie. 'It's a Hindu marriage necklace. Black beads are supposed to avert the evil eye.'

'I know,' Jasmine smiled.

'Are you a Hindu?' Natalie responded instinctively to the voice of friendship.

'I am a Hindu,' Jasmine told her. 'Though my father was English.'

'I've thought of becoming a Hindu,' said Natalie. 'Going on a pilgrimage.'

'My mother is in India now, with relatives,' Jasmine explained. 'On a pilgrimage to the temple at Pandharpur.'

Natalie crossed her hands over her chest as though cradling and nurturing a deeply held cherished ambition. Madden hated to bring her back round to the subject of her mother's murder. Hindu temples and pilgrimages could wait. Though he found it hard to see this vegan girl with her vegetable shoes and her desire to become a Hindu striking her mother down with a hammer in cold blood. But, as he well knew, strange dichotomies in human nature often existed. He remembered the case of little Bobby Brent, a four-year-old smothered to death by his dear doting white-haired Rottingdean grandmother because she was insanely jealous of the attention that her once devoted daughter had transferred to her offspring.

You just never knew what went on under the skins of families.

'Natalie, there are a lot of questions we need to ask you about your mother. I know it's going to be painful for you,' said Madden. 'But we need to know why your mother should have got up in the middle of the night to do a card reading. And in her nightdress.'

'That's simple,' said Natalie. 'She often read her own cards.'

Madden felt a *frisson* of horror. The thought of Lavinia getting up and dealing Death as her first card before being brutally murdered was almost unthinkable. And yet, it was a distinct possibility. Another was that she had actually been coerced into giving a reading for somebody.

'What was the routine? When somebody came for a reading?'

'Routine?' she looked perplexed.

'Yes. When people rang her up and she invited them to the house. Did they go through the house?'

'No. They always came through the courtyard into the kitchen. Never through the house. She kept the door to the living room shut and when they went out, it was through the back door. And then she bolted it. The lock broke years ago and she never had it fixed but she put this big bolt on instead. She always kept it bolted unless she had a client.'

'You're sure of that? She never changed her routine?'

'Never,' said Natalie.

'When did you last see her?' Jasmine asked.

'Only yesterday. About – about eight in the evening,' Natalie explained. 'I usually visit her about two or three times a week. More recently since—'

'Since what?' Madden gently pressed her.

'She'd been diagnosed as suffering from lung cancer,' Natalie expressed herself with considerable heartache. 'That's what is so horrible about this. She didn't have that long to live, she knew she was going to die. Why would somebody want to kill her?'

Why indeed, thought Madden. He recalled how cadaverous he had thought she looked, even in life. Lavinia must have known that she wasn't long for the world when she gave him that message from Jason on the other side. It made the message all the more poignant.

'When did she find this out?' he asked.

'About a month ago. She was terribly depressed about it. She just kept saying to me she didn't want it to drag out and be painful or to be hospitalised, and she hoped it would be quick.'

'Did she seem worried about anything else?'

'In what way?'

'Did she give any indication she was expecting a visitor last night?'

'No,' said Natalie. 'Why? Should she have?'

'Natalie, five days ago your mother asked me to come and see her. She described a reading she'd given to a young man. He was someone who disturbed her, gave her uneasy feelings. Did she talk about this person to you?'

Natalie appeared genuinely surprised. She shook her head.

'She said she got a feeling of occult evil from him. Is that something she would normally talk about?'

'She never told me about it,' said Natalie.

'I visited your mother on Thursday night. This person would have visited her on the Wednesday night. She never told you about a person she thought might have been a killer?'

Natalie's fingers went up to her necklace and grasped it. If it really did ward off the evil eye, she looked as though she needed every ounce of its power.

'What are you telling me?' she began to panic. 'Are you telling me she *met* the person who killed her?'

'She described him as a serial killer in embryo. She said he called himself David, but she didn't think that was his real name. She was concerned enough about him to phone me up and tell me about him, but what I don't understand, Natalie, is why she should keep such a thing from you. If you were as close as you say.'

Natalie shook her head again. She was clearly wrestling with something.

'How many times do you reckon you saw her between Wednesday night and today?'

'Three times.' Natalie didn't even have to think about it.

'And yet on none of these occasions she expressed the same worries to you that she did to me?' Madden indicated his surprise. 'Doesn't that seem unusual?'

'Very unusual.' She shifted uncomfortably in her seat and adjusted her skirt, and appeared actually put out.

'Can you think of any reason?' Jasmine gently probed.

'It might have been to do with Richard,' she snapped bitterly.

It was a sea-change in her manner. Interviews often worked like that. You thought the person you were questioning was one thing, and then it turned out they were something else. He had logged Natalie Blance as a quiet, sensitive, almost mousy young woman into all that New Age stuff, but the girl with the vegetable shoes had a bit of the wild animal in her.

'She hated Richard, you see. And Richard thought she was batty. And Mum thought that everything she told me got back to Richard, and so probably she decided if she told me about this person, I would tell Richard and he'd think she was even more crazy.'

Madden got the impression she was laying the blame quite squarely, if indirectly, at her husband's door.

'I take it,' said Madden, 'that relations between your husband and your mother were not good.'

'You take it,' she echoed.

And then it seemed as though she realised she had said too much. She was like a young woman who, forced to spend a night alone in a car in a dark lane, had suddenly become aware of two faces peering in at her through the windscreen. She retreated nervously.

'I didn't mean they were that bad,' she said. 'Richard wouldn't – I mean, he just wouldn't. You know. Do what you're thinking.'

'We're not thinking anything, Natalie,' said Madden. Which was a lie. 'We just need to know the truth.'

'It's a long story.' She looked as though she hoped they didn't want to hear it.

'We have plenty of time.'

'It goes back a year ago to when Mum used to work in our shop. Hubble Bubble.' Natalie unburdened herself. 'Mum used to do readings for customers in a room upstairs. We advertised her services at the counter. The trouble started when she began drinking. I don't know why she did it, but gradually it got worse, and – well – it wasn't very good for custom.'

'I imagine it wasn't,' Madden cut in.

He wanted to add something about toil and trouble but thought better of it.

'One day this lad came in,' said Natalie. 'He thought it was a bit of a game to have his cards read. Halfway through the reading, he told Mum he thought she was making it all up. Mum had been drinking and told him to – well, to fuck off. She ordered him out the shop. Then she – it's so painful recounting all this.'

'Don't look on it as talking ill of your mother, Natalie. Just look on it as telling us the truth.'

'She began insulting other customers. Telling them that she used to be famous on the pier. Which she was. Richard told her to leave and never to come back. Not even as a customer. He hasn't spoken to her from that day to this. She swore she would never set foot in the shop again.'

'And did she? Ever come into the shop again?'

'She came in a few times just to hang around, but Richard banned her again. She never came back. I do the readings in the shop now.'

So Natalie had the gift too. Like mother, like daughter, in many more ways than he at first imagined.

'What did Richard feel about your mother now?' Jasmine

brought the interview round to where it was inevitably headed. The discomfort set in. Natalie warded off the evil eye by twisting her necklace around and around.

'He resented me visiting her so often. He accused her of trying to poison my mind against him,' she said.

'Even though,' said Madden, 'she was dying of cancer? He resented you visiting her?'

Natalie looked away, bristled with what appeared to be a genuine grievance. She was angry with Richard for a multitude of reasons but she didn't want to land him in trouble. She was struggling between a desire to be frank and honest and her very real and natural fear that such honesty would incriminate the man she presumably loved.

'Have you studied much Hinduism?' Jasmine asked her.

'A little,' she said.

'Have you read the Taittiriya Upanishad?'

'No.'

'It says let your conduct be marked by truthfulness in word, deed and thought.'

Madden cleared his throat softly. He'd remember that one when next faced with some drug-crazed yob who'd just stabbed his mate in West Street on a Saturday night, or some drunken gay-basher. It sounded a useful book, if it was a book, the Taittiriya Upanishad. He could throw it at a few people.

'Richard didn't know. About Mum having cancer. I never told him,' she admitted. 'I thought it would just – make him cruel. Say cruel things. I couldn't stand that.'

'Did your mother try to poison your mind against him?' Jasmine asked.

'Mum was gentle and kind and loving.' Natalie defended her mother, her husband and ultimately herself. 'She wouldn't poison anyone's mind. She cared about people. And Richard wouldn't lift a finger to harm her because he cares about me.'

Madden could vouch for part of that at least. But then, he had only spent an hour in Lavinia Roberts's company, during which she had poured three full schooners of sherry for herself.

He didn't believe Natalie. There was poison in this family. He could practically taste it. It was bitter as hell.

'Sorry to have to ask you this question. But I'm sure you understand the reason for it, Natalie. About two o'clock this morning, where were you and Richard?'

'In bed. Asleep,' she said, as indignantly as though he had asked her if they'd had sex.

'Together? Or separately?'

'Separately,' came the one-word answer.

'Is that separate beds, or separate rooms?'

'Separate rooms,' she admitted, with more embarrassment than indignance. 'But Richard snores and I hear him. Now do you think you can find who killed my mother instead of wasting all this valuable time talking to me?'

'It's your valuable time too, Natalie,' Madden reminded her.

'I'm sorry,' she said. And then her eyes brimmed with tears. 'I've been through so much.'

She wiped her eyes. There was one final question.

'Did your mother practise spiritualism as well?'

'She went to the Spiritualist Church in Edward Street,' Natalie told him. 'She believed in it but she didn't practise it. Only sometimes—'

'Only sometimes *what*?'

'She would get messages very rarely from the dead, or so she said. When she did, she really believed in them. She reckoned that if she had trained herself to be a spiritualist more, she might have been more proficient at it. She thought it was a talent that was latent in her and which she'd never brought out. Why?'

Madden smiled casually.

'Just wondered,' he said.

6

Richard Blance was a very different character. He reminded Madden of a tranquillised squirrel.

'Any chance of seeing my wife?' he asked plaintively, almost ingratiatingly.

'Sorry. It'll have to wait.'

He couldn't see Richard Blance in vegetable shoes. He was definitely a leather soles kind of guy. Richard looked older than his years and was losing his hair dramatically. His eyes were tired, the skin around them sagged, and his cardigan, which bore all the hallmarks of being picked up in a charity shop, was not only ill-fitting but a mustard colour which clashed with everything else he was wearing. He was Mr-No-Clothes-Sense. Madden thought it would take a cleverer detective than he to work out how this man had ever got together with a long-legged, pretty New Age creature like Natalie. Then there was the matter of separate rooms, which Richard confirmed. Madden had a charge sheet already made out for that.

They lived in Hove, up near the railway station, in a district known as Poets Corner. Natalie, Richard explained, had read somewhere that it was bohemian and that was good enough for her. They had bought a house in Byron Street, which was sandwiched between Coleridge Street and Wordsworth Street, which had once been a corner shop and which Natalie had painted bright blue. As far as Richard was concerned, the whole area was a bit down-at-heel and he was waiting for it to become fashionable and for the house prices to rise. Richard Blance looked like the kind of guy who sat and waited for house prices to rise while everybody else went out and got a life.

'I need to speak to her,' he said. 'I need to see her.'

'You will,' said Madden. 'But first tell us about your relationship with her mother.'

There was nothing like launching straight in, he thought.

'What has she told you?'

'I want to hear it from you, Richard.'

Richard repeated at length and without reticence the story of how he had sacked Natalie's mother from the shop and barred her from entering, and how he had thrown her out of the shop when she had come back as a customer and upset the other customers. There was no need for the Taittiriya Upanishad here. If Richard knew what it was.

'When did you last see her? Or speak to her?' Madden asked.

'About six months ago. It was in the street. She crossed over to the other side to avoid speaking to me. She thinks that I try to poison Natalie's mind against her. Happy families.'

Madden didn't like suspects who made jokes.

'Let us do the humour,' he said.

'Sorry.'

'She said you resented her going to visit her mother every day. Did you?'

'You couldn't poison Natalie's mind. You've spoken to her. She's not that kind of person. She was really devoted to her mum. You have to understand what kind of girl Natalie is. She just doesn't see anything bad about anybody. I suppose that's why I love her.'

There were always surprises. Now Madden thought he saw the reason. Richard Blance just didn't look like the kind of guy who could ever love himself. Perhaps that's why he needed the sunshine girl who practised veganism and read the tarot cards and wanted to become a Hindu. But it didn't answer the more burning question. What had Natalie ever seen in him? He had to find out. They had, he said, been married twelve years.

'How did you meet?'

'On the pier.' Richard concocted a sly grin that wasn't exactly in keeping with the circumstances. 'She was standing in for her mum, who was Vina the Mystic. I think her mum had gone off to the pub and she was doing the readings. I was down from London with a crowd of mates one Bank Holiday weekend and I kind of just went in to the booth for a dare. She must have fancied me because we went out that night.'

There was no real mystery after all. The sea air, a bank holiday, a bit of booze. Brighton did the rest.

'She didn't need to see into your future then,' said Madden.

'I don't understand why you're questioning us,' Richard said thickly, turning his gaze on Jasmine. And it wasn't just a gaze either. He ran his eyes up and down her in the time-honoured tradition of all lascivious males.

Jasmine adjusted her skirt. Some suspects she just never took to, and Richard Blance was shaping up well.

'You don't look like a police officer,' he said with a partly concealed sneer.

'You don't look much like a New-Age shop proprietor,' Jasmine countered.

'It's a business,' said Richard Blance in his slow way. 'It was Natalie's idea. She does the spiritual side and I keep her grounded. I used to be an accountant and provided the financial know-how. Natalie wouldn't have a clue how to run a business. Her head's too up in the clouds. Mist in the mountains, mist in the head. She has all these crazy ideas. Like doing yoga on the Ganges. Or going on pilgrimages. The next thing she wants to do is the Inca trail in Peru. I have to keep telling her that we have a shop to run.'

He added dolefully, 'She's even talked about becoming a Hindu.'

'What's wrong with becoming a Hindu?' asked Jasmine.

Madden was getting to like Natalie Blance the more he heard about her. So she did yoga and climbed mountains. She was quite a girl. He leant back in his chair and decided to enjoy the show.

'Nothing's wrong. It's just one of these funny religions.'

Madden stretched his legs out. The job was hard. You took every moment of light relief you could get.

'I'm a Hindu,' said Jasmine.

'Yes, but you're a natural one,' Richard said, unfazed.

'I'm not sure what that is. You can be born a Hindu, you can also become one. There's nothing to stop anyone becoming a Hindu.'

Better and better, Madden thought. But it was time to put Richard out of his misery. Rather, it was time to add to it.

'To return to your question, why *we're* questioning you, you're family. That makes you both the logical prongs of any investigation.'

'Logical prongs,' echoed Richard. 'That's a funny way of putting it.'

'I have a funny way of putting things. Let me put it another way that's less funny. The way I see it, there was bad blood in the family. When there's bad blood and someone is murdered, the family's the first place you look. The first place I look. It might be better for you if there was someone else who could vouch for your whereabouts in the early hours of this morning?'

'Isn't Natalie enough?' he asked naively. 'She would've heard if I'd gone out.'

'She's your wife. You're her husband. Husbands and wives sometimes lie for each other.'

Richard looked as though he had never remotely considered that possibility.

'You see, you're the only person who had any grievance against Natalie's mother. I'm not saying I think you killed her. But I have to eliminate you and you're the only person who can help me do that.'

It wasn't strictly true but Madden wanted him to think that it was. Forensics would put him at the scene if he'd been there. Equally they might establish he'd been nowhere near the place, unless he'd been extremely careful not to leave so much as a fibre or a fingerprint. Richard Blance didn't look or sound that clever. He might have a financial brain but that didn't exactly make him The Talented Mr Ripley. On the other hand, Natalie, in her countless visits to her mother's house, would have taken there unknowingly scores if not hundreds of tiny pieces of evidence, hairs, fibres, the microscopic detritus of life that belonged not only to her but to her husband, and brought the equivalent amount of invisible stuff back from her mother's. Madden put a lot of hope in three things. Ivy hairs. Broken glass. And blood.

'Natalie wouldn't lie,' Richard said.

'I'm sure she wouldn't. But I have to be convinced of that. Natalie said you resented her going to see her mother every day. That slow drip drip of poison. Days, weeks, months of resentment, sometimes they mount up. Anger explodes. Happens all the time.'

He added, 'Even in outwardly happy families.'

Richard adopted a look that reminded Madden of something. Then he remembered what it was. In the old Laurel and Hardy films, when Ollie told Stan how he'd got him into another fine mess, the latter would bite his lip, look away, and embrace a mood of bewildered innocence. It was that kind of expression Richard Blance, sitting there in his mustard cardigan, now wore. Madden couldn't see anger exploding out of this man. He couldn't see anything exploding out of him for that matter.

'There's nobody but Natalie,' he said. 'Sorry.'

They had been out of the interview room only two minutes and had barely time to discuss their all-important impressions when the call came up from the front office. Madden didn't recognise the voice.

'Sir, there's a Professor Grimaldi downstairs. He says he has some important information on the Roberts murder case for you?'

'Professor *who*?'

He heard an exchange in the background.

'Professor Robert Grimaldi.'

'I'll be right down.'

He turned to Jasmine.

'You ever heard of a Professor Grimaldi?'

'Not lately.'

'Neither have I. Let's see what he wants.'

They went down to the front office. On the way, Madden asked her what she thought. She had a number of theories.

'The first thing that struck me was that Natalie might have done it as a mercy killing.'

'Don't you think aspirin would have been a little less violent? And a bit more mother-and-daughter kind of thing? You know, holding hands as she drifts away peacefully.'

'What a nice gentle species you think we are,' she teased him.

'I never thought that, not for one minute.' Then, 'What, by the way, is the—'

'Taittiriya Upanishad? It's an ancient Hindu text,' she said. 'They were given by gurus to their chosen pupils.'

'You learn something new in this job every day, Jaz.'

The man whom Madden supposed was Professor Grimaldi was standing erect. He was a tall, imposing and heavy figure with a bushy beard and strands of hair plastered across a bald, heavily freckled pate. His eyes looked sharp, so sharp they were almost piercing. He wore a brown corduroy jacket and olive green cord trousers that didn't match. Maybe today was a bad dressers' convention and nobody had told him. Professor Grimaldi must have been well over six feet. He carried a copy of the *Evening Argus* which carried a story about Lavinia Roberts's death.

'This is Professor Grimaldi, sir.'

Madden looked at the probationer behind the desk. He was in his very early twenties at most with blond hair, rosy cheeks, and blue eyes and probably didn't know what a razor was. His short sleeved white shirt dazzled like they did in those ads you never saw any more because people just didn't believe them. There wasn't so much as a hair follicle on his forearms. They were picking them up in cherry orchards these days, he thought.

'Professor Grimaldi. I'm DI Madden, this is DS Carol. You said you had some information for us.'

He presented them with his card. It read *Professor Grimaldi,*

Clairvoyant and Seer, Tarot, Crystal Ball, Palm Readings, Occult Specialist.

The professor looked proud of his range of occupations.

'Did you know the victim?' Madden asked.

'No. I've recently moved to Brighton from the west country. But after I read about it, I suddenly had a flash, I do have flashes suddenly, particularly I think because she was one of our own. It could happen to any one of us, after all. I saw somebody called Stephen, a white car, and there was a dog in the back of the car, a spaniel or a red setter, I'm not sure. I also got the feeling he lived somewhere further along the coast from Brighton, going west, maybe as far as Bournemouth. The white car is a Ford Capri, I'm convinced.'

Madden looked at Jasmine. She returned the look.

'Professor Grimaldi, thank you very much,' he said. 'But we're still on day one of this enquiry and we've got lots of other lines to follow up. Right now we don't really need the services of a clairvoyant. Please don't take it personally.'

It was clear that the Professor did.

'You will take a note of this information?'

'If we need you,' said Madden, 'we'll contact you.'

'You could also contact a Chief Inspector Andrew Fortune of the Yeovil CID. I helped him with a murder case about five years ago and my information turned out to be very accurate.'

'I'm sure it was,' Madden assured him. 'But right now we have a lot of evidence to gather, and we can't get bogged down with white Capris and dogs in the back just on the basis of—'

He chose his words carefully.

'—this kind of information.'

'Well at least I've put it in your domain,' said the Professor.

'You've put it in our domain,' Madden confirmed.

Professor Grimaldi gave them a pert little bow, shook their hands, and turned and left. Madden was reserving his bile for the probationer.

'What's your name, son?' he asked.

'Jeff Walker, sir,' he said, straightening up.

'Right, listen to me, Jeff Walker. You filter out clairvoyants when they turn up.'

'As they almost certainly will,' added Jasmine, putting Madden momentarily off his stride.

'I don't care what titles they have in front of their names, if they don't have any direct information I don't want my time wasted. Get it? I don't want to have to come down here again and be polite. Do I make myself clear?'

'Very clear, sir. Sorry, sir,' said Jeff Walker.

'How long have you been in the Force?'

'Five months, sir. This is my first week of operation work.'

'Done your IT at Sussex.'

'Yes sir. Just finished last week.'

'Who's tutoring you?'

'Sergeant Tony Collins, sir.'

Madden looked at the Blackstones Police Manual open on the desk. This baby-faced rookie had only had his handcuffs and baton and pepper spray a week. Madden remembered when he'd got his first handcuffs. He'd gone back and experimented on Clara. He wasn't unique.

'How old are you?'

'Twenty-three, sir.'

Twenty-three. Looked nineteen.

As they climbed the stairs back up to the office, Jasmine scolded him.

'You shouldn't have blasted him like that. We all have to begin somewhere, Steve.'

Jasmine had done her fair share of suffering as a probationer. Halfway through her two-year period as the only Hindu woman in an intake of all white, all male, intolerably laddish police trainees, she had considered leaving the Force. It was an experience she had never forgotten. She had been the butt at a time in her life when she hadn't yet learned how to kick it. She had been shouted at, cajoled and criticised far more than anybody else. If it had left her with anything, it was an inordinate capacity to feel for those others just starting out. It didn't matter what colour or sex or orientation they were. Straight Anglo-Saxon boys who just didn't happen to fit in to a group got kicked in the butt just as readily. Racism and bullying were just two sides of the same coin.

'He's got to learn,' Madden defended himself. 'Clairvoyants. We'll have them coming out of the woodwork over this one.'

'So what was so special about Lavinia Roberts that you rushed off to see her before a crime had even been committed, but now that we have an actual murder, clairvoyants are persona non grata?'

'Did you see Professor Grimaldi's knees?' Madden asked her.

'No. Did I miss something?'

Madden waited until they were back in his office, and then let her in on the secret.

'When Lavinia Roberts hung about Hanover in her twenties, I was a kid. She had the best pair of legs you ever saw. At least through the eyes of a twelve-year-old.'

'I get it,' said Jasmine. 'She was a formative sex object.'

'You could say that.'

'So presumably if a lady clairvoyant comes in with nice knees, you'll want to see her regardless?'

Madden treated her jibe with the contempt it deserved by ignoring it. If it had come from any other DS he'd have had them up for being insubordinate.

'Don't be facetious,' he said. 'I just wanted to see how she'd changed. Take a little trip down memory lane.'

'While she read your cards?'

'That's it.'

'And didn't get a description of the person she asked you to go and see her about.'

'Exactly.'

'Don't you think, Steve, you should keep your mind on the job sometimes?'

Madden rounded on her.

'Don't ever think, DS Carol,' he said, 'that I'm beyond putting you across my knee.'

'I would like to see you try,' she smiled.

7

Steve Madden hated autopsies. Ever since Jason's death, he had hated them even more. What was the difference, he wondered, in seeing a body cut up and mutilated by a maniac, as Jason's had been, and watching one dissected by a professional on a stainless steel table in a mortuary. The answer was not a lot. He had stood through many in his time, even made a point, as a lot of officers did, of squeezing in to watch one that was particularly fascinating. Like a case years ago in which a fairground worker on the pier stabbed his best friend to death and drank his blood and ate a bit of his brain in order to obtain the immortality of a vampire, and long before Buffy too. It didn't take rocket science to determine the guy was a psychopath. Madden had been a very junior officer on that one, but he remembered standing for three hours, fascinated, as the scalp was peeled back and the skull opened up, all to see what a partially eaten brain looked like. Like the dinner my wife made for me last night, one officer had joked. There was a Scottish officer on the Force who thought it looked like the tripe and onion his grandmother used to serve him up.

Madden had heard every gallows joke. There was nothing new. When you'd seen your own son with multiple stab wounds and his genitalia severed, you didn't want to hear any more. You wanted to blank it out. You certainly didn't want to stand in a room full of coppers with their mobile phones going off every five minutes and making sick jokes and popping outside for fags while some cadaver was cut open. That was why Madden now liked to avoid autopsies, and found every reason not to attend, like for instance the slightly more important task of interviewing a suspect or a relative. He was content to miss the big picture and come in just as the credits rolled. He trusted pathologists to do their work. He didn't expect them to stand and watch him while he did his.

The Brighton and Hove City Mortuary was a deceptively innocuous building at the entrance to the Extra Mural Cemetery, just off the Lewes Road, opposite Sainsburys. Madden knew officers who had watched the start of an autopsy, gone over to do their shopping, and come back to watch the end. It looked just like a chapel of rest as you approached, which, of course, in a way, it was. There was a tiny, sanctuary-quiet room, totally non-denominational, with a star on the wall, and a window through which relations could look at their loved ones. Behind that, away from the public gaze, were the fridges and the tables where the real work went on. Colleen Redman had just finished the autopsy on Lavinia Roberts when Madden arrived. Officers were drifting out.

'Good timing,' said Colleen.

'I'm a master at it.'

'Want to see her?'

Colleen had performed the autopsy on his son Jason. She knew how he felt. He hadn't been there. It would have been unthinkable and impossible for him to have attended. Although he had been called to the scene of the crime and had been one of the first to see his son's horrific injuries, Jack Fieldhouse had taken over the case. Madden's own wounds could be sewn up and covered over, but they would always hurt, always be there to remind him. You only got one shot at being a parent. He had missed by a mile.

'How are you coping?' asked Colleen.

'Just fine,' he lied.

'You get over it. You have to. You work on,' she said.

At least with Colleen there was little of *that sad business*. She called a shovel a shovel.

'I work on because I have to. It doesn't make it easier though.'

Lavinia looked alien compared to the last time he had seen

her. Shaved and unclothed she resembled a tiny emaciated bird stripped of its plumage. When Madden was a boy, he had once plucked a dead sparrow to see what it looked like under its feathers. Lavinia Roberts on the mortuary table reminded him of that pitiful sight. He looked at her legs. He wanted to cry at the thought of that childhood memory. Life was one cruel trick. The journey she had made from then to here, and his own, had been long ones. Yet you suddenly saw life for what it was – the blink of an eye.

'There were eleven head injuries in all.' Colleen brought him back to the present. 'Some of them caused depressed fractures of the skull, while others were fairly superficial; a few of them formed a cluster of wounds each about one inch in diameter. It was a heavy weapon with a rounded end. Like a hammer. They were all to the front as well, below the midline. She was hit from in front.'

'No sign she attempted to defend herself?'

'None. It was like she just sat there and took it. Normally you'd expect to find injuries to the hands where the victim raised them up to defend herself against the blows when the attack comes from the front. From behind it's a different matter. The first blow could render you unconscious and you wouldn't be able to do a thing about it—'

'Yet she was facing the door through which her killer broke in,' said Madden. 'Or at least that's how it appears. And she couldn't have been asleep because it's pretty difficult to give a card reading while you're asleep.'

'You have a mystery, m'duck,' Colleen smiled.

'She had cancer,' said Madden. 'Of the lung.'

'I know.'

'How long would she have lived?'

'I don't know. I treat the dead, not the living,' Colleen said with razor sharpness.

He let it pass. Lavinia's doctor would supply that information.

'You said some of the blows were superficial. How superficial?'

'Like tentative. Not delivered with very much force. In fact two of them were very light and barely cut the skin of the scalp.'

'Any explanation for them?'

'Could be any number of reasons. He met some resistance, though like I said there are no injuries to her hands or fingers to suggest she put them up to ward off the blows. Or maybe he didn't mean to kill her at first, just render her unconscious. I'd say it's more likely, given the set up, that she wasn't expecting the first blow.'

'I take it, in that case, that death probably wasn't instantaneous.'

'She might have lived on a few minutes after he left her. Not much longer than that.'

'No cadaveric spasm then?'

Colleen chuckled.

'Its more than likely she was just laying out the cards when her killer struck the first blow, then she lapsed into unconsciousness in a seated position, he went on striking her, and she eventually slumped forward over the table.

'She didn't put up any fight, poor duck,' Colleen added.

Madden thought of Lavinia just sitting there while she was battered to death. It sickened him. Then he thought of the blood-smeared telephone receiver lying on the floor and the cable that had been cut through. With the cards still gripped in one hand she must have reached for the phone with the other and, realising the futility of it, drifted into unconsciousness and finally death. Or that was how it seemed.

'Can you narrow down the time of death for me?'

Colleen gave a little shrug.

'The million-dollar question,' she said.

'I'll buy you a drink.'

'Roughly half a day. Say not much earlier than one in the morning, and not much later than four in the morning.'

'I'm sure your TV counterpart could give it to me to the nearest second,' he quipped.

'She can stick her head up a dead bear's bum,' Colleen fired back. 'Come to think of it, she probably will in some episode. You see the one where she put her hand up a twenty-five stone dead guy's backside and pulled out a packet of cocaine and then tasted it to see what it was? Jesus Christ, I said to Rosy, is she some kind of sick weirdo?'

'Narrow it for me, Colly. You say between one o'clock and four o'clock. What's more likely? Two o'clock? Three o'clock? Four o'clock—'

'Rock,' Colleen made the quick rejoinder. 'Bill Haley and the Comets, wasn't it?'

'Didn't think you were around.'

'I'm good at pub quizzes.'

'Then give me my answer.'

'The nearest I'm going to narrow it to is between one and four. Like I said, any pathologist who gives you the time exactly was there when it happened and probably did it.'

'Thanks.'

'Got a suspect in this case?'

'A loving daughter and a despised son-in-law.'

'Pretty good start.'

'You said you once had your cards read by Lavinia Roberts. On the pier. Was she in any way accurate?'

'I had everything. The full reading. Cor, that was about fifteen years ago. I had tarot cards, crystal ball, and she read my palm. Told me I had a long lifeline, that I was going to live a long time. Well, thirty-five years ain't bad so far.'

'What else did she predict?'

'That I was going to marry a bloke who had something to do with carpentry. That I would emigrate. That Sidney would come into it somewhere. Not sure if it was Sydney, Australia, or whether the carpenter I was going to marry would be called Sidney. Either way it didn't come true, thankfully.'

'Did anything?'

''Course not. You don't believe in that stuff, do you?'

'No,' said Madden. ''Course not.'

He left the mortuary, and as he was up that part of town,

drove round to the adjacent Bear Road Cemetery from the top end of which one obtained a panoramic view of Brighton, the sea, and the misty Downs. Jason lay in a plot of earth here, his grave marked by a white marble enclosure in which he and Clara had planted rosemary for remembrance. The white marble cross was inscribed with the date of his death and the words:

JASON MADDEN, AGED 19,
BELOVED SON OF STEPHEN
AND CLARA MADDEN.
TAKEN FROM US SUDDENLY.
MAY HE REST IN PEACE.

Madden had read those words countless times and on countless visits. They still didn't mean anything. What did rest in peace mean? Or taken suddenly for that matter? He would like to have engraved the stone with a thousand other words that summed up how he felt about his son's death and his own reaction to it, but convention demanded that you obey the unwritten law of mourning. Euphemisms served where anger required a stronger phraseology. Calmness was needed instead of rage. As a parent you could feel bitterness and hostility and guilt, but the dead had to lay untroubled by it, with no marker to indicate the level of human strife that had brought their offspring to this serene and untroubled place. Jason had not been taken suddenly, Madden told himself, kneeling by the grave and picking up and rearranging some flowers that Clara had left there. He had been savagely murdered and though his screams were long silent, they still went on in Madden's head. Unless you were there, you never knew how the living really died, how long it took, how many seconds or minutes passed before unconsciousness prevailed, how long these awful seconds and minutes seemed, how much pain and agony was involved. Or what they thought.

'Taken suddenly' didn't enter the equation.

So Clara had been here on her own, and recently. He should have been with her. He trusted Clive had not. He didn't want to think of her new husband accompanying her to *their* son's grave. Surely Clara would not do that. There was a card with the flowers. In her handwriting, it read simply, 'From Mum'. He took out a pen and wrote underneath, 'And Dad'. He put it back.

Such gestures, he knew, were to comfort the living, not the dead. Jason had no need of flowers. Or messages. He thought of Lavinia's last few words to him, about Jason forgiving him. He didn't believe in that stuff, he told himself. Comfort was all it was. Jason was a memory, his physical body was all there was, and it was six feet under the ground. The dead didn't speak to anybody.

He was still telling himself that when he walked into the front office the following morning and saw Natalie Blance standing at the counter. She was leaning over it with her back to him, and had one long leg gently crossed over the other. He could see the perfectly formed hollows in the backs of her knees. She was talking to the probationer in the Persil white shirt and with the cherry red cheeks who was still on front office attachment. She obviously knew him. For a second or two, they looked intimate. They drew apart as Madden approached the desk.

'Am I interrupting something?' he asked.

'Natalie – Mrs Blance wanted to see you,' said Jeff Walker.

'That's right. There's something I thought of that might be important,' Natalie told him.

'You two know each other?'

'Yes sir,' said Jeff. 'My girlfriend works in Mrs Blance's shop. Hubble Bubble. In fact, we just got engaged yesterday.'

'Congratulations.'

'She's a therapist there.'

'What kind of therapist?'

'Holistic therapist. And a Reiki practitioner.'

'Reiki?'

'Yes, sir. The – channelling of universal energy. For healing. I actually live in the flat over the shop with her.'

By this time, Jasmine had come down to the desk. Like most

people who came in halfway through a conversation, she took a few seconds to catch up.

'I didn't think you were here so I came down to see Mrs Blance,' she said.

'I'm here,' said Madden.

'It's not just a physical healing system,' explained Natalie. 'It's very good for curing spiritual and emotional problems. It's a very hands-on therapy.'

Madden felt none the wiser. What the hell was universal energy when it was at home? The only kind of hands-on therapy he knew was sitting down with a bottle of beer and watching Arsenal on the television.

'You should try it one day, sir,' Jeff suggested.

'You said you had some information?' Madden directed this at Natalie.

'Yes. I might know something about the person Mum said she was worried about.'

Within minutes, he had whisked Natalie Blance back to an interview room. Prior to that, he turned to Jeff Walker and said, 'Put your universal energy into studying your Blackstone's. Okay?'

'Okay, sir,' said Jeff with a smile.

'*Reiki healing*,' Madden intoned mockingly.

In the interview room, Natalie took a cup of weak herbal tea and refused a biscuit. She kept a box of camomile teabags in her handbag along with her tarot cards which she never went without. All they had to supply was the boiling water. Madden was tempted to ask if that was to her satisfaction, but he didn't. He liked Natalie Blance. She was probably a headache on a dinner date, but a girl who wanted to climb mountains in Peru and do yoga on the Ganges had something going for her. The yoga explained her obvious state of physical fitness. The energy spun off her like sparks from a catherine wheel.

Jasmine sat in with them. Madden was glad to have her. The Upanishad might come in useful again.

'It only occurred to me after I got back to the shop,' said

Natalie. 'You said this person called himself David and that he visited Mum on the Wednesday night?'

'I went to see her on the Thursday. She said he'd visited her the night before.'

'I had a client on the Wednesday, also called David,' she said. 'I checked it in my diary.'

'Was that his real name?'

'I didn't have any reason to doubt it.'

'What time?'

'Four o'clock in the afternoon. And he did look – well, a bit suspicious.'

'Suspicious? How do you mean?'

'I thought he might have been in prison. Or the army. He had really short hair, almost shaven, a skinhead I suppose you'd call him, and he had tattoos on his arms. It might just be coincidence, of course. There *was* something about him that made me feel a bit uneasy.'

'Couldn't that just be hindsight?' Jasmine pointed out, not unreasonably.

'What makes you think he might be the guy who visited your mother?' Madden asked.

'I asked him if he'd visited a clairvoyant before and he said loads.'

'Is it normal for someone to visit two clairvoyants on the same day?'

'I had a client once who'd visited three before he came to me,' said Natalie. 'He was comparing readings. It happens.'

'Can you give us a more accurate description?'

'Shaven hair, like I said, very shaven. Very dark eyes. Almost black. Piercing.'

They always had piercing eyes, thought Madden. Either that, or hypnotic. He never put much store in such details.

'He was about thirty. Quite short and skinny, about five foot five. And he had a slight mole on his chin. And he looked at you in a kind of – evil way. Almost penetrating. Oh, and he had his right ear pierced, and he had this upside-down crucifix hanging from it.'

'Can you describe the tattoos?'

'I didn't see them clearly. He kept his denim jacket on and I just saw them protruding from under the sleeves. But one person – I just thought – who would have seen them is Paula.'

'Paula?'

'Paula Needham. She's our holistic therapist. The one who's engaged to Jeff downstairs.'

Happy families, thought Madden.

'She gave him an Indian head massage while he was at the shop. She would have seen his tattoos, I'm sure.'

'Did he know you had a mother who was also a psychic?' Jasmine leant forward and asked.

'Oh yes.' Natalie blew on her tea before sipping it. 'I told him. I said, "Have you seen my mother? She does readings in Southover Street." He said he hadn't.'

'You mean,' said Madden, trying to get this straight, 'you sent a guy who looked at you in an "evil way" to see your mother?'

'I didn't *send* him there. I only told him about Mum. And anyway, I didn't think it was *that* evil until you mentioned the guy who'd been to see Mum and I remembered *my* client. Do you think they're one and the same?'

'Could be,' said Madden. 'I'd like you to go back to your mother's house. With Detective Sergeant Carol. We need to know if anything was stolen. You're the only one who can tell us.'

'I have to go – back inside?' she gave an involuntary shudder. At least it looked involuntary.

'I'm afraid so. Take a good look round. Anything that's out of place, anything moved or removed, anything that should be there but isn't, or shouldn't be there but is – let us know about it.'

'I'll do my best,' said Natalie.

Madden had no doubt she would. He was still thinking of those superficial blows to her mother's skull, as though somebody had picked up a hammer and been reluctant, maybe at first, to hit too hard. He was still thinking of Jasmine's loosely voiced theory about a mercy killing. Just because something was unthinkable and improbable, it didn't stop you considering such a motive. All things were possible. He took Jasmine aside, out of Natalie's presence.

'Study her,' he said. 'The moment you step back into that house with her, I want to know where she looks. Use your woman's intuition.'

'You know, Steve, there's a great myth about that. Woman's intuition. Men have it too.'

'I've no doubt.'

'It just needs developing in them a bit more.'

He'd asked for that.

'And get a team on to phoning up or calling on every clairvoyant in Brighton and Hove. Ask them if they've been visited recently by our skinhead with the tattoos and the inverted crucifix in his ear. Just as a precaution. And tell them to be on their guard. Until we know who or what we're dealing with here.'

'Do you want me to mention the evil eyes?'

Madden cast a pair of derogatory ones over his notebook containing Natalie Blance's description.

'No,' he said. 'Too subjective. Better leave that to them. How the hell, Jaz, do you assess whether eyes are *evil* or not?'

'You develop spiritual understanding,' she said, as she went out of the door.

8

Hubble Bubble was located halfway up Queen's Road, the main artery that ran in a straight line south from Brighton railway station towards the sea. It was the last lap of the escape route from London. On summer days, the station would disgorge crowds hightailing it from the capital. From the station forecourt, one could see the English Channel. Not much of it, admittedly, but enough to draw the throng down Queen's Road to the clock tower and from then on down West Street to the seafront. There was no escaping Hubble Bubble. The aroma of natural essences drifted out onto the pavement. The window was full of crystals and other brightly coloured rocks, model dragons, wizards and candles and piles of Hallowe'en merchandise. On the inside of the glass was a sign advertising Indian head massage, hopi ear candles, reflexology and Reiki healing. There was also a flotation chamber. *Float away into paradise in our flotation tank, one hour of indescribable relaxation. Eliminate stress, forget your problems, revitalise as you drift into a world of soft light and calming music and discover your own little corner of Heaven.*

It was the kind of place that was definitely *in*. And of course if it was in, it was in Brighton. Madden sometimes felt you couldn't walk down a street in the city without finding an alternative therapist. Even some small shops in the trendy North Laine had a parlour in the back where you could get a massage. Not *that* kind of massage either, though there were plenty of places delivering that service too.

He wasn't sure how an Indian head massage differed from an ordinary massage, but he was in no doubt that he would find out.

The ground floor was basically the kind of New Age shop he unconsciously avoided. Along with the ubiquitous soundtracks of dolphins and whales singing along to music, there were the usual crystals, indoor water fountains, mist makers, model unicorns, tarot cards, buddhas, books, magazines, even witches' paraphernalia. And of course candles. Hundreds of candles. Thousands of candles. And piles more Hallowe'en merchandise. There were stairs at the back of the shop that presumably led up to the treatment rooms. The stairway to paradise, he mused. A notice on the counter read *NATALIE BLANCE – tarot, runes, crystal ball, palmistry, clairvoyance – let Natalie, our highly gifted resident reader and astrologer, guide you in romance, career, health and spiritual matters. Appointments taken. Ask at the counter.*

Natalie Blance could guide him in all of these, he thought. Then he recalled Jasmine's advice to keep his mind on the job. It wasn't a bad idea. At the counter, his arms spread across it as he read the *Evening Argus*, was Richard Blance, as lugubrious as ever. He was wearing the same mustard coloured cardigan that he had been wearing the day before. Underneath he had a pink shirt. Mr-No-Clothes-Sense looked up.

'Hello,' he said.

'Thought I'd drop by. Look around,' said Madden.

He never ever dropped by and looked around, but it broke the ice.

'Feel free.'

'How's your wife taking it?'

'She's taking it okay,' Richard answered. 'You have to know Natalie to know what I mean by that. She spent all last night reading runes and crystals to try and figure out who killed her mother.'

'Sometimes we do that too,' Madden quipped.

There were South American pan pipes playing in the background and a handful of customers. Madden picked up a magazine. It was called *Pagan Light*. On the front was a picture of a glamorous young woman with long silky hair that flowed onto her shoulders like a waterfall. She was a witch called Holly. Inside was an article she had written on how to be a solitary pagan. Madden wondered if it was the sort of activity that made you go blind.

'Who buys this sort of thing?' he asked.

'We have a few pagans and witches come in,' said Richard. 'They don't burn them at the stake any more.'

Next to the books, where Madden noticed subjects ranging from Zen Buddhism and Divination to how to read the tarot and the means by which women could contact the earth mothers within themselves, he found himself staring at a locked cabinet containing paraphernalia for witches' rituals and covens. Ceremonial daggers, candlesticks, pentacles, packets of magic herbs, even cauldrons. So witches still used cauldrons. It was a revelation to him. There was a sign stuck to the glass which said PROTECTED BY WITCHCRAFT. The glass was cracked.

'The witchcraft didn't work then,' said Madden.

'We had a break-in a few days ago,' said Richard.

'Much taken?'

'Not much. Few pieces of witch stuff.'

'Sell any broomsticks?' asked Madden.

'Only at Hallowe'en.' He pointed to a corner in which there were – yes – broomsticks.

A plumpish young woman with blonde hair tied in a bow and sapphire blue eyes and wearing the fluffiest jumper Madden had ever seen in his life bounced down the stairs. She was expecting him. She was holding the hand of a pretty little girl of about four. He introduced himself to Paula Needham. The child appeared shy and buried her face in her mother's chest.

'Jacqueline, say hello to Mr Madden.' Paula tried to coax her daughter, but the girl remained resolutely opposed to looking at him.

'The police have that effect on a lot of people,' said Madden.

He saw that round her neck Paula wore a little heart-shaped pendant with a picture of Jeff enclosed within it.

She was just taking Jacqueline back to the creche, she said. She had collected her and brought her to the shop for half an hour to meet one of her regular clients who liked children. You couldn't have a four-year-old running around a New-Age shop all day, though little Jacqueline did have a thing about unicorns. She had a soft, stuffed one under her arm. It had a silver horn and was covered in red and green material. In most cities little girls would carry dolls. In Brighton they carried unicorns. Ho hum, thought Madden.

'Your employer told you what I wanted to see you about?' he said.

'Yes, you want to know about that chap with the tattoos.'

They went upstairs to talk. Paula left little Jacqueline downstairs with Richard. Madden wondered at the wisdom of leaving your child with a man who ran a New-Age shop and thought of Hinduism as a funny religion, but he put such doubts aside when he saw Richard pick her up and sit her on the counter and tickle her under her chin. He was in danger of warming towards the guy.

Upstairs, Hubble Bubble was much larger than it looked, extending upwards for two more floors. On the first floor were two rooms off a narrow corridor that smelt of furniture polish and incense. One was separated by a purple curtain covered in stars and was, he imagined, where Natalie did her guidance in romance and spiritual matters. The other was a conventional treatment room with a massage table, white sheet stretched across it, a chair and shelves full of bottles of aromatic oils. The walls were bare except for half a dozen small Japanese prints and a couple of posters advertising alternative treatments. Paula invited him in. She explained that she had a client in the flotation tank on the floor above and that unless he pressed the panic button beforehand they had ten minutes.

'By which time presumably he'll be done nicely,' said Madden.

Paula smiled but didn't seem to appreciate the joke. He decided not to try again.

'Natalie said you gave this guy an Indian head massage.'

'That's right,' she said.

'Did that entail him taking his clothes off?'

'He took his shirt off. He didn't have to but he did.'

'Can you describe his tattoos?'

'The one on his right arm was of a devil. I remember it distinctly. I asked him about them. It was like a cartoon devil with its tail curved round behind it and holding a pitchfork, and it had the name Tracy above it. The other one was of a dagger. And he had one on his back as well. That was really quite horrible. It was like a big tribal face. Like a witchdoctor.'

You couldn't get much better than that. Tattoos had become more elaborate since Madden's father had been a tattooist in Brighton. A tattoo *artist*, Madden always reminded himself. Sid Madden had been in the vanguard in the town, administering his singular talents to handsome if greasy Rockers who parked their bikes outside his shop while one of their number was adorned. Madden, as a young boy, had gone to watch his father at work. It fascinated him how and why people had pictures 'painted' on their bodies. His father had told him it was a primitive desire, that it was tribal, that it went back centuries to other lands and even beyond that into the mists of time when ancient man discovered dyes and decided to decorate himself. That was explanation enough for a young lad. His father was following in a tradition that had begun with ancient civilisations. That made you feel good.

'Did you ask where he'd had them done?' Madden asked.

'Yes, he said locally,' said Paula.

'How local?'

Madden knew most of the tattooists in Brighton.

'He didn't say.'

'You got many appointments today, Paula? The reason I ask is, I'd like you to come round a few tattoo studios with me, try and identify them. Tattooists always keep photographs of their work.'

'I'd love to.' Paula seemed instantly excited at the thought.

They waited fifteen minutes until Paula's client was 'done' in the flotation tank, during which time she cancelled a couple of appointments by phone and Madden perused a leaflet which told him that ear candles had been used as a natural therapy since ancient times. There was a picture of a lady lying on her side looking serene with a length of beeswax stuck in her ear and burning. The floater came downstairs. He was a young man, in his twenties, wearing torn jeans and a suede jacket and he had rings in both ears and hair that reminded Madden of a cockatoo's crest. He overheard the client telling Paula that the experience had been spiritually uplifting. Madden went upstairs and looked inside. There was semen floating in the water.

'They do that,' sighed Paula, angrily. 'It's not what it's for.'

Far from being uplifting, Madden reckoned it probably felt like being shut in a waterlogged coffin.

They walked Jacqueline back to the creche. Jacqueline hung on to her mother's hand, swinging it boisterously, while clutching the red and green unicorn under her other arm. She was still too shy to look directly at Madden.

'Say goodbye to Mr Madden,' said Paula.

'Goodbye,' said Jacqueline, staring coyly at the pavement.

On the way to the first of the tattoo studios, Paula showed him her engagement ring. It had a sapphire blue stone.

'Jeff said it matches my eyes,' she told him.

Nobody's eyes could be that naturally blue, Madden told himself. They had to be contact lenses. Madden wondered if she knew what she was doing, marrying a guy who in just over a year and a half would be a fully-fledged police constable, or a sergeant if he was fast-tracked. He had married Clara shortly after he'd joined the Force. She hadn't quite known what she'd let herself in for. Partners of police officers rarely did. He would never go so far as to say that his job had wrecked his marriage but it had been a contributing factor. No detective in similar circumstances could ever claim otherwise. This girl was, from her ecstatic expression, madly and completely and wholeheartedly in love, and wasn't into disillusionment. Neither was he today.

In the first three tattoo studios they visited, they drew a blank. Paula flicked through books and books of photographs but didn't recognise either of the tattoos she had seen on her client. Two of the owners thought the tribal witchdoctor face sounded like the work of Gentle John of Worthing. Madden knew Gentle John. He had once worked as an apprentice under his father.

Madden fetched his car and they drove to Worthing, ten miles along the coast. On the way, they stopped for a coffee and slice of cake in a seaside café. Paula seemed pleased that she was helping in a murder investigation. It wasn't something that happened every day to an ordinary person. The cake was stale, but then once you got out of Brighton you took on and accepted those kinds of risks. Paula tucked into it nonetheless. She wasn't worried about her weight. Madden put his to one side.

'You do Reiki,' he said. 'Jeff told me.'

'Yes,' she said. 'Have you ever had it?'

'I only just learnt to spell it.'

'It's a form of healing but it's much more than that. You're not doing the healing. The energy is doing it. Reiki is doing it. You can even do it mentally. It's like using God's power.'

'How did you meet Jeff?'

'Guess,' she giggled.

Madden guessed right.

'Often I combine it with a little massage,' Paula said. 'Jeff came in one day, thought he'd try it, and well, I don't suppose I need to tell you the rest. Richard and Natalie eventually let him move in to the flat with me over the shop. He's going to adopt Jacqueline when we're married.'

In two days Madden had met two couples, one of whom met over tarot cards on the pier, the other on a massage table above a New-Age shop. Brighton's reputation as a place of dirty weekends away from London might have been well earned but there was clearly something else in the air.

'Who was Jacqueline's father?' he asked innocently.

She looked down and stirred a spoonful of sugar into her coffee.

'Just a boy I used to know,' she said.

Madden decided not to pursue the matter.

'Did you know Lavinia Roberts, Natalie's mother?' he changed the subject instead.

'I met her one or two times, I didn't really know her,' said Paula. 'She'd left by the time I came to work here. But she came into the shop a few times as a customer.'

'Tell me about the few times.'

Paula appeared reticent at first.

'She was usually drunk. She annoyed the customers,' she told him. 'I had one woman coming up to me for ear candles and she nearly drove her away. I remember Richard literally shoving her out of the shop one day and telling her never to come back. There was a big fight.'

'Between who?'

'Natalie and Richard.' She added, hesitantly, 'I don't know if I should be telling you all this.'

'You should be telling me. Tell me about the fight. Between Richard and Natalie.'

'She just said that he couldn't treat her mother in that way. He said they were trying to run a business and that she had to leave the shop.'

'You witnessed it yourself?'

'Yes. I was just showing a client downstairs, and there were customers in the shop, and it was all acted out in front of them. It was horrible what Mrs Roberts did.'

'What did she do?'

'It was the way she swore at them.'

'What did she say?' He reassured her. 'Don't worry, Paula, I've heard the lot.'

'She was drunk, and she told – well, she told Richard he could stick his effing shop up his effing arse. Though she didn't say it quite like that if you know what I mean. And then she gave him two fingers and stuck her tongue out.'

'Nice,' said Madden.

It wasn't the Lavinia Roberts he knew. The woman Paula had described was a complete stranger. The good-time girl with the great legs and the remarkable gift who had found fame on the pier had obviously fallen on more difficult times. He wondered what had made her start drinking. He had seen it destroy policemen's careers. This was the first time he'd heard of it destroying a clairvoyant's. He found himself starting to feel deeply sorry for her. The declining years had clearly not been her happiest. It was a jump of some magnitude from celebrity status to resident seer above a shop that sold crystals and magazines for witches, and an equally enormous leap from there back to the bay-fronted little Victorian terraced cottage where she had been born, with adverts in the *Evening Argus* to pull the punters into her back kitchen. It was almost as though she had gone full circle.

He wondered how much of it she foresaw.

They drank up and drove on to Worthing. Madden didn't like Worthing. Even the name suggested a place that its inhabitants thought was better than its neighbours. Unlike Brighton, it was the sort of seaside town in which you couldn't imagine anybody spending a dirty weekend or even having sex. Unless, that is, you were somebody like Gentle John. He greeted Madden like a long-lost friend. He had owned a studio in Brighton but had relocated two years back. Gentle John had been anything but in his youth. A former Hell's Angel with a once fearsome reputation, he now ran the shop which bore his own name just off the seafront. His heavily illustrated arms looked as though they could crush an ox. It was rumoured that he had tattooed the name of every one of his girlfriends and their phone numbers on his penis and that at full stretch it looked like a telephone directory, but Madden reckoned it was probably an idle boast. One boast which wasn't idle was that he held one of the best portfolios on the south coast. And he specialised in tribal designs.

'Good to see you, man.' He gave Madden's shoulders a powerful squeeze with his immense hands. Love and hate were tattooed on the fingers.

'How's business?'

'Up and down,' he said. 'Different kind of clientele. Here you get loads of Tory middle-class ladies and retirees sneaking down to get little butterflies done on their bottoms and their ankles. Wanting to rekindle their love lives, get their husbands going again. Know what I mean?'

Madden introduced him to Paula. The holistic therapist in the fluffy jumper and with the heart-shaped pendant round her neck shook hands with the six-foot-six fifteen-stone ex-Hells Angel whose entire surface was ablaze with tattoos.

'She gave a massage to a guy who had tattoos and we're trying to identify him,' said Madden.

'A massage, eh.'

'Not that kind, John. We're talking therapy type massage. Get it?'

'I had one of them once,' said John. 'No offence, darling, but she came on to me something chronic.'

'You obviously didn't go to the right one,' said Paula, flushing.

'Oh, I went to the right one all right, darling.'

'Mind if she looks through your books? See if she can identify him?'

'Be my guest,' said Gentle John, putting a pile of albums on the counter. 'I had this woman in yesterday, late fifties she was, she wanted a face done on each buttock. I said to her does your husband know. She said it's my husband's face I want put on them. I asked her why, she said he likes looking at himself so much he might start looking at my bum again after fifteen years.'

'You must be popular among the Tory ladies in Worthing,' said Madden.

'Get invited to all their garden parties.'

Paula suddenly squealed. She was almost dancing up and down.

'That's the one!' she said. 'That's the one.'

Madden looked at the photograph. It showed a broad back with the picture of a tribal-looking face with a bone through its nose. He turned it round for Gentle John to look at.

'Ah. That one,' Gentle John said. 'Few years back.'

'Don't you keep consent forms that the customer has to fill out? The ones that say they don't have fainting fits or HIV?'

'Should be attached.' Gentle John withdrew the photograph and pinned to the back was a form. The name of the customer was Michael Bird and he lived at 22, Friars Twitten, Lewes, Sussex.

'You ever seen him around since?' asked Madden.

'No, but he must have been inside because I had a few ex-cons coming in recently asking for similar, saying they'd seen it. Nice to know your artwork gets a showing, even if it is Wormwood Scrubs.'

Ex-cons in Worthing. Tory ladies wanting to beef up their sex lives. It all happened in Sussex-by-the-Sea.

'I'd like to be a fly on your wall,' said Madden.

'I'd swat you,' said Gentle John with a big wink at both of them. 'You'd find out all my secrets.'

Madden left, taking Paula with him, promising that if Michael Bird was the person they were after they'd make sure Gentle John had another exhibition somewhere and that it would be permanent.

He drove her back to Brighton and dropped her outside Hubble Bubble.

'Hope I was of some help,' she said.

'You were of enormous help, Paula. Thanks.'

She was about to get out of his car when he put his hand gently on her arm.

'Marrying a policeman isn't easy,' he said to her. 'I know it might seem glamorous and exciting to you now, but you have to make sacrifices. Take it from me.'

She gave a nervous smile.

'We've discussed all that,' said Paula.

'Sorry for meddling,' he smiled.

'That's all right,' she said, and went back to her job.

Madden drove back to the police station, parked his car, hurried upstairs and fed Michael Bird's name into the computer. It wasn't bad for a few hours' work. Michael Bird of 22 Friars Twitten, Lewes, had form. He had served four years of a six-year sentence for his part in an armed robbery in which he had physically assaulted a security guard. With a hammer. Not only that. He had served in the Territorial Army, gained the rank of corporal, and been discharged for misappropriation of a rifle and twelve rounds of ammunition.

Jasmine had something interesting too. She had just returned from Southover Street with Natalie. Nothing had been stolen. There was money in a kitchen drawer which the killer had not taken. But the clairvoyants enquiry she had set in course had already borne fruit.

'Six,' she said.

'Six? Six what?'

'Six clairvoyants,' she told him. 'Our friend visited six clairvoyants. They all remembered him distinctly. And he went to see them all on the same day. The Wednesday.'

'Six?' said Madden. '*In one day*?'

'And there's something else, Steve. He gave a different name to every one of them.'

Madden was still looking at the computer screen, digesting the criminal career of Michael Bird of Friars Twitten, Lewes. There was something else on it that he thought he must be reading wrongly. But no, there it was. Two years before the charges connected with the armed robbery, Bird had been found guilty of stealing six human skulls from a London teaching hospital where he had been employed as a janitor.

'What do you think he wanted these for?' Madden asked. 'Medical research?'

9

They were driving over to Lewes, a small provincial Sussex town fifteen minutes by car to the north-west of Brighton. Madden knew it well. Not only was Lewes home to the headquarters of the Sussex Police, it also hosted the most notorious bonfire night of the year. Known simply as Lewes Bonfire, it commemorated an event in the town's own history when seventeen Protestant martyrs had been burnt to death in the High Street. It was hard to believe that in a small provincial Sussex town at the start of the twenty-first century they still mounted torchlit processions and blew up an effigy of the Pope. But they did.

Madden knew it well for two other reasons. The first was that his father had brought him here to watch the fireworks when he was nine years old. None of the religious connotations had been apparent to him on that visit. He remembered the excitement of the train journey, steam in those far-off days, with his mother and father to a crowded place thick with the smell of blazing tar pulled in barrels by people dressed as Vikings. He remembered his father perching him high on his scrawny shoulders and hoisting him up even further with his deceptively strong arms so that he could see the procession pass by. This was, he recalled, their first 'excursion' out of the town in which they had made their new home. When the fireworks went off at the end of the evening, his father had remarked that he felt the ground shake under his feet.

And twenty-five years later Madden had returned with Clara on his arm and his own son Jason, aged four, and like his own father before him he had perched Jason high on his shoulders to wonder at the processions and watch the fireworks. They were a happy family then, or so time seemed to paint. Jason's enthusiasm and excitement was as infectious as the torchlight processions were never-ending, with various 'bonfire societies' converging on the small, densely packed town centre. And when Madden and Clara, in love in those days – were they so long ago? – had taken Jason to see the finale where a gigantic tableau unleashed an array of rockets and then exploded into a thousand pieces, the ground had certainly shaken under their feet.

Madden drove while Jasmine provided him with the details.

'At ten in the morning,' Jasmine consulted a timetable, 'he went to a Mrs Eve Knott, she does readings from the back of a shop in the North Laine, and he called himself Peter, then at midday he ended up in Hove where a Mrs Lucy Harmer does readings from her home. He was John then. Then he saw a Barry Lee at one o'clock, as Paul, then a Miss Julie Jones at two o'clock, as Matthew, then at four he had his appointment with Natalie at Hubble Bubble – as David – followed by an Indian head massage. At half past five he was in Kemptown again having his cards read by a woman called Mystic Marian but whose real name is Dorothy Smith, and he called himself Simon.'

'All disciples,' said Madden. 'Except David.'

'None of them, I'm afraid, got vibes about occult evil, although they all thought he was a bit villainous looking.'

'Did you speak to Professor Grimaldi?'

'Yes. He wasn't one of those visited. He seemed a bit miffed that the day after you told him he wasn't needed we should be asking for his help.'

'I hope you apologised.'

'I didn't get the chance. He put the phone down on me. He's a bit tetchy.'

'I don't think I'll go to him for my next reading,' said Madden.

'Every other clairvoyant spoken to is horrified at one of their own being killed. Right now they're probably getting ready to bombard us with more red barns and dogs in backs of cars than we can handle.'

'I'm sure you can, Jaz,' said Madden. 'Handle them.'

'I looked at Lavinia's diary. When she made an appointment, she put down a time and a little cross. On that Wednesday, she put a cross against eight p.m. That was her only appointment that night and must have been the one she told you about.'

'So if this Michael Bird was her visitor, that would make *seven* clairvoyants in one day. That's one hell of a belief in psychics. How much does each charge?'

'About twenty pounds, average. And you may be interested to know what we found at Southover Street. Natalie and Richard didn't tell us everything.'

'They never do,' said Madden.

'Lavinia's will and a number of letters from her solicitor. Apparently she lent Richard and Natalie ten thousand pounds to start up their business. It was never paid back.'

Madden gave a little whistle.

'Bad blood *and* money. A potent combination. What were the solicitor's letters about.'

'She wanted the money back. Before she died. She left everything to a cancer charity, Steve. Nothing to Natalie and Richard.'

Madden whistled again.

'And Richard didn't even know she was dying. Natalie never told him.'

Jasmine had another theory to explain the bizarre crime scene. In fact, she had two. Just in case he didn't like the first one.

'Suppose he got her out of bed. They had an argument. About the money. Lavinia comes downstairs, in her nightdress, they carry on the argument. We don't know how it resolves but maybe it reaches a plateau of some kind. Richard agrees to pay her back some of the money, or she agrees to wait for it. Whatever happens, she sits down at her table and decides to do a reading.'

Madden had to admit, it was a good one. So far.

'One can use the tarot cards to ask simple questions, Steve. It doesn't have to be a full reading. Maybe she just wanted to know if she was right in whatever she'd agreed with Richard?'

'Wouldn't she wait until Richard had left?'

'Not necessarily,' said Jasmine. 'You know how when you

have an argument with someone, you sometimes busy yourself doing other things rather than face the person?'

Madden knew it well. Clara and he had done it countless times.

'Well, maybe that's the case here. She reads the cards while Richard stands there, still arguing with her. He sees his chance. He batters her to death and then stages the break-in.'

Madden thought about it.

'It didn't look like a staged break-in to me,' he said. 'Sorry to disagree. Did Natalie's mother possess any wire coat-hangers?'

'Everyone has wire coat-hangers.'

'So Richard would either have had to bring one with him, or go upstairs and take one from her wardrobe and plant it to make it look as though he'd smashed the window and used it to pull back the bolt. I don't think he's that clever. If he'd killed her, surely he'd want to get out as quickly as possible. Then there's the hammer. He either brought it with him or it was lying around. Did Natalie say her mother had a hammer?'

'She did, but it wasn't the type that caused the injuries. Forensic are examining it nonetheless.'

'Theory two?' asked Madden.

'Suppose Richard came intending to kill her. He doesn't use Natalie's key but breaks in to make it look like a burglary. She disturbs him. He loses his nerve, can't go through with it. Who knows what they talk about?'

'I think I'd probably scream for help,' said Madden. 'If my son-in-law broke in in the middle of the night with a hammer.'

'In real life, things sometimes don't happen that logically. Suppose she tries to talk him out of it? Sweet talk her way. Richard breaks down, can't go through with it. She's in a perilous situation – she needs to keep talking, to keep Richard from carrying out doing what he went there for. What better way than to bring down her cards and give him a reading?'

It sounded crazy but Madden had to agree it was the better theory. He could see Richard Blance being reluctant to go through with it. He could see Lavinia using every bit of her guile to charm and disarm him. They weren't strangers. They were family. Families moved in mysterious ways.

'I like it,' he said.

'I like it when you like it,' she said.

'How's your mother's pilgrimage?'

'I got an e-mail from her last night.' Jasmine changed topic. 'She was in an internet café somewhere in Maharashtra, that's in the west of India, with two of her cousins. She goes over there every November for the walk to Pandharpur.'

'She walks?'

'Oh yes. Two hundred miles. She says it's wonderful, all castes mix together and they sing devotional songs in groups as they walk. They had to negotiate a river that had flooded and a bridge that was falling down, plus a herd of buffalo. Some Hindus walk well over a thousand miles on pilgrimages.'

'Probably a dumb question, but with what purpose?'

'To experience physical hardship in order to obtain a goal. The exertion enhances the spirituality.'

'Sometimes, Jaz,' said Madden forlornly, 'I feel I'm missing out on something.'

They arrived in Lewes. The town with its winding, hilly streets wasn't a joy to drive in. Some of the streets were so narrow you couldn't park in them. They left the car at the top of the High Street and walked. Friars Twitten was a narrow lane of terraced houses in the centre of the town. Number twenty-two had peeling paint but the windows were bright and gleaming and were backed by pastel shaded floral curtains. There was no bell. Madden knocked. Michael Bird's mother answered the door.

Mothers by their nature usually saw no wrong in their sons. Madden had met many who, when confronted with the evidence of their sons as rapists, crooks or murderers, would still put them on a pedestal, insist the police were mistaken, complain that they were being victimised, or bring out scrapbooks showing little Johnny in short trousers and tell how he'd never been in a day's trouble in his life. Florence Bird was all of them, and more. In fact, she was in a league all by herself. Sweet, sugary and small, she stood there with a regal smile on her face and a soft quizzical look in her eyes.

'Can I help you?' she asked.

'DI Madden. DS Carol. Brighton CID. We're looking for Michael Bird.'

Michael was not at home.

'They're getting ready for the Fifth,' she said.

'Who are "they"?'

'The Barbican Bonfire Society. Michael's a member.'

'Where can we find them?' asked Madden.

'At the tab shed.'

Little Michael was with his pals. That was how it sounded to Madden. It was hard to believe that the woman was talking about a son of thirty who had served time for assault and armed robbery.

'At the what? Where is it?'

'It's a barn at Priory Farm, out on the Uckfield Road. But they won't let you in to see it.'

'See what?'

'The tableau. For Bonfire. It's always kept a secret till the last minute.'

'Mrs Bird, I'm not interested in what they're making, just your son.'

'What's he supposed to have done this time?' she asked, her face darkening slightly, as though Madden was asking why her son wasn't at school.

'Does your son visit clairvoyants?'

'Clairvoyants?' she said. 'Oh good Heavens, is that all this is about?'

She smiled sweetly. Her teeth were bad.

'No, it is not all this is about.'

'I've told him all that stuff is silly, but—'

She stalled, thought. She had obviously read about the murder because it now swept to the forefront of her mind. Still, her composure didn't drop.

'You want to talk to him about the murder of that clairvoyant in Brighton,' she seemed eminently proud of herself for being one step ahead. 'Michael wouldn't do anything like that.'

'We just want to talk to him.'

'He's not violent. Why do you people keep assuming he is?'

'He went to prison for hitting a security guard with a hammer while trying to make off with fifty thousand pounds in a stolen car.'

'It was self defence,' said Florence Bird. 'The security guard shouldn't have had a go. He hit Michael and Michael just tried to protect himself. As boys do.'

Nothing, thought Madden, would ever turf Florence Bird from the nest in which she sat protectively over her chick.

Jasmine stayed with her. Madden didn't want her making any quick calls to her son's mobile. He didn't want the bird to fly. He got back in the car and drove to Priory Farm. The track was heavy with mud and full of potholes. The car lurched from side to side. Outside a tall corrugated iron barn, a girl was standing smoking. She eyed him with undue hostility. She folded her arms and came towards him. There was even something insolent about her gait. From inside the shed came a loud banging, like a hammer on wood.

'Can I help you?' she asked.

It wasn't a question. It was a way of telling him to go away. Her face was hard as nails. Madden didn't like her. Some people had that effect on him.

He showed his warrant card.

'I want to see Michael Bird.'

'He's busy.'

She folded her arms.

'You'll be busy too in a minute. Facing a charge of obstructing police. Get him out here.'

'You can't come in,' she said.

'What's your name?'

'Caroline.'

Parked outside the barn was a lime green Subaru Impreza with an enormous spoiler. It had leopardskin covers on the seats and two fluffy dice hanging in the windscreen. It reeked of class.

'That his car?'

'Might be.'

Madden stepped forward. She blocked him.

'It's premises,' she said. 'You need a warrant to enter premises.'

'Don't tell me what I can or can't do, Caroline, just get him out here.'

'It's secret,' she said.

'Just call him.'

'Thought you were a reporter at first,' she thawed slightly. 'You'd be surprised at the number of people who try to sneak a look at the tab before Bonfire. Just a minute.'

She turned to go back into the shed.

'Call him from here,' said Madden. 'And don't say who wants him.'

She called.

'Michael, the law wants you.'

'Thanks,' said Madden. 'You're a sport.'

'You're welcome,' she said.

She threw the stub of her cigarette on the ground and mashed it into the mud with her shoe. Madden waited. He waited too long. She tried to stare him out. It didn't take that long for somebody to come out of a barn. Madden pushed past her and ran inside.

'You can't go in there!' she shouted at him.

A motley group of people were putting the finishing touches to a giant tableau. Madden only briefly registered what it was. The American president with a missile through his skull, mounted on a wheeled cart. It gave a new meaning to political correctness, he thought briefly. A pot of paint went flying as the artisan group scattered in front of him. Madden made for the open door at the back of the barn.

Michael Bird was running headlong down a country track between two hedgerows and disappeared through a gap in one of them. Madden flung himself down the track and through the gap after him. Bird looked back, caught his foot in some briars, spun sideways, almost pirouetted in the air, and went down into a steaming heap of fresh manure. It was an ignominious end to what had begun as a hopeless flight. Madden stared down at him as Bird extracted himself ponderously from the fuming sludge.

'Ever felt,' he said, 'in deep shit?'

10

Michael Bird sat with arms tightly folded. He was still in deep shit, though of a different kind. They had fetched him a blanket and he sat wearing that and just his socks. He scowled across the table with an air of arrogance tempered by a feeling of stupidity at having got himself arrested. Running out of the back of a barn while his car was parked at the front hadn't been his brightest move but legs sometimes moved quicker than brains.

Bird looked as described. He was handsomer in the flesh than Madden had thought he would be, with a short neck in which a vein seemed to throb perpetually. His head was shaved to the scalp and he had squared sideburns similarly cropped. From his left ear dangled an inverted crucifix. He fixed Madden with a pair of very dark, penetrating eyes. Madden wouldn't have gone so far as to say that they were evil, but they were certainly hypnotic. He could imagine a certain kind of girl – and a few blokes – desiring to jump into bed with this guy.

In Bird's pockets were a mobile phone, a packet of cigarettes, another of condoms, some loose change and a matchbox with 'Ratty's Bar' printed on it. Nothing incriminating. Madden knew Ratty's Bar, however. There was a mobile phone number scrawled on the matchbox. He made a note of it. They had retrieved three hammers from the tab shed. They had all been sent up to forensic, as had Bird's Subaru car, as had his clothing. Innocent people, in Madden's view, didn't do runners.

Bird maintained he had nothing to hide.

'I was stupid,' he said. 'But look at it from my perspective.'

He was intelligent, thought Madden. A thug with a perspective.

'I've been inside. The police always pick on you if you've been inside.'

Bird denied ever having visited Lavinia Roberts. He had never heard of her. He didn't know where Southover Street was. He had never contacted clairvoyants, he had never contacted her. He had never even seen a clairvoyant. He had never telephoned her, or seen her advert, or heard of Vina the Mystic, or walked down the pier when he was younger and seen her in her cubicle. The first time he ever heard of her was when Madden mentioned her name.

'I categorically deny knowing her,' he stressed.

'You can just deny it. That's good enough,' said Madden.

Jasmine passed him the timetable. The 'psychic times' he was starting to call it.

'Okay Michael, you deny ever going to see a psychic. How about last Wednesday?'

Michael Bird pretended to think back. Madden could tell he was pretending. That was why he was on one side of the table and Bird was on the other. Bird stroked his chin and said, 'Can't think.'

'We have six psychics, Michael, who all described you as somebody who visited them on that day. Between the hours of ten in the morning and half past five in the afternoon.'

'Must have been somebody who looked like me.' Bird folded his lean smooth arms. Madden gazed at the one of the devil and pitchfork on his right forearm.

'Oh I see. There are a load of skinheads with tattoos and crucifixes hanging off their ears wandering round Brighton, are there?'

'Must be,' Bird said. 'In fact every weekend you see loads of guys like that down from London.'

'This wasn't a weekend. It was a Wednesday. Keep thinking.'

'I am thinking,' said Bird. 'It wasn't me.'

'Let's take one of these visits. Hubble Bubble. Keep thinking.'

'Never heard of it.'

'You didn't go for a psychic reading there?'

'No.'

'You weren't told about another psychic while you were there? Lavinia Roberts of Southover Street?'

Bird was getting fidgety. As well he might, thought Madden.

'No,' he said again. 'And even if I did, there's no law against going to psychics.'

'Did you go to Lavinia Roberts' house at eight o'clock on that Wednesday night for a reading? Did you, Michael?'

'No,' he said firmly.

'I think you're lying.'

The vein in Bird's neck was throbbing faster. He wasn't aware of it.

'Okay, can I come clean?' he said.

No, thought Madden, just go on denying it for a bit longer. Don't spoil our fun.

'I did go to see those clairvoyants, okay? But I didn't have anything to do with that one that got murdered. I never saw her.'

'Why?'

Bird shrugged his shoulders.

'Why not?'

'Why lie about it?'

'I was embarrassed.'

'Michael, you don't look like the kind of guy to me who gets embarrassed. A little tough nut like you. Just tell us why you went to see seven clairvoyants in one day.'

'Six,' said Bird, not to be caught out.

'*Six*, then.'

'Promise not to laugh?'

Madden and Jasmine sat there with stony faces.

'Do we look like this is funny?' she said to him.

'I guess I'm superstitious,' Bird grinned.

'Why six?' Madden pressed him.

'My lucky number.'

'What?'

'I was born on the sixth day of the sixth month. It's always been my lucky number.' He looked smug as he said it. 'Six readings. Six *different* readings. Do you know what you can take from that? A whole life plan. And do you know the most incredible thing? There wasn't one reading that conflicted in any major way with another. They all saw the same thing. Don't you find that incredible?'

'Yes, Earth shattering,' said Madden. 'Why did you give a different name to each one?'

'It just seemed like a fun idea,' said Bird.

'A fun idea? To use six different names?'

'Yeh. To test them out. To see if they can guess your right one.'

Madden narrowed his eyes.

'There's got to be something to it, don't you think? By this time next year I'm going to be in love, and not only that, I'm going to be surrounded by beautiful women. And I'm going to have a place in the sun, maybe Spain or Greece. A villa. With my own swimming pool.'

Bird had clearly not just fallen in bullshit but swallowed some of it.

'I'm also going to have a fleet of cars and be immensely wealthy. There are business opportunities on my horizon.'

'The only business opportunity on your horizon,' said Madden, 'is laundry and kitchen work in some nick. That's my prediction. Now tell us – *why in God's name did you visit six clairvoyants in one day*?'

'It was to do with Bonfire,' Bird said.

'Bonfire?'

'Yeh. Lewes Bonfire. It's coming up in a few weeks. I wanted to know how it was going to turn out. What the weather was going to be like. How successful it was going to be.'

Madden blinked. Just in case he was dreaming. No, he was still awake and interviewing a guy who spent a hundred pounds on clairvoyants to get a weather forecast. He'd been given some answers in his time but that one took a whole packet of Rich Tea.

'You're telling us, Michael, that you went to six clairvoyants to find out how a *firework display* would turn out?'

'Not just any firework display, Mr Madden. Bonfire.'

'I know what it's called. I've been to it.'

'It's the biggest date in the calendar. We prepare months in advance. We've got a real surprise tableau this year.'

'I know. I've seen it.'

'Some years it pours, one year before I was born it was cancelled because of flooding. This year it's going to be huge. I know this sounds crazy to you, Mr Madden—'

'You're right, Michael. It does. It sounds like the biggest load of hogwash I've ever sat here and listened to.'

'Me too,' said Jasmine.

'I've never missed a Bonfire. Except when I was inside. I've been with the Barbican since I was a kid. It's like – the main event of the year. Bigger than Christmas. Okay, I just like visiting clairvoyants, they make you feel good, they tell you things you want to know. There's nothing wrong with that.'

Madden slammed his hand palm down on the table. He'd heard enough.

'I think you went to see Lavinia Roberts, Michael. I think you went to visit her at eight o'clock that night. I think she read your cards and you didn't like what she saw, or *she* saw something *in* you – or *about* you – that you didn't like, and that you went back a few nights later and killed her.'

'I didn't,' said Bird, fretting. 'I never met her.'

'Why stop at six clairvoyants, Michael? Why not seven? Eight? Nine? Where were you at eight o'clock that night?'

This time he didn't pretend to think. He really thought. He thought hard.

'With Caroline,' he said. 'At the tab shed.'

'Anybody else?'

'No. We were on our own. She does painting, you see, and I do carpentry. It's a hobby of mine.'

A song came to Madden's mind. *If I had a hammer.* He asked about the night of the murder. Bird said he'd spent the evening with Caroline again at the tab shed, though on that occasion there had been others present. The night he had spent at home. His own sweet mother could verify it. Madden had absolutely no doubt she would.

'So why did you leg it?' he asked.

'Come on, Mr Madden, I've got form. I know I got mixed up with these bad guys up London—'

'Bad guys? You make it sound like a western, Michael. You got involved with a gang who cut people's hands off and gouged their eyes out if you so much as said good morning to them. They were a vicious band of crooks.'

'All that's behind me. Come on, do one of these psychological profiles on me. Does any guy go from armed robbery to killing clairvoyants? It's nuts. If I'd wanted to kill one of them for money, I could've done it with any of the six. I was alone with them. What possible motive could I have?'

Madden caught Jasmine's expression. She was thinking the same thing, clearly.

'One last question, Michael. Why did you once steal six skulls?'

'Oh that.' Bird dismissed it with a grin. 'That's old stuff.'

'It may be old stuff to you but it's new stuff to me.'

'I went on the Bonfire parade as the Grim Reaper, you know, with a scythe over my shoulder. I wanted the skulls to hang from a chain round my neck.'

'Did you have to steal them?'

'What do you think I am, Mr Madden? A grave robber?'

Upstairs, in his office, Jasmine put her cards on the table. Literally.

'Try it, Steve,' she said. She threw down a pack of ordinary playing cards on the table. She had found them in his desk. Madden would claim until his dying day that he had forgotten they were there.

'Is this a game?'

'Shuffle them.'

Madden shuffled them. He knew the point she was making.

'I phoned up three of the psychics that he visited,' she said. 'They all told me he shuffled the cards when he visited them. You try to shuffle a pack of cards without leaving fingerprints on them. Lavinia's cards have all been tested for prints. Michael Bird's prints aren't on them.'

'Maybe he didn't shuffle them. Maybe in her case he made a point of not touching them.'

'Why? If he hadn't yet planned to kill her? Why would he go to six clairvoyants, shuffle the cards, and not touch them when he went to the seventh? It doesn't make sense.'

'Are we sure these are the cards she used?'

'Lavinia told me those were the cards her mother *always* used,' said Jasmine.

'If a lot of people had handled them since, the prints could have become obliterated.'

'She had ten clients, Steve. Between the night you said she had her visitor and the time she was murdered. I checked in her diary. Ten clients wouldn't obliterate a set of prints.'

She went further.

'He would have to have been careful not to leave any prints when he visited either time.'

'There's DNA,' said Madden. 'A porous object like a card might absorb the sweat residue.'

'Do you know how long it'll take the lab to extract every strand of DNA from each one of those tarot cards?'

'Longer than the time we can hold him,' Madden admitted.

He turned over the 'Ratty's Bar' matchbox in his hand. He dialled the number that was scrawled on it. The phone was answered. An abrupt male voice said *Hello*.

'Who's that?' asked Madden.

'Who's that?' asked the person on the other end.

Madden rang off.

'Go to Bird's house, Jaz, see what else you can find, question his mother. She's not all saccharine, I'm sure. Check his alibi. Ruffle a few feathers if you have to. Find out what you can about his army career from her, find out if his interest in the occult extends beyond visiting clairvoyants.'

'You're taking what Lavinia said seriously? This business about her sensing occult evil?'

'You know me, Jaz,' he said. 'Always open-minded.'

11

Madden went back to the tab shed. Miss Hardware was still there, standing outside, smoking a cigarette. She blew a plume into the air defiantly.

'Fuck you,' she said.

Nice girl, thought Madden. Finishing school. Probably Switzerland.

'Fuck you,' she said again as he got closer.

'I'd try and be a bit more hospitable,' Madden suggested. 'Your boyfriend's in trouble.'

The others were inside the shed, banging away, putting the finishing touches to the tableau.

'You've fitted him up, you mean.'

'He's already done a pretty good job of that himself. How long have you been going out together?'

'Six months,' she said. 'Since he got out.'

She worked in a chemist shop in the town. She was a trainee. Madden decided not to go there for his medicines just in case she put nails in them.

'He ever talk to you about visiting clairvoyants?'

'He's superstitious.'

'You mean like black cats and walking under ladders?'

'Something like that.'

'Did you know he went to see six clairvoyants all on one day last week?'

She didn't look surprised. She didn't look like the kind of girl who would be surprised at anything.

'So?' she said.

'Don't you find that a bit strange?'

'It isn't for him.'

'Any idea why he did it?'

'Why don't you ask him?'

'I did. I'm asking you.'

'Maybe it's like when, you know, you work on a ship or in the theatre. You get superstitious. Maybe prison does that to you. I don't know. I've never been inside,' she said.

'I never heard that it does.'

'I never heard that it doesn't,' she rejoined.

'The night before last, where was he?'

'With me,' she said.

'What did you do?'

'Fucked,' she said.

'At least that's a straight answer. Where, if you don't mind me asking?'

She indicated the tab shed with a twist of her head.

'We had a bottle of wine after the others had left,' she said. 'Then we did it underneath.'

'Underneath what?'

'Underneath the tableau. It's hollow. You want any more details than that? On the Fifth we put fireworks inside and blow it up.'

'Did he say where he was going later that night?'

'No, he didn't say he was going into Brighton to commit a murder or anything like that,' she said cheekily. 'I'd have remembered.'

'He ever been violent with you, Caroline?'

'In our sex life or how do you mean?'

Some things just weren't worth pursuing.

'Mind if I go in and talk to the others? Your tableau's a secret with me.'

'Be my guest,' she said.

Madden went inside. On this occasion he had time to stop and look. Guy Fawkes took a back seat in the preparations for Lewes Bonfire. The effigy of the President of the United States did not only have a cruise missile through his head, he was also riding one. The builders were a mixed bunch. A councillor, an artist, a painter and decorator, a girl called Polly who ran a craft shop and a politics student. They were all local, they all knew Bird, they all knew he had a prison record, but that didn't matter. The Barbican Bonfire Society wasn't prejudiced. He was a member of the society, he was good fun, a good worker, he was useful with his hands, and that was the bottom line. Michael Bird wanted to go straight and being a member of the society gave him something to do and kept him busy.

Warmed to the cockles of his heart, Madden thanked them and left. Sometimes you learnt nothing. He felt he'd learnt less than nothing. Caroline was seeing off two kids on Raleigh choppers who were trying to spy. It was serious business, this Bonfire stuff. The kids cycled off, poking out their tongues. She gave them two fingers.

'They all want to see,' she said. 'You're privileged.'

'I have that effect on people,' said Madden.

He drove back into Brighton and went to Ratty's Bar.

The pub was brand new, though the premises were old. It had opened in the summer behind one of the seafront hotels and was accessed by a flight of steps that went down into what had once been a large wine cellar. The walls were painted deep red and the theme, not surprisingly, was rats. Stuffed ones, papier mâché ones, rat facts displayed on the walls in wooden frames, and a huge mural of two dancing rodents under an archway. It was a sprawling place, cavernous and sleazy, the kind of haunt where lovers could secrete themselves in dark, hidden corners and illegal substances could be easily sold, in spite of a notice above the bar warning that anyone caught with drugs would be immediately barred. The sleaze, however, was manufactured, a deliberate attempt to create an atmosphere of seediness and decline in stark contrast to some of the flashier, chromier, more funky bars in the city. The seating was an eclectic mix of old armchairs, sofas and wooden kitchen chairs, the tables either trestles or upturned wine casks, and the lighting low enough to disguise almost anything you wanted to disguise. Like drugs.

And it had caught on. Tired of paninis and organic salads

and designer lagers and Starbucks coffee shops, the punter could pop down to Ratty's for good-old-fashioned piles of bangers and mash and fresh caught cod and chips, and wash it all down with a selection of red wines or try one of Ratty's cocktails. Rat's Castle, Rentakiller, Rodent Racer and The Black Death were just a few that caught Madden's eye.

'One healthy pair of adult rats can be responsible for a thousand descendants in one year', read a RAT FACT on the wall. *'On the Red Sea coast at Qusir al-Quadim a mummified cat was found to contain the remains of six black rats in its stomach'*, read another.

But if the bar was eccentric, its owners were even more so. Madden knew both of them. Lucky Maynard had been on the fringes of the criminal world all his life though he had no form, and had supplied Madden with a lot of information over the years. Lucky (nobody knew his real name, not even Lucky, he had been told it once but had subsequently forgotten) had never been a registered informer. Anything Lucky gave Madden was strictly off the record. And sometimes it had been good information. Lucky was not the brightest spark in the firmament, however. A business like this would have been beyond his ability. Lucky's partner was the love of his life, a Thai transsexual called Ming. It was the sort of relationship that had 'Brighton' running through it like a stick of rock. Ming was, outwardly if not completely inwardly, mostly woman, though sometimes her previous sex gave itself away in raw moments. And a stunning woman at that. Shoehorned into a fabulous cocktail dress, she lorded it – or ladied it one should say – over Ratty's. She had once been an escort, and a classy one too, but had put all that behind her. Rumour had it she had saved well and had sunk the money into starting the business.

'Hi, Honey,' she squealed as Madden walked into the bar.

'Hello, Ming. How's business?'

'Business is good. Has been good, all through the summer. You want to try one of our *fabulous* cocktails? On the house?'

'You can't go throwing money away,' said Madden. 'I'll have a coke if that's okay.'

She squirted it into a glass, but she still refused to accept the money. Madden put it on the counter. He had a rule about accepting free drinks. He didn't. You never knew when your loyalty might be challenged or the rapport compromised. A drugs bust at Ratty's – he hoped it would never happen – would put him in an awkward situation. He tried to avoid awkward situations.

Ming put it in a collecting box for a local AIDS hospice.

Another remarkable thing about Ratty's was its blend of customers. Brighton had a huge gay population and a fair number of them flooded down here for the drag shows and cabarets at weekends. But more by accident than design, the venue also attracted a straight crowd, among them a few criminals, drawn by the presence of one of their number behind the bar. Madden had never enquired how they'd got past the licensing authorities. Another rumour had it that one of Ming's ex-clients who was seriously into bondage was on the committee. At lunchtimes came the business crowd, looking for something more quirky. Two middle-aged men at Ratty's huddled over a table might be long-term lovers, criminals planning a job or local businessmen. That was the thing about Ratty's. Sometimes you just couldn't tell who slotted where. It was a pub for all seasons.

'Where's your partner in crime?' asked Madden. It wasn't a good approach and he regretted it. Instantly.

'I'll call him.'

Ming called up the stairs. Lucky came down. He looked tidier than when Madden had first known him. Ming had clearly worked a bit of magic on his appearance. In the past, Lucky had dressed like something even the cat disdained to look at. Now his hair was neatly coiffured, he wore a clean, bright shirt and a pair of pressed jeans. He still looked a bit like a piece of cheap furniture that had been polished and polished to make it look good, but which still betrayed its unspectacular origins. Ming had even persuaded him to visit the dentist and have a few holes plugged.

'Hello, Mr Madden,' he smiled.

'Hello, Lucky. Like a word with you. That okay?'

'I don't give information any more, Mr Madden,' Lucky said.

'We've got a business to run,' Ming added sharply. She could turn from being effusive to waspish in less time than it took to blink.

'This is information about a customer, that's all.'

Madden produced a photograph of Michael Bird.

'You ever seen this guy?'

'Yeh, I know him,' said Lucky. 'He's been in here.'

'Even better. How well do you know him?'

Ming grabbed a tea towel and started drying glasses, making an irritating squeaky noise as she rubbed.

'We're running a pub,' she reminded him. 'We don't like giving out information about customers. It's not good. Supposing it got around? Lucky doesn't do this kind of thing any more.'

'Lucky?'

Lucky looked at Madden. Then back at Ming. It was clear now who ran Lucky's life. Being transsexual didn't run to abandoning trousers.

'Ming's right,' he said. 'I can't give information about customers.'

'This is information that wouldn't go past me. There's a murder involved, Lucky. That psychic who was murdered. Lavinia Roberts.'

'He doesn't give information about *murders*,' Ming shuddered.

'This was a brutal murder, Lucky. If you know anything at all, I'd be grateful if you could help me. If not, I'll just go away and won't bother you again.'

'That sounds like a very good idea,' said Ming.

'Lucky?'

'What do you want to know, Mr Madden?'

Ming slammed one of the glasses back under the bar. It broke. She started to sweep it up.

'Somewhere we can talk privately?'

The bar was quiet. They sat in a dimly-lit alcove. There was another Rat Fact on the wall. *'Did you know? A brown rat can gnaw at a pressure of five hundred kilograms per square centimetre producing six bites per second?'* Madden didn't know. He didn't want to.

'When did he come in here?' he asked.

'About three weeks ago,' said Lucky. 'He was with someone.'

'Who?'

'I don't know if I should be telling you this, Mr Madden.'

'Lucky, you and I go back a long way. You've done me a lot of favours. And you can't deny, I've done you a few. I need you now.'

It was true. Lucky had done jobs for him beyond the call of duty. Lucky had helped him in the hunt for his son's killer. And Madden had saved Lucky's life once, taken him back to his own house to protect him from elements that at the time seemed hell-bent on snuffing out his life. They owed each other.

'Who was he in here with?'

'He met Ronnie Edgeware.'

Madden sat back. To call it surprise would have been an understatement.

'*The* Ronnie Edgeware?'

'Don't know another one, Mr Madden.'

Ronnie Edgeware was the most notorious member of a notorious family. The Edgeware family were traditional East End gangsters. There were three brothers, and a fourth who was dead. The dead one, Frank, had been hacked to death with a machete by one of the other three who had discovered his brother sleeping with his wife. Lance Edgeware was now serving life for murder. There was little honour among thieves, and even less among their families, it had been said at the time. The third brother, Peter Edgeware, was also doing life – for a gold bullion robbery and the murder of a policeman. The job had been a big one, well planned, involving a dozen people, most of whom had been rounded up. Like all big jobs, it had a name. The Havilland Barr Robbery, named after the security van company involved, had been only a limited success for the Flying Squad who had handled it. Hardly any of the gold bullion had been recovered. It was rumoured that most of it had ended up in South America.

And that Ronnie Edgeware was the beneficiary of, if not all of it, a sizeable part. He had a large place out near Pyecombe, a village just north of Brighton, called High Hedges. It was reputed to have been bought with the proceeds. Proving it was impossible, or at least not worth the time. Ronnie Edgeware had legitimate business interests, a string of garages and repair shops, a hotel in Dover and two pubs. He had only served eighteen months for receiving, but nobody at his trial – or subsequently, Madden was well aware – believed any other scenario than that Ronnie Edgeware was the brains behind the Havilland Barr job.

'You hear what they talked about?' Madden asked Lucky.

'Come on, Mr Madden, you think I'm going to sit in and listen?'

'How long did they spend?'

'About half an hour.'

'Did they come in together? Leave together?'

'Bird came in first. Then Ronnie. They had a drink, chatted a bit, then Ronnie left on his own.'

'Has either of them been in here since?'

'Ronnie hasn't. This wouldn't really be his kind of place. Mike Bird uses it a lot.'

'Thanks, Lucky. It might be important, it might not.'

'I don't really like Ronnie Edgeware using this place,' said Lucky.

'I know. Lowers the tone. A few fun loving criminals is fine, but the Ronnie Edgewares of this world – you don't want them. I suggest you put a sign up.'

Ming threw down some beer mats on the table as though she was dealing out cards at a casino.

'We want to keep a good mix of people at this place,' she said. 'We want it to be the sort of place where a queen can shriek her tits off in one corner while the straights play pool in another.'

'Is that possible to keep up in Brighton?'

'Anything's possible in Brighton,' she said.

As Madden left and walked back onto the seafront, he reflected on the sentiment. It was true. Brighton sometimes seemed to him like the most accepting place on the planet. Lucky and Ming couldn't have embarked on their venture in the dreary suburbia of Tunbridge Wells or in the centre of a city like Birmingham or Manchester. Brighton it had to be. Clara had once said that Brighton wasn't so much a place as an idea. That was rich, coming from someone who now lived with an accountant in the Marina Village and professed these days to get most of her excitement there.

He turned in his tracks and headed up to the gallery.

'I'm sorry I've been so busy lately,' he told her.

'I've been busy too. Don't worry.' She was sitting at her desk, drinking orange juice and fingering a chocolate biscuit.

'I'm on this Roberts murder.'

'Got anybody?'

'Got somebody. No motive, though. You doing anything tonight?'

'Yes, going home.'

'Just wondered.'

He missed it. Going home and talking to her about his day, about the job, even if she had often been too tired or disinterested. It was impossible to get used to going back to an empty house after so many years of marriage. Especially when that house held so many ghosts. He would often delay his return, have a couple of drinks in Hanover before walking the half mile home and putting his key in the door. He would never go to sleep without looking at least once in the bedroom that used to be Jason's. Clara was away from it, in a new world, a new marriage, new surroundings. He was left with the bricks and mortar and the memories that went with their old life. The room of their dead son felt like a shrine at times, but at other times it was a painful reminder of the relationship he had lost.

'Remember I told you about the scarf.'

'Oh yes,' she said. She was the only person he could talk to about this.

'Well, the other things Lavinia told me. About the guy she

thought might be a serial killer. She said she felt he'd been in the army and that he had an interest in the occult. Well, the guy we've got was in the Terries. And he's certainly a bit of a weirdo.'

'It doesn't take clairvoyance to guess these things about a person,' Clara told him.

'I know that. She also said when she was reading my cards that she saw an old relationship that I thought was over. How did she put it? That there were wonderful things to discover in it.'

Clara didn't reply. Instead, she fiddled with her pen.

'She also said I was to be very careful and not rush in.'

'Good advice,' she said.

'That's what I thought.'

She graduated from fiddling with her pen to searching in her desk.

'I can see you're busy,' he said. 'I'll leave you.'

'I'm not busy,' she said. 'In fact I'm bored. It's been a quiet day. Suppose I pack up ten minutes early and we go and have a glass of wine.'

A glass of wine and Clara was always an irresistible combination.

They went round the corner to the Basketmakers. It was one of Brighton's unspoilt gems. There were no rats here, and you didn't feel like you were part of a group experiment. The walls were festooned with tins in which regulars and some not-so-regulars left secret messages for each other. It brought back a few more pleasant memories. He and Clara had once left a message for each other here, just for fun, in the Johnny Walker whisky bottle tin just above the table to the right of the door. He bought two glasses of Merlot. It wasn't organic, thank God.

'I hope you solve it.' She raised her glass.

'Oh, I will. I just hope my judgement isn't skewed by what Lavinia told me. That's all.'

'Does he look like a serial killer?'

'What does a serial killer look like? He's got a criminal record for assaulting a security guard and making off with fifty grand.'

'I'd watch him,' said Clara.

'And he tried to run away when I approached him. And he denied ever going to clairvoyants when he clearly had been.'

'I'd watch him closely,' she said.

'He once stole six human skulls to wear round his neck as part of a Grim Reaper costume.'

'Now, I'd *really* watch him.' She leant closer to him.

'He's also recently had a drink with Ronnie Edgeware.'

'*The* Ronnie Edgeware?' She echoed Madden's own reaction.

'There's only one Ronnie Edgeware.' He was tempted to sing it. 'I don't know what to read into that if anything.'

'You always used to go on your instinct,' she said. 'Why distrust it now?'

'Because my instinct's been driven by the predictions of the sort of witness I would never normally listen to. In this case, the victim.'

'You don't often have that luxury,' Clara reminded him. 'In almost every other case you never know the victim. Here you've got evidence straight from her mouth. Why not forget for the moment she was a clairvoyant? She'd been meeting people for years, all her life, complete strangers, trying to tell them things about their lives. Magicians do it, they make things look like magic when they aren't. I'm sure Lavinia Roberts was a shrewd judge of character, I'm sure she could tell you a host of things about people just by looking at them. I suppose what I'm saying is – don't discount what she said just because of what she did for a living.'

Madden thought about it.

'And Jason's red scarf?'

'That's spiritualism. Don't get me onto that. That's something else entirely. And are you absolutely sure nothing appeared in the newspapers about it? I think I remember reading something once about Jason supporting Arsenal.'

'You mean you think she read that and remembered it? And assumed Jason would have a scarf with the colours? And used the information to impress me?'

'I don't think she was out to impress you,' said Clara. 'From what you've told me about her, I think she wanted genuinely to help. That's all these people want to do. Help. How they go about it is another matter.'

She finished her wine.

'Another?'

'Sorry, but I've really got to go.'

'Like old times, wasn't it?'

'It was.'

She got up. She slung her bag across her left shoulder, the way she always had done. She was maybe another man's wife, but the little things she did and the way she moved and the way she smelt still somehow belonged in his domain. Clara hadn't changed. He still felt as though she was his. How she felt was difficult for him to tell.

After she had left, it struck him that she had suggested the Basketmakers.

Madden tore a page out of his notebook and wrote on it the words 'I still love you'. Then he screwed it up and wrote instead. 'Thanks for old times, Clara. Maybe again? Steve.' He folded the note and put it in the Johnny Walker whisky bottle tin above the table.

He wondered if it would still be there on his next visit.

12

Some villains locked themselves away in mock Palazzo style houses behind security gates in deepest Essex, while many poured their wealth into hacienda style properties on the Costa del Sol and similar stretches of sun-drenched white stucco. Many did both, and more besides. Ronnie Edgeware aspired to class, Madden thought to himself, as he stepped out of his car on the edge of a golf course just outside Pyecombe and looked at the house called High Hedges. English-gentleman type of class. He had bought himself a Jacobean country house that might have been the residence of a pop star or a celebrity footballer or fat-cat company chairman. You couldn't get more Sussex-cream-tea than Pyecombe. Nestling undisturbed on the Downs, it was picture-postcard perfect, home to a smithy made famous by the manufacture of the Pyecombe Crook, the 'Rolls Royce' of shepherds' crooks, used by flockmasters in the nineteenth century from Sussex to as far as New Zealand. Madden thought it deeply ironic that Ronnie Edgeware and his wife should live in a village famous for its crooks.

Two Range Rovers were parked outside. His and hers, no doubt. As Madden walked up the drive, he heard the sound of cellos playing. It wasn't a recording. Whoever the musicians were, they were good. Very good.

There was nothing like a direct approach, he thought. He rang the bell. After a minute – longer it seemed – a well dressed middle-aged woman answered the door. She was a bleached blonde and reminded Madden of the actress who got pecked comatose in Hitchcock's *The Birds*. He couldn't for the moment remember her name. She wore a green pencil skirt and a white blouse and a buttoned green jacket and from her wrists dangled masses of jewellery. Madden thought at first they might be entertaining, but he was wrong. This was obviously thc jewellery she did her housework in.

'Detective Inspector Madden,' he said. 'I take it you're Mrs Edgeware. Is your husband at home?'

'Who is it, Patricia?'

The man who came to the door almost in her tracks was sunbronzed and wearing slacks and an open neck shirt. His hair was artificially black, as though he had rubbed boot polish into it. In his chin was a dimple the size of a five-penny piece.

'A Detective Inspector Madden,' she said.

'Well show him in.'

She stood aside and the jewellery jangled. Madden stepped inside. The lobby smelt of furniture polish and fresh air spray.

'Hope I'm not intruding,' he said. Frankly, he didn't care. He was an intrusive kind of guy.

'Of course not,' replied Ronnie Edgeware, lying through every one of his small pellet-like teeth. 'The police are always welcome here.'

The outward image of the English country gentleman evaporated as soon as Madden stepped inside. Ronnie Edgeware showed him into a lounge which was decorated in appallingly bad taste. The carpet was cream and the walls a regency stripe. On the floor was a tiger-skin rug, while the head of the poor beast glowered from a plaque above the white marble fireplace. Elsewhere it was a mixture of rococo and Ikea with a touch of the traditional thrown in and a bit of art deco for good measure. Madden wondered what it was about some criminals that made them aspire to class but miss style by a mile. He supposed you had to be born to it, not elevated to it by a million pounds' worth of hastily melted down gold bullion.

'Drink?'

'No thanks,' said Madden.

'Can you leave us, Patricia?' Ronnie Edgeware poked a cigarette between his lips and lit it. He didn't offer one to Madden. 'Well, what can I do for you, Inspector—?'

'Madden.' As though he needed reminding.

Patricia closed the door softly on them. This was obviously the kind of house where a visit from the law merited as much surprise as a call from the gasman, though there was something about Ronnie Edgeware's demeanour that was grimly unsettling. The man was being polite, but he wasn't being hospitable or accommodating. Presumably you didn't just walk in on the Ronnie Edgewares of the world. Madden wasn't sure what you did. He'd never usually bothered with niceties when it came to the criminal classes, especially where murder was concerned.

'I'm enquiring into a murder case.' Madden put his cards on the table. It seemed a good place to start. 'Lavinia Roberts, the clairvoyant in Southover Street who was killed two days ago.'

'I believe I read something about it,' said Ronnie.

'We're holding someone at the moment. A Michael Bird. I believe you know him.'

'Michael Bird. Michael Bird.' Ronnie said the name twice just to remind himself. 'What about him?'

'Where did you meet?'

Ronnie Edgeware sat down. He didn't invite Madden to. He looked into an onyx ash tray into which he tapped the ash from his cigarette.

'In prison,' he said. 'I did a spell for receiving which you're no doubt aware of.'

'I was aware,' said Madden.

'What else do you want to know?'

'When you last saw him.'

'I haven't seen him since I got out.'

'You sure about that?'

'I meet a lot of people, Mr Madden. Make your point.'

'I have pretty good evidence you've met up with him since. And recently.'

'I'd be interested to know what evidence.'

'Your telephone number written on a matchbox.'

'I could have given him that in prison.'

'But you didn't,' said Madden.

'Let me see.' He turned the matter over. It was a good performance but it wouldn't win an Oscar. 'Oh yes. About three weeks ago. I met him once. I offered him a job.'

'What kind of a job?'

'A garage job. I have a few repair shops and I thought I could do him a favour by employing him in one. I'd almost forgotten.'

'Has he taken you up on it?'

'The offer's still open,' said Ronnie.

'Would you have any idea why he might visit six clairvoyants in one day?'

'I have no idea. Why don't you ask him?'

'I did.'

'Then there's nothing more I can tell you.' Ronnie wasn't forthcoming.

'Pity. You see, he's not helping us very much. Or himself. I just thought you might be able to shed a little light on his character.'

'You want a reference, Inspector Madden? You know, you've got a very good name. Because you're beginning to madden me. Just a little bit.'

'That joke's been made before.'

'What makes you think it was a joke?' Ronnie smiled.

'Did you contact him about the job? Or did he contact you?'

'I can't remember. He just promised to keep touch when he got out.'

'You can't remember whether he phoned you or you phoned him?'

'I have a terrible memory. I make about fifty calls a day. That's your answer.'

The door opened and a teenage girl bounced in. She wore a school skirt and blouse and long white socks up to her knees. She obviously hadn't been told there was a visitor. She looked at Madden and then at her father. She was about fifteen but the woman in her was fast exploding. She had full developed breasts and a precocious air. She tossed back her auburn hair.

'Dad, you promised to help me with my essay,' she said.

'Later,' said Ronnie. 'This is Detective Inspector Madden. My daughter Clementine.'

Like the orange, thought Madden. And just as sweet.

'Hello,' said Clementine. 'Are you two talking business?'

'You could say. Now scram.'

Madden heard the sound of the cello quite clearly now through the open door. Clementine Edgeware was clearly as unfazed as her mother by the presence of the law around her father. It was probably business as usual.

'I haven't heard that piece before.' Her father stopped her.

'It's Boccherini – Cello Concerto in B flat,' she said.

'Play Saint-Saëns.' He looked at Madden. 'It's my favourite.'

'Will you *please* help with my essay?'

'Yes. Now do as you're told.'

He tapped her lightly on the bottom, and she went back upstairs.

'What's the essay on? My father's occupation?' Madden asked.

Ronnie Edgeware didn't rise to the remark. Instead he directed his visitor's attention to a photograph of two girls in what appeared to be a school orchestra.

'I have the most talented and gifted daughters. Claire is going to be another Jacqueline du Pré. Don't you think they're pretty?'

Claire and Clementine Edgeware were undeniably pretty. From upstairs there now came another piece of music, a duo. Ronnie Edgeware made a show of going into a rapture.

'The second movement of Saint-Saëns' Cello Concerto.' He poured a drink, but did not offer one to Madden as he had before. 'It's my desert island disc.'

'What island might that be? Alcatraz?'

'Bit touristy these days. Try St Lucia in the Caribbean.'

'I don't get on holiday that often.'

'You should. You should take a very long one. You might need it.'

It was a blatant threat. Madden didn't have to remind himself that this was a man who, in his youth, had nailed a rival's feet to the floor. Whose brother had picked up a machete and hacked his own sibling to death. Whose other brother had shot a policeman and would never likely see the outside of prison. Ronnie Edgeware might have legitimate business interests and a wife who looked like a Hitchcock heroine and two daughters who were musical starlets, but the grain was the same.

'I'm sorry I can't help you with respect to Michael Bird. Like I said, he was just an acquaintance I made in prison. I think he looked up to me as a father figure. And I suppose I wanted to help him as I'd help a son. That's all there is to it.'

Madden doubted very much if that was all there was to it, but without making himself unpopular he wasn't to get much further.

'Well, I'm sorry to bother you,' he said.

'Next time phone first, or make an appointment, or better still go through my solicitor.' Ronnie showed him to the door.

'I wouldn't want to cause you all that trouble,' Madden pledged.

'Oh, it's no trouble, I assure you.'

Then, 'Are you going to charge Bird?'

'I wouldn't keep his job open.'

'Shame. Thought he was a reformed character. You never can tell.'

Patricia came through the lobby with a tray of chintzy tea cups and buttered ginger cake on a plate.

'Mr Madden's just going,' Ronnie told her.

'I'm sorry your visit was so brief,' she said.

Tippi Hedren, that's who it was. Patricia Edgeware's bleached blonde hair was done up into the same sort of beehive. It was a style that had gone out. Though she dressed like she was giving a cocktail party to a room full of suburbanites, Patricia Edgeware's pose betrayed the fact she had probably begun life as a piece of arm candy. The road to middle class respectability was long and tortuous.

'I shouldn't give my phone number to people who write them on matchboxes,' Ronnie said, smiling, as he showed him out of the door.

'No you shouldn't.'

'You'll excuse me if I smell a rat.'

As Madden walked down the drive, he could still hear the two cellos. He thought over Ronnie Edgeware's parting comment. He had attempted to keep Lucky out of it, but might just have done the reverse. There was nothing he could do except hope that Ronnie Edgeware had the capacity to behave like the gentleman he aspired to be.

He phoned Jasmine. She had been over Bird's house.

'You won't want to know what I found,' she said.

'The murder weapon?'

'You don't want to know.'

'*I* want to know. *You* don't want to tell me.'

'Right,' she said, teasing him.

'Detective Sergeant Carol, if you don't tell me, I shan't take you out for dinner at some romantic little pub on the Downs.'

'Which pub?' she asked.

'We'll take pot luck.'

'I wasn't doing anything tonight,' she said. 'Except working on a murder.'

'Good. Now we've got that settled, will you tell me what you found in Bird's house?'

'It was in his bedroom. Under his pillow. A voodoo doll with two black pins through the eyes.'

Madden asked her to repeat that.

'It still doesn't make him a devil worshipper, Steve,' she said.

'What the hell docs it make him?' Madden asked. 'Mother Teresa?'

13

There was more. The voodoo doll kept company in a drawer of socks with what looked like a dog's skull. Vampire books by Anne Rice and novels by Stephen King were eclipsed by a well thumbed paperback about a real-life mass murder in Matamoros, Mexico. Madden read the description of it. *The horrifying true story of the murdering drug cult whose members committed ritual slaughter and human sacrifice on a scale that horrified the world.* Madden had never heard of the case. He reckoned that while the world was being horrified he must have been asleep.

Jasmine was right. It didn't make Michael Bird evil. It didn't make him anything. The lab had come back with nothing. There was no evidence he had driven into Brighton in the middle of the night and parked anywhere near Southover Street. There was no motive. Bird's mother was claiming he had played cards with her till the small hours and made her a cup of cocoa before going to bed at half past one. He was so clean, thought Madden, he was starting to squeak. You couldn't hold a guy for being simply strange.

'Let him go,' said Ray Millington.

Trouble was simmering. Madden could tell. Millington had Jack Fieldhouse in his office. Jack Fieldhouse had been on three days' leave and taken advantage of a booze cruise across the Channel plus two nights in Paris with his diminutive wife whom Madden had christened The Fieldmouse. Fieldhouse had only just learnt that Bird was in custody.

Fieldhouse had been attempting to diet but there was little sign he was succeeding. His extended belly was still locked in mortal combat with the belt of his trousers.

'Enjoy Paris?' Madden asked him.

They were always polite. But Madden loathed Fieldhouse. Not only had he messed up the investigation into Jason's murder but he was also a racist and a bully. Unfortunately, in spite of those shortcomings, he was also a good detective. Madden had the good grace to regard their differences as water under the bridge just so long as he didn't have to swim in it.

'Yes thanks. Very romantic.'

Madden couldn't see Fieldhouse being romantic.

'I've had a telephone call from Ronnie Edgeware's solicitor.' Millington got to one of the points of the meeting. 'Wanting to know why you harassed him.'

'I didn't harass him. I never saw a guy look less harassed in his life.'

'He says you did.'

'Some criminals are off limits now, are they, sir? Once they get to celebrity status and everybody knows their name, they can no longer be regarded as members of the public? I just went there to ask about his relationship with Bird.'

'Why didn't you ask Bird?'

'I'm going to ask Bird. And if he gives me the same story I'll know they're telling the truth, unless they knocked something up between them beforehand.'

Jack Fieldhouse shook his head, expelled a mouthful of air.

'No need, Steve,' he said. 'I can tell you Bird's side of the story. Edgeware was going to give him a job in one of his repair shops, right?'

Madden sat down. He didn't like people muscling in on his cases. Especially Fieldhouse.

'You talked to him?'

'Yeh. We just had a chat. I've known him some time.'

'Get to the point, Jack.'

'I knew Bird long ago. Before he went inside. I've met him again a few times since he got out. I'd heard he'd got friendly with Ronnie Edgeware in the nick and thought it would be interesting to meet up. He's pretty pliable, likes a drink, know how I mean?'

'Just tell me direct.'

'You know how valuable it would have been to have somebody on the inside, somebody that Ronnie Edgeware trusts? Bird might have been that guy. Might have told us stuff eventually that would have put Edgeware away for a lot longer than eighteen months. Might have been quite a coup.'

'You didn't waste your time in France, then.'

Fieldhouse didn't get it.

'You learnt a bit of French. *Coup*.'

Fieldhouse wasn't in a joking mood.

'That's all blown now, Steve. Edgeware isn't going to take Bird into his confidence now he knows we're interested in him. It's a great opportunity out the window.'

'Well, that's what happens when you leave windows open and birds flying around,' said Madden. '*Tant pis pour nous*.'

'Can't you be serious?' asked Millington. 'Just for one minute?'

'You're trying to tell me, Jack, that Bird was going to turn informer? Against Ronnie Edgeware? The Pyecombe Crook himself? I don't believe it. I don't believe Edgeware would be so stupid as to betray his secrets to some freak he met in prison.'

'This was more than just a friendship they had in prison,' Fieldhouse said. 'It was really close. Father and son sort of thing. Know how I mean?'

If Madden had not possessed a deeper faith in human nature, he might have believed that Jack Fieldhouse was making a cruel dig. Madden knew all about father and son relationships. And he knew about betrayal.

'So let's get this straight. Bird was going to go work for Ronnie Edgeware and eventually spill all his secrets, and you were going to be the personal recipient of information that the Flying Squad would love to have and haven't been able to obtain in years?'

'That's about it,' said Jack Fieldhouse with a boastful flourish. 'And by arresting Bird and questioning Ronnie Edgeware, you blew it, Steve. You blew it big time.'

* * *

Later that night, they let Bird go.

But not before Madden had found out why he possessed a voodoo doll with black pins through the eyes and the skull of a dog.

'I'm a witch,' said Bird.

'You're a weird bastard.'

'Okay, I'm not a witch. I was joking. Only joking. The voodoo doll's a joke, it was given to me as a present. The skull I found on the beach. Is there anything sinister in that?'

He didn't bother to wait for his mother or his girlfriend to bring him fresh clothes. Instead he put on his stinking ones, walked out of the police station, threw a sheet of plastic over the driving seat of his Subaru, and drove off.

'Follow him,' Madden told Jasmine.

'Where?'

'Wherever he goes. Don't let him out of your sight. I want to know where he goes and who he sees. Especially if he goes to visit any more psychics.'

'You know I hate surveillance,' she said.

She had good reason.

'I'm not Jack Fieldhouse,' Madden reminded her.

Jack Fieldhouse once thought it a great wheeze to send Jasmine out on a totally unnecessary surveillance job one day shortly after she had finished her training. It entailed her crouching behind the wall of a pig farm for eighteen hours. He made sure nobody relieved her. When she came back, feeling sick and in tears, he laughed. She played neither the race card nor the female one. Instead, one day in the station canteen she put senna pods into his curry. It was, according to station legend, the nearest the fat detective ever got to becoming an Olympic runner.

'You're convinced he's involved.' It was a question rather than a statement.

'Maybe policemen are a bit like clairvoyants, Jaz. We use instincts we don't fully understand.'

On his way home, Madden made a detour and called in at the Basketmakers. He bought a pint and took it to the table where he had sat with Clara. He opened the lid of the Johnny Walker whisky tin on the wall. Just to see if his message was still there. It wasn't.

There was another piece of paper, and in Clara's handwriting were the words, *I just want both of us to be happy. Clara. XX*

He couldn't have put it better himself.

14

Michael Bird did not go home to his mother. That night she had to forego card playing and cocoa with her adored and adoring offspring. Neither did he go to Miss Hard-as-Nails, who presumably was left still guarding the inner secrets of the tab shed while wondering why her lover had not returned to her. Both had rung the police station to find out when he was going to be released, to be told simply that he had been. It was not their job to tell family and friends why suspects had not returned home. Madden knew, because Jasmine phoned him that morning.

After leaving the police station in his lime green Subaru with its leopardskin covers and throaty exhaust, Michael Bird had driven straight to the home of Ronnie Edgeware.

'He's been there all night,' she told him.

She was currently parked in a tree-lined lovers lane by the edge of the golf course, talking to him over her mobile and watching High Hedges. It wasn't called High Hedges for nothing. Walls of dark coniferous leaves bordered it on three sides. Bird's car was still parked outside. It was six a.m. Madden was still in bed. She felt quite good about waking him up. She had sat all night in the car with Detective Constable Russell Evans who talked about sport incessantly and whose breath stank of onions because he cut them up raw and put them on sandwiches. She was not a happy bunny.

Madden was intrigued.

'Why didn't he go home? To see his dear old mother?'

'Want me to go inside and ask him?'

'No. Just stay where you are. You're doing a great job, Jaz.'

Madden tipped some muesli into a bowl, flooded it with milk

and ate it while looking at Clara's paintings. He still had her note in his pocket. He was tempted to frame it and put it up alongside. Half an hour after opening time he was at Hubble Bubble.

Forensically, there was as much against Richard and Natalie Blance as there was against Michael Bird. They had found matching fibres in Lavinia's house but nothing that couldn't be accounted for by innocent transference. That didn't mean they were off the hook. Madden was still chewing on Jasmine's theories that Richard Blance had gone round there and battered her to death over the un-paid-back loan. Ten thousand pounds was a good motive in anybody's book. He wondered how many readings Lavinia had had to give to earn that amount. A simple piece of arithmetic came out at five hundred. Besides, he wanted to see Natalie Blance again.

Richard was wearing a different cardigan. Like the man, it was grey. Madden waited until the shop emptied temporarily of customers. He glanced at some customers' notices on a board which advertised a Wicca workshop and an invitation to indulge in Spiritual Response Therapy. Pagan Pet Rescue had a homeless black labrador in need of a good earth-mother. He increasingly felt as though the planet he was on was revolving without him.

He watched the last customer close the door and brought up the very un-spiritual subject of the ten grand. Richard appeared unfazed.

'I would have repaid it to her. In time,' said Richard.

'How come you didn't mention it to us before?' asked Madden.

'It didn't seem important.'

'According to your wife, your mother-in-law had already contacted her solicitor about getting it back. Didn't you think that was important enough?'

'You think I killed her to avoid paying it?'

'I think you had a motive to kill her, Richard. By your own admission, you hated her. You owed her ten thousand. That isn't chickenfeed.'

'It wouldn't have done her much good. She was dying anyway, I've just discovered.'

'I know that. Natalie knew that. But you didn't. That's my point.'

'I don't know why Natalie didn't tell me about her mother,' Richard said sadly. 'We don't keep secrets from each other.'

There wasn't a couple on earth who didn't keep secrets from each other, Madden thought.

'How is business?'

'Okay,' said Richard.

'I thought maybe I'd get more of an accountant's answer. Like is it in the black or the red? Or somewhere in-between?'

Richard took some books out from under the counter and put them on top.

'Want to look through them?' he asked.

'I'll take your word for it. For the moment.'

'Business is good. All this stuff is a growth market. People's disillusionment with established religion. We had a vicar in here the other day ranting and raving.' He put the books away. 'I'm thinking of opening some more branches. Operating a franchise.'

'Yet you don't believe in any of it yourself?'

'You don't have to eat leeks to be a greengrocer,' said Richard.

'No, but it helps to sell the product.'

'The product sells, Mr Madden. Look at the crystals behind you. There are people who live their lives by crystals. Angels, fairies, North American dream catchers, you name it. I'd have paid her the ten thousand back in a year or so.'

'By which time it would have been too late, Richard.'

'Yes. Sad that.'

'Where is Natalie?'

'Upstairs.'

Madden left him, ascended the stairs to paradise, and heard Natalie's soft tones behind the purple starry curtain. The door to the treatment room was closed. He imagined Paula had a client. The curtain parted and a middle-aged woman in a green raincoat and carrying an umbrella emerged, looked slightly embarrassed at seeing Madden, and scurried down the stairs.

Natalie was sitting in a narrow, alcove-like space with a crystal ball in front of her.

'Mind if I squeeze in for a chat?' Madden asked.

''Course not,' she smiled. 'You can have a reading if you want.'

'No thanks.'

It was a squeeze. Natalie called it cramped. Madden thought it was cosy.

'Do you really see things in that?' he asked.

Her wide dark eyes were full of innocence, of childlike wonder.

'Of course,' she said. 'I see right now a man come to ask me lots of questions and who I hope has a few answers.'

'Right with the first, wrong with the second, I'm afraid. Still, one out of two is not bad.'

'You shouldn't mock, Mr Madden.'

'I'm sorry if it sounded that way. I didn't mock your mother and I wouldn't you. I have good reasons.'

'It's a gift,' said Natalie. 'Like musical talent. Artistry.'

'Richard told me how you two met in your mother's booth on the pier. How you chatted him up over a reading. Was that a case of you knowing the future you wanted?'

Natalie chuckled.

'I was nineteen. Mum was livid. She said getting off with a customer just wasn't the done thing. But I was young and just a girl.'

She was still young and just a girl. If Madden had been in Richard Blance's shoes, he would have done exactly the same thing. Hang any prediction to the contrary.

'How did your mother take the news that she was dying?' asked Madden. 'I know the answer to that is probably obvious, but I have a reason for asking.'

'She was depressed. As we all would be,' said Natalie, bowing her head a fraction. 'That's why I tried to see her as much as possible.'

'You see, I'm still trying to work out why she came downstairs in the middle of the night to read the cards. Could that be the reason? To find out how long she had? If it would be a painful end? Those sorts of things?'

'Maybe,' Natalie answered.

A person with a limited amount of time to live and a death sentence hanging over them might well want to know what the future held in the short space of time left. Madden remembered his father talking pathetically of 'sorting out his affairs'. He hadn't really known what that meant. In your teens, you didn't have affairs to sort out.

'Were you afraid she might do something?'

'How do you mean?'

Do something. Like kill yourself. Take your own life. Commit suicide. Another damned euphemism like 'that sad business'.

'Sorry, Natalie. I know it's painful but did your mother ever mention suicide as an option?'

Natalie looked straight at him, and nodded. Then almost straight away afterwards she shook her head.

'She didn't mention it as such,' she said. 'I mean, she didn't say she ever contemplated it. But you pick up things. Things like – she didn't want to suffer and would prefer to die quickly or in her sleep. As we all would.'

'Do you think your mother would have been capable of taking her own life?'

'I don't know. How can you know that about a parent? She had a horror of going into hospital, of never coming out,' she added.

'Which more than likely would have been the outcome.'

'More than likely,' said Natalie.

A strange notion was forming in Madden's mind. The hammer blows to her head – Madden remembered Colleen telling him that some seemed superficial, almost tentative, while others were killing blows. That had never made sense to him until now. Neither had the strangest feature of all, the appearance at the crime scene that Lavinia Roberts must have watched her killer break in through the door.

It was fanciful, almost impossible to put into any rational, realistic scenario. But a picture was slowly forming of Lavinia Roberts inviting her own hopefully quick death. And knowing her killer.

'Did you believe in her talents as a spiritualist?' he ventured into another area.

'I'm not a spiritualist.' Natalie put him straight. 'I prefer to believe in reincarnation. I'm more into Hindu and Buddhist philosophy.'

'Again, there's a reason I ask. A more personal one.'

He told Natalie about Jason's red scarf.

'My ex-wife thinks your mother was just trying to comfort me.'

'Did you need comforting?' asked Natalie.

She shifted her position ever so subtly, until she was leaning towards him, almost touching him with her knees under the table.

'Every day I need comforting. To lose a son you never got to know properly is hard to live with. I'm living with it. Your mother, I'll admit, did comfort me a lot by what she said. Only I found it very hard to believe. When she died so suddenly and so brutally, it hit me too.'

Natalie slid her hand across the table and rested it gently on his.

'Mum may have sensed that,' said Natalie. 'It's rather similar to reading cards. You're there to help the person, not worry them. You're there to guide them, give them some hope. The last thing I would ever tell a customer would be that something horrible was going to happen to him.'

'Even if you saw it?'

'Even if I saw it. There are positive aspects to everything that's negative. Suppose I saw a car crash, injuries, terrible injuries. I wouldn't tell the customer he was going to be involved in one, I'd tell him that I saw a period in which he should take great care while driving. To check his brakes, to make sure his car was properly serviced. To not drive so fast.'

She was better than a speed bump, thought Madden.

'Did your mother ever predict something that defied explanation? Natural explanation, that is?'

'Her claim to fame was a murder case she worked on once.'

'What was that?'

'It was about twenty years ago. When she was on the pier. A fourteen-year-old schoolgirl went missing and the search lasted months. Mum pinpointed the place where the body might be found. It was in Devil's Dyke. The police dug and found the body and that led to clues that convicted the murderer.'

'Do you remember the name of the detective involved?'

'She didn't talk about it much,' Natalie said. 'Mum was like that, she was just pleased to have been of some help. She wasn't the type to want publicity or accolades. In fact she hated that kind of thing. She did use to mention one name – Ray Millington, I think it was.'

Madden felt his spirits do a bungee jump.

'Thanks, Natalie. You've been really helpful.'

'I lost a son too, Mr Madden,' she informed him, just before he was about to stand up and leave.

Madden delayed his departure.

'I'm sorry,' he said.

'I never got to know him either. Though I would like to have done.'

'How old was he?'

'He was born three months premature but his heart was still beating. It went on beating for about six minutes. A six-minute life. There's not a lot you can do in that. I sometimes wonder what he would have been like if he'd lived maybe six years or sixty years. What he would be like now.'

'My son was nineteen,' Madden explained. 'I had more chances than you did.'

'At least you had nineteen years,' she said.

'Did you not try again?'

She shook her head.

'I didn't want to go through all that again.' She cheered up instantly, as though a cloud had briefly obscured the sun. 'I just couldn't have. But I still think about him, about those six minutes. And where he is now.'

Madden stared down at the crystal ball just as she was about to cover it with a piece of silk and put it away. He had seen an identical one in Lavinia Roberts' kitchen.

'Natalie,' he asked, 'if your mother told you she had *done a reading* for somebody, might she have used her crystal ball instead of cards.'

'She could have done,' said Natalie.

'Which the person wouldn't have to touch?'

'No.'

It proved nothing, but it might explain a great deal, Madden thought. Michael Bird could have walked into that kitchen and walked out again without leaving so much as a trace.

15

Madden and Jasmine made a vow not to talk about the case over dinner. They broke it. They found a place on the edge of the Sussex Downs with a window from which one could look out over hills and rolling green shoulders of grass towards the sea. Madden had fish and chips. The fish was advertised as fresh. Madden reckoned it had been once. The chips were the size of a wrestler's fingers and about as full of fat. Jasmine tucked into a green salad. It wasn't romantic, but they had a candle that spluttered inside a glass jar. Small mercies.

High Hedges was still being watched, although Jasmine was now off the job. She didn't relish going back on to it. Two detective constables, Toby Dyers and Mick Rush, had taken over. Madden didn't think they were the best surveillance team in the world. Rush was the older of the two and had failed promotion twice. Dyers was a golf fanatic so it probably wasn't a good idea to put him in a car next to a golf course.

'Bird's car's been there since last night,' she said. 'I saw only four people come out this morning. Ronnie Edgeware, a woman and two teenage girls. Looked like they were taking them to school. They got into a Range Rover and drove off. According to Rush and Dyers, they came back at four o'clock this afternoon. Looks like Bird has taken up residence.'

Madden sloshed some white wine into her glass.

'Curious,' he said.

'What's even odder is that Bird's mother's been phoning in. She's frantic with worry, she thinks we're still holding him, that he's topped himself in his cell and we're covering it up or something worse.'

'She has a nice opinion of us,' said Madden. 'But you're right. You'd think a guy who plays cards with his mother till half one in the morning would at least tell her he was all right. Got another job for you, Jaz.'

'What did your last partner die of?' she asked.

'Lack of stimulus.'

'This one could die from lack of sleep.'

'Go down to the basement and dig among the files. The Devil's Dyke murder from about twenty years ago. If my memory serves me right, the victim's name was Shauna Lewis and the murderer was a guy called Shilling. Colin Shilling. As in the coin. It was the case that Millington handled when he was a DI.'

'Wouldn't it be better to ask Millington about it?'

'Better not. It's the case Lavinia Roberts was involved in. He said she wasn't much help, that he solved it on his own. Her daughter tells another story. She says her mother provided the breakthrough after months of searching for the body. I want to know what happened.'

'Do you think it could be relevant?' she asked.

'Have I ever asked you, Jaz, to do anything that wasn't relevant to an enquiry?'

She sighed audibly.

'A few times.' She leant up close to him, and he detected a hint of irony in her voice. 'But we won't go into that now.'

Outside it was turning dark. From their window, across the car park, they could watch the sea turning dark purple. It was studded by tiny far-off fly-speck points of light. Madden stared down at his plate. He'd lost his appetite. He shoved it to one side.

'I met up with Clara the other day,' he admitted.

Jasmine frowned. He noticed but unwisely ignored it.

'How was she?'

'She was fine. We had lunch. Talked a lot. You know how it is. Jason's death brought us close together, made us realise I think what we'd thrown away.'

'It's too late.' Jasmine sounded a note of caution.

'I know. It's too late to get back what we had, but I sensed there was something there. A willingness. Given time.'

'A willingness to do what?'

'Get together again. As friends. Maybe a bit more than that.'

'Steve, she's married. She's got another husband. You can't just barge in and take your wife back.'

'I didn't say that. I'm not barging in, as you put it. Besides, she's in a pretty passionless marriage. That's the one thing Clara and I did really well.'

Jasmine pushed her plate aside too. She decided she no longer felt hungry either.

'I'm not sure what you're saying,' she delivered coldly.

'Sorry, I didn't mean to talk about Clara.'

'But you did, and now you might as well carry on.'

'It just seems a tragedy to let things slip away. We're closer now, I feel, than we have been for years. Clive and she don't have sex, I doubt she even gets a cuddle off him. They have a friendship, not a marriage.'

'Sometimes that can be just as strong if not stronger.'

'I know that, and I know her reasons for wanting it. We were too intense, too – fiery. All that jealousy stuff killed us. Now though it's different. We can meet like two ordinary human beings and enjoy things.'

'And you want to turn it all back again?' she smarted at the thought.

'You got it wrong, Jaz.'

'Put me right then.'

'I just thought Clara and I might learn how to – enjoy the best of both worlds.'

'What you're talking is completely immoral, Steve. And stupid. It doesn't move you on, it just keeps you in the same place. You can't just walk into another marriage and take your wife back for sex and then send her back again. This is what it's about, isn't it?'

'I value your advice, Jaz.' He dodged the brickbat. But her criticism had become trenchant.

'Is that why we're here? So I can advise you on how to go about sleeping with your ex-wife again? Well thanks. So much for the invitation to a romantic little pub on the Downs.'

She stood up.

'I cocked that up, Jaz. I'm sorry. I didn't mean to. I just got talking and sometimes it's hard to stop,' he said, realising his mistake.

They paid up and left. Out in the car park, he tried to make more amends.

'It was tactless of me.'

'And pretty unthinking.'

'I didn't realise you'd take it that way.'

'How do you expect a woman to take it?'

'We work together. We have a different kind of relationship.'

'You mean just because we have slept together occasionally it's like it's part of the job? In the morning, it doesn't matter? When you get invited out to "a romantic little pub" on the Downs, they're just words? You might as well be saying let's go up to the station canteen.'

'Okay, I should have chosen them more carefully. I didn't think we did romance anyway, you and I. Not in that way. You never expressed any desire to. That's what I meant by saying we have a different kind of relationship because we work together. That's all.'

'There are just some moments,' she said, 'when one wants things to seem a little bit different. Even if they aren't. Next time, try and master the art of making a woman feel just that little bit special.'

They got into his car. The lights out on the water were brighter now. Ships on the Channel, passing in the night, like people on their myriad journeys. Madden wondered if she wasn't right. He hadn't moved on. Lavinia Roberts had told him that as well. He was afraid to, afraid to launch himself into a new relationship that might mean letting go of the past. He was the hanged man in that damned tarot deck. Not going anywhere. The past was safe, the future wasn't.

The death of Lavinia Roberts was certainly proof of that.

16

Madden snatched half an hour at the Leisure Club down at the Marina. He promised himself at least three half hours a week. When your ex-wife started leaving messages for you in tins in pubs, that was the time to make sure your body didn't slip back a notch.

He looked at the young, fit, healthy blond-haired guy two treadmills along. He recognised the face. He towelled the sweat off his own and put a hand on his shoulder.

'Found me any more clairvoyants lately?'

Jeff Walker spun round, stood down off the treadmill. He still had the torso of a teenager, smooth, muscly, yet with no hint of a six-pack. The kid seemed caught off his guard.

'Sorry, sir. Didn't see you there, sir.'

'Fancy a drink?'

'That would be very nice, sir. Thank you sir.'

Madden would do something about the 'sirs'. They finished their routines, towelled and dried then dressed, and walked up to the Captain's Cabin, a nautical theme pub for the nautically challenged people who lived in the Marina. Jeff Walker had a half of bitter. Madden, painfully conscious of putting back in calories what he had just taken off, stuck to a slimline tonic. Life could sometimes be purgatory. He remembered what Jasmine had said about pilgrimages, that the whole point was to experience physical hardship on your journey. Did he really want to subscribe to the no-pain-no-gain school? He wasn't sure.

They sat outside at a table by the water, looking at the boats.

'Cheers, sir,' said Jeff Walker.

'Forget the sir. At least while we're here.'

'I'm supposed to be meeting Paula and Jacqueline. Mind if I call them?'

'Go ahead,' said Madden.

Jeff rang his fiancée on his mobile. She said they would be with him in ten minutes. As he was talking, an attractive girl skipped out of the pub. She was wearing iridescent Spandex health club gear. Madden recognised her. She smiled at Jeff and Jeff smiled back. It was more than just a casual glance.

'Jill. My personal trainer,' said Jeff.

'A lad as fit as you needs a personal trainer?'

'I have to pass my fitness test in twelve weeks' time. I want to be in top condition.'

She was still looking back and smiling. Jeff waved. Madden brought the subject back round to Paula.

'I had a long chat to your fiancée,' he said.

'I know, sir. She told me.'

'She helped me identify a suspect.'

'Was he the right one?'

'I don't know, Jeff. She told me that when you get married you're going to adopt the little girl.'

'That's right, sir.'

'Will you take a word of advice?'

'Of course.'

The boy looked too young to get married. But there was nothing he could do about that.

'You're going to make your career in the police force. That's great. I hope you succeed. There's one thing though that I'd say to you. Put your family first. It might not be easy at times but so many police marriages break up because of the demands of the job. I'm sure you don't mind me telling you that.'

Walker looked down into his half pint.

'No, of course not,' he said.

'Take it from one who knows.'

Walker seemed nervous about broaching the subject.

'They tell me – your son was killed recently.'

'That's right. He was.'

Madden liked it when people didn't talk in euphemisms. *They tell me your son was killed recently.* That was as straight as it got.

'I'm really sorry,' said Jeff.

'He was working as a male escort.' Madden never used the term 'rent boy' when he spoke of it. Jason had aimed higher than that, though the person who had killed his son had sunk pretty low. 'I didn't even know he was gay. My marriage broke up a few years ago and – well, to cut a long story short, Jason was much closer to my wife. I was too busy, too involved in my job to get to know him. That's what happens. Anyway, one night he turned up to see me, told me he was gay. I'd had a hell of a night. I didn't want to know. He stayed the night and in the morning he was gone. I didn't see him again.'

Madden waded about in the dark pool of his memory.

'That's not strictly true. I did see him again. I found him dead.'

'That must have been so awful for you,' said Jeff.

'It was after that I found out he'd been – well, selling his body. If I'd been a father who cared, I might have found out sooner. That's what I mean about putting your family first. It's not impossible. You just have to make the time.'

Madden spotted the name on one of the moored boats, a sports cruiser. It was blue and white and long and large and called the *Armadillo*. That rang a bell. It was Clive's boat, the one on which he had threatened to take Clara on a romantic sail down the Channel. Madden didn't know much about boats but he thought he knew a hundred thousand pounds' worth of fibreglass when he saw it.

'Another thing,' said Madden. 'Tell me to shut up if you like, but you've got a nice sweet girl there in Paula. Don't throw it away. Other girls might be nice to look at, but you've got a gem. That's the other curse of this job. Infidelity. It's too easy.'

'I wouldn't tell you to shut up, sir.' Jeff smiled, embarrassed.

'Good. Because you'd be on Regulation thirteen if you did.'

'I spent a day out in a response car yesterday,' Jeff told him proudly. 'We were first on the scene at a fight between two drug addicts. We had to separate them.'

'You want to watch these kind of incidents. Needles, that kind of thing.'

'I put my foot on his neck.'

'You want to do a little job for me?'

Jeff looked as though he would jump over the moon to do anything.

'How do you get on with Richard and Natalie?'

'They're okay,' he said. 'Richard wasn't too happy at first about me moving into the flat over the shop but Paula begged him.'

'What I'm asking you is to keep your eyes and ears open. If you hear them talking about anything or arguing, or you detect anything that's odd, out of place, I want to know.'

'You suspect them?' Jeff appeared astonished.

'Learn this. Over fifty per cent of murder victims are killed by someone in their own family. No, I don't have any real reason to suspect them. At the moment. But anything you hear that might be of interest – well, pass it on. I'm not asking you to spy, listen at doors or anything like that. Just keep your ears to the ground.'

'I'd be happy to, sir,' said Walker.

'Rest assured that anything you tell me will be in complete confidence.'

Jeff waved as Paula Needham came hurrying towards him with little four-year-old Jacqueline in tow. Madden bought them both orange juices. Walker put his arm round her and kissed her. She snuggled into him as though almost in need of protection. Jacqueline sat and looked sulky and played with the red and green unicorn. Jeff took her on his knee.

'Did you find the tattooed guy?' she asked excitedly.

'We found him.'

'DI Madden's been giving me some advice,' Jeff said.

'No I haven't,' Madden corrected him. 'I've been an old bore, telling him how to run his life, and now he's probably hoping I'll shove off.'

'Have you thought any more about coming up for some Reiki

treatment?' Paula asked. In the sunlight, her sapphire blue contact lenses made her eyes look almost feline.

'She gives a wicked Indian head massage,' Jeff said.

'I'll think about it,' Madden promised her, and left.

As he was in the Marina, Madden thought he would take the opportunity of calling at Clara's flat. This was one of her home days. He first checked that Clive's BMW wasn't in its parking bay. He would still be in London, at the offices of the publishing firm for which he was chief accountant. He pressed the intercom button. It was marked Westmacott. Madden wondered whatever had induced Clara to remarry a man with a name that sounded like Where's-my-coat.

Her voice sounded nervous.

'Steve, you shouldn't have come.'

'Can I come up just for a minute?'

The flat was spacious but sterile. A bit like their relationship, he thought. Not his and Clara's. Clara's and Clive's. He had once torn himself apart at the seams with jealousy at the thought of her living with another man, but since he had discovered it was only a platonic relationship he had felt a lot better. Clara had left him, not because she sought passion in another, but almost literally for a quiet life. She had swapped a sensual, sex-fuelled and acrimonious marriage that was stifling both of them for a friendship that let her breathe. How any man could not find Clara sexually desirable was beyond Madden's power of comprehension. But there it was.

'Thanks for the message,' he said.

'You could have replied. I'd have picked it up.'

'I want both of us to be happy too. I just wanted you to know that.'

Clara walked through to her studio which overlooked the sea. He followed her.

'I'm happy,' she said.

'I'm happy too,' he rejoined.

'Good. Then that makes two of us.'

She showed him her latest painting. It was an enormous canvas, a still life of objects found on the beach. A fishing float, pieces of wooden flotsam, an empty bottle of washing-up liquid, a piece of old rubber tyre, a pink plastic child's toy, an empty crate. There was something surreal about it.

'It's terrific,' he told her.

'It's not finished,' she said.

'When it is, it'll be even more terrific.'

'How's the case?'

'Our clairvoyant-visiting suspect just moved in with Ronnie Edgeware.'

Madden wondered if, when Clive came home, Clara asked him how the company accounts were and if they were balancing. He doubted it.

'What connection could someone like Ronnie Edgeware have with the death of a clairvoyant?' she asked. 'Isn't he in an altogether bigger league?'

'Absolutely. But there's something going on.'

'That's your instinct, is it?' she smiled, taking up her brush and continuing to paint, an activity which he gathered he had interrupted.

'That's my instinct.'

He watched her arm, slightly elevated, as she ran the hairs of the brush over the canvas, delicately applying a touch of emerald green to the orb of the fishing float. The tiny silken hairs on her own arm caught the sunlight and seemed to shine. He missed those little parts of her.

'I saw Clive's boat,' he told her.

'He seems to spend more and more time on it.'

'Don't you?'

'I like to paint pictures of boats. I don't want to paint the horrible things myself which is what he had me doing last Sunday.'

'What would you rather be doing on a Sunday?'

She didn't answer. He recalled idyllic Sundays of times gone by when they had picnicked out at Devil's Dyke. It was only a short drive out of Brighton, and a local beauty spot, and they had walked for miles. There was a legend that the Devil had dug it to let in the sea and drown all the good church-going villagers. There was a better story, a true one, and one that both Clara and he knew. It was the place where, one balmy autumn Sunday evening, they had conceived Jason.

'Steve, I think you'd better go,' she said. 'Sometimes Clive comes home early. He's been coming home early lately so he can play with his boat.'

'Not with you?'

'I told you. We don't have that kind of relationship.'

'Don't you miss that kind of relationship?'

'It isn't everything.'

'It was with us.'

'No it wasn't,' she said. 'We had a lot more than just that.'

She lay down her brush and for a moment it seemed as though the past blew by them, like wind through grass. He took her arm, that arm he had missed, and kissed it gently.

'I wish we still had it,' he said.

'You'd better go,' she reminded him.

'Let's go and put flowers on Jason's grave soon. Together. Like we did before.'

'We're not using Jason, are we?'

'No, of course we're not using Jason.'

'It would be wrong to,' she said.

Madden left the flat and returned to his car. What would it be wrong to use Jason for? He thought he knew but he didn't like to hope too much. He passed the car wash which, in one of her more unguarded moments Clara had described as one of the excitements of living in the Marina Village. It wasn't just any car wash. It was all done by hand and you got the Five Star Treatment. Traffic film remover, foam and wax shampoo, gelled tyres, anti-smear window cleaner on both sides and something called Interior Rejuvenation. Nothing was too good for the folks who lived in the Marina.

Madden saw the BMW first, being lathered and pampered by a teenage lad. Then he saw Clive standing by it. Clive saw him. It was too late for Madden to avoid him. Clive all but intercepted him in a way that made it look casual. He was tall, bald and had eyes as fierce as those of an eagle. He wore an immaculately tailored black suit and polished shoes. A Rolex watch too, Madden noted. If Clive Westmacott had lived in an age when the bowler hat was still in fashion, he'd have worn one of these, Madden had no doubt.

'How are you, Steve?' he asked, in a manner that did not suggest going for a drink.

'I'm fine, Clive. How are you?' Madden reciprocated. 'See your car's getting a hand job.'

'What brings you down here.'

'I'm a detective. I come down here, go up there, move sideways sometimes. Where the job takes me. How's Clara?'

'She's fine. Just fine.'

And she's mine, he might as well have added.

'You won't know, I bought a sports cruiser. Twin Volvo, one hundred and seventy horsepower, turbocharged. Teak side decks.'

'You'll have a lot of fun on that.'

'Well, good to see you.'

'Good to see you too Clive. Look after her.'

'Oh, I will,' he said.

'And Clara,' Madden threw in snippily.

17

Thirty-six hours after being released from police custody, Michael Bird's car was still parked outside the Edgeware home. Madden wondered what the Hell was going on there. Bird's mother was still persisting in the belief that the police had done something awful to her son and were covering it up. No one had heard from him. Madden decided it was time to do something.

Jasmine put a box file in front of him.

'The Devil's Dyke case,' she said. 'Read it.'

'I take it you have?'

'I've had a quick skim through.'

'Then give me the gist. How did Millington find the body?'

She put one of the statements in front of him. It was signed by Lavinia Roberts. It was very short, and dated ten weeks after the murder. In it, she described seeing a path leading into a copse where there was a scar in the earth. She thought that the number three and the Devil had relevance. There would be three of something, three trees, three bushes, something like that. There was also something that looked like a gun emplacement and she also thought horses were important. Millington must have been desperate.

'Look at the crime-scene photo,' said Jasmine.

The photo showed what were clearly the half-sawn up trunks of three large fallen trees that had been placed next to each other. The grave was only a few feet away.

'Could just be coincidence,' said Madden.

'That's what I thought at first. So I tried to find out what might have led Millington to where the body was buried. It was only through finding the body that Millington found the clues that led to the arrest of the murderer. Colin Shilling had taken her walking there, killed her, and buried her with his bare hands in a shallow grave. The following night he went back with a shovel and did the job properly. There are plenty of statements from witnesses – eleven of them in fact – who last saw Shauna Lewis, but none of them put her in Devil's Dyke. The nearest sighting was in Henfield, about twelve miles away, where a garage attendant thought he saw a frightened schoolgirl who resembled Shauna Lewis in the back of Shilling's car.'

'So what made Millington start looking in Devil's Dyke?'

Jasmine passed him another photograph. It was an aerial one. It showed the ramparts of Devil's Dyke, a hillfort built by the Celts two thousand years ago. Someone – presumably Millington – had drawn rings round a number of features. One circled what looked like a concrete base that jutted out from the ramparts, the second highlighted a horse trough, and the third pinpointed three felled tree trunks which were clearly the ones which featured in the crime-scene photograph. Against each ring were the words 'try here'.

There was no explanation as to why anyone should have tried there. Madden turned over the photograph. On the back were the initials LR alongside an illegible scrawl that looked like the word 'doubtful'.

'The concrete block,' said Jasmine, 'is actually the foundation for one of the pylons that used to carry a cable car across the Dyke. At first glance, if you didn't know what it was, you might think it was part of a gun emplacement.'

'If Millington got help from Lavinia Roberts, how come this hasn't gone down in the annals of crime as one that really *was* solved by a psychic?'

'Because Millington claimed he got the information through an anonymous tip-off,' said Jasmine.

'Oh, how very convenient.'

'He claimed that he got an anonymous letter which directed him to that part of Devil's Dyke. The letter said that the writer had seen a man with a girl in that part of the Dyke and that she had looked frightened. He hadn't wanted to come forward at the time because he was afraid of getting involved, and didn't want to even now, but he pinpointed three places where he might have seen Shilling with her.'

'Is the letter in the file?'

'No. It's missing.'

'Was it ever there?'

'You think Lavinia Roberts really solved it for him?'

Madden stared at the photograph. Millington had certainly struck it lucky. After ten weeks of fruitless searching he had dug in the right place and put a feather in the cap of his police career. A fingerprint taken from the inside of a cigarette packet found in the grave of Shauna Lewis had led to the arrest of her killer.

'Where is Colin Shilling now? Just as a matter of interest.'

'I thought you might ask that,' she said. 'It didn't take a crystal ball, Steve.'

He smiled at that.

'As a matter of fact, he was released on licence a year ago. He moved to a hostel in Chiswick in London. He died there about three months ago, just found dead in his bed. Passed away in his sleep. Natural causes.'

'The way to go,' said Madden. 'Just a shame his victim didn't have the same luck.'

They drove to High Hedges. Rush and Dyers were still parked in the lay-by watching the house. They were eating cheese rolls. Madden grabbed one, ate it hurriedly. He pretended he didn't see the golfing magazine under the seat.

'They're all at home,' said Rush.

'Nice cello playing, that,' said Dyers. 'Handel. Carries on the wind.'

Madden listened.

'That's not Handel,' he said. 'It's Elgar.'

'Elgar, sounds like Handel,' said the copper who knew more about golf strokes than he did about classical music.

Bird's Subaru was still parked in front of the door, parked

between His Range Rover and Her Range Rover. He had not been sighted since arriving there.

It was time to go in.

'What reason are we going to give?' Jasmine asked.

'Do we need a reason?'

'It might stop us standing around like dummies.'

'Okay, we just want to clear up a few points with Bird. Nothing more than that.'

'And what are the points?'

'Improvise,' he said.

Madden rang the bell. The sweet music drifted down from the upstairs window. He wondered briefly what it was in the genes of the Edgeware family, populated as it was by villains and murderers, that had spawned musical talent. Patricia Edgeware answered. The cool hostess with the Tippi Hedren hairdo was dressed in a scarlet silk dress decorated with birds of paradise. Her shoes were poppy red. She was drinking a cocktail. She had what looked like a hibiscus flower in her hair. For a moment Madden thought he'd landed in Tahiti.

'Mr Madden,' she said.

'This is my colleague DC Jasmine Carol. We'd like to see Michael Bird.'

'I'm afraid he's not here. He's gone,' she said.

'His car's outside.'

'His car may be outside but he's gone, I assure you,' she reiterated.

'Mrs Edgeware, we've been watching this house for the past thirty-six hours and he hasn't set foot out of this house. Now if we could kindly talk to your husband?'

'You'd better come in,' she told them.

She showed them into the lounge. After a few moments, Ronnie Edgeware joined them. This time, Patricia didn't leave. She sat down and crossed her legs and tried to look the perfect suburban wife. Madden had done a little bit of homework since his last visit. Patricia Edgeware was the daughter of an East End publican who had done time for theft. She had been a beauty queen in

Whitechapel – that took some imagining – at the age of eighteen. She had originally been the girlfriend of Ronnie's brother Frank who had been macheted to death by his brother Lance who was inside and not likely to be released for a very long time. Clearly naive and inexperienced in the ways of the criminal world, she allowed herself to be caught with a quantity of stolen jewellery in her car and had served three months in prison. On her release, she took up with Ronnie, and had thereafter slowly climbed the ladder to respectability. Patricia was part of the family.

Ronnie appeared charming. He didn't give the impression of a man who had requested that the police give him notice of the next intended visit. Madden was glad. He didn't like disharmony. Ronnie Edgeware was wearing a dressing gown as he had just had a bath, and was smoking a black Turkish cigarette.

'This is my colleague, DS Carol,' Madden explained.

'Delighted,' Ronnie said.

'We understand Michael Bird's not with you.'

'That's right. You could say the bird has flown. Much to my relief.'

'I don't see how that can be,' Jasmine put both feet straight in. 'He arrived here yesterday, he hasn't left, and his car's still outside.'

'You wouldn't by any chance be hiding him, would you?' asked Madden.

Ronnie laughed.

'I'll be honest with you,' he said.

'I'd appreciate that.'

'Birdy came to me for help. He was scared you were going to fit him up for something he hadn't done. I told him I didn't want to have anything to do with it. I have a family now, a home, businesses to run. I don't want any of that kind of trouble.'

He sat down and his dressing gown felt partly open, revealing strong, hirsute legs.

'I told him he could stay the night but I wanted him gone by morning before my two kids got up.'

'What about the garage job?' asked Madden.

'That's taken. I don't want trouble, Mr Madden. I've been in enough. Birdy was trouble. I could tell. You wouldn't have held him two days if you didn't have something on him. I just want to stay out of it from now on. That's why I said to him, I want you gone by morning. And he was.'

'That's crazy,' said Jasmine. 'I was watching your house all night.'

'Birdy guessed you would be. You don't think he was going to be stupid enough to walk out the front door, do you? He probably slipped out the back way when it was dark. Over the gardens, up through the meadows. Unless you had a dozen pairs of eyes and night goggles you'd have found it impossible to keep tabs on him. He'll probably lie low a bit then come back for his car.'

'You didn't make any arrangement with him?'

'What kind of arrangement?'

'You know what I'm talking about,' said Madden. 'Like helping him sneak out then promising to drive his car somewhere where he could pick it up?'

'I told you. I wouldn't help him.'

Patricia Edgeware got up and walked across the room. She helped herself to a cigarette. She lit it from a lighter shaped like a Buddha.

'He asked me,' she said suddenly.

Ronnie turned to her. He was evidently as surprised as anyone.

'You?'

'Yes. Last night before he went to bed. He asked me if I would do him a favour.'

'What did you say?' asked Jasmine. 'More to the point, what was the favour he wanted to ask you?'

Patricia Edgeware stood in the centre of the room and held the lighted cigarette close to her right breast.

'He wanted to know if I would drive his car up to London for him. He knew someone who had a lock-up garage. He wanted me to leave it there until your interest in him died down, or you arrested somebody else for the murder.'

'What was your reply?'

'I said no, of course. Like Ronnie, I wasn't going to help him.'

'Did he say who this friend was, or where the garage was?' asked Madden.

'No. We never got as far as that. To be honest, I wanted him out of the house as much as my husband did. His clothes were in a state so I leant him an old set of Ronnie's and he took both when he went.'

She sat down, and crossed her legs again. A pat of butter wouldn't have melted between her cool, graceful thighs.

'We have two daughters, Mr Madden,' she reminded him. 'Do you think we wanted them touched by something like that?'

'Something like what?'

'Murder,' she said. The syllables left her lips in a gasp, as though she had shocked herself by the very utterance of the word.

'If my wife says that's the truth, that's the truth.' Ronnie spoke up for her. 'Now, if you don't mind, we'd quite like to get on with our lives.'

Madden and Jasmine stood up, but Madden was still bothered.

'Can you offer me any explanation why he hasn't contacted his girlfriend or his mother?'

'You're the law. Use your imagination. The moment he calls from anywhere, you'll be listening in and you'll pounce on him.'

Madden heard the cello playing coming through the ceiling and looked up. If Edgeware was lying and Bird was still in the house, there was not a damn thing he could do about it without a search warrant. And getting a search warrant without any evidence against someone, let alone the fact that that someone was Ronnie Edgeware, ranked as almost impossible. They had released Bird without charge. He was entitled to go where he pleased. And for the second time he'd done a runner.

They left the house. Madden told Rush and Dyers to keep it under surveillance. When that Subaru left the house they were to follow it, whoever was driving.

'You let him go, Jaz,' he said accusingly to her in the car.

'I'm so sorry,' she said. 'Next time you send me on a job like that I'll get whoever I'm with to sit in the car and I'll surround the house myself.'

'Sorry,' he smiled.

'You'd have needed half a dozen people to stake out that place properly. There are probably twice as many places under the hedges he could have slipped through in the dark after sneaking out the back way. Who thought he was going to abandon his car and give us the slip?'

'So he goes to ground. Doesn't phone his mum. Not even to say he's okay. I don't like it, Jaz. Whether or not Edgeware helped him to escape, he's up to something. What the hell is he hiding?'

'Maybe nothing,' she said. 'Maybe he's just one of those people who finds himself in the wrong place at the wrong time and on the wrong side of the law.'

'And pursued by a detective who has all the wrong ideas, I suppose?'

'You said it. A clairvoyant can no more tell when somebody's going to become a serial killer than we can. If it was possible to do that, we'd have a world free of them.'

Madden took one lingering look back at the house before they drove off. He felt uneasy.

'Suppose Ronnie found out Bird was being set up to inform on him. And topped him?'

'Be a bit rash of him knowing we were watching the house,' Jasmine said. 'I'm sure Ronnie Edgeware didn't get where he is today by being stupid.'

Madden hummed to himself.

'You're right,' he said.

'And how would he get the body out of his house without us seeing?'

'Without *you* seeing, Jaz. The same way he says Bird legged it in the night. Out the back under cover of darkness.'

'Over his shoulders? Across neighbours' gardens? Maybe in a wheelbarrow.'

'Maybe he's buried in the cellar,' said Madden.

'Like me to calculate the odds of us getting a search warrant on that basis?' she asked.

'I've already calculated them,' said Madden.

They arrived back at the police station to find a familiar figure stepping out of the main entrance. With a briefcase under his arm, his bulky, ill-dressed figure reminded Madden of some down-at-heel college lecturer. Professor Grimaldi saw them and swept some loose, blowing strands of hair across his freckled pate. In his booming voice, he said, 'Ah, just the people I wanted to see. They told me at the desk to write to you, but this is far too important a matter to leave to the mail.'

'What can we do for you, Professor Grimaldi?'

The Professor smiled at Jasmine through a set of what appeared to be tightly clenched teeth that looked like he'd used them to rip into lesser mortals all his life.

'I trust you were successful in your enquiry? About the young man with the tattoos?'

'We were successful,' said Jasmine.

'Good. I'm only sorry I wasn't one of those he visited. I might have told you something about him the others didn't.'

'What do you have to tell us?'

'This time, I hope, you'll listen to me.'

He put down his briefcase and took out a copy of the *Evening Argus*, two days old with a picture of Lavinia Roberts on the front page.

'It's a particular gift of mine. I prefer gift to talent. Anyway, I pass my hand over the photograph—'

He demonstrated.

'Like so. And I pick up all sorts of information. I have picked up a great deal of information about this lady that I want to put into your domain. Information about her killer, about the night she was killed. I really do believe it's of some importance.'

Madden got the feeling that it was a case of the Professor believing himself important.

'Thank you,' said Madden. 'But please. Do as they asked you on the desk.'

'Oh I see, I'm only useful to you when I might have information you're interested in, not when I might have information that *I* think is bloody interesting?'

His tetchiness had reached a new level.

'Professor, I'm really busy now. But I promise you. If you put it in writing and hand it in at the desk, I will give it my fullest consideration.'

'When I lived in Yeovil, I was given courtesy *and* consideration,' Grimaldi pointed out.

He drew three sheets of foolscap paper out of his briefcase and shoved them into Madden's hand. Then he gave a *hmmph*, turned, and disappeared round the corner into Edward Street, his strands of hair soaring about in all sorts of directions as though they too were trying to escape from the Professor.

Madden looked down at the sheets of foolscap.

'Anything useful?' asked Jasmine.

'Dogs, white Ford Capris, and red barns,' he said in exasperation, turning the pages. There was writing on both sides. 'And that's just for starters.'

18

Pumpkin lanterns grinned from shop windows and the streets were full of hooded and costumed characters braving the stiff wind that had blown in off the sea bringing rain with it. Thunder and lightning were forecast. Almost every other pub in Brighton was advertising its own Hallowe'en party. In dozens of streets, children were knocking on doors and demanding money with menaces, letting down tyres and pushing eggs and bags of flour through letter boxes or throwing them at windows. It was only one night in the year, Madden thought to himself. The moment he took the call from Ming, however, he knew something was seriously wrong.

'Mr Madden,' said Ming. She sounded distraught, fearful. 'I told you this would happen. This is your fault. I told Lucky not to go giving information to the police any more but he wouldn't listen. You brought this on him.'

'Hold on, Ming. What's this about?'

'Don't you even *know*? Lucky's been injured. They cut off his—'

There was a shriek at the other end as Ming dissolved into choking tears.

'Cut off his *what*, Ming?'

'His little finger,' she said.

Scarcely relieved, Madden headed for the Royal Sussex County hospital in Kemp Town. Lucky had been rushed there in an ambulance with Ming clutching the severed digit in a tissue and weeping hysterically. Lucky Maynard looked in a sorry state. His face was bruised and one of his lips was almost the size of a sausage and approaching the same colour. A surgeon was sewing his finger back on. Jack Fieldhouse was there, waiting to interview him. After the operation, Lucky forced himself to smile. Half his hand was bandaged.

'Hello Mr Madden,' he said.

'Don't you be polite to him,' said Ming.

'I understand,' Fieldhouse put it as succinctly as he could, 'these two are friends of yours?'

'I do know them from some place, yes.'

Ming was no stranger to Jack Fieldhouse either. She had been interviewed as part of the investigation into Jason's murder which Fieldhouse had handled, or mishandled as Madden preferred to put it. Then, she had been a transsexual prostitute in Earls Court. Now, she was a respectable publican in Brighton. Madden often wondered what Ming had looked like as a boy. It was academic really, he thought. She would have been wasted in her former sex.

'I told him. And I told *you*,' she said, dabbing at her eyes with a mascara stained handkerchief. 'Lucky is finished with his old kind of life. This is what happens. This is what I told him would happen. You had no right to get him involved in this. No right at all.'

'What happened?'

'I was just putting some bins out the back,' said Lucky. 'We were getting ready for our Hallowe'en party tonight.'

'Don't speak,' Ming ordered him.

'I went out the back to put the bins out and they jumped me, Mr Madden,' Lucky ignored her.

'Who jumped you?'

'Two guys. They had Hallowe'en masks on. Like Satan, you know, red with horns. I didn't see their faces and they didn't say anything. They just kicked me onto the ground. And then one brought out this pair of pliers and cut my little finger off.'

Ming covered her face with her hands and shuddered at the memory.

'I found it,' she said. 'They put it in a bin. They put Lucky's finger in a bin!'

'I think I'll live, Mr Madden,' Lucky grinned.

'Lucky, you're a soldier.'

'No, he's not,' Ming begged to differ. 'He puts on a brave face because it's you and there's nothing he wouldn't do for you, but this is the last thing he's doing, you hear?'

'Ming, how do you know this is connected?'

'I *know*,' she said. 'I did not come from Thailand all those years ago on a rickshaw. I had a first-class ticket, paid for by a very rich admirer.'

'You upset anybody recently?' Fieldhouse asked Lucky. 'Throw any customers out? Stop them drinking?'

'No,' said Lucky.

'Call time a bit too rudely?'

Madden knew that disgruntled drinkers didn't usually remove publicans' digits with pliers. It looked like a warning.

'Sorry, Lucky,' he said. 'I hope I wasn't responsible, but there's a chance I might have been.'

'That's all right, Mr Madden. It was only my finger.'

'Only!' Ming shrieked. '*Only*! He could have layed out there and bled to death.'

'Don't be so stupid, woman,' said Lucky. 'Yak, yak, yak, she makes a bloody fuss.'

'I only make a fuss because I love you,' she said, kissing him lightly on his swollen lips.

Fieldhouse had seen enough.

'You reckon Ronnie Edgeware was behind this?' he put to Madden as they left the hospital.

'If he was, you'll never trace it back to him. Ronnie Edgeware's too smart for that. These guys probably came down from London to do the job. There'll be a chain of command with so many links in it you'll never get anyone to talk. They probably didn't even know why they were sent down to Brighton to do it.'

'Why would he want to warn Lucky off?'

'Because he's Ronnie Edgeware. He sussed that Lucky spilt the beans on him meeting up with your friend Bird. Nobody has ever crossed that guy without coming unstuck. He's a psycho.

The whole bunch of them are psychos. They have about as much moral sense as a family of hyenas, and that's probably being grossly unfair to hyenas.'

'Fancy a pint?' Fieldhouse asked.

Madden had a rule never to drink with Fieldhouse. Such an activity carried a health warning. Fieldhouse's distended stomach was ample testament to the amount of beer he could consume. This night he broke that rule. He wasn't sure why. Perhaps he needed to know more about where Fieldhouse was coming from.

They found a pub which mercifully wasn't having a Hallowe'en party.

'Look,' said Fieldhouse, sampling the head of his pint, 'I know you and I haven't seen eye to eye lately.'

That was putting it mildly, Madden thought.

'I know what you're thinking. I tried to set a guy up over Jason's death. It's not true, Steve. I believed I had the right guy, I really believed it. Like you're convinced now that Michael Bird had something to do with that clairvoyant's death.'

'Her name was Lavinia Roberts. Give her a bit of dignity.'

'Okay, with Lavinia Roberts's death. You know how it is. You get a fix on somebody and sometimes it's difficult to believe you can possibly be wrong. We don't like to admit being wrong. It's not good for the image. To you, I admit I was wrong. I fucked up. I was convinced I had the guy who killed Jason. I was doing it for you, Steve.'

'Let's talk about Ronnie Edgeware.'

Fieldhouse looked a little bit put out that Madden should want to cut off his apologetic stride so abruptly. He looked down wanly into his drink.

'You think he and Bird are somehow involved in that – sorry, Lavinia Roberts's death?'

'I just don't know. All I know is Bird went to see six clairvoyants in one day just a few days before Lavinia was killed. One of them was her daughter, who happens to tell Bird about her mother also being a psychic. Your friend Bird not only tries to run away but lies about these visits, and now he's legged it from Ronnie Edgeware's. What's he running away from?'

'You, maybe?' said Fieldhouse.

'This plan of yours, to infiltrate Edgeware's little empire. What did you hope Bird might find out? Did you seriously think Ronnie Edgeware was going to divulge all his secrets to some weirdo he met in prison and who was going to start repairing cars for him in a workshop in East London?'

'I told you,' said Fieldhouse. 'They got really close in prison. Like father and son.'

'And you expected the son just to go in there and betray the father?'

'It happens. You know there's no honour among that crowd.'

'What was Bird going to get out of it? A couple of pints and a ticket to watch Brighton and Hove Albion?'

'He would have become a registered informer. I was working on him.'

'Come on, Jack. Who's going to put their neck on the block over Ronnie Edgeware for the kind of pittance he'd be getting? Bird would have to be crazy. If a guy can get his finger snipped off for just putting Edgeware into the frame, imagine the fate that's going to befall an informer.'

'We'll never know,' said Fieldhouse. 'Because Ronnie Edgeware isn't now going to trust Bird, or want to be associated with him. You've seen to that. And now you've lost Bird anyway. Bit of a fucking cock-up if you ask me, Steve.'

'When I want your opinion, Jack, I will ask you.'

'What's more, I hear it was Jasmine that let him slip away. These Pakis are good at running corner shops, Steve, but at modern police work—'

'Can I just stop you there, Jack.' Madden put down his drink purposefully and rammed Fieldhouse solidly in the chest with his finger. 'You invite me for a drink, you keep your racist slurs to yourself. Or you'll have that drink over you. Savvy?'

''Course. I forgot. You two are a bit more than just – what's the word?'

'Colleagues.'

'That's it. Colleagues. Well, you certainly do your bit for racial harmony.'

'If that gets repeated round the station, you are dead meat, Jack.'

'I understand.' He looked down into his beer. 'Hey, Steve, do you remember that female copper you had a thing with long time ago. And not just you. I think she cycled round the whole fucking station. What was her name?'

Fieldhouse was treading on dangerous ground and he knew it. The man seemed to thrive on putting people's backs up. The hazard warning lights were blinking yet he sailed on into the conversation without a care in the world, like a motorist careering blindly into a pile-up. There had been a DC, but she hadn't been that loose, and she had contributed in part to the break up of Madden's marriage. Her reputation as a 'bike' had been unjust and undeserved, yet she had failed promotion, many thought because of it. Madden was determined Jasmine shouldn't suffer the same fate.

'Lay off the subject,' said Madden.

'Wouldn't want Jasmine to get the same sort of reputation,' Fieldhouse said wryly.

Madden picked up Fieldhouse's pint and did something he had never done before. He pulled out the belt of his colleague's trousers and tipped the pint inside. Fieldhouse's jaw slackened as the beer spread over the front of his trousers and ran down his legs and made puddles round his shoes. Madden was too angry to feel pleased with himself.

'Je – sus!' Fieldhouse swore at him. 'Look at me!'

'You just pissed yourself, Jack.'

'That was an assault. A physical assault.'

'Yes it was, wasn't it. Better than losing a finger, Jack.'

'You'll pay for it.'

Madden considered that.

'There's no price higher than the one I've paid already,' he said, and walked out of the pub.

Madden battled his way home via Southover Street. It was a wild night. The wind and rain came in squalls, chilling him to the bone. He needed to go past that house again. He wanted time to think. There were always far too many people at a crime scene to get a real overall picture of what had happened. Scenes of Crime collected the bits and pieces of evidence, and put them together, but sometimes you needed to stand alone.

He stopped at the top of the hill. It would have been deserted at around two or three in the morning on the night of the murder. This was a residential area, away from the bright lights of the seafront. He tried to imagine Lavinia Roberts's killer arriving, by car or on foot, checking that no one was around, letting him or herself into the courtyard garden, then quietly leaving after the commission of the deed. Was she sitting there when the killer arrived? Or did she come down subsequently?

Madden usually found it easy to read a crime scene. But this one gave off so many different interpretations. The answer was probably simple. The key was in discovering why anyone should want to remove a harmless elderly psychic from the face of the earth. As he stood in the wind and the rain, and watched a band of children dressed as goblins fighting against the elements as they knocked on one door after another, Madden remembered what she had told him.

A serial killer in embryo. I saw a child. A very young child. An evil murder for pleasure's sake. This interest he had in the occult came over very strong. Spiritual evil.

Madden hoped strongly that she had been wrong about a serial killer. Because her killer was still out there, and if he did have an interest in the occult, this was his night.

19

Madden's first caller that evening was expected. Jeff Walker had rung to ask if it was all right to come.

'Didn't want to just turn up, sir,' said Jeff Walker. He was out of his uniform.

'That's all right, Jeff. Come on in.'

He was driving a dark blue mini. The boy – Madden could scarcely think of him as anything else – stepped gingerly over the threshold. Starting out on a police career, you didn't expect to get asked into the home of a senior officer or be invited to address him by his first name. Madden realised that as much as he did.

'Want a beer?' Madden asked.

'I'm driving, sir.'

'Then share a can with me.'

Madden went into the kitchen, tore the top of a can, listened to the hiss of gas escaping, and poured the frothy concoction into two glasses. He carried them through. Walker was standing up, looking at a photograph of Jason on the mantelpiece.

'Was that your son, sir?'

'Yes, he was my son. Sit down. Make yourself at home. And don't call me sir. It's Steve within these walls.'

'Yes, sir.'

Jeff Walker obviously had a problem with authority.

'What have you brought me?' asked Madden, directly.

'You asked me to report to you if Richard and Natalie spoke about the case, or said anything interesting.'

'Have they?'

'I feel a bit of a traitor coming here actually, sir. Steve,' he said.

'Listen, Jeff. A few days ago a woman was murdered. A woman who did no harm to anyone in her life. She was hit repeatedly over the head with a hammer and bled to death. If you want, I'll show you the photographs or the crime-scene video. I don't have a clue yet who killed her or why, so forget your conscience. I need your help. Just tell me what you know.'

The last time he had sat like this, drinking beer with a young male visitor, was when Jason had come home to see him. It felt strange, almost reminiscent of that night. A sensation of déjà vu descended suddenly. Jeff Walker was sitting in the very chair Jason had sat in. Madden tried not to think about that night, to return to it, but it was impossible. How he wished he had listened, cared, not been so involved in his own problems. It all might have been different. He might have learnt about his son that night instead of having to wait until after he was dead. How he wished he could go back, turn the hands of the clock in reverse, wind back the months that had passed, have that night again.

'Cheers,' said Jeff, raising his glass.

'Cheers, Jeff.'

'Well, sir – Steve—' he began rather falteringly, 'because of Paula, I spend quite a bit of time in the shop and upstairs in her flat. The other night I heard Richard and Natalie arguing just after they'd closed up the shop. As though something had been simmering.'

'What were they arguing about?'

'According to Paula, ever since her mother's death it's got worse. She accuses him of not feeling anything, he accuses her of not doing enough to help run the shop. She wants to go climbing the Andes with some of her yoga friends and Richard won't let her. None of this will get back to Natalie, will it?'

'Anything you tell me is in confidence,' Madden told him. 'I told you that.'

'It's just that if they thought I was spying on them, they might take it out on Paula. And I'd hate that. She might lose her job.'

'Do they talk about the murder?'

Walker sat forward, rested his elbows on his knees and nursed his glass between his hands.

'It's more the mood,' he said. 'It's the things you pick up. The things they don't talk about. It's almost as though Natalie doesn't want to talk about the murder. Almost as though – she thinks Richard might have been responsible and she doesn't want to face it.'

'And I thought New-Age shops were full of peace and harmony and New-Age enlightenment,' said Madden.

'Some are,' said Jeff.

'How's your beer?'

'Fine, sir. Steve. There is more if you'd like to hear it?'

'I'd like very much.'

'This absolutely mustn't get back to Richard or Natalie. Or Paula, because she told me it. Paula left a book in the treatment room about a month ago. She has her own key to the shop and she went in and upstairs to get it. Richard was there, doing accounts, or at least that's what he'd told Natalie he was doing. Well, Richard had gone to the toilet and the computer was on, and Paula saw what was on it. He was writing an e-mail to some girl he'd met over the internet.'

'What did it say? Did she have time to read it?'

'What she did read was pretty pornographic. Paula's not exactly prudish but it even shocked her. She didn't let on she'd seen it but another time she caught Richard looking at some stuff on the internet and he was pretty embarrassed and made her promise not to tell Natalie what he did.'

'You mean what he did when he was supposed to be doing the accounts?'

'Exactly.'

'Care to tell me what kind of stuff he was looking at?'

'Lesbian Babes was the name of the site.'

Madden wondered why somebody like Richard needed lesbian babes when he had a very un-lesbian Natalie, but there was no accounting for people's sexual psyches.

'Anything else?' he asked.

'That's all,' said Jeff. 'I don't know if it's helpful.'

'In a murder case, you never know what's helpful. Sometimes some detail that seems insignificant at the time takes on major importance later in a case. Look at it like a jigsaw. You have a stray piece that doesn't seem to fit anywhere until all the other pieces are put together and then, bingo, you see how it fits.'

Jeff turned to looking displeased with himself.

'I was put on scene guard today,' he said. 'We found a body in a flat in Coldean. First body I've ever found. You feel kind of out of it when everybody takes over from you. I just wanted to be in there, doing something, instead of just standing about in my uniform. I got shouted at for touching a door.'

'Quite right,' said Madden. 'Can't have probationers contaminating crime scenes.'

Madden took a mouthful of his beer. It was good sitting here with someone you could talk to, someone who wanted to learn.

'Want to see the crime scene video of the Lavinia Roberts murder?' he asked.

'Could I?' Jeff was eager.

'Don't see why not.'

Madden switched on the television and shoved it in the recorder. He prepared the ground. He told Jeff of the client about whom Lavinia had entertained such bad vibes a few days before. How she was struck from in front, sitting at her table facing the door through which the murderer had broken in. And about how she had been dying of cancer. Then they watched the video. The camera moved around the room, taking in the body of Lavinia, the tarot cards, the blood-splattered wall, the telephone receiver lying on the floor, the broken window.

'The mystery is why she just seems to have sat there while he struck her over the head.'

'Why is she holding two cards in her hand?' asked Jeff abruptly, as puzzled as Madden had been.

'She may have been doing a reading for herself, or even for the person who broke in and killed her. We don't know.'

Jeff thought about it.

'Want to know what I think?'

'Give it to me.'

'This may sound far-fetched.'

'There's an old Sherlock Holmes dictum. Once you have eliminated the impossible, what remains, no matter how improbable, must be the truth. Or something like that.'

'Here goes,' said Jeff. 'Supposing she knew more than she told you. About this person. Or found more out about him subsequently.'

'That's a thought I've entertained.'

'What if she wanted to commit suicide? But didn't have the courage to do it herself? She knew someone who was a killer, who had no compunction about killing. She asked him to break in and do it for her. Murder by invitation.'

'Why not just let him in?' asked Madden.

'Perhaps she was to be asleep in bed when he did it. Imagine just going to sleep and not waking up? But she couldn't sleep. Could you? If you knew someone was going to break in and kill you? She came downstairs instead and – and decided to read her own cards.'

'What would be the purpose in that? If she was going to die.'

'Did she believe in an afterlife?'

Madden had no quickfire answer to that. Rather, a quickfire answer would not have done the question justice. It was a good point. One he had failed to appreciate.

'Yes,' he said. 'She believed in an afterlife.'

He wanted to tell the lad how she had given him a message from Jason, but didn't. He wasn't going to make a complete fool of himself.

Jeff went on, oblivious.

'She comes downstairs, reads the cards. He breaks in as they planned, but he finds her not in bed but sitting in front of him. He does the job, as quickly and as painlessly as he can. And then leaves.'

Not exactly quickly and painlessly, thought Madden, remembering the tentative blows that had probably first rendered her unconscious, though such blows would fit the scenario of an assailant ill at ease with his task and forcing himself to comply with the victim's wishes.

'Good theory,' he said. 'In fact it's a great theory. Almost every single thing fits. There's only one thing that doesn't. She was conscious enough to try and make a call after she was attacked because her bloody fingerprints were on the telephone receiver. But somebody had cut the cord.'

'Difficult one,' said Jeff.

Madden took the video out. Jeff looked down into his beer then up at his host.

'Did your son never want to become a policeman?'

'I think when he was about ten. I don't think he ever thought about it again.'

'Would you like him to have been?'

'I would like him to have lived,' said Madden.

'I'm sorry. I mean, that was a stupid thing to say.'

'No stupider than some of the things people say, Jeff. Like "you'll get over it". You never do.'

Jeff approached the subject cautiously, unaware of how Madden would react.

'Natalie told me about the red football scarf.'

'These things get around.'

'How Mrs Roberts gave you a message – from your son.'

So Natalie couldn't be trusted. Or else she just had a mouth she couldn't control. Madden couldn't find it in himself to hate her for it.

'If you believe in these things,' he said.

'Do you?'

'Come upstairs. I'll show you his room,' said Madden non-commitally.

Madden took him upstairs. He pushed open Jason's bedroom door. He still thought of it that way. It was still Jason's bedroom. It could never be anything else. The red Arsenal scarf was hanging over a hook on the wall where he had left it.

'Go in if you want to. Nothing's changed.'

'Mind if I—?' Jeff stepped in. Madden really didn't mind him taking an interest. What would have hurt would have been someone not taking an interest.

'You asked me if Lavinia Roberts believed in an afterlife. She must have done. To have talked about Jason and the scarf. I don't know how she knew about the scarf, unless she'd come into this room and seen it. Maybe she had genuine psychic powers, I don't know. All my training and experience leads me to the conclusion that such things aren't possible. But yes, I'd like to believe it.'

Madden sat on the bed. Jason's bed. Like Jason's room, it would always be Jason's bed. Jeff looked at the scarf and held it for a moment.

'You have nothing to feel guilty about,' Jeff said.

'Why don't I?'

'You seem to have loved your son. I never had one drop of it from my father,' he said.

'No?'

'Not for as long as I can remember.'

Jeff let the scarf drop back against the wall.

'Want to talk about it?' asked Madden.

'Got a few hours?' Jeff asked.

'Let's go down and have a few more beers, you can leave your car here, get a cab home. Or stay the night if you want.'

Madden turned out the light and they went back downstairs. Madden opened two cans. He thrust one into Jeff's hand. They sat and listened to the window shake in the gale.

'So what was it with your father?' Madden prompted him.

'My mother died after I was born,' Jeff began to open up. 'My birth caused her to have a mental breakdown. She committed suicide and my dad always blamed me. All through my life he never forgave me, like I was some curse somebody had put on him. I had two sisters and I think I was the mistake, the one that wasn't planned.'

Madden felt like saying something but he'd learnt that sometimes it was better not to. He let Jeff carry on.

'I remember one day, sir. Steve. I got bullied at school a hell of a lot. I came home one day really suicidal, you know how it is? I just wanted to talk to him, to tell him about it, but he always shunned me. He used to walk into another room. All through my life he used to do that. Walk into another room. I remember that night I wrote suicide notes to everybody in my family including him and put a polythene bag over my head in my bedroom and wanted to kill myself.'

'What stopped you.'

'I realised I couldn't breathe.'

'What about your older sisters? Weren't they any comfort? Couldn't you have gone to them?'

'I couldn't go to anybody,' Jeff said. 'That's why—'

He slugged his beer down.

'I think back to that night. You feel guilty about what you didn't do for your son, but believe me, Steve, you did a hell of a lot more for him than my father ever did for me.'

'Thanks. I appreciate that. You ever see him?'

'He lives over in Rye but I don't see him that often. No reason to.'

Jeff's mobile started ringing in his pocket. He answered it. It was Paula. She wanted to know where he was.

'I'm at DI Steve Madden's,' said Jeff. Then, 'She doesn't believe me. She thinks I'm at some Hallowe'en party without her.'

Madden grasped the phone. As he did so, the doorbell rang. Trick-or-treaters, he had little doubt.

'Get rid of them for me,' he said to Jeff. 'Nicely. I don't want them letting down the tyres of my car. Or yours for that matter.'

He spoke into the phone.

'Paula, it's Steve Madden. He's with me. The only party is at my place. I'll send him back safe and sound.'

'I was worried about him,' she said.

'No need.'

Madden looked up. Clara was standing in the room. She looked windswept even from the short journey she had made from her car to his front step. Madden felt stunned. She needed no invitation but this was the first time in two years she had been back to the house that had been theirs.

'Hello,' she said.

'Sorry, Paula. I'll hand you over to Jeff.'

He gave the phone back to Jeff. Jeff said he would be returning soon. Sooner than he had expected.

'Clara, this is Jeff Walker. He's a probationer. Just started doing his first ten weeks of operational work. This is my wife – sorry, my ex-wife Clara.'

'Pleased to meet you,' said Clara, overlooking the slip.

'I think I'd better go,' said Jeff.

'Am I interrupting something?' Clara asked.

'No, we were just having a cosy chat. Was there anything else you wanted to tell me, Jeff?'

'That was about it, sir.'

'Ever thought of applying for the HPD?'

'I have, sir.'

'You mean you have applied or you have thought about it?'

'I have applied for it. I've got an appointment with the Division Commander.'

'Good luck. I hope he supports it. Maybe I'll put something in your PDP.'

'That would be terrific.'

'Good. Well, thanks for your company. And your input. Some other time. See you in the morning.'

'Thanks for the beers,' Jeff said.

He left. Clara stood in the room she hadn't graced for a long time.

'HPD? PDP? What wasn't I supposed to know?'

'High Potential Development. Personal Development Portfolio. We talk like that, or have you forgotten? He just came round for a chat.'

Madden poured one of the glasses of beer away down the sink. Clara came into the kitchen after him. She looked around, at things familiar and at things unfamiliar.

'Very *cosy* little chat,' she said.

'It gets lonely here.'

'Since when did you invite police trainees back for a drink?'

'Since my wife left me to marry another man. Do you want to go on like this all night?'

'I can't believe, Steve, you're *that* desperate for company? How about what's–her–name?'

Clara hadn't forgotten. She just didn't like to validate the currency of any new relationship he might have in the same way that he didn't like to validate the currency of her marriage to Clive. A break-up was a two-way relationship. Most of the time they behaved civilly, as couples who had been together a long time should, but occasionally they danced around things. Like proper names.

'Jaz,' said Madden. 'And our relationship's strictly professional.'

'Most of the time,' said Clara.

'As a matter of fact, she hasn't been back here for a while. I've been too busy.'

'Obviously,' she said.

'To what do I owe this pleasure?'

She sat down, looked at her paintings on the wall.

'You never took them down?'

'No. They look good up there. Besides, I don't like bare patches.'

'Neither do I,' said Clara.

'Just say if you ever want them back.'

'No, I wouldn't want you to have bare patches,' she stated.

'My life is one big bare patch,' he said.

'Mine too,' Clara said, looking down at the floor.

She ran a hand across her eyes, not wanting him to see that she was crying. Madden had thought about this moment. Now that it was on him he wasn't sure what to do. Jason's death had brought them closer, but he had fought the temptation to use it for selfish means. Clara was another man's wife. He resented it, made a caper out of it sometimes, but he always respected it because he respected her and wanted her to be happy.

And yet he was only human. What man could resist the temptation to act when the one woman who had brought him the most excitement in life suddenly admitted she was not happy? Much to his surprise, he found that he was one.

'What's suddenly brought this on?' he asked.

He sat across from her, far enough away not to invade her space. To give her room. He had never given her that in the past. It was all part of why they had split up. Now he wanted to give her as much as he could.

'Nothing's *suddenly* brought it on,' she said. 'Oh, I'm being stupid. I shouldn't have come.'

'You should, and you did, and now you're here. And Jeff's gone so you can say what you like.'

'It's just—' she began, but was finding the words difficult, if not impossible to find. 'I love Clive, I wouldn't have married him if I didn't.'

'So what's gone wrong?'

'Nothing. That's the thing. Nothing's gone wrong. I'm happily married, Clive's very generous, in some ways, we enjoy doing things together, we go for picnics on Sundays like *we* used to do, we go sailing, I have my own studio in the flat, we look out to sea, we go up to the theatre in London quite a lot, we have a laugh, we share the same sense of humour.'

'Hang on, I thought life was a bare patch a minute ago.'

'You know what I mean, Steve.'

'No I don't know what you mean. Tell me.'

'Oh God, this sounds so unappreciative of Clive,' she said. 'And I feel a heel coming here to talk to you about it.'

'Maybe,' said Madden, 'you don't have anyone else to talk to about it.'

She sat straight, facing him. He wanted to touch her, to come over and hold her in his arms. He didn't need to. She wasn't going anywhere. He recalled what Lavinia Roberts had told him. *I see a woman who's been through torment, through a lot of problems, and you want to help her with them.*

Coincidence or clairvoyance, she had also advised him to

be careful and not rush in. He wasn't about to wreck the moment.

'Yes we had sex at first, of course we did,' she admitted. 'I may have given you the impression that our relationship wasn't based on that, when I found out how you were suffering over it. But it was stupid, Steve, because it was never sex like we had. How could it possibly have been?'

'I don't know,' said Madden. 'I wasn't a party to it.'

'After a while, we just sort of forgot about it. It didn't become necessary, if you know what I mean.'

'You mean it didn't become necessary for Clive or it didn't become necessary for you?'

'These things don't happen suddenly, Steve. They don't just – happen overnight.'

'You've only been with him two years, Clara,' he reminded her. 'That sounds pretty sudden to me.'

There was something else, something he was reluctant to bring up. It was too raw a subject. It had surfaced during his very personal investigation into Jason's death. Or rather, it hadn't so much surfaced as been dug out by him for reasons he now felt quite ashamed of. He had had Clive followed one day in London and discovered that he had visited a prostitute. Clara knew all about it too. She knew about it because he had told her. Still, her marriage to him had survived. It survived because, as Clara was now frantically trying to explain, there were things other than sex that cemented two people. Clara had never challenged her new husband. How could she have done? It would have meant confessing that her ex-husband, a detective inspector in the Sussex Police, had spied on him, a situation that might have exploded in both their faces.

Besides, Clara had had enough acrimony from their own marriage. She had gone to Clive to find peace and harmony, perhaps the kind you were supposed to find in a New-Age shop or lying in a flotation tank. Madden had never tried the latter but he imagined what it must be like. You didn't just throw away a second marriage at the first hurdle. But sometimes the second made you realise that not all was as perfect as it might be.

'Where is he tonight?' he asked.

'A board meeting followed by a dinner,' she said. 'Back late.'

'How late?'

'Late,' she said simply.

'Want to go out and grab supper somewhere?'

'On Hallowe'en? Everywhere's going to be full. Special events.'

'I could fix you something here,' he said. 'From the freezer.'

'Very romantic, Steve.'

'You know me. Romance at the press of a microwave switch.'

'I already ate,' she told him.

'Me too.'

She came over and sat beside him. His heart raced almost as fast as it had that night he walked up Southover Street at the age of twelve and knocked on Lavinia Roberts's door. There were precious few moments in life when you felt this kind of rush. This was one of them. She draped her arm in his lap and he stroked those tiny translucent hairs that excited him so much. Then he took her arm in his hands and kissed it gently. She did not pull it away. Every memory he had ever had of sex with Clara came pouring back into his mind. He kissed her, on the cheek. She turned her face to him and it was almost a different Clara sitting with him on the sofa. An innocent child, not a woman at all. Certainly not one that had been through what she had. Divorce, the death of a son. He had been through that too. They had shared it. How, he wondered, was she viewing him in that moment? He kissed her lips. It was like someone diverted the national grid through his veins. They fell into a clumsy embrace, the kind that lovers usually do on the first date.

'We're out of practice,' he said.

'Do you want to go to bed?' she asked.

'Do you?'

'Better than supper from the freezer,' she remarked.

'Are you saying cooking's not my strong point?'

'I know what your strong point is. I also know know what your weak point is. They're both mine as well. Let's just go to bed, Steve, and stop pretending we both don't want to.'

The doorbell rang for the third time that night.

'Unless,' she said, 'you've got another visitor?'

'People are like buses. Nobody comes for a fortnight then three turn up all at once. Trick-or-treaters this time definitely.'

He stood up and closed the curtains. The doorbell was rung twice more. Then the telephone.

He took it off the hook.

'I'm not answering the door again tonight. Or the phone,' he said, taking her by the hand and about to lead her upstairs. Not that Clara needed any leading. She rested her head on his shoulder and their mouths met again. He held her tightly in his arms. It was like this was a dream, not reality at all. He would wake up and she would be gone.

There was a loud *tap-tap-tapping* on the window.

'Bloody kids,' said Madden, then, more alarmed, 'It couldn't possibly be Clive, could it?'

'Oh God,' she said. 'No, it couldn't, there's no possible way he could know I was here.'

'You're sure of that?'

'Absolutely sure. Anyway, he's in London.'

'Wait in the kitchen.'

She stood, straight as a rod, in the kitchen doorway while Madden ran upstairs to the front bedroom. The *tap-tap-tapping* on the window went on, louder now, more urgent. It wasn't so much knuckles now as a fist.

In the darkened bedroom, Madden drew himself up close to the upper window, out of the view of whoever was in the garden. He gently angled his vision so that he could see who was standing there.

It was Jasmine. She was on her mobile, in his garden, knocking on his window. She stepped back and saw him and gesticulated with her hand. Open the door, she was saying. She did not look as though she was playing games.

Madden went back downstairs.

'Sorry about this,' he said. 'But she's not going to go away.'

'She?'

'It's Jaz. Maybe some urgent business. I don't know. Let me get rid of her.'

'It was always like this, wasn't it?' she said.

'No it wasn't and it doesn't have to be, Clara. I promise you. No matter how important it is, I'll get rid of her.'

Clara folded her arms. She was determined to stay in full view of the door when he opened it.

'She doesn't *have* to see you,' Madden told her.

'I know that. But it's best she knows what she's interrupting,' said Clara feistily.

Madden opened the door. Jasmine's gaze fell upon them. She was clearly surprised and not a little put out.

'Trick or treat?' she said, though she didn't say it as a joke.

'If this is a joke, Jaz—'

'It's no joke. I thought you ought to know. They've just found a child's body on the Rottingdean path.'

Madden pushed aside his deepest fears, just for a second. This was Hallowe'en. A night when even the imagination played tricks.

'Is there no other detective in the whole of Sussex that can deal with it?'

'Jack Fieldhouse is there. So is Ray Millington. You ought to get down there too.'

She stared at him for a few moments, not wanting to believe it herself.

'He's about three or four years old, Steve. And his heart has been ripped out.'

PART TWO

The Devil

20

Clara drove Madden as far as the Marina, just beyond which lay the start of the Brighton to Rottingdean undercliff walk. It was a popular stroll, about two miles long, with the chalk cliffs towering above on one side and the sea on the other. Jasmine followed in her car. On the way, Madden turned to Clara and said, 'I'm sorry about this.'

'It's your job. It's important.'

Sweet Clara, he thought. Always so understanding. Why had he thrown it away?

'It would have to be tonight. This night of all nights.'

'There'll be others. Maybe it was meant to happen. I don't know.'

'Is that your way of saying it shouldn't have happened?'

'No. And anyway, Steve, it didn't happen, did it?'

'You won't have second thoughts?'

'You'll have to wait and see,' she said.

'Clara, don't tease me like that.'

'Maybe we'll both have second thoughts. In the cold light of day, Steve.'

She stopped the car before heading off down into the Marina Village. Madden climbed out and transferred to Jasmine's for the extra few yards and watched Clara drive away without looking back.

'Did I interrupt something?' Jaz asked crossly.

'No,' he lied. 'She was visiting me, that's all. It was unexpected.'

'I saw her face when you opened the door. I know, Steve, this is none of my business but it looked to me—'

'She surprised me as much as you did, Jaz. I wasn't expecting her tonight.'

She looked at him, disbelieving.

'I just hope you know what you're getting into,' she said. 'And what you're doing.'

'I'm not doing or getting into anything, Jaz. Right now, I just want to see this kid. Has there been a report of one missing?'

'That's the peculiar thing,' she told him. 'There hasn't.'

It wasn't a good night to be on the undercliff walk. Whoever had placed the body there, assuming that it hadn't been thrown up by the tide, possessed a sense of the dramatic. Three teenagers had thought it a great dare to go down there, at Hallowe'en and in the storm, and brave the sea which whacked against the protective wall, sending walls of water sheer into the air. As they plummeted back, you ran away or got soaked. Madden had walked it many times himself. On this occasion, their adrenaline rush had been compounded by the discovery of something none of them would probably ever forget.

Madden first saw Ray Millington.

'No reason for you to be down here, Steve,' he said.

'We thought there might be linkage,' explained Madden, looking to Jasmine to back him up. She didn't, or at least wasn't prepared to for the moment.

'Can't see any possible link at the moment. Different ages, different sex, different method of killing, different everything. What's more we don't even know the identity of the victim.'

'All the same, sir, I'd like to see.'

Jack Fieldhouse had obviously gone home and changed his trousers. He wasn't pleased to see Madden there.

'Fuck off, Steve,' he said.

'Suppose we bury the hatchet. Just for tonight.' Madden attempted to make amends.

'In your head.'

'You asked for that earlier on.'

'What did he ask for?' Jasmine enquired, as they walked on out of Fieldhouse's hearing.

'He impugned your dignity,' said Madden. 'And so I tipped a pint of beer down his trousers.'

'A whole pint?'

'I don't do things in halves, Jaz.'

'No. I've noticed that tonight,' she said.

Acrimony was put aside, and any aggravation Madden felt earlier at his evening being curtailed paled into insignificance when they saw the corpse. A tent had been hastily erected against the wind and the battering waves and the squalls of tepid rain. There was a limited amount that SOCOs could do down here as much of the crime scene, including the body itself, had been swept by waves and rain.

Every officer who had a child must have been equally affected, Madden thought. He peered inside the tent, to where Dr Colleen Redman was bending over the tiny specimen. There was no better way of describing it. She glanced up, managed her usual workaday smile, though it was somewhat muted in the circumstances.

'Hiya,' she said. 'Poor little duck.'

Madden stared at the dead body of the child in front of her. He was naked, except for a pair of blue shorts, and lying on his side, pushed up against the base of the chalk cliff and resting on a bed of rounded polished pebbles. There was a bloody gaping hole in his chest where bone and flesh had been gouged away. It almost went through to the back. The killer had indeed removed his heart.

'Placed here or thrown from the top of the cliff?' asked Madden.

'Placed here, I think,' she said.

'By hand or by the tide? Could he have been washed up from somewhere else?'

'I'm not a tidal expert,' she answered.

Fieldhouse came up behind Madden, slammed a corpulent, fleshy hand on his shoulder.

'Okay, Steve, you've satisfied your sick curiosity. Now leg it and get out of my way.'

'There's nothing sick about my interest, Jack.' Madden felt like reminding him how heavily mutilated Jason had been, how they had both seen the body, how no approach Madden ever made to a corpse could be conceivably described as sick curiosity. 'I'm here because there might be a link between Lavinia Roberts' death and this one.'

'Your clairvoyant hater dislikes kids too, does he?'

'I wouldn't expect you to understand.'

'Try me. I'm a pretty reasonable fellow.'

'That's news, Jack. I must have missed it.'

'If you can make any link then I want to know. From the outset. Before I start rounding up every Satanic weirdo and paedophile on the south coast, I want to know.'

'Seriously, Jack, do you think this looks like a paedophile killing?'

'What does it look like to you? The result of some domestic argument? The kid's had his heart cut out, we don't know know what else has been done to him. Don't come down here and tell me this isn't some sicko killing.'

'That's not what I said, Jack. I said this doesn't look like a paedophile killing.'

Colleen came up to them.

'Boys, boys,' she said.

'There's one thing I'd like to know as soon as possible,' asked Madden. 'The way the heart was removed. Was it a skilful operation? Are we looking for someone with surgical skills or – pardon the expression Colly, was it a hack job?'

'*I* am looking for one sick fuck,' said Fieldhouse. 'That's my expression for it.'

'Tell you later.' Colleen looked at Madden as she spoke. 'At the moment, I'd say the latter. Anything else you're going to have to wait for. Got any report of a kid missing?'

'None,' said Fieldhouse.

'Something about the face,' she said. 'Doesn't look English. Could be foreign. Almost androgynous.'

'You're still saying he could have been washed up here from overseas?' Madden tried to pin her down.

'You guys are all the same,' she said. 'You want it yesterday. I'm not Sarah Mahoney, I don't do tides, I don't give orations at the crime scene, I just do my job. In short, you want miracles, you wait. But no, it doesn't look like he's been in the sea. You see that episode the other night?' she threw in. 'She stuck a thermometer up the bum of this woman that had been anally raped, which you should never do. Fucking shaking it she was like she was conducting the Boston Symphony Orchestra. And I told you that affair with the copper wouldn't work out. He finished it when he discovered she couldn't make a lasagna.'

After her departure, Fieldhouse turned to Madden and asked, 'What's she talking about?'

'*Dead Men Tell.* Her partner produces the programme.'

'Never watch it,' said Fieldhouse.

Madden went back up the path with Jasmine. There was little more he could do there. The Coroner's Transfer Service had arrived. A black van to take away an unidentified child with no heart on a wild, stormy Hallowe'en eve. It was as dark and surreal a crime as Madden could imagine.

'One thing puzzles me, Jaz,' he said.

'You're lucky,' she replied. 'A lot of things are puzzling me.'

'What made you call me out tonight?'

'I thought you'd want to be here. I have your best interests at heart.'

'You and I are the only ones who know Lavinia Roberts kind of predicted this. Apart from Clara, that is. And you were pretty cynical about it.'

'Get this straight, Steve,' she said. 'I'm still cynical. And she didn't predict this, according to what you've told me. She said she saw a child, that's all. This could be pure coincidence. Did she actually predict an occult crime?'

'No. That doesn't answer my question, Jaz. If you're still cynical, why did you call me out?'

'Let's just say,' she reminded him, 'that it's a good job I did.'

'What do Hindus believe in, Jaz?'

He took her by surprise. She didn't show it.

'Hindus believe in a lot of different things.'

'Such as?'

'Is this the time?'

'What better?' Madden had good reason for asking.

'It's a living tradition,' she said. 'Every Hindu adapts it to his or her individual needs.'

'How have you adapted it to your needs?'

'I was brought up with the stories,' she said. 'I perform my daily puja to my deity.'

'What *deity*?'

'I have a little shrine to Ganesha, the elephant God, who helps me overcome life's obstacles.'

Madden had worked alongside Jasmine for some time, but this was the first time he had ever learnt that she worshipped an elephant God.

'I worship through my personal deity, which all Hindus do. Many Hindus worship different deities, but we all believe in something higher. Whether it's God or some other principle.'

'How do you mean principle?'

'This isn't the time or place for a lesson on Hinduism,' she said as they got to the top of the path and were blasted by a particularly violent squall. 'Just tell me why you want to know?'

'Natalie Blance said you believe in reincarnation?'

'Yes,' she said, drawing out the simple syllable in a way that suggested it wasn't quite as elementary as Madden imagined it might be. 'I believe in *karma*, the idea that your actions in this life have a direct effect on the events in your next life.'

'There you have it,' said Madden. 'What's so different about believing in reincarnation and worshipping an elephant God, and believing that one elderly lady who's practised being a psychic all her life might not be right about a thing or two?'

'Because, Steve, I don't happen to believe it's possible to predict the future.'

'She had a guy sitting in front of her that she said gave her a sense of occult evil. Bird certainly had some strange interests. She said he was a serial killer in embryo, intimated that the victim, one of the victims, would be a child. Maybe that's not so much predicting the future as seeing something in the present.'

'You're still saying you think Michael Bird did this?'

'I don't know, Jaz. I wish I did.'

Madden saw Colleen about to get into her car. He hurried over to her, still battened up against the rain.

'Colleen, a word,' he said.

'Existentialism,' she said.

'Pardon?'

'I got pulled out of a Hallowe'en pub quiz tonight to come along here. That was the last answer I just put down. I take it you don't want to know the question?'

'Brighton pub quizzes are going up in the world.'

'What do you want to know?'

'I need a link, Colly. I need a link between this murder and the killing of Lavinia Roberts. Some common thread, there has to be one.'

'I don't *make* connections, I find them if they're there.'

'I know that,' he smiled. 'Same thing.'

'On the face of it, there isn't one. Different *modus operandii* completely, different weapons, two completely different crimes they look to me.'

'On the face of it.'

'What makes you think they're linked?'

'If they're not,' Madden explained, 'then I'm about to blunder into the biggest mistake of my career. Just do your best for me.'

'Can't have you doing that, m'duck,' she said. 'See you at the mortuary.'

As she went off, Jasmine put a valid criticism to him, not unreasonably he thought.

'You know what you're doing?' she said. 'What you once accused Jack Fieldhouse of doing. Going off in search of facts to support a theory.'

'I promise,' said Madden, 'never to do it again.'

She brought up another problem.

'How are you going to convince Millington these cases are linked?'

'I'm not. Millington's going to do the convincing,' he told her.

21

Thunder and lightning raged over the Brighton and Hove City Mortuary as Colleen performed the autopsy on the boy they had decided, in the absence of any identification, to call Alex. Madden stood with Millington and Fieldhouse and watched the grim dissection. He wasn't sure what had made him attend this one. Or rather, he *was* sure. He wanted to know if he was losing his mind. Colleen established that the boy had died by drowning and that the removal of the heart was post-mortem, and that he had been killed elsewhere and brought to the under-cliff path. The samples would be sent up to the County Hospital so that it could be established whether he had drowned in the sea, a river or in water from a domestic supply. There were fibres in the water, lots of them, which would go to the lab. Colleen suggested that the boy might have had a towel or cloth or some garment over his mouth and nostrils as he drowned and that his struggles to draw breath had sucked some of the fibres into his lungs. Inside his stomach were the remains of a burger and chips probably eaten, she estimated, about two hours before he died. There was no evidence he had been interfered with sexually.

Millington went outside during the autopsy for some fresh air. Madden found him standing under a big golf umbrella, looking at the dark clouds gathering in a primeval sky and the electricity that flickered like mortar fire. He had a daughter. This kid was somebody's son.

'Incredible thing, nature, isn't it,' Millington said.

'More things in Heaven and Earth.' Madden couldn't remember the rest of the line.

'I wish you and Jack Fieldhouse would put your differences behind you.'

'We have, sir. The trouble is they keep pushing from the front.'

The rain hammered on the umbrella. Madden slid under it.

'I'd like to talk to you. About the Devil's Dyke case, sir.'

'That was a long time ago.'

'I know. I don't suppose this is the right time.'

'My memory's very hazy on the details. Why?'

'How about the morning, sir? I won't take up too much of your time. No more than a few minutes, I promise.'

'If you think it's relevant.'

'That's why I want to talk to you about it, sir.'

Millington agreed, reluctantly, Madden thought.

With the autopsy over, Madden had little choice but to go home and try to snatch a few hours' sleep. Before he did so, he went to speak to Colleen. She was scrubbing down.

'Sorry,' she said. 'Unless you've got a murderer who's changed his signature completely. Most don't. Some try in order to fool us, but most give themselves away by repeating themselves somehow and in some way. In Lavinia Roberts' case, she was hit on the head with a hammer. In this case, something like a dagger was used, a long thin-bladed dagger.'

'Any guess as to his nationality?'

'Difficult to tell. Not English.'

'I agree. East European? There's just something about the face, Colleen.'

'Yes there is, isn't there. DNA and bonemapping tests will tell. Never been involved in a case where we had to use bonemapping. The diet is reflected in the minerals in the bones of the body and we can get what sort of diet he was brought up on, whether it was a western diet or from a different country of origin.'

'How long does that take?'

'Three to four weeks.'

'Can't see Jack Fieldhouse being that patient.'

'Sorry, Steve, but were you to ask me to put my hand on my heart and say there was any obvious linkage between these two crimes I'd have to say no.'

'How about the non-obvious?'

'Then they're still non-obvious to me, duck.'

'Maybe,' said Madden, 'when we know who he is that'll be clearer. I'm curious about one other thing. The fibres mixed with the water in his lungs. Surely if you wanted to drown somebody, you'd make it as quick as possible by keeping the airways open. Not smothering him with something at the same time.'

'Yes,' she said. 'Maybe there were fibres already in the water.'

'Maybe,' mused Madden.

The following morning, he caught sight of the tabloid headlines. Brighton had once again become the Queen of the Slaughtering Places, a nickname it had earned back in the 1930s when the infamous trunk murders had taken place. One read MYSTERY CHILD IN SATANIC DEATH RIDDLE, another somewhat innaccurately, BRIGHTON BEACH SACRIFICE HORROR. One of the broadsheets led with WHO IS CHILD IN BRIGHTON HORROR FIND? Madden wanted to know himself.

Ray Millington beetled his eyebrows and couldn't believe what one of his detectives was telling him. Every so often his gaze drifted to his office window, as though he wondered what the weather might be doing. When he returned it, Madden was still talking about clairvoyants and predictions and occult evil and Michael Bird's fugitive status and a prediction about a child as a victim. When Madden had finished, Millington pressed his fingertips together and delivered his opinion. It was not unexpected.

'Have you taken complete leave of your senses, Steve?'

'No, sir. I wouldn't be sitting here wasting your time if I didn't think there might be some connection.'

'On the word of a *clairvoyant*? That's what all this is about? You think because she predicted something like this, she was killed? And the same person might be responsible?'

'Not just any clairvoyant, sir. Lavinia Roberts. You said it yourself. She was famous in her day.'

'Famous doesn't make her right. Or clever. Or any wiser than we are. Otherwise we might as well all go home and leave it to a tribe of crystal-ball gazers and pendulum swingers. We have two major enquiries on our hands and I'm not going to jeopardise either investigation by following this lead. As for Bird, find him, and let's eliminate him, but without any concrete evidence you are really on very thin ground.'

Madden produced from a folder the aerial photograph of the Devil's Dyke murder scene from twenty years ago. Millington's face visibly darkened.

'I looked into the Devil's Dyke case, sir. The one you handled,' he said. 'Just in case it had some relevance.'

'I don't see what relevance it could possibly have.'

'It was the case Lavinia Roberts helped you on—'

'I told you, she didn't help me. She offered her help. That's a different thing.'

'Did you accept it, sir?'

He parried the question.

'Why did you think it might have some relevance?'

'I just thought the killer might possibly have concluded that Lavinia Roberts was responsible for his capture. After all, she seemed to regard the case as one of her claims to fame. Or so her daughter told me.'

'That's rubbish, Steve. She had no claim to any fame over that case.'

Madden pushed the photograph in front of him.

'She didn't make it public, sir. She wasn't that type of lady. She didn't want praise, or accolades. In fact she didn't really want to become a celebrity at all. She felt it interfered with her natural gifts. So few people really knew about it.'

Millington gazed down at it. His expression gave little away. He was content for Madden to finish.

'Anyway,' Madden said, 'I found this photograph in the file and I wondered what it related to.'

Millington took it in his hands, stared at it, then passed it back.

'It's a long time ago,' he said. 'I believe these were the places we dug for the body.'

'Which you found.'

'Yes. I can't remember now exactly which place we found the body.'

'It was there, sir.' Madden pointed to the three tree trunks.

'If you say so. I haven't looked at the file in twenty years. If you say so,' he repeated.

'I just wondered why you dug there?'

'If my memory serves me right, I received an anonymous letter from someone who claimed to have seen the killer with the girl in the Dyke on the day she disappeared.'

'This is a police aerial photograph, sir. Presumably it didn't come with the letter?'

He could tell Millington was getting edgy.

'Presumably it didn't. Where is this all leading to, Steve?'

'It's just that it must have been a very detailed letter. I've searched the file and I can't find it. I wondered who put the rings round various places and wrote 'try here' next to them?'

'It's my writing,' said Millington.

'Did the letter mention these places? I mean, I'm trying to get to the bottom of something here, sir. You don't mind me doing that?'

'I have other things to do. Like hold a press conference in an hour's time on what is looking like a ritual murder.' He looked at his watch. 'Can you make it snappy?'

'As a crocodile, sir. Just another minute of your time. If the letter simply described this guy *seeing* the killer in the Dyke with the victim, why should that automatically lead to you digging in these places?'

'I can't remember,' said Millington. 'It was a long time ago. What I think happened was that we went out to search the Dyke and found something and then started to dig.'

'Who suggested you dig in these places?'

Millington frowned.

'I've had just about enough of this, Steve,' he said. 'Make your point.'

Madden turned the photograph over and revealed the intitials LR and the scrawl that looked like the word 'doubtful'.

'Do you know whose initials these are, sir?'

'No.'

'They're in your writing, sir.'

'I wrote them twenty years ago.'

'Why "doubtful"?'

'I have no idea. I don't even know if that's the word I wrote.'

'I know what you mean, sir. I have trouble reading my own writing sometimes. You'll have to forgive me, but I thought at first the initials must have been those of Lavinia Roberts and you wrote doubtful because you didn't believe it would lead to anything. Apparently I was wrong.'

'Apparently you were.'

Millington put the photograph back into Madden's hands.

'So you don't know who the initials LR belong to?'

Madden felt he was pushing his luck, but he was pushing it for a purpose. If Lavinia Roberts had helped Millington solve the Devil's Dyke case, it made his own just that bit stronger.

'Probably the initials of whoever sent me the letter in the first place,' said Millington, with exasperation.

Madden nodded as though prepared to accept that, then stood up and went to the door. He imagined Millington couldn't wait for him to go through it. He was right.

'Sorry, sir,' he said, turning round, as though he had just remembered something. 'But I thought you said the letter you received was anonymous.'

Millington glared at him. Madden had pushed his luck too far.

'This meeting is terminated. For the moment,' Millington told him.

'Fine, sir. Understandable, sir You might like to know that Colin Shilling, the Devil's Dyke killer, is dead anyway.'

'I'm pleased,' said Millington.

Madden didn't go to the press conference. He didn't want to feel like a gatecrasher. Millington and Fieldhouse knew what they were doing. Afterwards it would be a case of rounding up the usual suspects. Or the *unusual* suspects in this case. Paedophiles were fair game, but the heady talk of Satanists hung in the air, of devil-worshippers, of sinister cults, of a Hallowe'en blood sacrifice. There had been reports of three 'Goths', youths dressed in black and crimson clothing, howling in a churchyard which had upset the local vicar, who had found vampire magazines and used condoms on a gravestone. Because of the missing heart, there was also fevered speculation of it being a muti-type killing, in which body parts taken by witchdoctors were used in traditional medicine. Madden had never come across witchdoctors in Brighton, but there was always a first time. Fieldhouse had hit the ground running and phoned South Africa, which possessed the only Occult Crimes Squad in the world, to ask advice. It was all go, and Madden was out of it.

Jasmine stepped into his office and closed the door. There was a hint of conspiracy in her actions. He thought she had been acting strangely for the past half hour, going out of the station to make surreptitious calls on her mobile.

'I don't know if you're going to like this,' she said. 'But I've found us an expert.'

'An expert? On what?'

'On the occult. He claims to be the foremost occult expert in the world, he's living here in Brighton, nobody else knows about him, and if we move fast enough he's ours.'

Madden was on his feet.

'Jaz,' he said, 'I love you.'

'Don't overdo the romance just yet. I haven't told you his name. It's Professor Grimaldi.'

Madden sank back into his chair and covered his face with his hands.

'It was on his business card, Steve. I've just spoken to him. Oh, and by the way, there's something else about Professor Grimaldi you ought to know. He's a practising witch.'

22

'Don't worry, I've prepared the ground for you,' said Jasmine.

They were turning the corner by Embassy Court, a big art deco building on the seafront which had enjoyed so many better days it was hard to see worse ones approaching other than a healthy dose of demolition. Crumbling and peeling and derelict-looking, it was one of the most famous eyesores in Brighton. Madden put it in the same league as the Marina.

'That's kind of you. What exactly do you mean?'

'I sweetened him up. Apologised to him for your brusque behaviour the other day, and told him that this time we really do need his help. It won't be as bad as you think.'

'Jaz, you're indispensable,' Madden complimented her.

'There's a *quid pro quo*, Steve.'

'What's that?'

'You tell me the truth about what happened the other night?'

'Nothing happened. That's the truth. I don't want to talk about it.'

'If I hadn't arrived at the door, would something have?'

'There's no reason for you to feel jealous,' he said.

'Jealous? I'm not jealous,' she said with a tinge of anger. 'I just care about you, that's all, and I don't want to see you hurting yourself like you did before over Clara. I thought you'd forgotten her, moved on.'

'I told you, I can never forget Clara.'

'She's a married woman, Steve. You've got to move on from that. You can't just go on living in the past. Just stop and think what you're getting into.'

He stopped and thought.

'I'm not getting into anything, Jaz. We're friends, that's all. Jason's death brought us together again and if there's one good thing that came out of it, it was that. She has a few problems and I was just helping her with him.'

'What problems?'

'That's personal.'

They turned into Norfolk Street, a little terraced enclave of attractive houses practically in the shade of Embassy Court and opposite a pub that advertised itself as the most haunted hostelry in Brighton. One of the houses was painted in black and white and had baskets of flowers hanging from what looked like gibbets. There was a small roof garden of yuccas. It was called Black Cat Cottage. There was a sign on the window which read: 'The Old Ways are Alive, I walk the Path of the Ancient Ones, Miracles Happen, Witches Heal, The Earth is our Mother, Treat her with Respect.'

'Do we have to go through with this, Jaz?' Madden asked.

She rang the bell. It made a cackling sound. Madden thought he needed a drink.

'How does one become an "occult specialist" anyway?'

The door was opened, not by the Professor, but by a tall, slim, elegant blonde in her late twenties. She wore a blue sweater with the sleeves rolled up and a pair of tight shiny black trousers. Around her neck was a gem encrusted pendant shaped like a crescent moon. Her hair cascaded about her shoulders and her lips were strikingly red. There was something immediately sensual about her. When she spoke, it was apparent she had been well educated. Roedean, perhaps, or some other public school. There was also something deeply familiar about her.

Madden forgot about the drink.

'You must be DI Madden and DS Carol. I'm Holly Elder. Robert's niece,' she introduced herself and thrust out her hand in the manner of a woman who had been taught how to receive guests. 'Come on in.'

As they entered, Madden remembered where he had seen her before. She had been on the front page of the pagan magazine which Madden had picked up in *Hubble Bubble*. When she walked, there was something of the breezy college girl in her movements. This was the young woman who had written an article on how to be a solitary pagan. Madden couldn't see her being a solitary anything. It occurred rapidly to him that, after what Jasmine had revealed about the Professor, this woman was probably a witch too.

'You've met my Uncle Robert,' she said.

There was no sign of a cat. Professor Grimaldi put down a cup of tea and a book and rose to the occasion. Madden saw the title. It was called Southern Baroque Revisited. Grimaldi did not at first look at Madden but embraced the presence of their other visitor.

'Ah. Sergeant Jasmine Carol. Thank you for your call. This is my niece, Holly. This is her house and I thought I'd ask Holly to be here because she's not as old and useless and as much of a damned pest as I am, and she might add a bit of colour to the proceedings.'

Madden thought a bit of colour was putting it too mildly.

'As for you, Mr Madden,' the Professor turned his stony gaze on him, 'I trust that on any third occasion I come to you with information, since I am about to give you an unlimited amount of my time, you will at least grant me a few minutes of yours.'

'Point taken,' said Madden.

'If it wasn't for your colleague explaining to me, I might not have been so amenable.'

'I assure you, I'm humbled.'

'Good. Well, I'm glad that's out of the way.'

So was Madden. He looked about the place. It was full of *things*. Cupboards, chests, trunks, cabinets, packing cases, some unpacked, some with the contents half spilled out, a stuffed cobra that looked as if it was about to lunge and bite, books by the hundred, most of them leather tomes, a collection of witch-doctor masks which adorned one wall, a pair of shrunken heads in a box lying open on a table by the window. If you looked beyond all that, the room was traditional English country cottage, right down to oak beams and wicker-back chairs.

'I only moved in a month ago,' said the Professor. 'The removal company didn't want to touch half of my stuff, they said it gave them the vapours. I haven't decided where everything's going to go yet but I'll get there in the end. Would you like some Moroccan mint tea?'

'Just had some,' said Madden.

'Good. Then you'll have some more.'

Holly made it in little silver cups, and it was green and tasted sweet. The Professor explained that his wife had recently died and he had decided to depart the west country and move nearer to where his niece lived as she was his only surviving relative, though not by blood. She was his wife's brother's daughter, but they had always been close. Almost like father and daughter. He himself was of Italian extraction. His grandfather had been an Italian count, which was no big deal he said, as there were so many of them.

Holly worked in London where she ran an occult bookshop with her partner Brendon. She was indeed a witch. She ran a local coven in Brighton called the Coven of the Celtic Moon which included elements of traditional Irish paganism as her partner Brendan came from Connemara, with some Scandinavian pagan concepts thrown in for good measure.

'Let me assure you from the outset,' she said, 'we have nothing whatsoever to do with killing babies, strangling cats, or indulging in wild sexual orgies. I was extremely disheartened by the news of the child. Witches get a bad press and this sort of thing only stirs up more prejudices.

Neither did she particularly approve of her uncle's collection which she regarded as 'gross in the extreme'.

'A lot of the stuff you see around you came from my grandfather,' Grimaldi said with inordinate pride. 'He was born in Friuli in Italy and had a great interest in witchcraft. He spent his life collecting hundreds of bizarre and unusual objects and I inherited them. You will be fascinated by *this*, I'm sure.'

He was addressing Jasmine. She looked somewhat nonplussed as he produced from a chest a number of items.

'Must you, uncle?' said Holly. 'I'm sure they don't want to see *these*.'

'I'd like to know,' said Madden, 'how you become a specialist in the occult, Professor.'

'Travel and study,' replied Grimaldi, now so wrapped up in his own world that Madden saw little chance of stopping him. 'Now then, do you know what this is?'

He thrust in front of Jasmine a sealed jar containing what looked like a lot of charred items.

'Am I allowed to guess?' Jasmine smiled.

'The ashes of a human skull, the flesh, nails and hair of an executed assassin – don't ask me who he assassinated, the Italians were always killing each other – the feather of an owl, the first menses from a virgin plus the first seminal liquid of a young man, and a snake's placenta.'

'Every home should have one,' Madden commented.

'It belonged to a magician. If one wanted to control the mind or the heart, one would rub it on a thorn and pierce the left hand with it. But *this*—' he said, '*this* is the most remarkable item in the collection.'

It was suspended in formaldehyde and was a demonic little creature with wings and an enormous penis.

'This is probably a forgery, though my grandather was convinced it's genuine. It was called an Osel and it harassed young women, especially country girls while they were asleep, in the eighteenth and nineteenth centuries. Pleasant little fellow, isn't he?'

'Yes. Charming,' said Jasmine.

'Professor Grimaldi,' said Madden, 'I would appreciate your advice on the body of the child we found last night.'

'I'll help in any way I can.'

'Do you know what a muti killing is?'

'Yes, it's a murder which takes place with the aim of obtaining body parts for use in medicine. I've known a witchdoctor who actually practised it.'

'*You've* known a witchdoctor?'

There were moments in a detective's life when you realised that nothing surprised you. This was one of them.

'Yes. In the Congo. I've travelled extensively in Africa. I spent three months with him in the jungle. Fascinating man. Wouldn't like to upset him, though. Mind you, what he didn't know about natural medicine wasn't worth knowing.'

'What would signify a muti killing to you?'

'Were the genitalia of this lad removed?'

'No. They were intact.'

'Then I doubt very much it was a muti-type killing. I say *muti-type* because this child isn't African, he's European, and besides in a muti murder you would have the complete disembowelling of the victim and most of the organs removed, *especially* the genitalia. Of course, you could have a human sacrifice.'

'What would be the purpose of it? A human sacrifice?'

'You might remove the heart and brain for the purpose of obtaining supernatural powers, so you would be successful in some field. Like business or politics. There was a case in America once where a young computer engineer who got into black magic cut out the heart of his nephew because he thought the possession of it would make him more successful at his job. Now that isn't black magic, that's something else, psychosis, call it what you will, but it has nothing to do with real magic.'

'Though he might think he was some kind of magician?'

'There are some weird people around,' said Professor Grimaldi.

Madden was tempted to agree but did not think it would advance their improved relationship in any way. Holly looked upset.

'Witches have one important maxim,' she contributed to the discussion. 'Do what you will so long as it hurts nobody. No witch would do anything to hurt a child or – or anyone. We don't believe in Satan. Satan was an invention of the Christian church and has nothing to do with us.'

'I know that,' said Madden.

'But I imagine you people are going to start questioning every single one of us over this.'

'You people?'

It always caused Madden severe irritation when the police were referred to in that way.

'Prejudices are hard to shift,' he said. 'In both directions.'

'I'm sorry,' she said.

'My colleague who's dealing with this case probably won't understand the finer points of pre-Christian religion. In fact I'd happily bet on it. But what we're left with is this. A kid's dead, we can't identify him, and it looks as though he's been sacrificed by somebody with an interest in the occult, and that's something we've all got to deal with.'

'Even so,' said Grimaldi, 'I can't see any *group* doing this. I've met a number of Satanists and even they would say they don't kidnap children. There's a lot of rot talked about Satanic abuse put about by Christians and social workers, and most of it's come from America. Poppycock, most of it. Evangelical hysteria. And you can forget Dennis Wheatley as well. He gave Satanists a very bad name.'

'I didn't know they had a good one.'

'Your killer might think he's the Devil or some kind of magician, but in the end we come back to a form of psychosis.'

Madden recalled the three cards on Lavinia Roberts's table. *Death. The Devil. The Magician.* They seemed increasingly apt.

'Holly,' Madden asked, 'if this was some kind of sick individual, if he's got this interest in the occult, is it possible he might apply to join a coven?'

'Oh yes,' she said. 'It happens all the time.'

'To you?'

'Yes. To every coven. You get people that are not suitable, that want to join for the wrong reasons, lots of weird people. You have to spot them. Sometimes they get in before you do and they can wreck a coven. I've seen it happen.'

Madden showed her the photograph of Michael Bird.

'Did you ever see him before?'

'Is that the tattooed gentleman?' asked Grimaldi, straining to look.

'I know him,' said Holly.

Madden's heart skipped a beat.

'How?'

'About three months ago,' she answered. 'We turned him away.'

'Why?'

'He came to us and wanted to join our coven. We never turn anyone away if they're genuinely interested. We sometimes like to hold open rituals so the public can come along. He'd done some reading but he had no tradition of his own, he couldn't even define his own religion or what he believed in. He was mixed up. Experimenting. I'm not even sure he'd gone into the broom closet let alone come out of it.'

Madden stifled a smile at that.

'In the end, why did you turn him away?'

'Because,' she said, 'he was interested in the *dark side*. Like a lot of people he mixed us up with Satanists. He hadn't wanted to admit it at first. He brought this dreadful girl along, wanted her to join too, thought we did things naked and had sex orgies. We had to tell him to go.'

'What was the girl's name?'

Holly Elder thought for a moment.

'Caroline,' she said.

23

'Well, I think he's a poppet,' commented Jasmine outside.

'Jaz, he's got shrunken heads in his house and a demon in a jar with a large cock. How can you call a man like that a poppet?'

'You'll just never know what a woman sees in a man,' she needled him.

'I'm not sure what a woman would see in that man.'

'He's been around. He's intelligent. He's witty. I don't think one could ever get bored in his company. Doubtless you were more interested in the niece.'

'Well, she was kind of fascinating.'

Jasmine said nothing, just gave him a look.

'I'd go further,' he said. 'And say she was *bewitching*.'

He went further still.

'Find out all you can about our friend Grimaldi. He mentioned living in Yeovil, in the west country, and some detective he knew there. Andrew Fortune, I think his name was.'

'You don't think he's genuine?'

'Oh, he's genuine all right. Just seems too keen to help us, that's all, to steer us on a certain track. And when a kid's heart gets ripped out and I see a collection like he's got, I start to imagine all sorts of horrors.'

Madden drove out alone to Lewes. Piece by piece, like a jigsaw, his picture of Michael Bird was growing. Of course the fact he had applied (did one *apply*?) to join a witches' coven didn't make him a killer, but it added to his conviction that Lavinia Roberts had guessed right about her visitor. If she had guessed right about that, what else had she surmised correctly? Perhaps Clara was correct. There was something of the magician's trick about it. He had once gone to a magic show where a playing card with a random twelve-digit number written on it had disappeared from the pocket of a contestant and rematerialised in the handbag of a woman at the back of the audience. Other than the whole thing being a swindle and the members of the audience being plants, Madden couldn't work out how it was done. He had seen a guy on the television levitate in the street in front of a crowd of shrieking, confused and totally mystified onlookers, and it had made him shake his head in disbelief, yet it *had* happened. Or so it appeared.

But again, that was a different thing from forecasting the future. And the more he thought about them, the more he couldn't get those three cards out of his mind. *Death. The Devil. The Magician.* What were the chances of Lavinia Roberts dealing those very cards in the last minutes of her life?

He found Caroline Gray at Bird's mother's house. The two of them had seen a lot of each other since Bird's disappearance. Florence Bird was as dyed-in-the-wool a member of the Barbican Bonfire Society as her absent son. They were sitting in front of an open fire and wearing striped jerseys and stitching a banner in preparation for the bonfire celebrations in a few days' time. It read ENEMIES OF BONFIRE. Madden didn't feel inclined to ask what it meant. They got funny in Lewes if you asked too many questions. It was a bit like that film *The Wicker Man*, he thought. As a stranger, you didn't go around asking what time the barbecue started. On the drive in, Madden had witnessed huge pyres being built and sensed that something important and almost mystical was about to happen. In Lewes, it was said, the inhabitants of the town spent three hundred and sixty-four days of the year preparing for just one. That one was almost upon them.

Florence Bird shot to her feet the moment he entered the room. She remained convinced that the police were lying, that something terrible had happened to her son in a police cell and that the police were covering it up. She had gone to the trouble of contacting a solicitor who had made the requisite enquiries and assured her that such wasn't the case, but Florence Bird, in spite of her sweet, motherly exterior, was turning out to be a conspiracy theorist of some proportions.

'You can't believe a thing anyone tells you,' she complained. 'It wouldn't surprise me if you have all the solicitors in your pay. You hear about these things happening. I was reading a book once about a police force in Tennessee, they killed this black man and buried his body and framed someone else for it.'

Madden pictured her digesting the contents of the book over her evening cocoa.

'Mrs Bird, I can assure you your son walked out of our police station. There are procedures that would prevent such a thing ever happening. He was eliminated from our enquiry. He went straight to the house of Ronnie Edgeware, a known villain, and his car's been there ever since.'

'You could have driven it there,' she said. 'You people are in league with all these major criminals.'

Oh please, thought Madden.

If Florence Bird was a conspiracy theorist, Caroline was just plain angry.

'You come into people's lives,' she shouted at him, 'and you just fuck things up. Michael was going straight before you took him away.'

'With respect, Caroline, sometimes people's lives are already that way when we step in.'

'What do you mean by that? You mean *my* life's fucked up? Is that what you're saying? Well just say it.'

'Do you know why he went to Ronnie Edgeware's? Either of you?' Madden thought he would try and nail them to a constructive answer.

'They're friends,' said Florence Bird. 'They made friends in prison.'

'Why go to see Edgeware before coming home to see you? Wouldn't he at least call, Mrs Bird, to tell you he was all right?'

'He's probably scared to,' Caroline interjected. 'He knows how the police trace calls. You'll go out and try and find evidence against him and then arrest him again and plant it on him, he's not stupid.'

'You sure you don't know where he is?' Madden put to her bluntly. 'If he has any other friends, any associates, up in London maybe, people who might be protecting him? Giving him the use of another car?'

'If I did, I wouldn't tell you,' she said.

No, thought Madden, he was sure she wouldn't.

'Can we talk outside? In private?' he asked her.

'I'm not going outside with you,' she said. 'You can say what you want to say in here. In his mother's presence.'

'All right,' he said. 'If you want it that way. I'd hoped to spare his mother this, but did you and Michael ever attempt to join a coven of witches?'

'Oh good heavens,' Florence Bird laughed.

Caroline didn't.

'What of it?' she almost spat at him.

'Did you or didn't you, Caroline?'

'It was a lark,' she said. 'Nothing more than that.'

'I'm told you and Michael thought they had something to do with black magic and sex orgies and that's why they turned you away.'

'Michael, never!' said Florence Bird, appalled at the suggestion.

'You don't know your son, I'm afraid.' He turned back to Caroline. 'Well? Is that true?'

'Tell him it's a lot of lies,' Florence said. 'Like the police always tell.'

'It's not a lot of lies,' Caroline confessed. 'But it was just a laugh, nothing more.'

'You think it's a laugh to go to a coven of witches and express an interest in black magic and romping naked and having sex orgies and then get turned away because that's not the sort of thing they do?' Madden piled it on.

Caroline's face darkened. Her lips seemed to shrink.

'I can't believe Michael would *ever* do a thing like that,' said Florence Bird.

'Yes, well he did,' Caroline admitted. 'And he dragged me along too. We thought it would be good fun, you know, the sex thing, he was interested in the black magic, not me.'

'How interested?' asked Madden.

At that point, the alarm bells must have rung.

'Why are you asking?'

By now there probably wasn't a person in the country who hadn't heard about 'Alex'.

'It's my job,' Madden answered.

'You think he was responsible for that kid now, don't you?' Caroline almost flew at him like a harpy.

'I don't *think* anything. I want to know what his interests and yours ran to. Where he got his interests from. You can tell me.'

'Go find him and ask him yourself,' she said. 'Because you're getting nothing out of me.'

'You won't help him?'

'Help him? Is that what you call it. Look, he's a bit weird, but that's better than somebody who's straight and boring. He got his ideas out of books, he thought it would be fun if we got stoned one night and met some real witches and – just had a laugh. We weren't going to strangle chickens or do anything like that.'

'If you know where he is, Caroline, I'm prepared to talk to him. Over a phone if necessary. No trace, I promise you. I'll agree to any arrangement you want. All *I* want is the chance to talk to him, to assure him I'm not going to arrest him. I just need to know what he's so scared of, what he's running from, who's hiding him.'

'You're lying,' she said.

Somehow, he had predicted that answer.

'I'm not lying,' he tried to assure her. 'I'm not interested what you two do in your spare time. You can join the Ku Klux Klan for all I care. But unless you can put me in touch with Michael I'm never going to be convinced of anything.'

'I don't know where he is.'

And neither, or so she said, did his mother. She reiterated her belief that there was a police cover-up. Madden didn't feel he was going to get any further on with either of them. By the time he left, he fully expected Florence Bird to accuse the Sussex Constabulary of colluding in the death of Diana, Princess of Wales.

He arranged to meet Holly Elder again. She was more than pleased. Madden had never knowingly met a witch until that day. He invited her to have a glass of wine with him down on the boardwalk cafe by the beach. Although it was the first day of November, the sun was strong and the air was still and one could have believed it was much earlier in the year. Holly said she had arranged it that way. She was joking. Witches, she said, had terrific senses of humour.

'There used be a TV programme about a witch,' he said. 'She twitched her nose and made things happen.'

'I'm too young to remember it,' she answered pointedly. 'But I have heard of it. Didn't she have a mother who kept getting her spells wrong?'

'That's right,' said Madden.

'My parents were Catholics. I was going to become a nun when I was a little girl, but I soon got disillusioned. Then I did the rebellious stage all teenagers go through and discovered I had this great affinity with nature and animals. I used to collect animals and bring them back to my house. I used to talk to them!'

'When did you decide to become a witch?'

'When I was sixteen. My parents were horrified. They're still horrified and we have a very uneasy relationship. That's when I got close to Uncle Robert. He was always the black sheep of the family, the uncle who had lots of money and did unorthodox things and went to strange places. I was absolutely fascinated by him. The "Italian" side of the family, though it's three generations back. We just got on so well. It turned out we were both following the same sort of path through life. He gave me a piece of advice I've never forgotten. Be yourself and never be afraid.'

'Not always easy.'

'No,' she agreed. 'I organised a convention in Brighton a few years ago and it was picketed and broken up by fundamentalist Christians. I got hate mail from them, telling me they hoped I would die a horrible death and get killed in a car crash, and things like that. I got really upset. Sometimes I wish I could twitch my nose and make people like that go away.'

Madden looked at the green tinged waves breaking on the shore. There were quite a few people on the beach, though it wasn't warm enough for swimming. A girl who appeared lost and alone led a tiny puppy on a lead which was shaped like a string of pink sausages. A fat bald man in a sweatshirt and floral Bermuda shorts was swinging a metal detector over the pebbles. Two young gay men flaunted their sexuality as they paraded along the boardwalk. A family of four clutched fluffy dolphins which they had won at the Dolphin Derby on the pier and worked their tongues into ice creams. There were a lot of different people under the skin of this city, which had a reputation for tolerance, but tolerance itself could sometimes be only skin deep.

'I interviewed Caroline. Michael Bird's girlfriend. She told me they just wanted to join you for a lark.'

'That's not the way it seemed to me,' said Holly. 'He wanted to know if we took drugs, and seemed to have done a lot of reading about the Church of Satan in America. What really rankled was when we got into this discussion about sexual freedom and he poured scorn on the fact we use robes in our ritual instead of going skyclad.'

'Skyclad?'

'Naked, sweetie.' She grinned.

'I should have guessed.'

'I said to him if you want to watch naked bodies, go buy a magazine.'

'When you told me Michael Bird was interested in the dark side, how far do you think that went? I've met the guy, interviewed him, but you must have summed him up in a way I don't feel qualified to do.'

'Why do you think that?'

She twiddled the stem of her wine glass. He sensed she was playing a little game with him.

'Because I deal in human evil. Spiritual evil is something I've never encountered.'

'Nor I,' she answered. 'You're perfectly qualified, Mr Madden. Because human evil is all there is. I don't believe in the Devil. Witches don't. Forget all these images of old crones riding to sabbats on broomsticks. Mankind doesn't need Satan for evil to flow out into the world. Human beings are perfectly capable of being their own Satans.'

She asked the obvious question.

'This Michael, you think he killed that child?'

'I don't know what to think,' said Madden. 'I'm not in charge of that case.'

'But you wish you were?' she asked perceptively.

'I think it's connected to another crime I *am* investigating. The murder of Lavinia Roberts, the clairvoyant. But I don't have any evidence. And it's becoming very hard to find. I feel like I'm chasing phantoms.'

She told him that in the interim period she had been contacted by DI Fieldhouse, and that the police wanted to interview her, her uncle, and every member of their coven.

'A waste of time,' she said, 'because we were all together at Samhain.'

'What is Samhain?'

'Sorry, you call it Hallowe'en. We regard it as a festival to celebrate the end of summer and the dying of the old God, when the worlds of the living and the dead meet.'

'The murder didn't happen at Hallowe'en. The body was found then, but the killing took place the day before.'

'I suppose,' Holly remarked, 'that we shall just have to bite the bullet.'

'Something like that,' said Madden.

He finished his wine and stood up. She walked with him as far as the pier, where they parted. There was something comforting about her presence. A warmth, a glow, a radiance that he couldn't quite account for. He wondered if she'd put a spell on him.

'You still put spells on people?' he asked.

'Of course. We're not that dull and goody goody.' She laughed, and as she did so a breeze sprang up and blew her long straight hair so that it gently brushed Madden's face. 'I hope you get what you want and find what you're looking for.'

And with that she was gone, along the front, the wind taking her hair and turning it into burnished, luminous streamers that caught the autumn sun.

24

Jack Fieldhouse was furious. Madden knew he must have overstepped the mark because Fieldhouse started the morning by shouting at him. Fieldhouse never usually started the morning shouting at anybody. Usually he was too hungover from the night before and spent the first hour reading and checking statements so that nobody could see he was hungover. He was frustrated because 'Alex' had not yet been identified, and it was well nigh impossible to track down a killer when you didn't even know the identity of the victim. Neither were they any nearer establishing the nationality of the child. The wonderful new science of bonemapping couldn't be done overnight. The scientists were talking about three weeks. Three weeks was a long time in a murder enquiry. The most likely theory was that he had been brought into the country from abroad and that his mother probably didn't even know where he was. Immigration was involved, but there were so many thousands of immigrants that they had lost, not to mention the illegal ones, that hopes of a quick identification receded even further. Somebody had fed the boy a burger and chips two hours before his death, and initially every burger establishment within twenty miles of the city was being visited to see if anyone could remember a small boy wearing blue shorts being fed such a meal. It was clear from the start that this one wasn't going to be cracked in a day.

Fieldhouse's anger, however, was not simply the product of his intense frustration, but a direct consequence of Madden going behind his back.

'Why the hell didn't you tell me?' he boiled over.

'I didn't think of it.'

'You found an occult expert here in Brighton, and had me wasting time phoning South Africa?'

'I didn't know he was an occult expert until I went to see him. He might have turned out to be a charlatan. Anyone can call themselves an occult expert.'

'He had it on his business card!' shouted Fieldhouse. 'Which you possessed.'

'Anyone can put occult expert on their business card. I could put occult expert on mine, you could put it on yours.'

He caught Jasmine's eye. She was applying liner to it. She looked stunning this morning in a smart grey outfit with a cream chiffon scarf. If Madden didn't know her, he would have sworn she was going off to a power breakfast. She was staying out of the discussion. Jasmine had a knack of doing that.

'I don't care, you took it on yourselves to go and see these two bloody devil worshippers and didn't even tell me.'

'They're not devil worshippers. They're witches. There's a difference.'

'Difference my arse,' said Fieldhouse.

'The difference is probably the size of your arse, Jack.'

'You think you're so much cleverer than me.'

'I don't think.'

'You never did like working as part of a team. Always going off, doing things your own way, pursuing your own agenda, well let me ask you something.' He jabbed him in the shoulder with his finger. 'If you have one shred of evidence these two murders are connected, spill it now, because I'm sick and fed up trying to second-guess what's going through your mind.'

'What's going through my mind is trying to find the evidence. And don't prod me. I don't like being prodded.'

'Different MOs. Different weapons. Different ages. There's nothing to link them. Nothing. Not even Colly can find a link. So what do you know the rest of us don't?'

'You wouldn't believe me if I told you, Jack.'

'Then stay out of it. Just because you managed to lose *your* number one suspect—'

'I didn't lose him. We let him go because there was no evidence against him.'

'Then you should have found it. I always do.'

'Like when you found the person who killed Jason?' said Madden.

'That's water under the bridge.'

'Is it? I'm glad you think so. I wouldn't call your handling of the case water under the bridge. I'd call it a bloody big stain on my conscience and a blot on my career.'

Fieldhouse ran a fat finger under his collar. He was sweating profusely.

'You'd better take that accusation back, Steve.'

'I don't take things back. I give them in good faith.'

'Take it back. Or you and I don't share this office, this station, this town. I did the best for you. I made a mistake, an honest mistake.'

'You did your best for me? *Your best*? If that was your best, Jack, don't ever do your worst for me.'

Fieldhouse expelled a gasp of breath and crumpled suddenly to the floor. When you were the size of Fieldhouse, you didn't go down without making a noise like a felled cow. The floor vibrated. Jasmine leapt from her desk. Fieldhouse had gone a grey, sickly colour.

Madden loosened his tie and shirt collar.

'Call an ambulance!' he shouted across the office.

Somebody dialled for an ambulance. Madden raised Fieldhouse's knees. Jasmine felt for his pulse.

'You're going to be okay, Jack,' Madden said.

'I can't feel a pulse,' said Jasmine.

She took a mirror out of her bag, held it to his lips. Nothing. No mist, just clear glass. Madden leant over him, gave him cardiac compression.

'You know what you're doing?' asked Jasmine.

'I know what I'm doing.'

Jack Fieldhouse started breathing. Within ten minutes, paramedics had arrived.

'You might just have saved his life,' Jasmine told him.

'Tell that to me at the hospital.'

An hour later, Jack Fieldhouse was in intensive care at the Sussex County. The prognosis was not good. He had suffered a massive heart attack.

Madden and Jasmine, who had gone with him, were soon joined by Millington. Fieldhouse's wife Lesley had been informed. Not for nothing had Madden christened her The Fieldmouse. She was small but she wasn't weak. Neither was she ill-informed. News travelled fast.

'I hear he was having an argument with you, Steve,' she said.

'That's right. We were standing up and he just fell. Crumpled to the floor.'

'I'm sorry,' she said. 'Don't feel bad about it.'

'I do,' said Madden.

'Nobody blames you.'

'Except me.'

She smiled a little smile and went to sit by her husband, or as near to her husband as they would let her. Fieldhouse wasn't conscious but he was breathing through a mass of tubes.

'What was the cause of it?' asked Millington. 'I know it's probably academic now but I would like to know.'

'It was nothing, sir.'

'You and Jack Fieldhouse don't have stand-up rows about nothing.'

'I was trying to link up the two cases. He resented me treading on his territory and then it got onto Jason.'

'I don't like acrimony between my officers,' said Millington. 'Can't everyone work together as a team?'

'That's what we all desire,' said Madden.

'Have you found any connection between them?'

'No, sir.'

'Then drop it. That's an order. I've had just about enough of this obsession of yours.'

'It's not an obsession, sir. It's a reasoned analysis. We've discovered Michael Bird had an interest in black magic and attempted to join a witches' coven and got turned away because they don't do that sort of thing, and now he's missing and nobody's heard from him. Plus we've got an unidentified kid at Hallowe'en with his heart removed. Even without Lavinia Roberts's prediction, that's a pretty strange coincidence.'

'Then concentrate on finding Bird,' said Millington.

'From my enquiries, I don't think you'll find that anybody who has a serious interest in witchcraft was responsible for the death of that boy.'

'What do you mean serious? You think we should be looking for somebody who *doesn't* take it seriously?'

'We're looking for a sick loner in my opinion.'

'Thank you for that opinion. You'll excuse me if I cast the net a bit wider than that?'

'You must do as you see fit, sir.'

Millington went off to do as he saw fit, which was probably *not* to listen to Steve Madden's opinion. Madden couldn't blame him. He got back into his car with Jasmine. There was nothing more they could do at the hospital. He felt lousy. It started to hit him.

'I shouldn't have got into such a temper,' he said.

'It wasn't your fault,' Jasmine squeezed his arm. 'Steve, it really wasn't. Jack Fieldhouse came in this morning and his clock was already ticking.'

'Yeh, and I stopped it.'

'I mean his *time*. It could have happened at any moment. When he was climbing upstairs, or driving his car, or in the middle of a conference, or in bed even. It was going to happen. It just happened when he was talking to you.'

'Not talking. Shouting.'

'He'd abused himself all his life. He knew the risks. He'd been told to lose weight.'

'Doesn't make me feel less guilty. Sorry. But thanks for trying, Jaz.'

'Want to know what I found out about Professor Grimaldi?'

They left the hospital and went for a drink. Madden needed one.

'Fire,' he said.

'Well he's not a very good clairvoyant,' she told him. 'I spoke to Andrew Fortune of the Yeovil police. Grimaldi seems to have bombarded him over the years with all sorts of stuff, none of which ever remotely helped him to solve a case. He thinks Grimaldi is a bit of a self-publicist.'

'So much for that,' said Madden.

'But I wouldn't write him off just yet. He's a member of both the Magic Circle and the British Order of Druids, a world authority supposedly on southern baroque architecture as well as being recognised as one on the occult, he lived for a year in a Tibetan monastery, and he founded a local coven in Somerset which got involved in psychic wars with another local coven. That's why he decided to move to Brighton.'

'What are psychic wars?'

'I hoped you wouldn't ask.'

'Pretend I didn't.'

'But his greatest claim to fame was as an expert defence witness in a murder case in Tennessee about ten years ago. A child was found murdered in a river and four teenagers were arrested and charged and – wait for it – were suspected of being members of a satanic cult. There was a lot of hysteria at the time, with social workers giving evidence that these lads had lured other boys into the woods and carried out satanic rituals, and there were other young boys that came forward and said they'd been made to urinate on babies and kill them and drink their blood. Anyway, Grimaldi went over there and demolished the entire thing. He even took on the local detectives and did his own investigation. In the end, the boys were acquitted.'

'How Salem came to Tennessee,' Madden ruminated.

'The real murderer turned out to be a preacher.'

'I take back everything I said about the Professor,' Madden told her. 'Maybe we could do with him on our side.'

The parcel had been waiting for Madden since that morning. It was sitting on his desk among a pile of mail he hadn't had time to open. It was lumpy and about the size of a hardback book, but soft round the edges. He tore off the string and opened up the brown paper. Inside, folded up, was an orange T-shirt. There were some objects wrapped inside it. It wasn't until he unfolded the garment that he saw the blood. It had already adhered to his fingers and felt sticky.

He got up from his desk and shouted to Jasmine. She hurried into his office. She looked in astonishment at the array of items on his desk.

'Get SOCOs in here quick,' he said. And then more reverently, 'This office just became a crime scene.'

Wrapped up in the T-shirt was a small blue bottle of ribbed glass, of the kind poison once used to be sold in, and inside it appeared to be a piece of paper. Through the glass, Madden could see what was written on it. His name. There was also a ceremonial-looking dagger with a pentacle on the handle, the long thin blade of which was encrusted with blood. But it was the third item that made Madden reel with horror. At first glance it looked like an enlarged fig bloated and covered with blood.

It was not every day that you opened your mail and found a human heart.

25

Ray Millington peered at Madden over the steepled tips of his fingers. He and Jasmine were sitting in the Chief Superintendent's office. It was eight o'clock in the evening. The news had come through that Jack Fieldhouse's condition was stable. Madden never knew what that meant. It always sounded like a euphemism for something. Like when things were really bad you couldn't say they were really bad or that so-and-so was in a worsening condition, so all you said was 'stable'. Fieldhouse was in a coma. That, to Madden, sounded serious. It sounded like he wasn't coming back for a considerable time. If at all.

He was thinking of Holly's parting words to him.

I hope you get what you want and find what you're looking for.

Hallowe'en was past but Madden felt spooked.

'Why you?' asked Millington.

'I don't know,' Madden shrugged. 'Somebody thought I'd be interested.'

'It was posted in central London last night, sir,' Jasmine informed him. 'Which means the killer kept the heart in his possession for at least twenty-four hours.'

'The dagger, sir,' said Madden, 'is identical to others I've seen at Hubble Bubble. They're used in witchcraft ceremonies. Not for sacrificing children or animals, I might add, but for drawing down energy. They have symbolic uses.'

'And that's not all the uses they have,' Millington pointed out.

'All roads lead back to Hubble Bubble,' Madden said, recalling something Richard Blance had told him about a break-in.

'It could just be coincidence, of course.'

'It could just be coincidence that the day after Lavinia Roberts' murder I went to the shop and was told they'd had a robbery. In Richard's words, some "witch stuff" was taken.'

'The T-shirt was a child's?'

'Yes, sir. It's at the lab now with everything else, sir. There were no prints on any of the items, other than the ones you'd expect from postal staff on the outside of the wrapping. We're having those eliminated. I think we can take it that the T-shirt belonged to Alex. Whoever he really is.'

'The bottle is the really unusual item,' said Jasmine. She shot a glance at Madden. 'It had a piece of paper inside with DI Madden's name on it.'

'That's right, sir. Just said Steve Madden. Nothing else,' confirmed Madden.

'Any explanation for that?'

'None I can think of straight away.' Madden shook his head. 'The bottle was of a pretty common type. You can pick these things up in antique shops and at antique fairs for a few pounds. But why my name should be written on a piece of paper and stuffed inside is beyond me.'

'What is beyond me,' said Millington, 'is why the killer should single you out for such preferential treatment.'

'He – or she – wants me to connect the crimes, sir.'

'This might seem like Christmas to you, Steve, but there's nothing about any of those items that remotely connects the two crimes.'

'Early days,' said Madden.

Millington stood up and looked out of the window. Something else seemed to be bothering him, Madden thought. Something unconnected with the present discussion. He wondered if it might have something to do with Devil's Dyke. He thought it better not to reopen that. For the moment, anyway.

'It's a great pity we let Bird go,' Millington admitted.

'It was your decision, sir. The right one at the time. We had no evidence against him, nothing to hold him on. It isn't a crime to visit clairvoyants.'

'How convinced *are* you he was Lavinia's eight o'clock appointment that same night he went to the other six?'

'Pretty convinced, sir. He lied about the others, and he did know about her because Natalie suggested he might go there. He needn't necessarily have touched the tarot cards. He could have had a crystal ball reading and left without touching anything. Unfortunately, Lavinia never made that clear to me and I never asked.'

'He hangs over this case like a phantom,' said Millington. 'Where the blazes is he?'

'My guess is London, sir. He has friends and associates up there, though they've all been visited and nobody admits to having seen him. Similarly his mother and girlfriend down in Lewes. And Patricia Edgeware says he asked her to drive his car up to London and leave it some place for him, but she refused.'

'Wherever he is,' said Jasmine, 'staying on the run is more important than retrieving his car. The last signal from his phone was from the vicinity of High Hedges. It's been off ever since.'

'You are absolutely sure he is not still in the Edgeware house, Steve?' Millington put a question that Madden had asked himself many times.

'It's a possibility, sir. But without a search warrant we won't know.'

'And without hard evidence, you're not going to get a search warrant to go into Ronnie Edgeware's house and start looking in the attic and pulling up floorboards. His lawyers would have us filleted. Get something concrete on Bird, and we'll try.'

'Difficult to get something concrete on Bird when we don't know where he is, sir,' said Jasmine. 'But we'll try.'

Madden was tempted to say that there was one person who might be able to provide a few extra answers, someone whom he was increasingly convinced hadn't been entirely forthcoming. That person unfortunately was lying in a coma as they spoke and was saying nothing.

From their meeting, he went straight to the Blances' house in Hove. Natalie was in, Richard was at the shop doing the accounts. She distracted him, Natalie explained. She seemed genuinely pleased to see him. It was a pleasant, airy house, full of candles.

Natalie had brought in a Feng Shui consultant which had annoyed the hell out of Richard as he had had to move all the furniture. It was, thought Madden, a very Natalie Blance thing to do. She was practising yoga in a white leotard when he walked in and looked as graceful as a swan on a millpond.

'Sorry to interrupt,' he said.

'That's all right,' she smiled. 'Have you brought any good news?'

'Do you recognise that?'

He showed her a photograph of the dagger.

'It's one of the kinds we sell. Why?'

'Richard told me you had a break-in a while ago. I need to know, what was stolen?'

'A similar one to that,' said Natalie. 'And a few other things.'

'I need to know if it was this one, Natalie. Where do you get them from?'

'Just one supplier. Glastonbury Products. In Wiltshire.'

'Presumably they're sold in a lot of other outlets.'

'And by mail order,' said Natalie.

'We have reason to believe one was used on the body of that child that was washed up.'

Natalie shuddered. She put her knuckles to her mouth. For a moment it seemed to Madden as though she wanted to scream. First her mother, now this. How bad could it get?

'Richard will know exactly what was stolen,' she said. 'He did an inventory. I can't remember.'

She tried phoning the shop but there was no answer. Neither was Richard answering his mobile.

'That's strange,' she said. 'He only left an hour ago.'

They got into his car and drove round there. It was a pleasure to drive with Natalie Blance next to him. She looked the kind of girl who would be oblivious to any man's attentions, even those of her husband. She lived on a different plane. Mist in the mountains, mist in the head, Richard had said of his wife. Yes, she was up there somewhere. Natalie fondled her necklace of black beads as he drove.

'Did you report the break-in?' he asked her.

'No. Richard didn't want to. I'd forgotten to set the alarm and he called me all sorts of names. He said there was only about two hundred pounds' worth of stuff stolen, plus the glass in the cabinet, and we could have had bad publicity about it. Selling stuff for witches' rituals is just a small part of what we do. We just wrote it off.'

'When did this happen, Natalie? Can you remember?'

'It was the same day that that guy with the tattoos came in for a reading. The one you asked about?'

Madden almost crashed the car into the back of the one in front. He had a fist shaken at him out of a hastily wound-down window.

'You're sure about that? It was the same day?'

'It was that night. After he'd been in the shop. You don't think—?'

'I don't want to be in any doubt about this, Natalie. It is important. You're saying that after Michael Bird had been to your shop, that night there was a break-in and one of these daggers was stolen?'

'Ask Richard if you don't believe me.'

'I believe you.'

'There's something I have to ask you,' she said.

'Go ahead.'

'When will I be able to cremate Mother?'

'Soon. Whenever the coroner releases the body.'

'There's this company in Chicago. The only one in the world. They extract the carbon from ashes and make it into a diamond. That's what I want to do with Mother. Wear her round my neck so she'll always be a part of me.'

The thought made Madden shiver. But then he'd never subscribed to New-Age thinking.

'I don't want her to just disappear,' Natalie said. 'I want her to be there, always. Catching the light. Shining.'

'It's a novel idea.'

'Richard doesn't like it.' She turned glum and introspective.

'He says if I do that, he's going to hide her and I'll have to search for her. He's like that.'

They arrived at the shop. The front door was locked. They went round the back and in by the service entrance.

'Richard must be here,' she said. 'I'll look upstairs.'

Madden glanced in the locked cabinet, at the daggers and other paraphernalia. He saw one identical to the one he had received. He quickly followed Natalie upstairs.

They passed the little office where Richard had his computer and where presumably he should have been doing his accounts. The computer was not on. Madden thought that a pity. He had entertained thoughts of walking in on Richard accessing some very dodgy websites, though he wasn't sure he wished that on Natalie. Some days he felt like a good guy.

There was a dim glow from the top floor. It emanated from the room which contained the flotation tank.

'Richard must be using the flotation tank,' said Natalie, sprinting up ahead of Madden on her lean athletic legs. 'He never uses the flotation tank.'

Never say never, thought Madden. In his experience, people frequently did things they never did. He heard Natalie's scream before he entered the room behind her. The lid of the tank was up. It was like a large capsule from which came the greeny glow of light on water and soft music. There was a terrible splashing as two bodies, as naked as babes, but a lot older and a lot guiltier, rose from the tank like two Venuses rising from that shell in the painting Madden couldn't quite remember the name of. At least one of them was a passable Venus. She had perfectly formed breasts and covered her pubic region with a pair of small, wet, trembling hands. She looked about eighteen. In contrast, Richard Blance looked less shapely.

Madden looked away. He wasn't a voyeur.

'Oh Christ. Christ, Christ,' said Richard. 'Natalie, I'm sorry.'

At least he didn't shame the occasion further by saying he could explain.

'I can explain,' he said.

Madden was wrong. He waited for the explanation. He wondered if Richard, being an accountant at heart, could cook the books over this one.

'I really am sorry,' he said again.

'I'm Ginny,' said the girl.

She was a tonic.

'You bastard!' Natalie screamed, and launched into a high-pitched aural assault. 'How could you do this? Lie to me and – and with this little floozy!'

'I'm not a floozy,' said Ginny.

Natalie picked up a towel and threw it at him. Then she picked up another one and threw it at the girl. Madden chose the moment to restrain her before she propelled something harder.

'Natalie, why don't we go downstairs,' he said. 'Let them dress. Then discuss this.'

'I'm not discussing this!' she cried. 'Discuss it? With either of them? Get your clothes on and get out of my shop.'

'It's our shop,' said Richard, forcing his flabby wet pale legs into his trousers and forgetting his pants.

'I'm not talking to you, I'm talking to her!'

'You didn't tell me you were married,' Ginny said, pulling on a pair of tight white shorts and flicking back her hair and making things worse by the second. 'Filthy liar.'

'He'll get called a lot worse when you've gone.'

Ginny pulled over her a T-shirt on which was written MY-BOYFRIEND-WENT-TO-THE-BRIGHTON-SEA-LIFE-CENTRE-AND-ALL-I-GOT-WAS-CRABS. Natalie nearly exploded.

'At least if you're going to shag around,' she yelled at Richard, 'shag around with some girl that isn't a tart.'

'*You're* a tart,' Ginny spat at Natalie, and flounced down the stairs with a face as crumpled as a used table napkin. Madden went after her.

'I might be a tart but I'm his fucking wife!' Natalie screamed after her.

Downstairs he learnt that her name was Genette Silverton, she came from Portslade-by-Sea, she worked in a fish-and-chip restaurant and she was sixteen and a half. She had met Richard over a chat line where he had told her he was twenty-eight. They had arranged to meet, and she discovered that he was nearer thirty-eight. She was about to end the brief association when Richard had asked her if she'd ever had sex in a flotation tank. She hadn't. After a few brandies in a pub (it was Ratty's Bar, unfortunately) she was ready to consider it a good idea. When you lived in Portslade and hated your job, sex in a flotation tank with soft lights and music and a talkative man sounded like Heaven. The rest was history.

Natalie and Richard came downstairs, their exchanges still heated and the mood extremely volatile. It would have been proper to withdraw, but Madden still had a job to do.

'I know this isn't the right time, but I have a question to ask.'

'You're right. This isn't the right time,' said Richard savagely. It was the first time Madden had ever heard his voice raised in anger.

'That day the tattooed guy came in, had his cards read, Paula gave him an Indian head massage, did he look round the shop at all?'

Natalie threw herself into a chair, crossed her legs, and refused to look at either of them. She opened her hands and closed them repeatedly. Madden wondered if it wasn't some yoga exercise to relieve tension.

'What of it?' Richard asked.

'It's important, Richard. I'll leave the two of you alone just as soon as you give me an answer.'

It was so important, he was determined not to lead him.

'He looked round the shop while he was waiting,' Richard said. 'For his appointment. With Natalie.'

'What did he look at?'

Richard was looking at Natalie. Natalie wasn't looking at him. Her hands were still springing open and shutting tight. Madden didn't want to be in Richard's shoes that night.

'I don't know,' answered Richard belligerently. 'He just looked round.'

'For God's sake, did he take an interest in the cabinet? With all the witchcraft stuff?' Natalie suddenly snapped and fired at her errant husband.

'Oh yes. He looked in that. He took quite an interest in it,' Richard remembered.

Natalie stormed over to the cabinet, unlocked it with her bunch of keys.

'Which was stolen?' she asked him. 'One like this? One like this? One like this?'

She held up a handful of daggers until she looked like one half of a circus knife-throwing act. Madden was tempted to step in in case she started hurling them at Richard.

'For God's sake!' Richard was almost in tears. 'Is this important right now?'

'It's important,' said Madden.

Richard pointed.

'One like that,' he said.

It was identical to the one Madden had been sent.

'Anything else?'

'A couple of goblets. A packet of dragon's blood. It's not real dragon's blood.'

'I'm glad to hear that.'

'And a packet of tarot cards. That's all.'

'And that's all I need to know,' said Madden. 'In the meantime, don't either of you touch the cabinet. There might still be a print somewhere in it or around it. I'm sending a fingerprint team round.'

Natalie put the daggers back. Madden made sure she locked the cabinet. He didn't want a third murder on his hands.

At least he had got the answer he wanted. The night after Michael Bird had visited Hubble Bubble, and taken an interest in the cabinet of magical paraphernalia, the shop had been broken into, and a dagger, two drinking goblets, a packet of dragon's blood and a box of tarot cards had been stolen. Not the computer upstairs, or anything else, but just those items. And that was the same night Lavinia Roberts had received her mysterious visitor. It was far from being concrete evidence of anything, just one more intriguing detail.

'Look after yourselves,' he said, and left the shop.

He phoned Jasmine, told her he wanted a SOCO to take fingerprints and without delay. She had news for him too.

'I'm sorry to tell you this, Steve,' she added to his store. 'But Jack Fieldhouse just died at seven forty-two this evening. Without regaining consciousness.'

Madden fell silent.

'Are you there?' she asked.

He was, but he couldn't say anything. He switched off the phone. For the next hour, he didn't want to talk to anybody.

26

He went to Ratty's Bar. It was midweek and early evening and there was a happy hour that was due to end in two minutes. Madden didn't feel like being happy. Lucky insisted on buying him a whisky. He bought it himself – a large one – and went and sat in a corner and tried to think of a good reason why he shouldn't feel guilty about Jack Fieldhouse's death. He couldn't think of one. Jasmine's contention that Fieldhouse's time was somehow written in the stars and that he was just the catalyst didn't work any more.

If the row had been about anything else – anybody else – other than Jason, he might have felt marginally less bad about it. As it was, it seemed as though the past had come back to haunt him. Madden remembered Lavinia Roberts's dictum that murder altered the whole fabric of space around a person. Perhaps something of that disturbance attached itself to the people most affected, to those left behind. Murder never cleared the air. Instead, it infected the air, it went on destroying, like some poison that seeped through the atmosphere, lethal, invisible, dormant even. Murder went on killing. Madden could think of numerous instances where one death had not been enough.

Like the case of the ten-year-old schoolgirl Alison Betts. Instead of uniting her parents in grief, the murder by a twenty-eight-year-old hospital porter George Anthony Mooney had driven them apart, resulting in the father's suicide three years later and the mother's death by a drugs overdose. Murder went on killing, like it had done in the case of the Rottingdean grandmother who had murdered her own grandson out of filial jealousy. Two more members of that family had died within a month of each other, struck down by 'unmanageable grief' as the papers had expressed it. Then there was the case of fifteen-year-old Darren Westwood, killed by his stepfather in a drunken rage. The youth's two brothers had simultaneously taken their own lives because they might have stopped it but failed, neither of them able to live with the guilt that had blighted the remaining ten years of their lives.

And now Jack Fieldhouse was dead because he, Madden, had been unable to forget the past, to bury the dead. Murder went on killing, a kind of emotional rampage that stemmed from the very moment of the violent act. The dead rested in peace but the living never did. They were not allowed to.

Lucky came over. His hand was still bandaged and his face still bruised but he and Ming had a business to run. Madden felt guilty about Lucky too. He would never be sure if he hadn't inadvertently tipped Ronnie Edgeware off about the source of his information.

'How's your hand?'

'Throbs a bit, Mr Madden. But it's okay. We've got a pub to run.'

'That's good. Dunkirk spirit.'

'Don't have any of that, Mr Madden.' Then, 'You don't look too happy.'

'Lost a colleague, Lucky.'

'I'm sorry to hear that, Mr Madden. Where's he gone?'

The lights were off tonight.

'Lost as in dead, Lucky. And it was my fault.'

'Surely not, Mr Madden.'

'I was arguing with him and he had a heart attack. The argument was about my son, Jason.'

Lucky sat down next to him. Madden told him the whole story.

'He'd have probably had a heart attack some other time. You just probably brought it on quicker than it would have done.'

'Thanks, Lucky.'

'No, I mean, you know what I mean, Mr Madden.'

'I know what you mean, Lucky.'

'You got to be philo—'

'Philosophical?'

'Yeh, that's it. You've got to be phil-sophical about these things.'

'If Phil Sophical ever comes in here, I'll buy him a drink.'

'Naw, he never comes in here.' Lucky laughed, sending himself up. He knew he wasn't the shiniest pebble on the beach. 'You got to stop blaming yourself, mate. What are you going to do? Go through life not arguing with anybody?'

'Right now, Lucky, that would be a pleasant option.'

He owed Lucky something.

'You had a guy in here earlier with a sixteen-and-a-half-year-old girl,' he told him.

'Did I, Mr Madden?' Lucky seemed genuinely surprised.

'Brighton Sea Life Centre T-shirt.'

'That one? She looked about nineteen. He was about forty.'

'She wasn't yet seventeen. You want to be careful, Lucky.'

'I said to Ming, he's a dirty bastard.'

'He's a very repentant bastard right now. But that's another story. I'm just warning you.'

'Thanks, Mr Madden.'

Ming came over, just to make sure Lucky wasn't providing him with any more information. Next time, she was convinced, it wouldn't be just his finger.

'You caught the guys yet that did it, Honey?' she said.

'Not much to go on. They wore masks and didn't speak. Probably came from London. I reckon Ronnie Edgeware was behind it but proving that isn't going to be easy. But I promise you, I'll find those responsible.'

'You've got more important things on your plate, Mr Madden,' said Lucky.

Ming slapped Lucky on his arm as a caution.

'Don't you be so understanding,' she scolded him. 'Look at you. A bloody wreck. What other priorities have the police got? Giving out parking tickets? I heard this story the other day, and it's true. This woman had her car broken into and the police said they were too busy to come out and investigate it, so she drove into Brighton to report it and there were two cops waiting in a lay-by who saw her going over a mini-roundabout and gave her a ticket.'

'I lost a colleague tonight,' Madden told Ming. 'I was arguing with him and he had a heart attack. He died about an hour ago. To say I feel guilty would be an understatement. And I need to find Michael Bird. He wouldn't happen to have shown up here again?'

'Sorry,' said Lucky.

'And he wouldn't tell *you*, Mr Madden, if he had. Would you?' said Ming.

'I'd tell Mr Madden anything if it helped solve a murder.' Lucky gazed at Madden as though he meant it. Madden had no doubt he did. 'I mean, I got beaten up but that woman lost her life. You can't get one of them back, can you?'

'No, Lucky. You can't,' said Madden. 'You said you knew Michael Bird. How well?'

'Just met him a few times. Through some guys I used to know. Long time ago. He was going to do this job years ago, but it fell through.'

'Oh God,' said Ming. 'Here we go again.'

'You wear the dresses round here, I'll wear the trousers,' said Lucky assertively, making a forceful gesture with his thumb. 'Customers at the bar, woman!'

Ming stood with jaw-dropping incredulity at Lucky's militancy. She trounced off, clearly unused to being spoken to in such a way. Lucky looked pleased with himself.

'Well she wanted to become one, she shouldn't complain at being called one,' he said.

'You were telling me? About Bird.'

'Yeh, it was a funny business. Like I said, years ago he was going to do this job, just outside Brighton, with a guy called Minky. They were going to turn over this electrical warehouse on an industrial estate together but the night before, Mike Bird pulled out. This Minky, he asked me if I would do the job with him, but I said no. I was too busy.'

'Very wise. How long ago was this, Lucky?'

'About ten years ago. As it turned out, Minky, he got this other guy to do the job with him, a guy called I can't remember what his name was, and they did the job together.'

'Successful?'

'Well sort of. They loaded this van with about thirty thousand pounds' worth of gear, drove it up to London, and discovered they were all rejects.'

'What were all rejects?'

'The stuff they'd stolen. It was all stuff returned by customers 'cause it was faulty. I tell you this, Mr Madden, it made me laugh.'

As it was still just happy hour, Madden shared in Lucky's amusement.

'You know this Minky's real name?'

'No, Mr Madden. Just ever knew him as Minky. He got killed in a car smash-up long time ago.'

He wasn't sheltering Bird then.

'Why do you think Michael Bird dropped out?'

'No idea.'

'Think he set them up?'

'He could've done, Mr Madden. I'll tell you this, though, he was a funny bugger. He was – what do you call it – superstitious?'

'Really?'

'He used to carry this rabbit's foot about with him. Told me it was lucky. I said what for? The rabbit?' Lucky laughed a second time. He liked his own jokes. Usually he didn't get them.

'That's interesting, Lucky,' said Madden.

'And if you had a meal with him and he spilt the salt, he'd throw it over his left shoulder. He said that's where the Devil sits.'

Madden remembered what Caroline – Miss Hardware of the tab shed – said about Bird being superstitious. Like it was when you worked on a ship or in the theatre. Something began to make sense. It was good when you suddenly saw something that was staring you in the face but you hadn't been able to see it because the blinkers were on. They were beginning to come off.

'Thanks, Lucky,' said Madden. 'You might just have helped me resolve part of this case that was really bothering me.'

'Really, Mr Madden?'

'Really, Lucky.'

Madden rang Lesley Fieldhouse. She had just returned home from the hospital. Jasmine was with her, but she wanted to see him. He said he would be there in fifteen minutes. He got there in ten. Jasmine opened the door to him.

'Where have you been?' she asked.

'I needed to be alone,' he said.

He hadn't been, but she gauged his mood.

He had never been to the Fieldhouses' home. Sometimes you imagined what a colleague's place would look like. The Fieldhouses' was a three-bedroom detached bungalow in Saltdean. There was a loft extension and a painfully neat front garden. Inside, it looked like the sort of home where a policeman went home to sleep and got up in the morning. It was ordinary, so dead ordinary that Madden wondered if anything exciting or passionate had ever happened here. They had no children. Madden had never asked why. It was none of his business.

Lesley Fieldhouse looked even tinier in the confines of her own home, a small, bowed woman with peephole eyes and a drawn face whose whole life, it seemed, had been dedicated to supplying the domestic needs of her hard-working, hard-drinking husband. She got up from the end of a long pale green settee and hugged him. He hadn't expected to be hugged. It was nice.

'I'm sorry about Jack,' he said.

It felt inadequate, but then whatever you said always did. Jasmine returned to the armchair where she was drinking a cup of tea and eating from a plate of ginger snaps.

'I really am sorry.' He needed to say something else but he wasn't sure what. It just came out. 'I feel responsible, Lesley. If I hadn't been arguing with him it might not have happened.'

'It did, Steve,' she said. 'And you can't turn it back.'

'I feel bad about it. Terrible, in fact.'

'Don't feel terrible. I could have been arguing with him,' she said. 'Any one of you could have been. This could have happened any time. Anywhere.'

It was good of her to feel like that, Madden thought. He wished he could be as generous with himself. He felt as guilty as though he had been in the driving seat and Jack Fieldhouse was a passenger and he had crashed the car.

'Is there anything I can do?' he asked.

'You can sit down and stop blaming yourself,' she told him.

She made him a cup of tea. It was strong and brown, so strong he couldn't drink it. He said nothing but just put it to one side. When you'd just hastened the end of a colleague's life it seemed insensitive to complain about his widow's tea. That was probably the way Jack liked it.

'He had high blood pressure,' she said. 'He'd had it for years. And the doctor had told him to knock the drinking on the head. I suggested he stick to halves but Jack could never be seen with a half pint in his hand. He said it looked stupid. He thought he had a reputation to keep up.'

'He had a reputation as a good detective,' Madden said.

It wasn't the time to say that her husband had a reputation for cutting corners in investigations, homophobia, sexism, bullying and racism. It wasn't the time to mention that Jasmine had suffered frequently while working alongside him because she was a woman and a coloured one to boot. It wasn't the time to bring up Jason's death and the mistakes that had been made in the investigation. It was Lesley who brought that up.

'Jack would have wanted you to know this,' she said. 'I don't think he could have told you himself, Steve, because he always found it difficult to admit mistakes. But he really did genuinely feel awful about what happened.'

'I'm sure he did.'

That wasn't the right thing to say, but it came out nonetheless.

'He even cried over it. I know you'll find that hard to imagine.'

Madden did. So did Jasmine. Nobody had ever seen Jack Fieldhouse cry. It wasn't part of his image.

'After you found who had really killed Jason, he came back home that night and poured his heart out. It was the first investigation he'd ever messed up and he knew he had. He felt so guilty about it. He wanted to do it for you, Steve, because you were a friend and a colleague. He *felt* he had to. The fact he failed cut him up more than I've ever seen him. It destroyed him, in fact.'

Murder went on killing. Those crushing and devastating after-effects of a murder that lasted for years and involved dozens of people included policemen. It was assumed by much of the public that when you were a policeman you didn't get emotionally involved with cases, that you did your job, helped to bring it to trial, and then went on to the next case. It wasn't true. Madden knew detectives who had lived and breathed cases and never got over them. Success or failure was irrelevant. In the most extreme cases, they saw and touched and felt pure evil in a way that few people ever did in their ordinary jobs. How many city stockbrokers or company accountants or shopworkers ever had to sit face to face with a cold-blooded multiple rapist or a child killer after seeing their victims and then go home to tea? It wasn't easy.

Sometimes it made you physically sick, or exceptionally angry, or just plain horribly depressed. But you had to go on being a professional, doing the job, taking the pay.

'Are you sure there is nothing we can do, Lesley?' asked Jasmine.

'That's very sweet of you.' Lesley Fieldhouse placed her hands in her lap and looked over at her. 'I don't suppose Jack made your life very easy. He didn't like women officers, I suppose you gathered that?'

'I did gather that,' said Jasmine tactfully. 'But then we all have prejudices.'

'Jack more than most. I'll let *you* into a secret. He was actually quite scared of them.'

'I find that hard to imagine.' Jasmine mustered up a laugh that was in perfect keeping with the sobriety of the occasion.

Her husband had been dead only a few hours, but Lesley Fieldhouse seemed to be undergoing a catharsis. Maybe she had lived with the truth so long she needed to share it.

'It's true,' she said. 'Jack had had a problem with it for years. Women, that is. Me included. He just couldn't – what's the popular way of putting it? He couldn't get it up, I suppose you'd say. It frustrated him terribly. Then when he saw an attractive colleague like you it would just bring it home to him and make him so angry. Oh, he thought I couldn't see it, but I did.'

'Lesley,' said Madden, 'you don't need to tell us this now.'

'Oh, but I want to,' she said. 'It helps me and it helps you to know Jack. I don't want you to walk out of here without knowing why he was the way he was. Don't you see?'

Madden said that he saw.

'This might not be the right time, Lesley. Tell me if it isn't. But did Jack discuss the job with you much?'

'Sometimes,' she said. 'When he wasn't too tired or drunk.'

'Did he ever talk about his relationship with a guy called Michael Bird?'

Jasmine flashed an angry look at him. He could tell that she disapproved of him using a comfort visit to expand his knowledge of the case.

'I think he mentioned the name once or twice,' she said.

'In what context, Lesley?'

'He was just someone he'd had a drink with late one night. Said there was a big job afoot.'

'A big job? Did he expand on that?'

'No, he just said it was a big job. To be honest, Steve, I rarely listened. Especially if he was drunk. He said something about going to St Lucia in the Caribbean, us going, I mean, but I didn't take it in.'

'You mean a holiday?'

'I assume that's what he meant. But we've never had a holiday for years. Not a proper holiday. He took me to Paris for a few days this year as you know, but that was the first time we've been abroad in ten years.'

She wiped a few tears from her eyes. It hadn't escaped the attention of either of them that she was still talking in the present tense, as though Jack was alive. And she was sounding ungrateful. Jasmine sat beside her and held her hand. Death brought out strange reactions in people. He imagined her going to bed alone for the first time in years, perhaps not altogether sadly. She had suffered, but the shock would still hit her.

Something nagged at the corner of his mind about St Lucia. Ronnie Edgeware had mentioned it in passing. He had called the island fashionable. Maybe it was irrelevant, a tiny detail which at the end of the day he could discard. Right now Madden would hang on to it, like a piece of jigsaw in the corner of the board that didn't seem to belong or fit anywhere. For the moment.

27

Jasmine came home with him and invited herself in for coffee. He was glad. He didn't want to be alone. He wondered if she would spend the night. He'd have been less than human if he hadn't wondered it. These things were never planned.

'Well, that was a revelation,' she said, as Madden switched on the percolator. They were standing in the kitchen, at opposite ends, still pretending that this was just about coffee.

'I still feel bad. He might still be alive if it hadn't been for me trying to sidestep him, to get one over on him. That's what made him mad. He was ringing about trying to find an expert and we had one, Jaz. We had one, and it made him furious. Then it got onto Jason.'

'I contacted Professor Grimaldi,' Jasmine reminded him. 'Blame me too.'

'I was in charge. I have to take full responsibility.'

'How long are you going to carry this burden of guilt around with you?' she asked.

'As long as it takes to go away.'

'That might be never,' she said. 'Unless you make it go away.'

'How do you make guilt go away, Jaz? I've tried and it doesn't work.'

'You move on. You don't look back.'

'Easier said.'

He poured out the coffees and they went through to the lounge. She crossed her legs and he thought that next to Clara she had the finest knees he had ever seen. They were a weakness of his, but then everyone had their weakness. He preferred it to guilt. Jasmine was right. He had to move on, and he had tried to do that since Jason's death, and failed.

'I think I know why Michael Bird went to six clairvoyants,' he said.

'We're talking about the case now, are we?'

'That's what you came in for, isn't it?'

'Of course,' she said.

'Everything we've found out about him suggests he was superstitious. Lucky Maynard told me he used to carry a rabbit's foot about with him. That he once backed out of a job unaccountably at the last moment. Jack said Bird might have been prepared to turn informer against Ronnie Edgeware. Suppose Bird visited all these clairvoyants to find out if that was the course of action he should take? There were dangers involved, after all.'

'But why six?'

'Why not? Six readings probably helped him more than one would. Put them all together and what do you have?'

'Probably six very different sets of advice.'

'Maybe that's how he ran his life. Maybe he went to see psychics before he suddenly dropped out of the job Lucky told me about. Our Michael Bird's a weird character. The question is, what advice did he receive this time? And was our Lavinia Roberts the seventh?'

'And why kill her if she was?' Jasmine made an even more important point.

Madden told her about his visit to Hubble Bubble, about the theft of the dagger, and about Richard's indiscretion.

'They were *in flagrante?*' she gasped.

'They were in the flotation tank.'

'Having sex?'

'It's probably quite exciting. Maybe we should try it one day. The salt stops you sinking and you just – well – bob around I imagine.'

'I can't imagine doing anything of the kind, Steve. In *water*?'

'Forget I mentioned it, Jaz. What's important is that Michael Bird visited Hubble Bubble the day before they had a break-in there. He looked round the shop. One of the items stolen was a dagger identical to the one sent to me. The coincidences are adding up.'

'Why break in and steal it? Why not buy it?'

'If you worked in a shop like that, you'd remember people that bought ceremonial witches' daggers. I don't imagine they sell a hundred a day.'

'Why not just use an ordinary kitchen knife?'

'Good question. Our friend Grimaldi answered it for us. He's looking for power. Ritual. He wants the right equipment. He keeps the heart for a while to give him that sense of power, of control over somebody's life. The heart is the powerhouse of the body.'

They looked straight at each other. They were both thinking the same thing. It was a case of which one of them was going to be the first to say it.

'Steve, that doesn't exactly square with a guy going to clairvoyants to seek advice on whether or not he should turn police informer.'

'I know. It doesn't, does it? Still, we're making progress.'

'Are we?'

'It's late,' he said. 'Maybe we should leave psychological profiles till the morning.'

'Steve,' she said, broaching what was clearly a difficult matter for her. 'You're making a big mistake.'

'How?'

'Planning to sleep with Clara again. It'll bring you problems. Big problems.'

'I'm not planning it, Jaz. Nothing's happened.' It was part true, part lie. The first part was the lie, the second part true.

'I have no right to tell you what to do, to order your life, but – should something happen between you, and these things do happen, then it would bring you all sorts of problems.'

'I can handle them.'

'No, you can't. I don't need a set of tarot cards to tell you that it's like taking a step back and that it'll cause you a lot of grief. You know how much pain it brought you before.'

'The pain was in not having her.'

'Is this some kind of – primeval conquest?' she challenged him. 'Just because she's some other man's wife, you now want to show you have the power to bring her back?'

'I don't have that kind of power. I don't want it. She came back. All I did was just open the door.'

'Don't kid me, Steve. That's how you might tell it to yourself but you know that's not how it is.'

Sometimes he felt she knew him too well.

'You're right,' he said. 'That's not how it is. I don't know how it is. All I know is if Clara and I go on being friends like we are, I'm not going to be able to stop myself. I find myself manipulating her though I don't want to. I know it's wrong. But what can I do?'

'Where's it going to lead to?'

'I don't know. Does it have to lead anywhere, Jaz?'

She came and sat beside him and snuggled into his arm. It wasn't a sexual snuggle. He knew what those felt like. This was a protective one. Theirs was a relationship that wasn't going anywhere either, or at least if it was he was blind to the signs. Jasmine's mother and family wanted her to marry a Hindu boy eventually, and Jasmine had not expressed herself averse to falling in with their wishes, though her own mother had married an Englishman. At least her mother had gotten past the stage of placing matrimonial advertisements in Hindu newspapers. Jasmine wanted to concentrate on her career. She would make her own mind up. She had been born in the west and she was half English, and though her religion was important to her, she had no intention of sacrificing her freedom. Just yet.

'How's the pilgrim?' Madden asked.

'Mum rode a horse for the first time in her life.' Jasmine recounted the contents of her latest e-mail. 'They were singing on horseback when the heavens opened and the road flooded and they nearly got swept away.'

He drew her close to him. He tried to imagine her mother sitting in internet cafés in India between coping with collapsed bridges and surviving floods and herds of buffalo. She laid her head on his shoulder.

'We have to keep this a working relationship,' she said.

'It's working for me.'

'Me too,' said Jasmine.

'Jaz, if you were any other woman, you'd storm out of here right now after I admitted to you about Clara. Not sit here with me like this.'

'I'm not any other woman. You can do what you like. We're free agents. We don't do romance.'

'So why did you take such umbrage before?'

'Because,' she said, 'you played the game wrong.'

'What are the rules tonight?'

'You ask me to stay, I agree, we don't talk about Clara.'

'Okay. I agree.'

'Good,' she said. 'Now did I see an open bottle of wine in the kitchen?'

Ray Millington said, 'You can wipe that smirk off your face, Steve.'

'I wasn't smirking, sir,' said Madden.

'Well you will be when you see the lab report on that little Christmas parcel of yours. That's why I thought I'd get it in first.'

Within minutes Madden and Jasmine had joined him in his office. Millington looked penitent. Madden didn't think that so extraordinary as Millington was a Methodist, and he reckoned that Methodists must surely on occasions be penitent about some things. They read the lab report. The smirking could come later.

The fingerprinting of the cabinet at Hubble Bubble had turned up nothing except Natalie and Richard Blance's own prints. But that disappointment faded when Madden saw what they did have, courtesy of the police laboratory at Aldermaston.

'They found ivy hairs on the orange T-shirt,' said Millington. 'The ivy hairs match the species of ivy climbing up the window outside Lavinia Roberts's kitchen. They also found a fragment of glass caught in the weave that has the same refractive index as the glass from the window that was broken.'

'I don't understand. What are we supposed to read into that, sir?' asked Jasmine. 'That this unidentified boy climbed in through Lavinia Roberts's kitchen window and murdered her?'

'Cross transference,' said Madden. 'Whoever killed Lavinia Roberts wore an item of clothing that picked up the ivy hairs and the glass splinter. Nobody could commit a murder in those circumstances and *not* take something away with them. He wore the same article of clothing when he murdered and undressed the boy, and those things transferred onto the T-shirt.'

'We have linkage,' said Millington. 'Whoever killed Lavinia Roberts killed the boy. That's undisputed. Now all we have to do is find out who the hell he is and why nobody's missing him.'

'And find Bird,' said Madden.

He went back to his office feeling giddy with fulfilment. He was tempted to believe that the killer had made his first mistake. But was it? You didn't present evidence on a plate unless you wanted it be consumed. And Madden was hungry. There were words almost burning his ears.

I hope you get what you want and find what you're looking for.

He hesitated before picking up the phone and dialling Holly Elder's number. He couldn't tell her everything, of course. In fact he couldn't tell her very much. But he did explain that they had found the evidence to link the crimes and that he was now handling both cases. That much would be in the papers the next morning. More pointedly, he mentioned Jack Fieldhouse's death.

'You think I did this with a spell? Twitched my nose?' she said. 'Let me tell you something. Have you ever heard of the threefold law?'

'No, but I've got a funny feeling you're going to tell me it.'

'Any spell cast is revisited on the sender three times over. A bad spell resulting in a person's illness or death would come back on me threefold. It's a witches' maxim.'

Madden breathed a sigh of relief.

'That's what I hoped you'd say,' he said.

28

The press were calling it a breakthrough, but for Madden it was a chance to get on with the job. He had spotted a French and a Japanese television crew in Brighton that morning, had been asked to make a statement in front of the cameras in which he appealed for anyone with information about a three- or four-year-old boy who had worn blue shorts and an orange T-shirt to come forward, and politely declined the services of three more psychics, one from Holland who believed that the boy was Russian and that the answer would be found at an address in St Petersburg. The father of a boy who said his Greek-born wife had abducted his son ten years previously said that Alex might be his, until it was explained to him that Alex was four at the very most. More sickeningly, there had been an anonymous confession that morning written on bloodstained paper and decorated with pictures of skulls and pentacles and something that looked like a large octopus. Madden felt distinctly underwhelmed.

There was a promising lead. In fact, it sounded too promising. A newsagent in North Moulsecoomb, an estate on the northern outskirts of the city, claimed that a 'foreign girl' had visited his shop regularly with a little boy who had worn an orange T-shirt and that recently he had seen her but not the child. He had no idea where she lived or what her name was.

To outsiders, North Moulsecoomb conjured up images of thatched cottages, village pubs and smoke drifting sleepily from crooked chimneys. Nothing could be further from the truth. Madden knew North Moulsecoomb as a 'no go' area. The estate had been built in the 1920s to house the slum dwellers that the Brighton corporation wanted shipped out of the new, bright, shining town centre, and half a century later it had become a dumping ground for problem families. It was rare for a North Moulsecoomb resident to voluntarily phone up the police and offer information to do with any enquiry, let alone one concerning murder. So when it did happen, it was worth seizing on.

The shop was in a semi-derelict, dead-end row at the foot of a hill. Albert McKendrick was a small, droopy man who ran it single-handedly, and had done so since the death of his wife a year past. He had bars on the window and a stock that consisted of newspapers, magazines, cigarettes, chocolate bars, a few cheap plastic children's toys, and not much else. Madden wondered how such shops ever made a profit. Next door was a boarded up Post Office still advertising 'Car Tax Here' and covered in graffiti.

'Want to buy a shop?' asked McKendrick, rolling a cigarette.

'Tell us about the girl,' asked Madden.

'She comes in here from time to time. Foreign girl she is. One of them immigrants.'

'Nationality?'

'I don't know. Just foreign sounding. Can't speak much English. Reckon she came over in a lorry.'

'What do you mean?'

'Well, one of them that shouldn't be over here. Too many of them if you ask me.'

He looked at Jasmine. Jasmine looked at him. Neither flinched.

'I'm not a racist,' said McKendrick.

'You don't sound like one,' said Jasmine.

'Do you know her name?'

'Nope. She just used to come down here with her kid, buy a packet of cigarettes and go. You don't get into conversation with them.'

'When did you last see her?'

'She came in yesterday and the day before. Didn't have the kid with her. I asked her where he was but she either didn't understand me or she just didn't want to talk. She had a cut on her eye and a bruise on the back of her neck as though she'd been beaten up.'

'I thought you said you didn't get into conversation.'

'I was being affable,' said McKendrick.

'Any idea where she lives?'

'Somewhere local.'

'Can you describe the boy?'

'He was a small lad, about three or four. Black hair. Pretty, bit like a girl. Thought he was at first. Had that sort of foreign face that made it difficult to tell. Wore an orange T-shirt.'

'Shorts?'

'Don't remember. Didn't see. He only came up to the top of the counter. She used to buy chocolate for him. Thing that made me suspicious – you listening?'

'I'm listening,' said Madden.

'Last time she came in, I said, here's a bar of chocolate for the kid. I didn't want any money for it. It was a present. A gift. Goodness of my heart. I said, take it, for the kid. She wouldn't take it. She just turned and went. You listening?'

'We're still here,' said Madden.

'That was yesterday. I thought to myself, it's funny. That's why I rang you.'

He lit his rolled up cigarette with a plastic disposable lighter.

'Can you describe her?' asked Jasmine.

'Who?'

'The mother.'

'Foreign looking. About eighteen. Black hair. Foreign kind of eyes, you know, the way they don't look straight at you. Odd mouth. Nice ears. Pretty, I suppose, in a kind of a way. Unmarried mum, I reckon. Never saw a bloke with her, anyway.'

'When does she normally come in?'

'Usually about six o'clock. Never earlier. Buys her cigarettes then goes. Like I say, you try to be affable but they don't look at you. They want asylum but they don't want to integrate. Know what I mean?'

'Yes, scandalous,' said Madden.

They left the shop, realising they had two choices. Start knocking on doors in North Moulsecoomb, which was not a good idea as almost certainly most would stay shut. North Moulsecoomb residents didn't readily open their doors to the police. Or go back for six o'clock.

They returned with an hour to spare. McKendrick was his affable self. He had decided to sit down so he was almost invisible behind the counter. He asked them if they wanted a cup of tea. They declined. He invited them to open a packet of biscuits on the house.

'Sure you don't want to buy a shop?' he reprised.

'Absolutely sure,' said Madden.

'Things haven't been the same since my wife died,' he said, looking at the floor and shuffling his feet.

Almost exactly on six o'clock, by which time it had turned dark, a spare, white-faced girl with prominently arched eyebrows and a smooth complexion and rich black hair parted in the centre, entered the shop. She looked straight ahead at McKendrick and opened a plastic purse. She did indeed have a gash over her eye and a few-days-old-looking bruise on her neck.

'Twenty Marlboro,' she said, in an accent that sounded East European.

McKendrick flashed a look at his visitors and tossed his head. Madden and Jasmine stepped up to the girl, showing their warrant cards. She looked like a startled rabbit. She spun round and tried to run out of the door but Jasmine caught her.

'We only want to talk to you,' she said.

'*Nuk kuptoj*,' said the girl.

'Can you speak English?'

'*Nuk kuptoj*,' she repeated in panic.

'What's your name?'

The girl understood that. Madden could tell.

'Where are you from?' Jasmine asked.

The girl just looked terrified. She understood that too, he was sure.

'You got an atlas of the world?' Madden asked McKendrick.

'What do you think this is? W.H. Smith's?' he replied.

'Sorry I asked.'

'Albania,' said the frightened girl in almost perfect English.

They found an Albanian interpreter. Her name was Dr Yolanda Terzi and she taught at the School of Slavonic and East European languages at University College, London. She was a trim, bustly, energetic woman in a serge blue trouser suit and looked the type who would stand no nonsense. Within an hour, they were sitting with her in an interview room, facing the girl whose name turned out to be Delina Vllasi.

'Ask her where she's from in Albania,' asked Madden.

'She's from Tirana, the capital. Where I come from,' said Dr Terzi.

'How long has she been here?'

The two engaged in what seemed a rather long conversation. Eventually, Dr Terzi said, 'About six months. She initially didn't want to tell me even that. She's quite scared.'

'What's she scared of?'

'You,' said Dr Terzi.

'Tell her she has nothing to be scared of.'

'I've already told her that.'

'Ask her how old she is.'

'She's seventeen.'

'Does she have a son?'

Another long conversation ensued in which Delina began to shed tears and looked about the room at the walls as though searching for a means of escape.

'She says she had a son, but he is back in Albania.'

'Ask her who the little boy was that accompanied her to the shop where we arrested her.'

Dr Terzi put that to Delina. Delina shook her head wildly.

'She says she doesn't know anything about a little boy.'

'I don't speak Albanian but body language says she's lying. Try again.'

Dr Terzi tried again.

'Now she's changed her story. She says she does have a son

in this country. But he was taken away from her when she arrived. By the immigration authorities.'

'That doesn't make sense. She had a boy with her a few days ago. We need to know who he was and where he is now.'

Dr Terzi put all this to the girl. There were more tears and more wild head shakings.

'She sticks to her story,' said the interpreter.

It was frustrating when you had to rely on a third party to conduct an interrogation. Madden wondered how forcefully Dr Terzi was putting the point. A quarter of an hour later, they were still no further forward. Delina Vllasi was still denying that she had visited the shop with a small boy, and continuing to insist that the immigration authorities had taken him into care.

It was easy to check. Or so he imagined.

'Might help if we knew what port she arrived at,' said Jasmine. 'And which social services took him into care, if they did.'

Dr Terzi found out a little bit more.

'She says she arrived at Dover. But she doesn't know which social services were responsible. She just says it was the immigration authorities.'

Jasmine went out to check with the immigration services, to see if they had ever heard of a Delina Vllasi. Madden had the blue shorts and the orange T-shirt which the boy was wearing brought into the room. He spread them out in front of Delina. It wasn't the kind of thing he liked doing, but it did the trick. Delina let out a long, penetrating wail and jammed her knuckles into her mouth and would not look at them for more than a second.

'She recognises them,' said Terzi.

'I know she does. Ask her who they belong to.'

After what seemed an interminable time, Delina came up with the boy's name and a little bit more information besides.

'Dana,' she said, over and over again. 'Dana – Dana—!'

'His name is Dana,' said Dr Terzi.

'I got that much.'

'He's three years old. She had him when she was fourteen. She was raped by a soldier.'

'We need to know what happened to Dana. And where she's living and who she's living with.'

Dr Terzi tried her best. The story changed.

'She says Dana went missing a few days ago. She was scared to report it in case she was sent back to her own country.'

'Why should we have done that?'

'She's seventeen and in a foreign country. I should think that's a good enough explanation.'

'Okay, ask her about the circumstances in which Dana went missing.'

Delina spoke for a long time. Occasionally she seemed to ramble. Dr Terzi began taking notes. Madden couldn't tell whether Delina was telling the truth or not. That was another problem with suspects who couldn't speak English and where you had to rely on the services of an interpreter. Eventually, Dr Terzi got the story. It sounded plausible.

'She says she was walking back from the shop at about six o'clock in the evening and cut across a piece of land called the Wild Park.'

'I know it,' said Madden.

'Dana was with her, and he liked to go and play in some bushes near the road. She used to let him. He would play aeroplanes, and run about in the bushes with his arms like this. So,' Dr Terzi demonstrated. 'Five nights ago she was sitting waiting for him—'

'Hang on, she sits and lets a kid of three disappear into bushes at night?'

'I asked her that. She thought he was safe. She was sitting only a few yards away. When she called him, he didn't come. She went to look for him and somebody attacked her from behind. She didn't see who. A man, she thought. She was knocked unconscious, by a large piece of wood she thought, and as she lay on the ground she had a tennis ball rammed in her mouth before being gagged and tied to a tree.'

'Tied, what with?'

Dr Terzi asked her.

'Rope,' she said. 'She heard a car driving away. Whoever it was took Dana.'

'She didn't see the car?'

'She didn't see it. She only heard it.'

'Ask her – was this a routine? Did she do this every night?'

Dr Terzi asked. Delina nodded.

'She says she did it every night. She would go and buy cigarettes. It was the only chance, she said, for Dana to have a run around.'

'Who freed her? What happened after that? Where was she going back to? Where does she live?'

Dr Terzi put all those questions to Delina, but Delina wouldn't say much more. She kept looking at Madden as though he was going to hurt her.

'All she will say is that her boyfriend found her.'

'Her boyfriend? Who is he? Where does he live?'

'May I make a suggestion?' said Dr Terzi. 'You frighten her.'

'I frighten myself sometimes.'

'If I could talk to her on my own, gain her confidence, she might open up to me.'

Madden agreed, and left them to it. After an hour, they were still in there. He gave instructions for them not to be disturbed. Jasmine had been on to the Immigration Service. She was waiting for them to call back. They had not done so by the time Dr Terzi came out, with a broad but rather business-like smile on her face.

'I have what you want,' she said. 'She wouldn't tell me until I told her her son was probably dead. Did I say the right thing?'

'You said the right thing.'

'She wouldn't have understood any of the English papers about the boy being killed. I think now she feels she has nothing left to lose. From what I can make out, she lives with someone she's scared of. I assume he's a boyfriend but she's clammed up, even on me. I did get his name. Kostandin Motolese. And where he lives.'

She wrote it down and gave Madden the address.

'Go back in there, Dr Terzi. See what else you can get out of her.'

'I will try my best,' she said.

'Try to assure her that if she's telling the truth she has nothing to be scared of.'

'I have told her that.'

'And tell her we're not scared of this – Kostandin Motolese,' Madden said.

29

Number one hundred and seventy Bluebell Avenue, North Moulsecoomb, was at the end of a cul-de-sac where there was a parking bay in which few people parked any more because most of the houses were boarded up and unoccupied. It was only a few minutes' walk from the Wild Park, a green, wooded and popular picnicking spot that was one of the small mercies of the area. It was where urban decay met nature of a sort. Number one hundred and seventy had floral curtains and fresh flowers in the windows, in stark contrast to the wooden slats and corrugated iron that covered the others in the street. There was a little seesaw in the garden made out of a plank of wood and an oil drum. A plastic cat weathervane spun on a pole. The front door and the window sills were painted bright blue.

Madden rang the bell. The night was bitterly cold. This was where Brighton met the South Downs, in an area where houses had been designed to integrate into the landscape and create a feeling of rural bliss. It hadn't happened. Tree and brick had remained on their own sides of the concrete divide. The planners forgot one thing. A slum was a slum wherever you put it. In the gardens of the boarded-up houses that stretched alongside there were pieces of rotting timber, remains of an old rusty bicycle and a broken pushchair, the detritus of modern living.

A spy hole in the door opened. This, after all, was North Moulsecoomb. Then the door opened a fraction. A face poked through. In the darkness, it was difficult to make out features, though they could discern that the man had a moustache.

'Yes?' he asked. It wasn't welcoming.

'Detective Inspector Madden. Detective Sergeant Carol,' said Madden. 'We'd like to speak to Kostandin Motolese.'

'I Kostandin,' he said.

'Do we have to talk like this?'

'What you want to talk about?'

'Delina Vllasi.'

'Wait,' he said. 'I talk.'

He shut the door. Madden and Jasmine waited.

'Think there's a cup of tea and a biscuit waiting for us on the other side?' he asked.

'Doubt it,' said Jasmine.

A few minutes later, the door was opened again. Kostandin Motolese was a stocky individual with a moustache that looked like a caterpillar and rather hunted-looking eyes. He was wearing a white shirt and baggy jeans and carpet slippers that had blue and green sequins on them. He invited them into the front parlour and invited them to sit down. Madden was right. There was no tea and biscuits.

Madden skipped the pleasantries.

'Is Delina Vllasi your girlfriend?' he asked.

'Yes.'

'Did she live here with her son, Dana?'

'No, no son,' said Kostandin Motolese, gesturing rather dramatically with his hands.

'Mr Motolese, we know Delina had a son. She's told us he was abducted the night before Hallowe'en.'

'Okay, okay, I know nothing about that.' He was growing increasingly nervous.

'She says you found her in the woods, untied her.'

'Not me. Not me,' said Kostandin. 'My brother Mustapha.'

'Can we talk to him?'

'He don't want to talk. I answer for him. He get call, go to the woods, find her, bring her back. I don't want any trouble.'

'The boy's dead, Mr Motolese. You couldn't be in much more trouble.'

Madden's mobile rang. He answered it. Kostandin Motolese

stared down at the carpet. It was covered in cigarette burns. Millington was on the phone. He suggested that Madden not speak, just listen.

'Is your brother Mustapha at home?' Jasmine asked.

'No, not at home,' Kostandin said all too quickly.

'Where is he? We'd like to speak to him.'

It was a simple enough question but it made Kostandin very edgy. He kept looking at the door. Madden finished his call and looked at her.

'My mother's dead,' he said.

It took her just a second to catch on. She knew exactly what he meant. It was a code they had used only once in the past. It meant stop the questioning. It meant they'd walked into something they hadn't been quite prepared for. In short, it meant stop whatever you're doing and get the Hell out.

'I'm sorry,' said Madden. 'But we're going to have to come back later.'

Kostandin lit a cigarette. His hand was shaking. There was a movement in the passageway outside the door. A teenager with handsome swarthy looks, muscular arms and curly hair stared into the room. He looked alarmed.

'Who's that?' asked Madden.

'My brother,' said Kostandin. 'Mustapha. He come home.'

Kostandin shouted something at his brother in Albanian. The boy ran up the stairs.

'He don't want to come in,' said Kostandin.

There was a clattering on the stairs. Madden and Jasmine left the room. Madden glanced up the stairs and saw the boy trip and almost fall in panic. He was holding a gun. Madden couldn't see what kind of gun it was, but when you were in that situation, you didn't much care. Unfortunately, Kostandin caught his look of alarm. He also saw his brother. He shouted something else in Albanian. The boy shouted back.

'You better go,' Kostandin said.

Madden experienced a surge of adrenalin and his mouth went bone dry. Kostandin tried to keep up the pretence of showing his visitors out while the boy ran back up the stairs. Madden would later think that his best course of action would have been to walk straight out of the front door, get into the car with Jasmine, and drive off. But like Lot's wife, he looked back again. He looked back to check where the boy was standing, if he was still in range. Big mistake. The boy was on the landing, halfway up the stairs, and he was still holding the gun in his right hand. It wasn't good to lock eyes with a scared kid holding a gun. Madden swung his head round.

They were almost out of the door when he felt it. Like a violent punch to his shoulder. The shot blast temporarily deafened him and made his ears ring. The air smelt of cordite. Everything after that happened so fast he wouldn't remember in which order the events occurred. The youth leapt over him. Jasmine fell down in a heap on top of him. Blood was pouring down his arm, soaking into his shirt. He was aware of Kostandin grabbing the gun from his brother. Jasmine pulled out her phone and called for help. There was a screech of tyres as the two Albanians leapt into a car and sped away from the house. Madden felt a searing, burning pain on the top of his shoulder. Jasmine removed her chiffon scarf and tried to staunch the blood.

'Guess we won't be having that cup of tea and biscuit after all,' he told her.

30

An ambulance arrived plus three squad cars and an armed response unit. Madden was able to walk into the ambulance himself. A paramedic called Roger looked at the wound and said it was just a flesh nick. Bloody, but a flesh nick just the same. Madden had always wondered what it would be like to be shot. He didn't want to try again. The call had gone out for Hotel 900. That meant the police helicopter.

Jasmine travelled to the hospital with him. He told her the rest. Dr Terzi had got it out of Delina after their departure and Millington had called him immediately.

'They're Albanian gangsters,' he said.

'In North Moulsecoomb?'

'They're known to the Met. They were running that place as a brothel. A sort of off-shoot from Soho. They cleared the other girls out after Delina's son got taken. They knew there'd be trouble.'

He went on, his shoulder giving him agony.

'Kostandin was her pimp. Delina Vllasi was a prostitute.'

'How does it feel?' she asked.

'Sore,' he said. 'Am I going to live?'

'It looks like the bullet only grazed you. Don't be such a baby.'

'It feels worse than that. It feels like I've had half my shoulder shot off.'

'You were lucky. That was a Walther P38. Popular with terrorists. They use them for assassinations and kneecapping and that kind of thing.'

'Thanks, Jaz. That's the kind of information that's nice to have.'

'I did a firearms course,' she said.

At the hospital, a male nurse called Simon who had ginger hair and freckles and smelt of sweet cologne, dressed the wound and told him that he was on the local radio.

'You're a hero,' he said.

'I'm not a hero. I got shot.'

'That's a hero in my book.'

'In mine, it's a bloody fool.'

Two hours later, Millington turned up at the hospital. Madden was told they wanted to keep him there for a few more hours, just for observation.

'What do they think I'm going to do?' he asked. 'Dance a jig?'

'It's for your own good,' said Millington. 'You could be in shock.'

'I had the shock. When I was shot.'

'The doctors know best, Steve. We picked up the two Albanians. Mustapha Motolese is only nineteen.'

'I hope he has a great future ahead of him.'

'You're lucky he wasn't a very good shot. That was a Walther P38 he pointed at you.'

'He didn't just point it, sir. At least we've identified the boy, sir. His name is Dana Vllasi.'

'What you don't know, Steve, is that somebody telephoned the Motoleses after his mother was attacked and the boy taken. They were told exactly where to find her. They untied her and took her back to the house.'

'Do they know what he sounded like?'

'They're Albanians, Steve. Every English accent sounds the same to them.'

'What did they do with the rope she was tied up with? The gag – and there was a tennis ball too.'

'Burnt them,' said Millington. 'In the garden.'

'You reckon she's telling the truth? That she's not covering up for the Motoleses?'

'The stories match up too well. Looks like it was well planned. Whoever did it probably guessed he'd have plenty of time to get away with the boy. Phoning the Motoleses guaranteed that she wouldn't be found by anybody else. Albanian gangsters running a brothel, an immigrant girl working as a prostitute and scared witless, none of these people are going to run to the police.'

'I reckon she was stalked,' said Madden. 'And that her killer was probably a client and that's how he got to know her and the set-up.'

'Don't you think I already worked that out, Steve?'

'Ask them about Michael Bird. If he was a client—'

'Don't you also think that's one of the first things I asked *all* of them before I came here?' Millington said. 'I'm sorry, Steve, but they don't recognise him. And she would certainly have remembered those tattoos.'

'They could be lying.'

'They've every reason to want to help us. Now.'

Simon, the male nurse, brought him a cup of tea and a chocolate biscuit. Madden devoured both rapidly. It was strange how being shot and ending up in hospital made you suddenly ravenous.

'You're convinced this was Bird's doing?' Millington sighed.

'I'm not convinced about anything.'

'But you are about Lavinia Roberts's conviction that he was a – how did she put it?'

'A serial killer in embryo,' he said.

'If I tell you something, Steve, I want you to promise me you'll keep it to yourself.'

'You have my word,' said Madden.

'I want more than that.'

'You have two words. "Trust" and "me".'

'That's good enough,' said Millington, drawing up a chair by the bed on which Madden was resting. He pulled the curtain for privacy. 'How do I start?'

'This is your confession, sir.'

'Confession.' Millington seemed amused by the word. 'Yes, I suppose that's what it is. You were very near the mark when you quizzed me on the Devil's Dyke murder. There *was* an anonymous letter, but it was very vague, and the truth is I don't know what's happened to it. If it isn't in the file, it's got lost. It scarcely matters. The letter writer simply said that he'd seen a man answering Colin Shilling's description with a girl in the Dyke on the day she disappeared. I had no more than that. Where was I to start?'

'An aerial shot of the area. To look for fresh movements of earth.'

'The murder happened in the early spring. It was midsummer by that time. Everything had grown. We went out with dogs but found nothing. Then, when I thought it might just have been a hoax, Lavinia Roberts offered her help. She said she could try dowsing.'

'Isn't that for water?'

'Apparently not. You can dowse for anything. Minerals, even people. I didn't believe in it, of course, but to tell you the truth, I was desperate. She came into my office and went into some kind of a trance and hung this pendulum over the photographs we'd taken. She identified three places where she felt the body might lay.'

'Try here, try here and try here,' said Madden.

'We tried. If in the very first place we dug we hadn't found anything, I was going to pack it in.'

'You found the body.'

'We found the body.'

'I'm surprised you didn't arrest her,' Madden smirked. His shoulder was starting to throb, as if there was something inside it, expanding and contracting. He wondered where the bullet had gone.

'Well, I thought about it. I'm just an old-fashioned Methodist, Steve. I don't believe in divination and fortune telling and tarot cards and all that mumbo-jumbo. Even after that breakthrough, I wasn't sure I believed in it. I put it down to just sheer luck.'

'Like winning the lottery at thirty-two million to one? I imagine the odds were probably even higher than that.'

'It helped me get promotion, that case,' Millington said. 'I was hardly going to give credit to a process that would have branded me – well, having relied on a psychic. I'm sure you understand.'

'How did you cover your tracks, sir? Or perhaps I should say, how did you cover *hers*?'

Millington glanced around guiltily. Simon, the male nurse, was pottering about on the other side of the curtain. He moved away. Millington leant closer to the bed.

'I said I'd gone for a walk in the Dyke. Discovered a patch of earth under some nettles that looked as though it had been disturbed,' Millington admitted.

'Shame on you, sir.'

'You think I should be ashamed?'

'I think you should feel very ashamed, yes.'

'Well, that's what elevates us above the animal kingdom,' said Millington. 'A guilty conscience.'

'I wonder if our killer has a guilty conscience.'

'Get some rest,' said Millington, standing up. 'Come in when you feel ready.'

'I feel ready now, sir. I want to confront the guy who shot me.'

'Tomorrow, Steve. Tonight go home and rest. That's an order. Damn it, you're not the only detective in Brighton!'

'I didn't think old-fashioned Methodists swore, sir.'

'This one does,' said Millington.

After he had left, Madden lay there and for some reason – no, not just some reason, there was a reason – began thinking about the tentative claw hammer attacks to Lavinia Roberts's head and the white fibres mixed with the water in the child's lungs.

There was a pattern. Not a very discernible pattern, but one nonetheless. You couldn't even call it a signature. And Colleen had missed it.

31

They had sent him home with his shoulder heavily bandaged. He had a laceration of the soft tissues, that was all, but it was enough. He had taken pain killers and they were making him feel groggy. He sat through an episode of *Dead Men Tell* in which Sarah Mahoney tracked down a killer from the species of dead insects scraped from his car windscreen (she was an entomologist), escaped from a trunk in a burning car (she was an escapologist) and fell in love with another policeman (she was a fool).

He dialled Colleen in the middle of it. He reckoned she would be watching.

'How's the hero?' she said.

'In a pain-killer enduced stupor. You got a minute to talk?'

'Seen this one before,' she said. 'I know how it ends. Rosy only ties me to the chair and forces me to watch them when they're new.'

'Kinky.'

'Well, a girl's got to have fun.'

'I've got a theory.'

'Try it on me.'

'Our killer has a conscience.'

'That's a great one,' she said. 'Why didn't I see it? I specialise in consciences.'

'Seriously. You said the tiny fibres in the boy's lungs mixed with the water suggested he was smothered with something while he was being drowned. Why should anyone do that unless they didn't want to look at his face? And might not these superficial hammer blows have been made by someone who had never killed before and couldn't quite bring himself to do it? As though he feels he has to kill but doesn't like doing it.'

'Odd slant.' She took a moment to think about it. 'It makes sense. Not sure where it takes us, though.'

'It doesn't take us anywhere,' he said. 'But at least it's better than going nowhere.'

A few minutes after he had put the phone down, Jasmine arrived. She had a bunch of flowers. He hated flowers in the house but didn't like to tell her. They reminded him of funerals.

'How's the patient?'

'Recovering.'

He told her his theory. She liked it. She rummaged in one of his cupboards and found an old vase, which he determined he would throw out at the earliest opportunity, cut the stalks and thrust the flowers in water.

'The trouble with a killer with a conscience,' she said, 'is that he's possibly more dangerous than a killer without one. Something's driving him to kill, maybe against his will, and that's spooky.'

'Voices from heaven?'

'Peter Sutcliffe. The Yorkshire Ripper.'

'You believe that?'

'Some people do.'

'The Yorkshire Ripper killed just young women, most of them prostitutes. Our killer picked two victims that were totally different types. An elderly lady, then a child of three. There's no way of predicting who or what type his next victim will be.'

'You think there will be one?'

'I'm convinced of it.'

Jasmine helped herself to a glass of wine.

'Be my guest,' he said. 'It's happy hour. You get two for one.'

'I got the rest of Delina's story. It's a sad one. Want to hear it?' she asked.

'Might cheer me up.'

'The immigration authorities lost her. Happens all the time. In Delina's case she arrived in the UK with her son and because she was seventeen she was classified as an unaccompanied minor. That means they both had the right to remain in Britain until she was eighteen when they'd assess her claim. She was put in foster care in Acton up in London with a Mr and Mrs Canfield under the supervision of Hillingdon social services.'

'Her and the boy, I take it.'

'Her and the boy. I got on to Hillingdon social services, then on to the Canfields, then on to a Detective Inspector Bill Tyler. Apparently the Canfields – they were also fostering a Kosovan boy – took all three of them into London on a sightseeing trip the very first day Delina and Dana came to live with them. They went to the Tower of London and the Houses of Parliament, and in Trafalgar Square Delina and her son just vanished. They've never been seen again.'

'Until now.'

'She was lured to Britain by human traffickers.' Jasmine told him so matter-of-factly it was as though she accepted that was the way the world went round. 'Balkan gangs lure about two hundred thousand women to brothels in Europe every year. What normally happens, I'm told, is that they're made to memorise a telephone number and they're threatened that something will happen to their families back home if they fail to ring it. Everything goes fine for a while. In Delina's case she was taken into care, then one day she just vanished, taking the boy with her. She made the phonecall, met the Motoleses, and that was it.'

'Sexual slavery.'

'The Albanians are ruthless,' she said. 'They control about eighty per cent of off-street prostitution in Soho apparently. If Delina had ended up in a massage parlour there, she might have ended up being used by between twenty and thirty men a day. The Motoleses gave her a little time off. Time just to walk down to the shop and buy cigarettes and exercise her lad.'

'What do they want? Degrees in humanity?'

'The kid was the perfect victim, Steve,' she said. 'The mother was too scared to go to the police. She was probably threatened with her life if she did.'

She looked as though she was about to touch his shoulder. He flinched.

'There's something I don't understand, Jaz. We had an unidentified boy with his heart removed, we put out a description of him, all these people must have known this mother and boy had gone missing, how come nobody connected it?'

'That's the part,' she said, 'you're really going to love.'

'Try me. I'm in a romantic mood,' he said sourly.

'Immigration had Dana down as a girl.'

Madden remembered McKendrick telling them that he'd thought the child was female at first. And he recalled his own immediate impressions of the slightly androgynous features as the child lay on the Rottingdean path in the rain.

'Dana is also a girl's name. She wouldn't let anybody else touch him,' Jasmine said. 'That included the foster parents. They only had them in their house for a few hours before they took them sightseeing, and they naturally were convinced also that the child was a girl because they'd been told that. And they told DI Bill Tyler, who's handling the case, that Dana was a girl.'

She was reading Madden's face.

'I know what you're thinking, Steve.'

'I'm thinking what a cock-up. Immigrants get lost and the authorities don't even know what sex they are. Great.'

'Still sore?'

'If you want to rest your head on it, just make sure it's the other one.'

Someone rang the doorbell. He answered it. It was Clara. She rushed in as though she'd been told he had only minutes to live.

'I heard about it on the radio,' she said.

Clara saw Jasmine. For a moment, she ignored her. The gesture was returned.

'How are you feeling?'

'Just great. I've lost my chief suspect, been responsible for a colleague's death, and now I've been shot in the shoulder by a teenage Albanian gangster. Things couldn't be better.'

'You could be dead,' said Jasmine. 'We both could be dead.'

'I take it you were with him,' said Clara, sitting down on the other side of her ex-husband and taking hold of his right hand and squeezing it.

'That's us,' said Jasmine breezily. 'The crime-fighting duo.'

'I almost felt sick with worry when I heard.' Clara pressed his hand tighter. 'They said you'd been shot and injured. I thought it was more serious than it looks.'

'It feels that way right now.'

Clara took off her white silk jacket and appeared to make herself at home. He remembered the jacket. He had bought it for her. He didn't think she still had it. She laid it over the chair and went through to the kitchen to make some tea. She saw the wine instead.

'May I?' she asked. 'Do you want one?'

'Better not mix drink with pain killers.'

She sat down again with a glass of wine in her hand. Jasmine still had hers.

'Well isn't this nice,' said Madden.

'You shouldn't be on your own,' Clara told him.

'He's not on his own,' Jasmine reminded her sharply.

'I hope I'm not interrupting something. I mean, you're here talking about the case, I suppose.'

'We've done that,' said Jasmine.

'Good. Well, when you go, he won't be on his own. That's why I'm here.'

'That's why I'm here too,' said Jasmine.

The two women smiled at each other. You could have cut the smiles out with a pair of scissors and pasted them up on the wall.

'I'm so glad you kept my paintings,' Clara reprised from her previous visit. 'You could have sold them or thrown them away. But you kept them. That's lovely.'

'I'm a lovely guy. Except when I indulge in self-loathing and pity.'

'Which you don't do very often,' Jasmine put a hand on his knee as he didn't have another hand available.

'Steve and I went through a lot when Jason was murdered,' Clara explained, unnecessarily at that moment. 'It forced us to re-evaluate what had happened to us. Why it had happened. I shared the guilt with him. We were both Jason's parents and we both had a responsibility for him. It's maybe shocking to say, I don't know, but Jason's death made us realise what we had together. Though too late.'

Madden was aware of her scrutinising him for a reaction.

'Yes, it's a pity when these things happen too late,' said Jasmine.

'Still, it's better that way than not at all.' Clara still hoped to get some reaction out of him.

'How long have you been remarried?' Jasmine asked. She made it sound very casual.

'Two years,' Clara answered. 'Steve tells me you're putting your career first.'

'We have to put first what's most important,' Jasmine told her. 'If I got married, as a Hindu, I'd feel obliged to put my husband first.'

'I got the impression from Steve that you weren't a practising Hindu.'

'I never gave you that impression, Clara,' said Madden.

'It's the impression I got. I'm sorry. My fault.' Clara looked bemused.

She looked from one to the other. Clara never got wrong impressions.

'I practise the parts of my religion that are right for me,' Jasmine explained. 'Even if I wasn't a Hindu, I still believe that when a woman marries she should put her husband first. Call me old-fashioned.'

'How exemplary,' said Clara.

'Call me old-fashioned too,' said Madden, getting up. 'My place is at the station. I've got work to do.'

Clara and Jasmine shot to their feet almost simultaneously.

'You can't. You've been ordered to rest,' said Jasmine.

'Steve, you're not leaving,' said Clara. 'Don't be ridiculous. You've just been shot.'

'Not in my leg,' he said. 'I can still walk. Besides, I never felt finer. Why don't you two sit and chat, and I'll be back later. There's nothing like the good old work ethic to purify the body and mind. Come to think of it, I might pop to Hubble Bubble tomorrow for a bit of healing. Help yourselves to the wine.'

He walked out of the front door. Jasmine called after him from the doorstep.

'Steve, you're mad!' she shouted after him.

'Today I may be mad but at least tomorrow I'll be sane,' he smiled back at her.

There was a lot he could do. Like read the statements of Delina Vllasi and the Motolese brothers. See if there was anything the others had missed. He might even pop down to the cells and have a chat with Mustapha Motolese, the handsome young punk who had shot him, and thank him for not ending his life in North Moulsecoomb.

Then he saw the car following him. It was a dark green Vauxhall Astra and he knew it was following him because he had seen it parked outside his house and now it was crawling along behind him at about ten miles an hour. Whoever was driving didn't watch cop shows. Madden stopped walking and turned back. The car stopped abruptly. Madden leant against the window. The driver wound it down. He was a lad of about nineteen, white-faced and very nervous. Madden had seen him before but he couldn't place where.

'Nice evening,' said Madden.

'Yes,' said the boy.

'Looking for something?'

'Yes,' said the boy. 'I was looking for Sussex Street.'

'You're in it.'

The lad looked across at the road sign.

'Of course,' he said.

'What's your name, son?'

Madden showed him his ID. It usually worked.

'Kevin Taylor,' he said.

'And what do you, Kevin Taylor? When you're not following me?'

'I work at the car wash. At the Marina,' he blurted out.

Madden remembered. He had last seen the boy washing Clive's BMW.

'Go home,' said Madden.

The lad turned the car round in the road, and drove off fast in the opposite direction from which he'd come. Madden waited until he was out of sight. He knew that yet another trouble had just been added to his already heaving burden.

32

Madden slept the night in temporary accommodation at the police station. It was comfortable and had the basic necessity he needed – privacy. He switched his mobile off so as not to be disturbed, but he still slept fitfully. The pain kept him awake. In the morning, his shoulder was still throbbing like crazy.

He went down early to the front office. It was November the Fifth and although he didn't know it the fireworks were about to start. Jeff Walker was back on front office attachment. He looked at Madden and said, 'I heard what happened to you last night, sir. You were lucky.'

'My middle name,' said Madden, picking up his mail. Just in case there were any more blood-soaked confessions or strange bottles. He still had to work out the meaning of that.

'I heard about Richard and Natalie, sir.'

'How are they?'

'Not speaking. You could strike a match on the atmosphere in the shop.'

'Did you know anything about the break-in?' Madden asked him.

'I was away at Sussex. IT training,' he said. 'I only heard about it later.'

'You didn't think to report it yourself? I mean, there you are, two weeks after your passing out parade from training school, living on top of a crime and you didn't even think to report it or investigate it. That wouldn't look very good on your PDP.'

'They didn't want it reported, sir. And I didn't want to antagonise Richard. Like I said to you, he was never very happy about me moving in with Paula. It's their flat.'

'Sorry,' said Madden. 'I had a bad night.'

'I wanted to ask you a favour, sir,' said Jeff. 'Paula and I discussed it and we'd like you to be Jacqueline's godfather.'

Madden put down his mail. He looked at Jeff. He felt sorry for being so grouchy.

'It's just,' said Jeff, 'that when she was born – because of the circumstances – Paula never had her christened. When I adopt her we're going to have her baptised, and well—'

'I accept,' said Madden.

Jeff smiled broadly.

'Thank you, sir. I hoped you'd say that.'

Madden smiled back.

'What else could I possibly say?'

Jeff Walker noticed him before Madden did. Clive Westmacott strode through the door into the front office. Madden turned round and they came literally face to face. His own timing could not have been worse. He had expected something to happen but not this soon, and not here. Clive's fermenting anger seemed to spread up onto the dome of his head which was bright pink. He was dressed in an expensively cut and tailor made business suit and was looking anxiously at his Rolex watch as though he had another appointment to keep. Madden, if he ever changed his profession to that of clairvoyant, would tell sitters always to be wary of angry men wearing Rolex watches. They usually had fists to match.

'Hello, Clive,' he said. It never hurt to be polite.

'You know why I'm here,' said Clive.

'I think I know. Shall we go for a walk?'

'I'm late. What I want to say I'm going to say here.'

Jeff Walker gave a nervous cough, and looked down at his *Blackstone's Police Manual* which lay open on the front desk. Madden reckoned he was about to add to the probationer's experience in ways that they didn't teach you at training school.

'You've got the wrong idea,' Madden said.

'My wife has visited your house twice in the last five days,' he shouted. 'I want to know why.'

'Did you ask her? And there's no need to yell, Clive, I'm standing only a few feet away.'

'I haven't asked her, but I'm asking you!'

'If you'd asked her, she would have told you that last night I got shot in the shoulder, and she came round to see how I was. That's all.'

'Oh I see, she came round to see you.'

'Yes.'

'And she stayed in your house and then you left. What was that all about?'

'If you're going to have your wife tailed, Clive, at least have the decency to hire a private detective. Using the boy that washes your car is a bit demeaning.'

Clive took a step towards him. Madden kept his eye on the Rolex watch. If that got anywhere near his eye line, he was in difficulties. Bringing an assault charge against your ex-wife's husband after a row in a police station was not a good career move.

'I want a straight answer, Madden,' he said.

'Okay, I'll give you a straight answer. I left her with a female colleague of mine who was also visiting at the same time. I expect they had a drink together and then she went home. Next question?'

'And the last time? What about the last time?'

Madden was thinking of an answer when Ray Millington walked in. That was great, he thought. The timing just got better and better. A row with your ex-wife's husband in the front office and in front of the super. You just couldn't beat that.

'What last time?' Madden asked.

'The last time she visited you, Madden.'

'She called on me just to clear up a few things about Jason's death.'

'What things? Everything is cleared up, Madden. I want to know what things?'

'Like visiting his grave together. Putting flowers on it. He was our son, or do you forget that?'

He felt pretty dreadful bringing Jason into it. As though he was using his son's memory to get himself out of a scrape. If Jason was looking down on him, he wondered how his son would react. '*Cool, Dad*' was probably what he would have said. Another thing flashed through his mind. Lavinia Roberts had predicted a serious argument with a rival. Well, he had already had one of these. You couldn't get much more serious than an argument that ended in a death. And now, here he was again, this time with Millington listening in.

'You're lying,' said Clive. 'Clara could telephone you if she wanted to go and put flowers on his grave with you. She doesn't have to visit you and stay two hours and twenty minutes.'

The car-wash boy had been doing his stuff.

'That's the truth,' said Madden.

'I shall quiz Clara and if she tells me a different story, you are in a lot of trouble, Madden.'

'That's a nice way to run a marriage, Clive. Why don't you just trust her?'

'Because,' he said, 'I don't trust you.'

Millington stepped into the fray.

'I think the two of you had better continue this conversation in your own time and somewhere else,' he said gravely.

'It's all right. I'm going,' said Clive, turning to Millington. 'Just make sure your officers keep their trousers zipped up in future.'

He looked back at Madden squarely like a bull sizing up ramblers crossing a field.

'Stay away from Clara,' he said. 'Or I mean this, Madden, I won't be responsible for what I do.'

With that, Clive Westmacott stormed out. Madden didn't need a crystal ball to predict what was going to happen next.

'I want to see you in my office. Now,' said Millington.

Madden winked at Jeff Walker as he turned and left reception. The blond-haired rookie gave a conspiratorial smile. There were no winks or smiles in Millington's office. As a Methodist, Millington didn't believe in extra-marital relationships, especially when they encroached on work. They were as much the work of the Devil as tarot cards, and probably dowsing.

'You were shot yesterday, you're supposed to be resting.'

'Home was a little complicated, sir.'

'What was going on down there?'

'It's a misunderstanding, sir.'

Madden's shoulder was causing him considerable pain. He sat down.

'What, a misunderstanding between you and him over his wife?'

'My ex-wife, sir.'

'I don't care. I'm not going to pry into your private life, that is your business. I know you've had a lot of problems, but—'

'That's right, sir. I've had a lot of problems. Clara and I got close again after Jason's death and her husband doesn't like it. That's all.'

'I don't like it when these things spill over into police time.'

'Almost every minute of my day is given over to police time, sir.'

'And in the front office, where the public walk in. Couldn't you at least have gone out into the street?'

'That was my intention, sir.'

Millington glowered at him and looked as though he was about to hammer his fist on the desk. Instead he just sighed with exasperation.

'I'm a pretty tolerant man,' he said. 'I shared a secret with you yesterday, something I've never told anyone else in twenty years. I want you to know that if you have a personal problem, Steve, you can share it with me. In confidence. That's only fair. You'll find me a sympathetic listener. We're all prone to temptations. Well, most of us, anyway. I'm the first to accept that.'

And you might as well say 'fight the good fight' thought Madden.

'That's very good of you, sir,' said Madden.

'You look tired. In fact, you look as though you didn't sleep last night.'

'I didn't, sir. At least not very well. But you know how the body clock kicks you into gear.'

'It won't just be the body clock, Steve.'

Millington passed him a letter. It was from Lesley Fieldhouse. She had written thanking Millington for everything he and his officers had done for her husband, and particularly requested that Madden should not feel guilty about his part. She was as gracious as Jack Fieldhouse had been bellicose and antagonistic.

'I'm not going to have another officer work himself into the grave,' he said. 'Now go home and rest that shoulder. That's an order.'

'Is that the kind of order I can disobey, sir?'

'Damn you, Steve.' Millington swore. 'Just go away and stay out of disagreements!'

33

Madden drove up to St Catherine's School on the West Blatchington side of Hove and waited. It was the best girls' school in the city, if one discounted Roedean to the east. It also had the reputation of being one of the most prestigious schools for music on the south coast, and had an orchestra which had cut its own CD, which was on sale in local shops.

Patricia Edgeware turned up in her Range Rover at precisely twenty past eight. Claire and Clementine Edgeware got out with their cello cases. They were dressed in neat, well-pressed green school blazers and skirts. Patricia Edgeware was wearing a white jacket with purple buttons and a short skirt that showed too much of her thighs for a St Catherine's parent.

'Good morning,' he said.

He was sure he had just ruined it for her.

'Good morning,' she replied politely, with a hideously strained smile.

Madden had never met Claire Edgeware before, only seen her photograph and heard the dulcet tones of her cello playing. She was the image of her sister, if a little harder in the face. She looked precocious. Clementine just appeared morose.

'You're that policeman, aren't you?' Claire said.

'Yes, I'm that policeman.'

'Daddy's going to be furious with you. He says you people never leave our family alone.'

'That's the way it happens sometimes.'

'Well, we're going to tell him,' promised Claire Edgeware with a little arrogant toss of her head that revealed the young, brash woman lurking inside the schoolgirl.

Clementine flashed Madden a much more conciliatory look, and turned toward to the school gates with her instrument.

'Yes, you do that,' said Madden to her sister.

Patricia Edgeware packed them into school, turned to Madden and asked him outright, 'Why are you bothering us?'

'Because I have a job to do.'

'I've already told you, we know nothing.'

'You'll know about the child that was washed up on the undercliff path.'

'Yes,' she said, 'and I think it's appalling.'

'Yes, I think it's appalling too, Mrs Edgeware. I saw his body, what was done to him, and it was one of the worst things I've ever seen. I don't think I ever want to see anything like it again.'

'I think paedophiles should be castrated and hanged,' she said.

The woman obviously had a highly developed social conscience, thought Madden.

'Not a lot of point in doing that, Mrs Edgeware.'

'I didn't think about it,' she said. 'But you know what I mean.'

'I know what you mean. That's why I need to find Michael Bird. We know the two crimes are linked. I need to rule him out of all this, once and for all.'

'The police don't search for people they want to rule out.' She demonstrated that when it came to the business of being wanted for questioning she was quick off the mark.

'Sometimes they do.'

'Not in my experience. Which, of course, isn't vast,' she added, hastily.

'No, I'm sure it isn't. But Michael did ask you to do him that favour. To drive his car up to London where he could pick it up later. Why did he ask you, do you think?'

'Because, I presume, he had nobody else to ask.'

'He could have asked your husband Ronnie.'

She fumbled in her handbag for a tissue and blew her nose. Madden reckoned it gave her time to think.

'He asked me after Ronnie had gone to bed,' she said. 'Ronnie told him he wanted him to leave, that he didn't want to have anything to do with him. That he was to be gone by the morning.'

'That means you gave him a bed for the night?'

'I – I gave him a bed.' She stumbled over her words. 'I was to make it up, and when we woke up, he wasn't to be there. My husband said.'

Madden blinked. Perhaps he hadn't heard correctly.

'I'm sorry, but that sounds really odd, Mrs Edgeware. I mean, why not just tell him to go there and then? Why make him up a bed if he wasn't going to stay the night? It doesn't make sense.'

'It makes perfect sense to me,' she replied.

'Did you sit up and talk to him?'

'When do you mean?'

'After your husband – after Ronnie went to bed. Did you sit and chat?'

'I think we did, yes. We must have done.'

'If he asked you to drive his car up to London for him, you must have done.'

'Yes. We must have done,' she repeated, staring straight at him like a deer caught in headlights.

'It wasn't so long ago.'

'Then we did. Does that satisfy you?'

'What else did you talk about?'

'What else?'

'Yes. I take it your daughters had gone to bed by this time?'

'Yes, of course they had. Ronnie wouldn't involve them in anything like that.'

'So what else did you talk about? Did you make him tea? A cup of cocoa? Sit and have a fireside chat?'

'We talked about this and that,' she said vaguely.

'After Ronnie had told you and him that he wanted him gone by morning?'

'We are hospitable people,' she answered.

'Did you like him?'

'Meaning?'

'Did you like him? Can't think of a clearer way of putting the question.'

'I didn't dislike him.'

'He's a randy character. Not unattractive, I suppose. In a rough kind of way. I just wondered maybe if there was anything more between you?'

'Are you suggesting,' she said, 'that I would be unfaithful to my husband?'

'No,' Madden lied. He was good at it. She wasn't.

'That's what it sounds like to me.'

'He's not still in the house, is he?'

'Good gracious, no. What a thing to say.'

'You're not hiding him?'

'Don't be ridiculous.'

'I mean, if we got a warrant and came in and ripped up the floorboards and searched the attic, we wouldn't find him?'

'Oh how ludicrous. And if you had any evidence against him or us, you'd have done that.'

She sounded almost prim. It wasn't a trait he thought came naturally to her.

'I read about this American case once. Philadelphia, I think it was. The wife hid the sewing-machine repairman in the loft for twelve years and the husband never suspected a thing. Until the sewing-machine repairman got fed up playing second fiddle and came down out of the loft and killed the husband.'

She bristled and adjusted her skirt.

'What an amusing story,' she said.

'It's true. I never make these things up.'

Like you're making all this up, he felt like saying.

'He asked me the favour, and I said no, and then he went to bed. That was all there was to it. If you think I would let him hide in the house with our daughters present, then you're mad.'

'Didn't you ask him what he was running away from?'

'He was running away from you.'

'Did you help him sneak out of the house? Under cover of darkness?'

'No,' she said emphatically.

'Look at it from my point of view, Mrs Edgeware. He asked you to drive his car to an unspecified location in London, you refused, he sneaked out of the house under cover of darkness whether aided and abetted by you or not, his car is still there in front of your house, and you say he's never been in touch since. It's hard to swallow, isn't it?'

'Not for me,' she said firmly.

'One final question, Mrs Edgeware. Where is he?'

Madden reckoned he was pushing his luck, but then he'd had so little of it up until now he reckoned some push was in order.

'I haven't the faintest clue,' she said.

'Wherever he's disappeared to, he hasn't got his car. Do you know if he has access to another?'

'I thought you said that was the final question.'

'I lied.'

'I don't know where he is, who he's with, if he has a car, I don't care. I just want to be left alone. If you don't mind.'

'Neither of your daughters would know, I take it? I mean, if I wanted to question them, you wouldn't object?'

'I told you. I'll tell you again, Mr Madden. And I'll keep telling you until you get it into your head, we wouldn't involve our daughters in anything like this. Okay?'

'Your daughters might choose to involve themselves. Bird wasn't a bad-looking guy in a rough kind of way. Teenage hormones and all that.'

'That is a disgusting suggestion,' she threw at him. 'Claire and Clementine had gone to bed. I was alone with Michael. He went to bed, then so did I. End of story. Now, if you'll excuse me?'

She climbed into the driving seat of the Range Rover, once again exposing far too much leg for a St Catherine's School parking bay. Her skirt rode practically up to her crotch revealing a pair of pink panties.

'I suppose,' said Madden, 'if I were to ask you if you tucked him in for the night, it would spell the end of a beautiful interview.'

It did. She drove off at speed. Madden felt pleased with himself. If evidence was king, a gut feeling was a good throne, mate. He was convinced that Patricia Edgeware knew the whereabouts of Michael Bird. She was also, he knew, a very scared woman.

The pain from the wound in his shoulder seemed to be getting worse. He looked at his bottle of pain killers. One thirty-milligram tablet every six hours. He took two. Driving was uncomfortable but at least they hadn't put his arm in a sling. The discomfort was making him sweat as he pulled up round the corner from Holly Elder's house. Both she and her uncle were at home. They both knew of the shooting. It was good to be famous.

'You look ill,' she said.

'I need answers,' he said.

'You need a tonic. I'll fix you something.' Professor Grimaldi loomed over him almost as soon as he stepped over the threshold.

'No, thank you,' said Madden, unsure of what would be in it.

Holly Elder was wrapped in a pale blue robe that revealed long elongated ankles. When she sat down on the settee next to him her knees protruded beguilingly from between the folds of the gown. Grimaldi, by contrast, seemed out of sorts, behaving like some bothered academic, which was nothing new in Madden's book. He wondered if there had been further aspersions on his psychic abilities.

Grimaldi had made himself at home in his niece's house. Much of what she called his clutter and what he referred to as his foremost archive of the occult had been squirrelled away into cabinets and drawers and under his bed since Madden's last visit, much to her relief. She told Madden that no self-respecting witch could have people walk into her house and be confronted with demons possessing large appendages. He was, she said, hoping to get it all out of her hair once and for all by setting up his own small museum in Brighton, of which he would be the curator and resident expert. Madden vowed to give it a wide berth.

'You told me that cutting out a heart and keeping it was a

way of obtaining supernatural power.' He came to one of the purposes of his visit.

'Let me tell you this,' Grimaldi said, appearing to choose his words carefully. 'There is no such thing as the supernatural.'

'If you don't mind me saying so, that surprises me. Coming from a witch.'

'Don't confuse magic with the supernatural, Mr Madden. Nothing supernatural can exist. Magic isn't evil, neither is it inherently good. It exists in accordance with the laws of the universe, that's all. Which is why today's magic is often tomorrow's science.'

'Do you know why witches were burnt at the stake?' Holly put to him.

'Because people were frightened of them.'

'Because they had *power*. Or appeared to have power. This person you're looking for isn't a witch. But he is taking power from murdering. Power for himself. What he intends doing with it is something I can't say. I find the whole thing quite sickening.'

'Murder usually is quite sickening.'

'I mean, the fact he should taint our religion like this.'

'I need a psychological profile of him. We have experts but contrary to what people think they're not always right. And none of them know anything about the occult. I don't need to be told that this guy is a loner, aged between twenty and thirty, and probably lives with his mother. That's where you two can help me.'

'We shall do all we can,' the Professor assured him. 'Calling yourself an expert on the occult is easy, but you have to differentiate between what *is* and what is *not*. Doubtless you have heard of the case I was involved in in Tennessee.'

'We are aware of it,' Madden admitted.

'I thought you might have checked up on me,' Grimaldi grinned knowingly. 'To see if I was just a harmless eccentric or something much worse.'

'The thought never crossed my mind,' said Madden.

'In that case, the police got themselves into a terrible lather over black magic rituals and baby eating and child abuse, fuelled by a bunch of evangelists and social workers who should have known better. Just because the kids were in a band that called itself "Satan"! The real devil in the case was self-made, a man who killed for pleasure, for the sexual thrill it gave him. And he was a Holy Joe, one of the very evangelical preachers who'd whipped up the madness in the first place. He lived in a nice American house behind a white picket fence and was regarded by everybody as a good neighbour. Now *that's* true evil, Mr Madden. The wolf that comes in sheep's clothing, not the mumbo-jumbo of black magic rituals and the like.'

'In that case,' said Madden, 'am I justified in getting into a lather about this?'

He showed them the poison bottle and the slip of paper with his name written on it. At the same time, he studied their reactions closely, just to see if either of them recognised the items.

'I received this from the killer,' he told Holly. 'I want to know what it means. The piece of paper was inside the bottle. Nothing else.'

She seemed to be taken aback. Madden could see that she recognised them, or at least their significance. So did Professor Grimaldi.

'Good heavens,' she said.

'Now you're worrying me. What do they mean?'

'It means, Mr Madden, that he has power over you,' Grimaldi told him. 'Or *believes* he has power over you.'

'Over me? How?'

'It's a way of him telling you that he has control over you, your life, your emotions, everything you do. In a more primitive society, the belief of the recipient that some sorcerer had power over him would be enough to make the spell work.'

'You're telling me this is a sorcerer's spell?'

'I've seen it done in parts of the Caribbean,' Grimaldi said. 'Malaya as well. Writing your victim's name on a piece of paper and putting it in a bottle is – well, symbolic of having that power over him.'

'He could also have read about it in any number of books on witchcraft.' Holly put it into perspective. 'Including the pop-wicca literature. You know the sort of thing. How to be a teenage witch and turn your boyfriend into a toad.'

Madden confessed he'd never read any. Professor Grimaldi went to make some tea. Not Moroccan mint, Madden was thankful. Just plain Yorkshire.

'What did your uncle mean by saying he has control over my emotions?' Madden asked Holly after he had left the room.

'Oh dear,' Holly said. 'You drive me to a terrible confession.'

'I'd love to hear it,' he said.

'When I was a teenager and just learning the craft – that's what we call it – I had a great passion for this boy who worked beside me. We were in an insurance office. I was in love with him, almost infatuated. So I worked a number of spells to bring him under my control.'

'You needed *spells*?'

'Probably not.' She gave a little toss of her shoulders and swept back her hair in a gesture that indicated she knew perfectly well that she had more commonplace talents. 'But I was young and impressionable and wanted to prove that I could make him fall in love with me. And I did.'

'How?'

'I made this likeness of him, cut round a photograph of him and used it as his head, collected strands of his hair when they fell on his jacket. I even used a raw egg for his heart because it was a living, organic substance. Then I kept it in a box and over a period of weeks cast spells to bring him under my control and make him fall in love with me. I even sent it to him.'

'How long did it last?'

'Oh, only a couple of weeks,' she said. 'He was Jewish and when his parents found out I was a witch and that my parents were Catholic they sent him to a kibbutz in Israel. Still, it was fun.'

'And your present boyfriend – Brendan, is it? Did you acquire him the same way?'

'Oh good heavens, no,' she laughed. 'We met in a witches' chatroom.'

'*A witches' chatroom?*' Madden wondered if he'd heard correctly.

'A perfect example of magic becoming science,' she said.

'So my name in a bottle is his way of telling me he thinks he has control over my life?'

'I'm absolutely convinced of it,' she said, speaking for both of them. 'This has become personal between you and him.'

'Or her,' said Madden.

'Or her.'

'Give me that profile.'

'I see a very strong person.' Holly went into a reverie. 'A person who needs to have control over others. A dominating person. I see him or her in some job, managerial perhaps. A professional person. A person who likes telling other people what to do. The popular expression is control freak, I think.'

'Whoever said psychological profiling wasn't witchcraft?' Madden smiled.

'Whoever said it was?'

Professor Grimaldi came through with the tea. In the interim he had taken a phonecall which had made him even more out of sorts.

'I've been taking damned impertinence and experiencing gross prejudice all lunchtime,' he told Madden.

'I'm sorry to hear that,' said Madden. 'Happens to me a lot.'

'Uncle Robert's been looking for a pub where we can hold our moots,' Holly explained.

'Moots?' He looked bewildered.

'They're nothing sinister.' Holly laughed at his perplexity. 'Just get-togethers. Where members of our coven can meet socially and have a drink and where new and interested members can come along.'

'We also thought it would be a nice idea,' said Grimaldi, 'to hold an open coven, especially now. Where members of the public can come and watch and learn that it's not about human bloody sacrifices! All we need is a back room in a bar somewhere or an upstairs function room, but what do you get? "We don't want that type of person here." "Attract all the nutters, won't it?" I said, this is Brighton, the city is full of nutters, but do they listen? This murder has been really bad for us, Mr Madden.'

He shook his head and puffed with annoyance as he poured the tea into delicate china cups. Madden was tempted to say that murder was usually bad for everybody.

Madden fished a Ratty's Bar matchbox out of his pocket and handed it to the Professor.

'Tried this place? For your "open coven"?' he asked him.

'No. I haven't,' he beamed, gratefully.

'It's pretty cavernous. Probably the right kind of atmosphere for you. Mention me. The owners are friends of mine. Ignore the rats. The place is quite hygienic, I assure you.'

'You think they'd be sympathetric?'

'They're pretty live-and-let-live kind of people.'

Madden thanked them and left, but not before Holly told him that she was worried about him.

'I'm okay,' said Madden. 'I have a charmed life.'

Out in the street, he swallowed his third pain killer in six hours. The throbbing in his left shoulder was starting to make him feel sick and faint, although it was preferable to being dead. He knew that he ought to be in bed, but in a few hours' time darkness was going to fall. It was bonfire night and Madden recalled Michael Bird's strong connection with the Bonfire Society of which he was a member. It was a shot in the dark, but worth taking.

He looked at his watch. He reckoned he had enough time. He had scoffed at it, but what the hell, he thought. Give it a try. He phoned up Paula at Hubble Bubble and made an appointment for one hour of Reiki. Now that he could spell it, he might as well experience it.

On his way, Madden called in to Ratty's Bar and said that some friends of his who were white witches were looking for a regular meeting place and as Ratty's hosted gay drag nights and other events would they mind if a coven met there once a month? Ming at first threw her hands up in horror until Lucky reminded her of all the prejudice she had suffered as a transsexual and a prostitute, at which point she succumbed and said that as long as they didn't frighten the other customers or sacrifice animals they could have one of the secluded archways which would be cordoned off with a notice saying 'Private Party'. Madden expressed his gratitude and departed.

Sometimes he loved this town.

34

He was standing outside Hubble Bubble. Jasmine had been trying to get hold of him. He could tell from the caller display on his mobile. This time he answered. Doubtless she was trying to track him down to tell him he shouldn't be wandering round Brighton with a wounded shoulder, that he should be lying flat and resting. Madden didn't feel inclined to tell her that for the next hour, he was going to be just that.

'In a few hours from now, the Lewes bonfire societies are going to be marching,' he reminded her. 'If Bird's going to turn up anywhere it's going to be in Lewes tonight for the celebrations. With the exception of the period he was in prison, he never missed one. I don't believe, Jaz, he'll miss the chance to melt in with the crowd and try to make contact with his girlfriend or his mother.'

'Steve,' she said, 'do you know how many people cram into that town?'

'Last year it was thirty-five to forty thousand. What's your point?'

'Your shoulder is the point. You'll be crushed.'

'We've got to do it, Jaz. If he shows, I want to be there. What's the point of a pilgrimage without a bit of suffering and hardship along the way?'

'You're mad,' she said. 'Just as mad as last night.'

'Hope you and Clara had a nice evening,' he remarked. 'Meet me at the station at five. I'll let you drive.'

He went into the shop. Gregorian chants were playing. They soothed him.

'I came for some Reiki,' he explained to Natalie.

He reckoned he owed it to himself. Maybe there was something to this 'universal energy'. If it was going around, he could do with a share of it. Natalie Blance was alone downstairs. She had decided she could manage on her own, which was her way of telling Richard not to come near her. He was at home. Doing the accounts. He would be doing them there from now on.

'I heard you got shot,' she said.

'Wounds heal.'

'Some do,' she said.

'All do, Natalie, if you give them time.'

'How much time would *you* give a partner you found screwing some sixteen-year-old on your own business premises?'

'I'm not a marriage guidance counsellor,' he said. 'But I'd consider this. You not only have a marriage to make work but you have a business to run as well. It might be better for both if you settled your differences.'

'That's easier said.'

'What's the alternative? Lose the two?'

'I'm contemplating that,' she said, as though she was deciding between holidays in a travel brochure.

'I feel kind of responsible.'

Guilt again. Though this time he consoled himself with the fact that had he not been instrumental in the discovery, Natalie would not have learnt what a lecherous cheat her husband was.

'I'm grateful to you,' she said.

'Any time. Let's hope there won't be another.'

'Paula's ready for you. I never took you to be a Reiki kind of person, Mr Madden.'

'Hidden depths,' Madden smiled.

He went upstairs to the treatment room. Paula Needham was ready for him. She was wearing blue slacks and a pink cardigan with the sleeves rolled up. She looked desperately unhappy, as though forcing herself to smile through a prism.

'You'll know?' he said to her.

'Trouble downstairs,' she muttered softly.

'The trouble was upstairs. I don't suppose that's what the flotation tank is for.'

'No,' she agreed. 'Are you ready for your treatment?'

'As ready as I'll ever be. Never had Reiki before. Do I have to take my clothes off?'

'No,' she said. 'Just your shirt and your shoes and socks. Your trousers you can keep on. Clothes don't present any barrier to energy. And lie face down. And it might be a good idea if you turned your mobile phone off as well.'

He already had.

'You sure this will relax me.'

'Never fails,' she said.

Madden took off his shoes and socks and his shirt and lay face down on the bed.

'Watch the bandaged shoulder. It's just a flesh wound but it's still quite painful.'

'I heard you got shot.' She looked at it. She was curious.

'It's nice to be a celebrity. It could have been a lot worse. A few inches further down and across and I might not have been here. That's what made me think I'd better try some of this stuff, just in case I'm not so lucky the next time.'

'I can't heal wounds, they take their own time, but I can do something about pain,' Paula said. 'Just relax. Do you know anything about Reiki before we start?'

'I know more about atomic physics, and what I know about that wouldn't fill the back of a postage stamp.'

'Think of it as a whole body treatment,' she said softly. 'If you have disorder in one part of your body, it affects every other part in time. You have six major chakras in the body and ten minor ones, look on them as energy points. Although I'm placing my hands over them, it's you who draws the energy in. Okay?'

'I'm drawing,' said Madden.

He tried to believe. He really did. After the last few days, he needed energy. Or just a half hour in a position to do absolutely nothing, as he was now. He was aware of Paula resting her soft plump hands ever so gently on his neck. At times, he could not even feel her hands. He was aware of them, gently suspended above him, of that subtle movement of air as she brought them down but did not quite touch. Then for a period of a few minutes it seemed as though nothing was happening. Yet it was. He caught her in the mirror, her hands held about half an inch above his bandaged shoulder. She had her eyes closed. Madden thought it best not to interrupt her. He was aware of her moving about him, suspending her hands above his chest, his stomach, his groin, finally his feet.

'You can turn over now,' she said.

He turned over. He was about to make a joke about doing the other side, but she had her eyes closed again, as though praying. Then he saw tears running down her cheeks. Again, he resisted comment. He tried to believe. He stared at the ceiling, felt a tingling in his feet as she held her hands over them. It was weird. She wasn't touching him but he *felt* something. When the thirty-minute session was up, he did feel relaxed, though how much of that was due to being forced to lie still for that period instead of rushing around he couldn't tell. Madden knew little about the power of Reiki, but he knew a woman's tears when he saw them.

'How did it feel?' she asked him.

'Not what I expected. I thought it would be more of a massage.'

'You have a lot of blockages. Where the energy isn't being allowed to flow through your body. I did some unblocking and some smoothing out.'

Madden said he felt the difference.

'And how are *you* feeling?' he asked.

'I'm okay,' she said.

He sat up on the massage table. His shoulder didn't throb so much. He wondered if it was down to her.

'You cried while you were doing that. Is that part of the service?'

'No. I was just thinking about something.'

She lifted her hand to her eyes and turned away from him. He stepped down off the table and went towards her. As he did, she let go a flood of tears. He put out his hand and rested it on her shoulder. Paula stiffened at his touch.

'Look, I know this is kind of weird, Paula, but I think it's you who needs unblocking right now. Luckily I don't charge for my services. That's a way of saying, do you want to talk about it?'

'No,' she said.

'Suppose I say I'm not paying you or walking out of here until you tell me?'

'I can't,' she said. 'Please just go.'

'Is it about Jeff?'

The ensuing silence persuaded him that it was.

'He asked me to be Jacqueline's godfather,' he told her.

'I know,' she said.

'So that gives me a kind of responsibility for her. And if I'm to be responsible for her, I want to make sure that everything is all right with her parents. But it's not, is it?'

'I just can't stand it,' she shuddered. 'I can't stand it any more.'

'What can't you stand?'

'He says she's just a friend but I don't know whether to believe him or not.'

'Believe what? Who's just a friend?'

'Her name's Rebecca. She's an old girlfriend and just a friend now or so he says, but I don't know if it's true.'

He sat her down. He sat down with her. He'd been here before.

'You're telling me Jeff's seeing an old girlfriend? And you think he might still be sleeping with her?'

'I couldn't stand it if he was,' she cried. 'I'm sorry. This wasn't why you came—'

'Never mind that. I'm here now. And if you want me to find out for you, I will.'

'He mustn't know,' said Paula, suddenly frightened and deeply anxious. 'He mustn't know I told you.'

'He won't know anything. Except what will hit him if I find out it's true. What makes you think it is?'

'Just—'

She broke off. There were clearly things she didn't want to talk about. Perhaps things she couldn't.

'Little things,' she said.

'What little things?'

'Just little things.'

'Listen, Paula. I know what it's like, feeling jealous. Distrustful. I've been in that situation myself. I know the agony it can cause. And you're not even married to him, yet.'

'Can you find out? Without him knowing?' she pleaded.

'Part of the service,' he smiled.

'We're taking Jacqueline to the bonfire celebrations at Lewes tonight,' she said, wiping her eyes.

'I'll be there too. Which bonfire are you going to?'

'There's more than one?' she appeared ignorant.

'There are a number. The town has about four or five different bonfire societies. After parading through the streets, they all hold celebrations in their own grounds. If you want to do me another favour, go to the Barbican. I'll be there. If you see that guy with the tattoos, call me.'

He gave her his mobile number. He took hers.

'Whatever you do, don't approach him. Just call this number.'

'Do you think he's dangerous?'

'He could be.'

'Okay,' she said.

'And you leave Jeff to me.'

Paula turned to him and threw her arms round him and gave him a kiss on the cheek.

'Thank you,' she said.

He paid her, and went to the Marina, where she assured him he would find Jeff. Madden found him, just off duty, at the Leisure Centre. He was in the snack bar, sitting in a window seat, his arm draped around the shoulders of a girl Madden did not recognise. She was stunning looking in a cheerleader kind of way, nineteen or twenty years old, and if it had been possible to bodyspray on a leisure suit in gloss, this girl had gone for it. They weren't talking workouts, or at least not the kind of work-outs one went there to practise.

Madden saw Jeff before Jeff saw Madden. It was hardly

surprising really. Jeff had his face only a few inches from that of the girl. They were almost touching noses. Madden went up to them and coughed.

Jeff looked up. He appeared startled. As well he might have done, thought Madden.

'Am I interrupting something?' he asked.

'No,' said Jeff.

He wasn't only a cheating bastard, he was a lying bastard as well.

'This is Becky. She's an old girlfriend of mine.' Jeff introduced them. 'This is Detective Inspector Madden.'

'Mind if we have a private word? Outside?'

Jeff excused himself and they stepped out of the club. Madden didn't waste a second in coming to the point. He grabbed hold of Jeff's collar and shoved him against the wall. His shoulder smarted but he didn't care. It was turning into quite a day.

'What's going on?' he asked.

'What do you mean, what's going on?'

'Who is she? She doesn't look like an old girlfriend to me. You were practically on the point of eating each other.'

'There's no law against that,' said Jeff.

'You've got a sweet little girl in Brighton already, one that clearly worships the ground you walk on, and whose little daughter is going to call you Father once you're married. You call yourself a responsible husband and dad? You haven't even walked down the aisle with her yet!'

'And when I do – and when I do—' Jeff looked at the clenched fist that was scrunching up most of his collar.

'And when you do, then what? You'll go on cheating on her and hurting her? I gave you some advice a few days ago and I'm going to give you the same advice again, only I'm not going to mince words this time. Are you sleeping with that girl?'

'No.'

'Tell me the truth.'

'No. Let go, Steve.'

'It's *sir* out here. And it's *sir* to you in future. Are you sleeping with her?'

'It's not a crime,' said Jeff.

Madden was tempted to hit him, but there were people about, and being arrested for assaulting a probationer in public only a few hours after being physically threatened in the police station by your ex-wife's jealous husband was certainly no path to advancement. He wasn't even sure it would do much for his street cred either. He restrained himself.

'Now you listen,' he said. 'From one who knows. You start messing your life up now, before you're even married, and it'll go on and never change. You saw what happened this morning, it happened because I played around once and lost my wife and ultimately my son, and because I'm a stupid fool who can't let go of the past. If I were in your shoes, I'd appreciate what I've got. Paula loves you. She's hurting already because of your stupid actions. If that's the way you treat a fiancée, God help her when she's your wife.'

'Okay, you've made your point,' said Jeff.

'The point isn't whether I've made it or whether you've just listened to me. The point is, what are you going to do about it?'

'You expect me just to go in there and do what?'

'Might not be necessary for you to do anything.'

The girl called Rebecca had followed them out and was looking closely at them, her mouth opened wide in a gape of almost innocent astonishment.

'Don't read too much into this,' Madden said. 'Part of his training.'

'Are you all right, Jeff?' she asked.

'You know he's got a fiancée? And a kid he's going to adopt?'

'A *what*?'

She obviously did not.

'Curse my big mouth,' said Madden. 'Now you do.'

Rebecca stepped up to them. Madden instinctively stepped out of the way. Rebecca slapped Jeff across the face. Jeff appeared to be the most surprised of the three. Then she turned on the heels of her white trainers and marched off. If Madden had been thirty years younger, he'd have followed her. But now wasn't the time to even think such thoughts. Jeff was looking hurt and angry.

'Thanks, *sir*,' said Jeff angrily, nursing a reddened cheek.

'One day you will say thanks.'

'She was an old friend, that's all. Since when did my private life have anything to do with my career? Or you?'

'Since today.'

Two rude boy skateboarders in baggy blue jeans and back-to-front baseball caps whizzed past them, demonstrating their prowess as they kicked down hard on their boards and leapt up three steps board and all. It looked easy. Madden's shoulder was killing him. He took another pain killer.

'And perhaps the reason is I don't have anybody else's welfare to take an interest in.'

Jeff was sulking heavily. The humiliation was just starting to set in. He watched Rebecca as she looked back briefly with an expression of contempt. Madden thrust his arm out to stop him running after her.

'I want you to make me a promise, Jeff. You'll call Paula and tell her you love her. And that you'll never hurt her.'

'Who says she's hurt?'

'Just promise.'

'What do you want me to tell her? That you caught me at it?'

'Tell her what you like.'

'Okay, I promise,' said Jeff in the truculent manner of one forced to apologise.

'You could do it now in front of me if you wanted.'

'I'll do it,' said Jeff. 'Just don't embarrass me any more. Please?'

'Good. See you do.'

Madden stepped back. Jeff wasn't going to let him leave without sticking his own oar in.

'Can I ask you a personal question? About this morning?' he asked.

'I might tell you it's none of your business.'

'Are you having an affair with that man's wife?'

Madden considered the question for a moment.

'No, Jeff,' he said. 'That man is having an affair with mine.'

Work it out, he thought.

35

They were on the A27 dual carriageway driving through to Lewes. The traffic was heavy. Jasmine was at the wheel, Madden was slouching back in the passenger seat, about to pop another pain killer. She grabbed them from him. For a moment he thought she was going to throw them out of the window.

'You'll overdose,' she said.

'Better than being in agony.'

'If you're in agony, you shouldn't be doing this,' she said. 'Millington's not happy either. He thinks you're crazy to believe Bird would show up there.'

'The Reiki helped,' said Madden.

'Good. I'm glad.'

'So what did you and Clara talk about after I left last night?'

'You,' she said.

'Couldn't you have found a more interesting topic?'

'Not last night,' she said. 'Why did you just go off and leave us?'

'Because I couldn't handle two women fighting over me.'

'Fighting? You flatter yourself, Steve.'

'That was what it seemed like to me. If the two of you had claws, I'd have thrown a bucket of water over the both of you.'

'We had a civilised discussion. It's a good job I came round last night. Because I might have stopped something happening.'

'Clara came round to offer me support and sympathy.'

'You expect me to believe that? She's still in love with you, you know that?'

'I don't know that, Jaz. It's interesting you think that.'

'I could tell,' she said, not just a little put out.

'She's never said as much to me, and I don't want her to be in love with me. Love is what created all the problems between us to start with. I just want her as a friend.'

'And her husband as an enemy?'

'I can handle Clive.'

'No you can't!' she fired the words at him. 'Clive can make a lot of trouble for you. She's his wife, and if you start messing around with her, and don't say that isn't in your thoughts, Steve, it could ruin your career. Just think about that. What happened this morning is all round the police station.'

'I am thinking about it,' said Madden. 'Seriously.'

An enormous bonfire was already blazing high on the hill to their left, lighting up a portion of the sky like part of some pagan celebration. Fireworks were already going off, lighting up the sky.

'Besides which, I might be jealous,' Jasmine admitted, not without reluctance.

'Come on, Jaz. We don't do that scene. We don't do romance. Remember? It's written on the contract.'

'I never signed that contract.'

'Neither did I. Look, the bottom line is, we agreed very early on not to get involved.'

'I don't have to be involved to feel just a little jealous,' she said.

'We do companionship. We do sex. If we keep it that way, nothing can threaten us. I don't want to get hurt again, I don't want you to get hurt, and I don't want Clara to get hurt. I hurt her enough in the past. I just want us to behave like responsible adults.'

'Responsible adults don't have feelings?'

'Yes, and sometimes they learn to keep them in their place.'

'That's what I'm worried about. You not keeping yours in their place.'

'If you want to give me an ultimatum, Jaz, do it.'

'You mean me or her? I wouldn't want to make it that easy for you. The next time you get shot at,' she said, with her tongue loosely planted in her cheek, 'I might not be so quick to get you attention.'

'A guy's got to know where he stands,' said Madden.

He took a call on his mobile. It was Millington.

'Bird's Subaru car is on the move,' Millington told him. 'Rush and Dyers say it was driven away from the Edgeware house about ten minutes ago.'

'Who's driving it, sir?' Madden lurched forward in his seat, finding it hard to contain his excitement.

'Ronnie Edgeware. And his wife is following in a Range Rover.'

'Which way are they heading?'

'Same way as you, Steve. They're following. Keep your eyes open. How's that shoulder of yours?'

'Still attached to the rest of me, sir.'

He relayed the news to Jasmine. It wasn't news to her.

'They're in our rear-view mirror,' she told him. 'I've been looking at them for the past thirty seconds.'

A few moments later, Bird's lime green Subaru with its massive spoiler overtook them on the dual carriageway, with Ronnie Edgeware driving. Behind it was the Range Rover with Patricia Edgeware at the wheel, and coming up behind that were Detective Constables Rush and Dyers in an unmarked police car. Jasmine pulled out in front of the third vehicle, causing them to brake suddenly. Madden felt his shoulder jerk painfully.

'Where did you learn to drive like that?' he asked. 'This is surveillance, not a grand prix.'

'Sorry,' she said. 'I forgot. Though they're not stupid, so they're bound to know we've been watching that car.'

'In that case, Jaz, where are they leading us?'

At the outskirts of the town the road was closed. Lewes Bonfire necessitated the stopping of traffic from entering the town centre so that the place could slope back to the seventeenth century, something of which Ronnie Edgeware was clearly not aware. Madden watched as he got out of the Subaru and began an altercation with a police constable. Patricia Edgeware remained in the Range Rover. Ronnie Edgeware was gesticulating wildly. It didn't matter how much money you had, thought Madden, life just didn't go how you wanted it to sometimes. Ronnie Edgeware climbed back into the Subaru, pointed it in the other direction, and gunned it into a field which was being used as an overflow car park where he backed it up next to a hedge. Patricia Edgeware followed it, pulled up alongside, while Jasmine parked as far away as possible but within sight. Detective Constables Bob Rush and Tony Dyers, who had followed the two vehicles from the Edgeware house in Pyecombe, drew up alongside Madden and Jasmine.

Ronnie Edgeware sat in Bird's car for a few minutes, flashing the lights.

'What the hell's he doing?' said Madden.

'Signalling to somebody, I think,' she said.

Ronnie Edgeware climbed out of the car. He stood there in the rapidly filling overflow car park and shouted Madden's name.

'Madden, I know you're here! Show yourself!'

Madden and Jasmine glanced at each other, shrugged, and decided to play the game by the changed rules. They got out of their car and walked over to the Edgewares. Ronnie Edgeware threw the bunch of keys at Madden. They landed in the mud. Madden picked them up.

'Here,' he said. 'It's all yours.'

'What makes you think I want Bird's car?' Madden asked.

'It was either bring it back to his house and park it outside, which was what I intended to do tonight, or have it towed away for scrap. As it happens, we've been a bit thwarted. Have to leave it here. When he shows himself, you can tell him where it is.'

'I'm more interested in knowing where *he* is, Ronnie,' Madden replied.

'I told you. My wife told you when you forgot your manners this morning and insinuated things that upset her. He's probably in London. Sorry to hear about your near demise, by the way. I would have sent you a sympathy card but I ran out of sympathy,' he added.

'That's all right, Ronnie. I ran out out of manners.'

'Not a good thing with me, Mr Madden,' said Ronnie. 'I'm a bit of a stickler for them. Good manners, that is. That's why I send my daughters to the school I do. Maybe one day when we're in less of a hurry I can teach you some.'

'I'd like that,' said Madden.

'Good. It's a date.' Then he added, as though unable to resist, 'Another date, Mr Madden. Remember, Remember, the Fifth of November.'

He opened the passenger door of the Range Rover and climbed in. Patricia reversed quickly so that mud flew up from the wheels and splattered them. They drove off with a spin of tyres and disappeared into the night. Rockets were already exploding in the sky over the town. There was the sound of distant drum-beats and the smell of smoke in the wind as the Lewes Bonfire Societies prepared to march. Jasmine looked down at the Subaru keys in Madden's hand.

'That wasn't a good idea,' she said.

'No, it wasn't, was it?' Madden agreed.

'You just don't offend people as big as he is.'

'He's big?' Madden tried to play it down.

'He's got money and he's got power, Steve. And contacts. What did you say to his wife?'

'I suggested she might have bedded Bird.'

'You really do have a suicide wish, don't you?'

'I was in my rights, Jaz,' he said. 'Patricia Edgeware knows where he is. Ronnie Edgeware knows where he is. The question is, Jaz, why are they prepared to get involved in enquiries into two murders just to protect some third-rate villain? The Ronnie Edgewares of this world, they don't need that kind of thing.'

36

Madden was still contemplating the answer to that question when he and Jasmine arrived at the Haywain Pub in Lewes, the headquarters of the Barbican Bonfire Society. For bonfire night in that small Sussex town, you had to think not only *Wicker Man* but the Orange Day marches in Northern Ireland. A bull-necked individual wearing a bowler hat and a yellow jacket with a skull and crossbones and the words BARBICAN – MARCH OR DIE just about summed it up. Madden bought a programme off him. He noticed that Bird's girlfriend Caroline was listed under officials as Captain of the Tar Barrel. He wondered what foreigners would make of it all.

About five hundred people were preparing to march. Madden remembered that Lavinia had seen her 'evil sitter' marching. Bird had also been in the Terries. It was a tantalising piece of the jigsaw. The Barbican was only one of the town societies, each of which had its own historic route through the narrow, hilly streets. There was an air of carnival mixed with one of intense expectation. In the garden of the Haywain, children wearing flashing antennae and neon wands and dressed in costumes ranging from devils to princesses munched into burgers as their elders raised banners proclaiming SUCCESS TO THE BARBICAN. There were pirates, red-robed cardinals, erect ladies in Elizabethan gowns, a pair of undertakers in black silk top hats, and Roman centurions. Madden even counted a Napoleon, a Genghis Khan and a Henry the Eighth with his entourage of six wives. But the standard costume of the vast majority of the marchers was the ubiquitous striped jersey, worn by men and women alike, which gave a menacing edge to the proceedings.

There was no denying the erotic charge in the air as hundreds of serious-faced marchers picked up torches made of pitch and prepared to light them for the procession.

'Look for Bird,' Madden said.

'And if he's in costume?' asked Jasmine cynically.

'Then look more closely.'

There was something unquestionably Anglo-Saxon about the whole affair. Jasmine hadn't seen another coloured skin since their arrival. There was a banner slung across the pub. NULLI SECUNDUS, it read. Madden asked a woman holding the hand of her portly little son, who was dressed like a weasel, what it meant.

'Bonfire night,' said the boy.

'Don't be silly,' said his mother. 'They didn't have bonfire night in Latin times.'

She looked at Madden

'It means "No Popery",' she told him.

Madden was sorry he asked.

'Imagine if it said "No Hindus",' Madden said, turning to Jasmine.

'Incitement to religious hatred.'

'When in Rome,' said Madden.

'Not the best analogy, Steve.'

The defenders of Bonfire claimed such sentiments were celebrated out of tradition, not religious fervour. Madden wasn't so sure. In a town where once a year they ceremonially burnt an effigy of the Pope and where people dressed as cardinals to have fireworks thrown at them, you could never be one hundred per cent sure of your neighbour.

He saw, near to the head of the procession, awaiting orders to march, Caroline Gray and Florence Bird. Behind them, on a cart, was the tar barrel which Madden quickly gathered from his programme would be set alight and thrown from the town bridge into the River Ouse. Both women wore striped jerseys and carried torches of pitch. They saw Madden.

'You're not welcome here,' said Caroline.

'It's a public spectacle. We're here to see if Michael shows. I take it he hasn't.'

'If he had, I wouldn't tell you,' said Caroline.

'Bad attitude.'

'You've got a cheek,' said Florence Bird. 'Haven't you done enough damage to our lives?'

They turned their heads away, Florence Bird with an audible sniff.

The sound of another march grew closer, coming up behind, and now there was the sound of drums and brass and whistle. It was composed of the children of the Barbican holding flaming torches and dressed as Red Indians and sundancers, while a youth band led the way. Mothers drifted along by the side to make sure the little darlings didn't incinerate themselves. Madden wondered at the sanity of letting a kid in feathered headgear wield a blazing pitch torch, but in Lewes on bonfire night you held your breath because what came round the next corner usually knocked it out of you.

The adult members of the Barbican were now preparing to march. Huge crosses made of pitch were set alight and held aloft. More torches began to blaze. A group of characters appeared in Zulu warrior costumes. A company of lads gathered, dragging dissected barrels of burning debris on carts. It looked scary. And it was. Hundreds now began parading, with the burning crosses making it look like a Ku Klux Klan family outing. Everyone held a torch. Sparks flew off the tar barrels and massed in the air like fireflies. The beating of drums preceded the arrival of Guy Fawkes, who Madden was pleased to see at least putting in a token appearance on his own night of the year. Behind that was yet another banner, one which Madden recognised. Bird's girlfriend and mother had been stitching it in front of the fire the last time he visited. It read ENEMIES OF BONFIRE.

And then Madden saw it. At first he didn't quite believe it. Affrontery was slow to turn to flattery. Every year in Lewes, they paraded images of councillors and anybody else who had stood in the way of the celebrations, and there were many. There were three papier-mâché heads of lesser mortals, but mounted on a cart was a figure of a policeman. It had Madden's face. Underneath it was a placard that read POLICE – NOV 5TH LEWES – REMEMBER REMEMBER MICHAEL BIRD, BARBICAN BOY, DRIVEN AWAY AFTER BEING FALSELY ACCUSED OF MURDER BY BRIGHTON PIGS. COME BACK SOON.

'Quite a likeness,' said Jasmine, producing her camera from her pocket and snapping it for posterity.

'Pity about my nose.'

'You know they're going to burn it, don't you?'

'Remind me not to be around when it happens.'

'That was the point in coming here. To be around.'

They walked alongside the procession, one on either pavement, scanning the crowd for Michael Bird. Madden began to think it was a forlorn hope. The crush of people became greater as the procession turned up towards the bridge and the High Street. His shoulder pulsated with pain. He swallowed another pain killer. He wasn't counting. Someone knocked against his left side and he reeled with the agony. The crowd got even thicker until it was virtually impossible to move forwards. He lost sight of Jasmine. There were half-consumed flaming torches lying abandoned in the gutter. He grabbed one and dived into the ranks and began walking. He saw Jasmine struggling to keep pace. He ran back and hauled her in, and grabbed a torch from a youth who was carrying two and thrust it into Jasmine's hand.

'There's no running in the ranks,' said the youth angrily.

Madden thought of flashing his warrant card but didn't think it a good idea in a parade of five hundred people which had *en masse* proclaimed him as one of its enemies. Madden looked to the left. Jasmine scanned the crowd to the right. There was no sign of Bird.

At the bridge, the tar barrel was set alight and thrown into the river where a great explosion of steam rose up. Then the procession moved to the war memorial where there were bonfire prayers concluding with the words:

By God's Providence he was catched,
With a dark lantern and burning match.
Holler boys, holler boys, ring bells ring.
Holler boys, holler boys, God Save the King.

Wreaths were placed, then there was a silence punctuated by an ill-timed sky rocket followed by the playing of the last post. A band started to play *Land of Hope and Glory*. They didn't do anything by halves in this town.

All the time, Madden scanned the faces in the crowd who were kept back behind metal barriers.

'He's not coming,' said Jasmine.

'It's not over yet,' said Madden. 'This is just the start.'

He reckoned they had chanced their luck enough by 'running in the ranks' as one had put it. They had started to get hostile glares and not a few shoves, and Madden wasn't at all sure that a burning torch thrown down between his legs was entirely an accident. Madden wanted to see the dawn and preferably well outside of Lewes. They took up a vigil halfway up the High Street. Madden was convinced that if Bird was there he would want to march.

It was the grand procession that he remembered so well, when most of the bonfire societies later that evening merged into one huge, seemingly never-ending snake of people, almost, it seemed, the entire population of the town. The Borough, the Commercial Square, the Waterloo, the Barbican, they all conjoined to create a spectacle of fire and passion. It was almost on this very spot in the High Street that he had stood with Clara and Jason, Clara hanging onto his arm while Jason perched high on his shoulders, swinging his feet against his father's chest. Fifteen years ago. His memory was hazier about further back, when he was the small boy elevated onto his own father's back to watch the pageant. Bonfire night in Lewes held memories that were both painful and dear. For a few seconds he forgot why he had come back, to solve a double murder, a murder about which he had little more idea than when it was a single crime. Even such dreadful events seemed to be eclipsed by this enormous outpouring of reverence and loyalty to a centuries-old tradition. The enormous figure of Guy Fawkes in stovepipe hat now made a reappearance to cries of 'burn him, burn him' from the crowd. Banners proclaiming DEATH OR GLORY and LEST WE FORGET were followed now by the Barbican's grand tableau, the President of the United States of America astride the cruise missile, with another through his head. There were even more voluble cries of 'burn him'.

The 'enemies of bonfire' returned as part of the final grand procession, after being carted halfway round the town. There was rowdiness among the crowd. Someone threw a firework at Madden's effigy and it exploded with a deafening bang between its legs. 'BURN HIM, BURN HIM!' the cry went up, even louder than before. Madden sank back a bit, feeling queasy. He was jostled by the people around him. Someone banged him on the shoulder trying to squeeze past. The anguish made him feel sick and faint.

The air was now thick with the smell of paraffin and smoke from the blazing tar barrels which were pulled on wheels that screeched every inch of their tortuous route round the town. Jasmine stepped behind him to protect his left side. There was no getting out of this place in a hurry. The effigy of the Pope trundled by, accompanied by a retinue of doctrine-spouting cardinals in red robes at whom the crowd went berserk, throwing bangers and jeering. By this time, Madden just wanted to be home.

Then he saw the figure in the flapping black hooded cloak, with the scythe over his shoulder. The grim reaper was staring straight ahead, but it was what dangled in front of the cloak that caught Madden's eye. Four human skulls were linked together by a chain that hung round the wearer's neck. He remembered the picture of Bird wearing human skulls. He pushed forward, and elbowed his way into the procession. Two of the marchers tried to grab him but he flashed his warrant card at them.

'Enemy of bonfire,' he introduced himself. 'Flesh and blood version.'

To the cloaked character with the skulls he said more mundanely, 'Police. Remove that hood.'

The wearer tossed back the hood. He had a red beard and a scar that ran from the corner of his mouth to his right ear. The grim reaper was smoking a cigarette out the corner of his mouth. He grinned at Madden. A number of teeth were missing. The ones that had departed his mouth were luckier than the ones which remained.

'Problem, officer?' came a voice that was halfway between a broad Sussex accent and a growl of displeasure.

'Sorry. Mistaken identity,' said Madden. Jasmine pulled him aside as the red bearded skull bearer with the scythe carried on his way.

'This isn't getting us anywhere,' she said.

'The night's young.'

'He's either not coming, Steve, or he's been among the crowd and we just haven't seen him. There are thousands of people cramming into these streets. You need to go home. You're not well.'

She felt his forehead. He had a temperature.

'And suppose he turns up? At the end? When the fireworks are going off and the bonfires are being lit and when everybody's looking in one direction, supposing then he decides to drift into Lewes. I'm staying to the finish, Jaz. I can't believe he won't attempt to show up.'

They made their way, following a large part of the crowd, to the Barbican fire-site. It was a large meadow on the edge of town and there were hundreds already milling behind the cordonned-off area and hundreds more pushing in and driving the existing crowd around the perimeter. It was almost impossible to see faces unless you got to the front and had a high vantage point. Madden was beginning to sense the futility of spotting Bird anywhere in this crowd when the tableau, round the base of which stood the 'enemies of bonfire', was ignited and destroyed piece by piece in a series of loud explosions that made the ground vibrate. Flames poured from the structure. Madden just caught his own image before it was shrouded in a pall of smoke, only to be consumed moments later by the blaze. And then the fireworks began. The sky crackled as though with gunfire, one display among many in the town that put the word 'remember' in November the Fifth. Madden couldn't hear his phone, but he did feel it vibrating in his pocket.

He whisked it out and put it to his ear but the voice on the other end was drowned out. A firework detonated and ripped the air overhead. From the number on the screen, he knew it was Paula Needham.

'Paula, can you shout? I can't hear you.' Madden yelled into the phone, with his spare hand pressed over his other ear. More explosions. It was impossible to have a conversation.

'Damn, I can't hear her,' he said.

'Who?'

'Paula Needham. From Hubble Bubble. She's here somewhere.' He shouted into the receiver, 'Paula, if you can hear me, send me a text. Where are you?'

He wasn't sure whether she heard him or not. He waited, and then a text came through. It read simply, I SEE BIRD. BIRD IS HERE.

Bird was somewhere in a crowd of up to three thousand. He read Jasmine the text.

'He's here. I knew he would be. Trouble is I don't know where Paula is.'

He texted her back. There was no reply. Madden and Jasmine despatched themselves from the back of the crowd. It seemed to stretch about quarter of a mile around the fire-site and was twenty deep in places and densely packed. There was a belt of thick woodland and scrub behind them, and beyond that the main road. Madden slipped behind a tree, phoned Paula back, cupped his other hand over his ear.

Her phone went on ringing.

'Come on, come on,' he said. 'Answer. Where are you?'

There was no answer. Just her messaging service. He told her to ring him back straight away with her whereabouts. There was still no reply to his text.

'Let's find her,' he said.

They searched. They spent the next hour pushing through the mass of people, many of whom became angry as Madden and Jasmine elbowed their way in front and peered into their faces. A father became irate as Madden stepped on his daughter's toes. He didn't stop. The fireworks seemed to go on and on, the noise sounding like a whole battalion opening fire. People gasped, heads raised upwards. The huddle of spectators seemed to grow more compressed as Madden and Jasmine squeezed and pressed their way methodically from one side of the meadow to the other.

All the time Madden waited for his phone to ring again. It stayed silent.

He began to worry. Perhaps Paula couldn't call him. Perhaps she had found Bird and was standing behind him, keeping him in her sights. Then why didn't she send him another text? He sent her yet another. WHERE ARE YOU? it said simply. There was no response.

The display came to an end. The crowd batted their hands together in a collective applause, there were cheers and happy oblivious faces and kids with little battery-operated electronic necklaces hoisted on their fathers' shoulders. The gathering began to break up, families went home.

'Christ,' said Madden, 'we're going to lose him.'

And then, in the silence after the display, they heard the scream. It was that of a little girl. She was standing in the belt of trees about thirty yards away. They ran over, to where the child was standing. Madden would later learn that she had gone into the woods to have a pee and that her father was standing nearby, but that he hadn't seen what she had, only heard her scream. There was no moon that night and the wood was thick and overgrown and almost pitch black. As they stumbled towards the girl and her father, Madden heard the mobile phone ringing. The phone was Paula's and it was lying in the long grass by his feet. It was ringing repeatedly with his message.

A few feet away, Paula Needham was lying on her stomach, face down in the undergrowth. Madden shone a torch in her face. She was only a few yards from the main road. Her arms were stretched around the base of a tree, her wrists bound tightly with rope. There was a large red weal on the back of her neck and one to her cheek and her blonde hair was covered in bracken. She looked as though she had been dragged. There was a strip of duct tape across her eyes, making it impossible for her to see. It was also over her mouth and wound tightly round the back of her head. Under the tape, rammed in her mouth, was an object that looked like a tennis ball.

Madden started to removed the duct tape and the tennis ball from her mouth while Jasmine untied the rope which was cutting into her wrists.

'It's okay, Paula,' said Madden. 'It's okay.'

Madden knew that it wasn't okay. Behind those pretty eyes with their cobalt blue contact lenses there was panic and distress. A portent of what was to come occurred when he finally yanked the tennis ball from her mouth, and a stream of saliva came out with it followed by a heart-rending scream.

'Where's Jacqueline?' he asked her.

Paula went on screaming hysterically, beating at him with her hands. Madden grasped her wrists gently. He turned aside and stared in horror as Jasmine picked up something from the ground.

It was, he noticed, a green and red unicorn, and it had a silver horn.

PART THREE

The Magician

37

The first minutes in any child abduction were vital. Within five, Madden had every police officer who had been drafted into Lewes for Bonfire alerted and involved in the hunt. But Jacqueline Needham had been gone now for an hour and a quarter. Seventy-five minutes had been lost. You could drive a long way in seventy-five minutes. And it took only a few seconds to snuff out a life.

Paula was hysterical, petrified with fear. Madden went over and over the story with Paula, to make sure he got every detail. She had lain there for an hour, unable to see or cry out, knowing that her cries would not have been heard even if she could, the rope burning into her wrists as she tried in vain to free herself. For the whole of that hour she had been unaware of what had happened to Jacqueline.

'Find her! Please! Find her!' she pleaded with them. 'Oh God, find her!'

'You said you saw Bird.'

'It was him, I swear it was!' Paula clutched his arm so tightly she was almost pulling it off. It scarcely bothered Madden that it was attached to his injured shoulder. 'I watched him for about fifteen minutes. I think he recognised me too. Then I rang you. I looked for you.'

'We searched for you too,' said Madden.

'I couldn't hear you so I came into the woods to make the call. I had Jacqueline with me, I was holding her hand. *Really tight.*'

There was a small cobalt blue patch on her cheek. It was one of her contact lenses, which had become dislodged. Jasmine carefully caught it in a tissue before one of her tears washed it away.

'Oh God, find her, please. Before – before—'

'Where's Jeff? Why wasn't he with you?'

'He didn't come. He stayed behind to study. He has this exam—'

'We've got every police officer searching for her,' said Madden. 'We'll find her.'

They were comforting words. He wanted to take comfort from them himself but couldn't. The *modus operandi* was exactly the same in the abduction of little Dana Vllasi, he noticed. The tape, the tennis ball, the rope, the physical violence used. In neither case had the mother been killed whereas that might have seemed the most logical thing to do. Leave no witnesses. In Delina Vllasi's case, she had not seen her assailant. But Paula had.

'Did you actually see Bird? In the woods? Did you see him attack you?'

'It must have been him,' she said.

'Paula, this is vitally important. I need to know *exactly* what happened.'

'The last thing I remember was going into the woods to phone you. To make myself heard. I was standing there – with Jacqueline holding my hand – and then there was this blow. To the back of my head. And then I was hit in the face while I was lying on the ground. I remember trying to call out to Jacqueline but this tape – was being put round my mouth and eyes—'

He held her hand tight. Only a few hours before she had tried to take away his pain. Now he felt himself sorely ill-equipped to take away hers.

'You mean you saw him in the crowd when you phoned me first, but you didn't actually see him attack you in the woods?'

'It was dark,' she said, scrunching up her face in distress.

'Did you see him follow you into the woods?'

'No,' she said 'But he must have done. Why would he want Jacqueline? *Why*?'

'I don't know,' said Madden. 'I know these questions are hard right now, Paula, but I've got to know. Who is Jacqueline's father?'

She went rigid. He felt her fingers tighten around his.

'Just – just a boy,' she said.

'Paula, it might not be important. But it just might.'

'It's not,' she said.

'You want us to find her, we need to know.'

'It's not important!' she screamed at him. 'Just find her! Please!'

It confirmed Madden's worst fears and his best reasoning. It also gave him a sick feeling in his stomach, because he had asked her to look out for Bird. Madden wasn't ready to face being responsible for another death.

The local radio was reporting that upwards of forty thousand people had descended on the town this night. Cars were being stopped and searched on the roads out of Lewes, dozens of police and visitors and residents were scouring the rest of the woods and adjacent parkland. CB enthusiasts had put out an emergency call to other receivers. Householders nearby were being knocked up and asked to search their gardens and outhouses. The police helicopter with its thermal imaging device was in the air within ten minutes of Madden and Jasmine finding Paula tied to the tree, noisily flying its grid pattern over the surrounding countryside. The railway line was being searched and police tracker dogs were out. Of particular attention were the members of the Barbican Bonfire Society, especially Florence Bird and Caroline Gray. Madden wanted to know if Bird had contacted either of them. They may have burnt Madden's effigy as an enemy of bonfire but they were going to discover very soon it was not just phoenixes who rose from the ashes. Madden was hitting the ground running on this one.

The ambulance arrived. Madden decided to travel with Paula to the hospital. Her reticence to name Jacqueline's father bothered him a lot. It was true that it might not be important, but there were a lot of things in this case that at one time hadn't seemed important. Like Lavinia Roberts' prediction. He remembered something else she had said.

I'm seeing a child. A young child. The child of a friend, or someone you know. The child needs to be careful, to be looked after.

That chilled Madden to the bone. For little Jacqueline was

much more than just the child of someone he knew. He told Jasmine of Paula and Jeff's invitation for him to be the child's godfather.

'Don't tell Millington,' he said. 'Keep that between ourselves. I won't have them take me off this case as they did with Jason's.'

'You think he would?'

'Jaz, I'm investigating the disappearance of a girl who's going to be my godchild. I don't want Millington telling me I'm too emotionally involved and that my judgement might be impaired. I am and it might be, but I don't care.'

Paula was being encouraged into the ambulance by two paramedics. She was screaming that she wanted to stay and look for Jacqueline.

'If anything happens to that child, I only have myself to blame as well. I asked Paula to look out for Bird.'

'You couldn't have foreseen this,' Jasmine told him. 'Nobody could.'

'Lavinia did. She was right about Bird and so was I. I'm not so much concerned how. The question is *why*?'

'Steve, she didn't actually see Bird attack her, or take Jacqueline.'

'But he was *here*. Right *here*. And she was convinced he saw *her*. Suppose he followed her into the woods.'

'He would've needed a car waiting. On the other side. Or someone to pick him and Jacqueline up. And if he had a car waiting, how did he know that Paula would go into the woods? Why did he let her watch him for fifteen minutes before he attacked her?'

Bird hadn't used his Subaru. That was still under surveillance in the field where the Edgewares had left it.

'Bird must have had access to another car. Or someone picked him up. Maybe he intended to abduct Jacqueline among the crowd.'

'And he has a rope with him, and a tennis ball to shove in her mouth, and a roll of duct tape? Just like he did when he assaulted Delina Vllasi? How was he going to get her into the woods if she hadn't gone of her own volition?' Jasmine was trying to work out how just one person could have been responsible.

'Maybe,' said Madden, 'there *was* someone else.'

It was a chilling thought, but the more Madden considered the prospect, the more it seemed possible.

'What was Jacqueline doing while her mother was being beaten unconscious and tied up? Is it beyond imagining, Jaz, that the original plan was to lure Paula away from the crowd. She just made it easier for them. What better place than in a crowd of thousands, at night, when every other head was craned upwards looking at the fireworks?'

It raised yet another frightening possibility. If Paula was to have been lured away from the crowd, how much easier that would have been if the accomplice was a woman.

'The Edgewares are at the bottom of all this,' said Madden, climbing into the ambulance. 'Get the whole lot of them in custody. I want High Hedges turned upside down. And while we're at it, let's do the same with the mother and Caroline Gray.'

Jasmine looked at her watch. It was now ninety minutes since Jacqueline Needham had vanished. Precious, vital seconds were ticking away. She phoned Millington, who was on his way to Lewes as they spoke, and her voice was at first drowned out by the clatter and whirr of the police helicopter as it hovered almost directly overhead.

In the back of the ambulance, Madden phoned Jeff Walker. Jeff was oblivious, his head down in among his police manuals at the flat. Paula was desperate to speak to him. Madden broke the news.

'Jesus! When?'

'An hour and a half ago,' Madden told him. 'Meet us at the Sussex County.'

'I'm on my way.'

'I'm sorry, Jeff. I really am.'

Before Jeff could hang up, he passed the phone to Paula. She seized it and put it to her ear but could not speak. Her face was racked with anxiety to the point where she was too shocked to even cry or talk. She went on grasping the phone as though it was a lifeline to her fiancé.

Madden was still wondering about the identity of Jacqueline's father when they arrived at the hospital. He had a very good idea who that person was.

38

Jeff Walker turned up at the Sussex County practically in the wake of the ambulance. Paula wasn't badly hurt but they wanted to X-ray her skull. She had been unconscious and there was a possibility of a fracture. Jeff held her hand throughout. Madden had a brief encounter with Simon, the male nurse who had dressed his shoulder the previous night. He told Madden that he shouldn't be working, that he'd undergone a severe trauma and should be resting at home. Madden explained to the nurse that he wouldn't tell him how to do his job if he didn't tell Madden how to do his, and then asked him if there were any stronger pain killers as the pain was quite literally killing him.

'None that you can be sent home with,' said Simon.

Madden declined to tell him that he'd doubled the dose. As soon as the nurse was out of sight, he popped another to the back of his throat. He'd lost count.

Jasmine phoned him with more bad news. High Hedges was shut up. The Edgewares had not returned home since depositing Bird's car in the farmer's field just outside Lewes. The Range Rover they had used was gone. She had circulated a description and the registration number, and was at that moment on the way to a magistrate with an authority under the Regulatory and Investigatory Powers Act, signed by Millington, in order to obtain a search warrant.

'A child's missing!' Madden's voice rose in anger. 'Just tell him to break down the door.'

'He's playing it by the book,' said Jasmine. 'Ronnie Edgeware isn't just some nickel-and-dime villain. He's one of the most dangerous criminals in the country. He could make a lot of trouble if he's not involved.'

'All the more reason,' said Madden. 'We wait over a week to get some excuse to get a warrant to go in there and now we have to wait for it to be signed by a magistrate. Jacqucline could be dead.'

'That's the procedure,' Jasmine reminded him.

'To hell with the procedure. I'm tempted to go over there myself now and smash a window.'

'Bricks and crowbars standing by,' she said. 'Just as soon as the ink's on the paper. Bird's mother is in custody and screaming the place down and accusing us of mounting a vendetta against her son, but Caroline is missing.'

'She's *what*?'

'Nobody's seen her since before the firework display.'

Madden felt a tingling sensation down his spine. The thought that had occurred to him in the woods at the back of the fire-site, that two people might have been involved, one of them possibly a woman, ran through his mind again. Two hours had now passed since Jacqueline's abduction. He wasn't a believer in miracles but sometimes you had to hope and pray for one.

Jeff Walker came out of the ward, joined Madden in the corridor. He was as torn in two as Madden was frustrated by the delay in finding the Edgewares.

'I should have been with her,' he told Madden.

He collapsed onto a bench in the hospital corridor and buried his face in his hands. His whole body was shaking. Madden sat with him.

'I should've been with her, I should've been,' he repeated, over and over.

'Why weren't you?'

'I needed to catch up on my studying.'

'Is that the truth, Jeff?'

Jeff stared at him as though he couldn't quite believe what he was being asked.

'Don't you believe me?' he said.

'After what happened earlier,' said Madden, 'can you blame me?'

'You think I was out with that other girl?'

'I'm not into guessing games.'

'I feel guilty enough,' said Jeff. 'About what happened. You were right, sir. I have the sweetest girl in the world and if anything ever happens to her I'll be lost. I just don't want anything to happen to Jacqueline.'

He stared down at the floor and his breath came in short, almost painful gasps.

'I stayed in the flat to study because – because I'd spent too much time with that Rebecca. I needed to catch up. If I hadn't messed around with her and done the studying I needed to do, I'd have been with Paula and this—'

He looked up at Madden, his eyes bulging with tears.

'—this wouldn't have happened, Steve.'

'That's something you'll have to live with.'

'I don't want to live with it. If anything happens to Jacqueline, I'd rather die than—'

'Than what?'

'Does Paula have to know?'

'There are only two people, Jeff, who could tell her. You and me. And I'm not likely to. That just leaves you. If you want my advice, right now she needs your support, not your guilt.'

'She's got that, sir.'

'We all wish we'd done things differently.'

'I want to be sick,' said Jeff.

Madden accompanied him to the toilet. Jeff threw up into a bowl. He sluiced the vomit away with a jet of water from the tap. When he stood up, he was crying. He was just a kid, thought Madden. Out of his depth. Too young to have to live with such a burden of guilt for the rest of his life. If anything had happened – that euphemism people used as a protective shield against the unthinkable – to Jacqueline, he couldn't see a way in which Jeff could escape from it. Benefit of hindsight was great, but benefit of foresight was, after all, what one craved. Maybe, he thought, in the end, only psychics have that.

'I feel guilty too,' said Madden. 'I asked Paula to keep an eye out for Bird.'

'I know. She told me.'

'I told her not to approach him. Or do anything to alert him.'

'Did she?'

'It appears not. But he might have been ahead of the game.'

'I want to catch him,' said Jeff. 'I want to help catch him and find Jacqueline before—'

'Like I said, Jeff, your place is with Paula.'

'I need to help catch him. I can't just sit and do nothing. I want to get in on the search team. I want the satisfaction you had when you caught your son's killer.'

'You think that was satisfaction?'

'What was it?'

'Justice,' Madden told him. 'Simple as that.'

'If he harms Jacqueline, he will get justice. From me. I'll see to it personally.'

'There's no certainty he will. Harm Jacqueline. We just don't know. He could have killed Paula. He didn't. He could've killed the mother of the Vllasi boy. He didn't. His motive is still a complete mystery, but the net's closing, believe me. Everything's being done. Right now his description is being circulated to every police force in the country.'

'Why wasn't that done before?' asked Jeff almost bitterly.

'Because I didn't have a shred of evidence. Just the word of a clairvoyant, who turns out to have been right in her instincts all along. Or knew more than she told me. Now, thanks to Paula, we have that evidence. Though she didn't see who attacked her, she saw Bird in the crowd, or at least she's pretty positive she did.'

'What does this guy want with Jacqueline?' Jeff asked plaintively. Madden wished he had an answer.

'There's one matter I talked to her about. I asked her who Jacqueline's real father was. It might not be relevant but she's refusing to give me his name or tell me anything about him. Which makes me think it might be important after all.'

He pressed him.

'Could you try and coax it out of her?'

'I don't need to,' said Jeff. 'I know. At least I know the circumstances.'

'Mind sharing them with me?'

'I don't think she'll mind me telling you. Shortly before she went to work at Hubble Bubble, long before I knew her, she went to a party and these boys raped her. Four of them. She only told me after I'd known her six months. I think she was afraid I'd go off her.'

'Did she know the boys?'

'She said she didn't know any of them. It was a gang rape. They held her down in a bedroom. She was so shocked and traumatised she didn't report it but when Jacqueline was born, she knew it had to have been one of them.'

'Why didn't she report it?'

'Why do you think?' He qualified that. 'I tried to encourage her to give me more details so I could track down the boys who did it but she just wanted to forget the whole thing. Looking back I can't blame her.'

'Are you absolutely sure in your own mind that she doesn't know the father?'

'How could she? With four guys? I told her it didn't matter to me. That I would love Jacqueline just the same as if she was my own daughter.'

Madden put a comforting hand on his shoulder. He had perhaps been wrong in his suspicions. Now wasn't the time to voice them.

Jasmine phoned back. She had better news for him.

'The ink's on the search warrant,' she said. 'Do you want us to break in without you?'

'Break in now. I'm on my way,' he told her.

As he got up, he said to Jeff, 'Your place is with her. Go to her, be with her. She needs you to help her through this.'

Jeff stood up, turned back to the ward door. He shook Madden's hand.

'Thanks, mate,' he said, then followed that up instantly with an apology. He was, after all, still just a probationer.

'Don't apologise,' Madden told him, then smiled. 'I spent my time as a father hoping Jason would call me mate one day. He never did. Just don't make a habit of it, eh?'

39

By the time Madden arrived at High Hedges, a window had been forced open and entry made. The burglar alarm was blaring and somebody was trying to find a way to switch it off. The house was empty and in darkness. It had the look of a place to which the owners weren't returning for some time. Madden went from bedroom to bedroom. The beds were all made and as neat as apple pies. The furniture was all dusted and smelt of polish. In what were obviously the two girls' bedrooms, the cello cases stood up against the wall. Madden opened one up and strummed the strings with his fingers. It made a hollow, discordant sound.

'You'll never make a musician,' Jasmine told him. 'What exactly did you expect to find? Bird sitting downstairs bouncing Jacqueline on his knee?'

Madden went back downstairs. There was a note on the kitchen table addressed to a Mrs Harcourt. From the content of the note, it seemed clear that she was the housekeeper and was expected to let herself in.

'Find her,' said Madden. 'And while you're at it, check all airports, especially those with flights to St Lucia in the Caribbean.'

Jasmine delegated the job to two detective constables. She wasn't leaving Madden's side. He had driven there on his own from the hospital and he was, she felt, almost asleep on his feet. She wasn't taking the risk that he would jump in his car and try to drive again that night.

He went down through into a large utility room adjoining the kitchen. It smelt of lemon disinfectant. There was a pool table, a great pile of logs for the English country gentleman to burn in his English country fire, and a chainsaw hanging up on a hook. A mattress was propped up next to it. Nothing seemed out of place anywhere. Everywhere was tidy, ordered, immaculate. He sat on the pile of logs and looked at his watch. Jacqueline Needham had now been missing five hours. Dawn would be breaking in three. That terrible night was slipping away, like sand through his fingers, and he was still chasing phantoms. He had slept badly the previous night, what sleep he had tormented by dreams. Tonight he hadn't slept at all. And his shoulder was still pulsating. For a few moments he was aware of slipping out of consciousness. A dream crept out of the night side of his brain and crossed over into his awake state. He dreamt Michael Bird was standing there, telling him that his son wanted to see him.

And then Jasmine snapped him back to reality.

'You look dreadful,' she said. 'You need to sleep.'

'I can get through it,' he told her.

'So can we. Look at you, Steve, you look like a ghost.'

'I have to find that kid. Before anything happens to her.'

'Millington just called. Caroline Gray has turned up. She's been taken in custody. She says she didn't see Bird, that he didn't try to contact her. She went off to one of the pubs in Lewes before the fireworks started.'

Madden got to his feet.

'She's lying,' he said. 'Somebody else saw him. Somebody must have done.'

They left High Hedges in her car. Jasmine drove. He didn't argue.

'Nobody ever asked me to be a godfather before,' he said to her on the way back to the police station, putting his head back and resting it on back of the seat. 'What does it entail?'

You had to have hope. He clung to this one.

'I think you have to be at the baptism, as a sponsor to the child.'

'Sponsor? What do you mean "sponsor"?'

'I don't know. We don't have any equivalent in Hinduism. When Hindu babies are born, they're very much family affairs.

You'll be expected to buy her presents at Christmas and on her birthday.'

'Do you have to believe in God to be a godfather?'

'It might help,' she smiled. 'But I don't think anybody's going to be watching.'

'Has your mother completed her pilgrimage?'

Madden felt himself sliding again. His words slurred. He wasn't even sure what he had asked.

'I got an e-mail from Pandharpur yesterday. With a picture of her and her three cousins standing outside the temple. They didn't walk the whole distance, but they did most of it.'

'Must be satisfying,' he said. 'To get there in the end.'

'Yes,' she said. 'It always is.'

Madden began to wake up when he was confronted with Caroline Gray. She was spitting venom, angry that she had been dragged away from Lewes on the most important night of the year, bitter that Michael had been driven away from the town, furious that Madden should now be persecuting his friends and family.

'Michael's not a child killer,' she said adamantly.

'Then tell us why he might have come back to Lewes for Bonfire yet not even attempted to contact you or his mother?'

'I don't know,' she said.

Florence Bird was equally intransigent. Both she and Caroline were still wearing their striped jersies, which smelt of smoke and pitch. Gone were the nice sweet smiles. In their place was a termagant, a woman who despised the police. She had lost her son. If the police hadn't killed him, then they had driven him away and terrified the life out of him so much that he would probably never come back.

'He would never have done any of the things you're accusing him of,' she told Madden. 'But you police, you just never leave people alone. Never leave people's families alone. Michael made one mistake in his life and we all have to pay for it, time and time again. I'm sick of it, Mr Madden. Sick of the whole lot of you.'

Madden reminded her that it was one huge mistake for her son to have become involved with Ronnie Edgeware in the first place.

'They aren't involved in charity work together,' he said. 'So what are they involved in?'

With that she folded her arms and refused to say another word.

They drove back out to Lewes and searched the homes of Florence Bird and Caroline Gray. Caroline lived in a flat above a craft workshop. It was full of tortured looking metal objects. There was a poster on the wall for a band called The Dark Ones. It pictured five men with shaven heads, large inverted crucifixes hanging round their necks and malevolent eyes staring straight ahead. They seemed to be standing in some kind of pit of flame which reflected on their semi-naked sweaty bodies.

Michael Bird wasn't hiding out in either of the places. Madden and Jasmine looked under beds and in the attic. It had been a long shot, but with a child missing you couldn't afford to be complacent.

The police helicopter was still quartering the sky. Lewes was in the grip of a child hunt, with not only police but residents and visitors scouring the streets and backyards and gardens and parkland. Bonfire torches had been relit, and down by the river it was as though a cloud of fireflies had descended, as dozens of searchers combed and searched the banks and the surrounding fields.

Madden felt the chill of dawn on the back of his neck, a cold, creepy feeling that made him shiver. He began to feel more awake, as though his body clock was adjusting itself as he went along. He realised he had run out of pain killers. The cold seemed to stab at his wounded shoulder. He found himself praying for a miracle, even though he wasn't sure who or what he was praying to. Sometimes you did that as a detective. There came a point in an investigation such as this where you knew in your heart that the worst was yet to come, but you had to keep hoping, to believe in miracles. Jasmine had her Ganesha, the remover of obstacles. If Madden could have got down at that moment and prayed to an elephant God, and thought it might have done any good whatsoever, he probably would have done.

The search for four-year-old Jacqueline Needham was called off officially at six forty-five a.m. The driver of a fish lorry found her. He had pulled into a lane on the Lewes to Brighton side of the dual carriageway to read his paper and have a cigarette and had noticed what looked like a large doll lying about ten yards from the road, in undergrowth and at the side of a railway bridge. It wasn't a doll, of course, but a flesh and blood child. The girl was dead and fully clothed.

Madden knew all about the pain of losing a child. This was the kind of crime that brought it all back. The horror, the sense of outrage, of bewildered anger. He had felt these things as a parent and carried them with him at all times, unable to separate them now from the job. You couldn't stand at a crime scene like this and not ask the question that hundreds of others asked. *Why?* If there was one small crumb of comfort to be taken from that grim morning, as they stood in the drizzle that had started to come in off the sea, it was that Jacqueline Needham had apparently not been defiled in the same way that little Dana Vllasi had. There was no sign of blood on her undisturbed clothes. Beneath them, her little heart was still, but it was there.

'Perhaps he didn't have time,' said Jasmine. 'Assuming he took her for the same purpose. Perhaps someone disturbed him. Or maybe he was afraid of being stopped with the child in his car after the alert went out. It was on local radio pretty quickly after we found Paula.'

'Or perhaps he just got spooked,' said Madden. 'Like he's spooking me.'

Madden crouched down by the child. He wanted to cry. Her face looked white as porcelain.

Dr Colly arrived and carried out her examination. She was shivering too in the cold drizzle. A roadblock had been set up in both directions and early-morning drivers along the road were already being stopped and questioned.

'There's froth in her nostrils and mouth, poor duck,' said Colleen. 'Classic sign of her having been drowned. Her clothes and hair are wet too, wetter than I would have expected. How long's this drizzle been on?'

'About half an hour,' said Jasmine.

'Fresh water or sea water?' asked Madden.

'No idea.'

'Pathologists aren't supposed to say "no idea". I need to know if she was drowned in a river or in a house. I need to know soon.'

Colleen put her nose to the child's face and clothes.

'Can't smell sea water on her, but then that's not a very scientific observation. You linking it with the other child?'

'We're linking it,' said Madden.

'He was drowned in tap water. Chances are this is the same. Did you know, incidentally, that death from drowning takes about five times longer in salt water?'

'I do now,' said Madden. 'I'll remember that when I find who did it.'

'That would mean,' Jasmine said, 'that he drowned her in Lewes shortly after abducting her and dumped her here as he drove back into Brighton. Which means he had to have access to a house, probably in Lewes.'

'Placed her here, Jaz. Not dumped her.'

'Sorry, Steve,' she said. '*Placed* her.'

Madden thought of the two homes they had just visited. He was trying to figure out how and why Bird might have run that risk and not killed the child instantly. Unless these *were* ritual crimes. But that raised another question.

'How did he get a child single-handedly through a town swollen with thousands of visitors and in which cars had been banned for the night? He had to take her somewhere out of Lewes town centre, Jaz. And who's keeping Jacqueline quiet? She must have seen her mother attacked. What you said earlier about somebody else being involved, possibly a woman, is starting to make more and more sense.'

Dr Colly glanced from one to the other.

'Anything more you want from me right now?' she asked.

'No thanks, Colly.'

'Last episode next week. Sarah Mahoney gets stalked by a serial killer who has a psychotic hatred of pathologists. This guy's signature is to dissect them while they're still alive. Really. Gets through twelve of them in ninety minutes. All in a day's work.' She hummed softly as she watched the Coroner's Transfer Service vehicle pull up. 'I worry about living with a woman that produces stuff like that. Don't hold your breath, though, F.W. comes back for another series next year.'

'F.W.?'

'Fucking Wonderwoman, I call her. By the way, I think when you move the body we'll find there's something underneath. It looks like a card.'

There was indeed something pressed into the grass underneath Jacqueline's body. When it was lifted it stuck to the back of her coat and came up with it, quickly dropping off and fluttering back onto the ground. To Madden's mind, it was not accidental. It demonstrated a touch of arrogance, the same monumental egotism that had led the killer – or killers – to send him the heart of little Dana Vllasi, and the bottle with his name written on the piece of paper inside of it. Every serial killer had a signature. Often it was unconscious, unplanned. This was deliberate, less of a signature than yet another indication of the power which the murderer believed he had, and wished to convey.

For it was a single tarot card depicting a red-robed figure holding aloft a white staff. The card was the Magician.

40

Paula Needham was sitting up in the private hospital ward where she had spent the night under observation, ready to go home. Jeff had stayed with her all night. They looked up hopefully as Madden and Jasmine stepped into the room. Jeff shot to his feet. You could tell, Madden knew. Sometimes, as a parent, you just didn't need to be told. You looked at the faces and *you knew*. He had travelled this journey himself. And in a way, this was the same journey, or just another lap of it. Only twenty-four hours earlier Jeff had asked him to be Jacqueline Needham's godfather, but like Jason before she had been snatched away, cruelly, unnecessarily, as though one punishment was never enough to bear. Since Lavinia Roberts told him of his son's message and described Jason's red football scarf, he had thought a lot about a possible hereafter. Now he wondered if Somebody Up There just turned the screw and enjoyed the show.

'I'm sorry,' he said. 'Jacqueline is dead.'

Paula buried her face in her hands and wept bitterly. Jeff put his arm around her, held her tight. For a few minutes, they said nothing, just stared at each other, as though there was a pact between them.

'Was she—' Jeff began, his voice cracking. 'Was she *like the other*?'

'No,' said Jasmine. 'Not like the boy.'

'We talked about it through the night,' Jeff finally said. 'What we would do if this happened. We're going to get married next week and we're going to have a child of our own. In fact we're going to have three children of our own. Three wonderful children.'

Paula's breath seemed to come in chunks, interspersed with sobs of increasing despair.

'Why didn't he kill me too?' she asked. 'Why did he let me live?'

'That we don't know,' said Madden. 'He treated you just like the other mother. It gave him time to get away.'

'I don't care what you say, sir,' Jeff rose to the occasion manfully. 'I want to track him down. I want to be part of the investigation. I want to be there and I want to look him in the face and I want to ask him *why?* Why us? Why Jacqueline?'

And then there was somebody else in the room. Jasmine stepped aside as Richard and Natalie Blance entered.

'We heard on the radio,' said Natalie. 'Just this morning.'

'Is there any news?' asked Richard.

Natalie rushed forward and embraced Paula while Richard Blance seemed to hover in a state of uncertainty as to what to do. He had dressed hurriedly, it seemed. His tie was crooked and didn't match his silk waistcoat or the shirt underneath, which had been tucked roughly under the band of his trousers. His hair wasn't combed. But there was something new about him this morning, Madden noticed, something he hadn't seen before in the proprietor of Hubble Bubble. Gone was the lugubrious, doleful laid-back air that Richard had adopted on learning of the death of his mother-in-law. Vanished were his attempts at detachment. He was feeling something.

'Jacqueline is dead,' Jasmine told him. 'We just found her.'

Madden watched Richard's face crumple. And then he knew. He had suspected as much but the rape story had deflected him. He remembered the first time he visited Hubble Bubble and watched Richard Blance bounce little Jacqueline on the edge of the counter as he went upstairs to talk to Paula.

Richard stepped forward and he saw the confused look on Paula's face as she wrestled with grief and lies. Richard squeezed her hand and burst into tears. Paula was crying. They hugged each other. Natalie was looking confused and so, understandably, was Jeff.

'There's something you all ought to know,' said Richard.

'I think we know it already,' said Madden.

'Know *what*?' Natalie almost screamed.

And then it was as though, without anyone needing to say anything else, as though the truth collectively dawned.

'I couldn't tell you,' Paula poured out her admission of betrayal to Jeff. 'I just couldn't tell you. I didn't think you'd want to live with me if you knew. I'm so terribly sorry.'

Natalie brought her hands up to the side of her head as though to prevent it from bursting. Jeff shook his head in disbelief and bewilderment.

'You mean I've been living with you for two years with *his* child?' he exclaimed angrily.

'It was over between us,' said Richard.

'I had to tell you that story of the rape,' said Paula. 'It was the only way.'

'I want to be sick,' said Natalie.

Jeff looked poleaxed. 'You told me you were raped, and all the time you're living in a flat paid for by Richard and working for him, and I was going to adopt her as my own and never know about it, is that what you're now telling me? Paula? Is it?'

Jasmine took a step forward and tried to calm him.

'Let's not forget the child's dead,' she reminded not only Jeff but them all. 'Whatever the circumstances, let's not forget that.'

'How could you do that to me, Paula?' Jeff took no heed and shook her off. 'How could you do that to *me*?'

Paula was weeping into Richard's arms. Richard was trying desperately to stem the flow of his own tears.

'Think of me,' Richard said, addressing them all. 'She was my only daughter. Natalie never had any children.'

'I had one,' Natalie reminded him bitterly.

'And you lost that. You as good as killed it,' he accused her in a sudden bitter rage.

'Oh God,' she retaliated, 'don't go down that road again, Richard! I just can't stand it!'

Madden made a mental note to ask what it was she couldn't stand.

Jeff suddenly stormed from the room, banging the ward door angrily behind him. Madden left Jasmine to mop up the remaining mayhem and ran out after him. He caught up with him in the hospital car park, leaning over the bonnet of his vehicle.

'What the hell's going on in there?' Madden asked.

'You heard. You heard everything. She told me she was raped. By four guys. At a party. At a fucking party! I believed her. I was going to track them down, bring them to justice, and all the time she was lying to me. The bitch was lying to me!'

'Don't you think there was a good reason for that?'

'So I'd happily move in above the shop while the real father was downstairs all the time?' Jeff threw back at him. 'How do I know it was over between them? How do I know anything any more? What the truth is. For all I know, she's been having it off with him all the time I've been living there.'

'Somehow I doubt that,' said Madden. 'It's probably why Richard was reluctant at first to let you move in but I think from that moment on it was probably all over.'

'How can I be sure?'

'You can never be sure of anything in this life, Jeff. Trust is something that comes hard. But it's worth striving for.'

'She deceived me for two whole years!' Jeff sounded more distraught over that simple fact than he did over Jacqueline's death.

'I deceived my wife,' said Madden. 'Once. We both got over it and now we're good friends even though we're no longer married. Life's like that. There probably isn't a couple in the world who haven't lied to each other at some point.'

'This isn't "some point",' said Jeff. 'This is now. I told her I would marry her next week. Now I'm not so sure.'

Madden wasn't sure what made him do it, but he suddenly struck Jeff Walker. Not hard. Just enough to startle the boy. It hurt his shoulder more than it hurt Jeff's cheek. On this occasion, his timing was faultless. Striking a probationer was one thing, striking the fiancé of a girl whose daughter had just been murdered was quite another, but they were – he realised thankfully – this time alone.

'Grow up,' he said.

'I am grown up, Steve,' he said. 'And how dare you do that.'

'I dared because you are going back into that ward and you are going to damn well support her through this. Forget that Jacqueline was Richard's daughter. She's dead, she'll never see the rest of her life but you've all got lives to live, including me. Move on.'

Jeff rubbed his cheek where Madden had belted him with his hand. He was almost shaking with rage.

'I can't,' he said.

'You can. Who else has she got? You think Natalie is going to let Richard be her comforter? You think Paula wants that? You're the person she adores, Jeff. I can see it in her eyes. I saw it the day she came to meet you at the Marina. She'd do anything for you.'

He didn't want to remind Jeff of his own indiscretions, but he saw no option.

'Love is all about making sacrifices sometimes. You said it yourself. You betrayed her too. Nobody else knows about that except you and me, and nobody ever will. Now get back in there and stop behaving like a spoilt kid. Wearing a police uniform might make you feel important but it doesn't make you a man.'

Jeff stared down at the ground. Then he looked up at Madden.

'I can't look at Richard,' he said. 'I can't bear to go back in there and see him being the way he is with Paula. I just don't know if I can look at that.'

'There won't be any need to,' said Madden.

As they turned, Richard and Natalie came out of the hospital entrance. She was walking fast, storming ahead, while Richard attempted to make up the distance from behind, but it was as though she had erected an invisible barrier between them.

'Take your chance,' said Madden. 'Go on.'

He pushed Jeff gently. Jeff began walking back to the hospital entrance. He paused for just long enough to size Richard up, and for Richard to be made to feel even more despairing and uncomfortable than he already was. Then Jeff disappeared inside, without so much as a glance back. Madden wondered again about putting up the 'marriage counsellor' sign.

He produced from his pocket a Polaroid photograph of the tarot card they had found by Jacqueline's body. He showed it to Richard.

'Is that from the set that was stolen? Along with the other stuff?' he asked.

'That was from the set,' answered Richard forlornly. He was watching Natalie who had stopped in front and who, like Jeff, was too disgusted to look back at him. Madden began to feel sorry for Richard.

'Thanks,' he said. 'Just filling in details.'

'It's called The Tarot of Wisdom,' said Richard.

'Not a lot of that going around.'

'I want to know who killed her,' Richard begged him.

'So do I.'

Natalie swung round.

'I'm going home,' she said. 'You can do what you like.'

'Natalie, we need to talk,' Richard pleaded with her. 'It's why I gave her the job in the shop. And let her live in the flat over it. To support her. And Jacqueline. There wasn't anything between Paula and me.'

'What do you mean, there wasn't anything between you?' Natalie yelled at him. 'Don't treat me like an idiot!'

'What I mean is, there was nothing between us afterwards. When she started to work in the shop.'

'Oh, don't give me that.'

'Okay, there was for a while,' he said, digging his own grave deeper and deeper and poised to leap into it with both feet, 'but not since she met Jeff. I realised I couldn't carry on deceiving you like that and so I was glad when she – when she met Jeff.'

Madden made another mental note. If he ever got himself into a similar situation, he would keep his mouth shut. He made a third. Never get into a similar situation.

'Are you telling me,' said Natalie, 'that if Jeff hadn't come on the scene you'd have carried on having an affair with her under my nose?'

'It cooled off long before that,' Richard tried to claw back some of his ground. 'It really did.'

Madden interrupted.

'The child is dead,' he reminded them, as though they needed reminding. 'To me that's the greatest tragedy.'

'The greatest tragedy, Mr Madden,' said Natalie, 'is that I have been a fool.'

'How do you think *I* feel?' Richard stormed at her. 'Jacqueline was *my* daughter regardless of how you feel. Why don't you try and put some of it aside and think how *I'm* feeling right now. This isn't exactly the easiest day of my life, Natalie.'

He went on, saying things he had perhaps been building up for years.

'Nothing's been easy for me. What do you think I am, some kind of monk, some kind of individual who enjoys being celibate? When did we ever have sex? Not for years and years, not since you lost Harry, not since you decided you never wanted another child.'

Natalie pushed her hands over her ears but Richard pulled them away.

'I have needs, you know!' he berated her. 'You spend so much time up in the clouds with your yoga and your Hinduism and your trekking in Peru, do you ever stop to ask yourself what I want? What I need? Stuck running the shop while you flutter about like a butterfly on ecstasy? I have a life too, though you've never wanted to see it.'

'You have your accounts,' she said.

Priceless, thought Madden. Truly priceless.

'You really think that's what excites me?' Richard obviously thought the same.

'You could have done something with me. You could have done yoga, you could have done anything. I gave you plenty of chances.'

'Yoga's no substitute for a marriage,' he lambasted her. 'It was all these stupid New-Age ideas of yours in the first place that killed our son, remember that!'

Steady, thought Madden, as he put a hand on Richard's shoulder. Steady.

'Don't, Richard, please!' she turned away.

But Richard had his audience, and he was going to have his say.

'She practically starved herself,' he said. 'First she became a vegetarian, then she became a vegan, the doctor told her she was malnourished but did she pay any attention? No, she knew best.'

Natalie had her hands over her ears, shutting out the sound of her husband's voice. Madden had noticed her do that quite a lot.

'That's when she was carrying our child. Some women eat for two, you've heard that expression, Mr Madden? Natalie didn't even eat enough for one to live on.'

The tears rolled down his cheeks as he brought up the past to justify his present.

'Six minutes, he lived,' Richard collapsed onto an ivy-smothered wall at the side of the car park. 'Born six months early and lived six minutes. And then that was it. End of our marriage. All for what?'

He looked up at Natalie, whose hands were shaking as she took their car keys out of her bag.

'All for some stupid diet.'

The words barely registered with Natalie. She unlocked the car door.

'If you have anything else you want to say, Richard, say it now.' Natalie gathered up all her emotional strength and cocooned herself in it. 'Because I wont be here much longer. I'm going. Don't ask me where. Peru maybe. Somewhere far away from *you*!'

And as she delivered that final, stinging rebuke to Richard, she got into the car and drove off. Hell had no fury like a woman humiliated. Richard sat, emotionally wracked, a pitiful object.

Madden flopped beside him. He gazed up at the sky and breathed deeply. The sun had dawned on what looked like being an otherwise pleasant, very autumnal-feeling November day.

'Just find who killed my daughter,' Richard said, straight out.

'I believe I know one of those responsible. The other is still a mystery to me. But then, as I say, sometimes motives are not always obvious. Like the perpetrators, they live in shadows.'

'Why?' Richard asked the perennial question. '*Why?*'

'There are sometimes very strange motives under the skin, Richard,' Madden told him. 'Motives we are never aware of. Jealousies, rivalries, passions that get totally out of control. Obsessions that cloud our judgements. Love that gets too strong, hate too extreme. Things that fester.'

Richard blinked at him.

'That's why,' Madden continued, 'when I investigate a murder, I look for the hidden things. The unthinkable things.'

Jasmine emerged from the hospital main entrance, searching for him. Madden got up, placed a hand on Richard's shoulder.

'Looks like you're taking a bus home,' he said.

'Home?' said Richard Blance. 'I don't know if I can call it that any more.'

Madden took his leave of Richard, thinking that he looked one of the most dispirited and dejected people he had ever seen. Murder went on killing, and it was already taking its toll on Richard Blance. Everyone had skeletons, but not everyone expected them to come crashing out of the cupboard all at once and to have such painful and immediate repercussions. Unlike Jeff Walker and Natalie Blance, Madden did look back, with something that embraced concern. Richard was walking away, and not in a very straight line. He seemed to zigzag as he contemplated his direction. The day was barely new and he had lost his child and his marriage and any second chance he might have been given.

Jasmine saw Madden and hurried over to him.

'They traced Mrs Harcourt, the Edgewares' housekeeper,' she said. 'You were right, the Edgewares were booked on a flight this morning. All four of them. To the Caribbean.'

'How did I know that?' Madden induced a smile.

'Telepathy?'

'What time is their flight?'

'It was ten minutes ago. From Gatwick.'

'Shit!' Madden kicked the ground. The pain shot right up his left side and bedded itself in his shoulder. He cursed a second time.

'Don't worry, it's delayed,' she explained. 'Right now the plane is sitting on the tarmac and the Edgewares are enjoying champagne and canapés in first class. The airport police have been informed. It'll be delayed until we get there.'

'Talk about the skin of your teeth. Which island in the Caribbean were they flying to?'

'St Lucia,' said Jasmine.

41

They were ten miles up the M23 motorway taking an adrenalin-fuelled drive towards Gatwick when they heard the news over the radio. There had been been a major heist at a security depot near Heathrow. The details were only just coming through, but a professional and well-organised gang had carried out what was already being described as the 'robbery of the century.' They were always robberies of the century, thought Madden. Then he heard the figure. Eighteen million pounds in cash – 'ten tons of money' – a whopping sum by anybody's standards, had been taken in a dawn raid on the headquarters of a company called Global Security. The plan had involved a hijacked lorry and two cars.

Madden whistled.

'That's somebody's retirement fund.'

He continued listening. Two security guards had been shot but were not described as being in a critical condition. The victims aside, the plan appeared to have been carried out with near faultless precision. The crooks had got clean away. These were no amateurs. There were only a handful of professional criminals in the country capable of financing and organising a robbery of such magnitude. A Detective Chief Superintendent from the Flying Squad was mentioning no names, but one of those he had in mind was, Madden knew, currently sitting on the tarmac at Gatwick with a glass of champagne in his hand, waiting to take off for St Lucia.

'Now there's a coincidence,' said Madden.

'You don't think – surely?' Jasmine quickly caught his wavelength.

'I do think. A job that size? Like the man says, there are very few people in this country with the money and the contacts and the organisational skills to pull off something like that. This has the Edgeware stamp all over it. And by a strange little coincidence, if it wasn't for us he would be thirty thousand feet up and over the Atlantic by now.'

'But surely, Steve – he wouldn't have had time—'

'Ronnie doesn't get his hands dirty. Not these days. He bankrolls. He's Mr Big. I'll lay any odds you like he set this up and recruited the gang and has plans in place already to get his share laundered and out of the country as quickly as possible. That's why he's leaving. Till the storm dies down.'

'He's not going to be a happy bunny, then,' said Jasmine.

'The Flying Squad will be. Let's hope they appreciate who it was that stopped their guy escaping.'

'Didn't Lesley Fieldhouse say something about Jack promising her a holiday – in St Lucia?'

'Yes. Interesting, isn't it.'

'You think there's a connection?'

'Could be. Or maybe it was just a name Jack overheard. I think, Jaz, that Michael Bird and Jack Fieldhouse's roles in all this are very different from what we first imagined.'

They arrived at Gatwick closely followed by a car containing four other detectives, two of them women constables. You didn't remove people like Ronnie Edgeware and family from an aeroplane that was standing on the runway waiting to depart without back-up. Not unless, that is, you wanted to be reassembled. They were passed through the security channels and onto the tarmac. The plane was a Boeing 747 and like four of its occupants it wasn't going anywhere, or at least not for the next few minutes. They boarded and went straight up to first class, where Ronnie Edgeware, his wife Patricia and their two daughters, Claire and Clementine, were sitting waiting for take-off. Ronnie Edgeware appeared to be irritated, as well he might. When he saw Madden, his irritation turned to fury.

'I've just about had enough of this,' he said, tersely, staring out of the window.

'Sorry to delay your family holiday,' said Madden. 'But something's come up.'

'Why don't you go away and stop bothering us!' shouted Claire Edgeware.

'We need to talk about Michael Bird,' Madden told him.

'Not that idiot again. For God's sake, won't you people take anything for an answer? I haven't seen him since the day you released him from custody.' Ronnie was showing signs of increasing volatility.

'Somebody has,' Jasmine explained. 'And he's now wanted for questioning about the murder of three people. Two of them children.'

'Jes-us Christ!' Ronnie exclaimed. It was anger over his own predicament rather than any gesture of sympathy. 'Can't you just accept my word? And let us fly out of here? I hope you find him. I hope you lock him up. I hope I never have to see him again. I wish I had never heard his name. There, does that convince you?'

'Not entirely,' said Madden. 'Because I think your wife or perhaps your daughters know something.'

Ronnie Edgeware leapt from his seat and was about to assault Madden when he was restrained.

'You leave Patricia out of this, you bastard, and my daughters, or I'll kill you.'

'That's funny. You normally get other people to do your dirty work, Ronnie. Like hiring thugs to put on Hallowe'en masks and snip off publicans' fingers. That was a stupid move, but then you never could stand anyone getting in your way. I don't smell one rat, Ronnie, I smell a whole sewer full of them.'

'I'll see you rot in hell, Madden.'

'I'll wave,' he smiled.

In the end, Ronnie went off the plane peaceably if with strong reluctance, demanding his solicitor. Claire and Clementine refused to be touched by anybody, and stomped off angrily behind their father with faces like sewn-up purses. It was Patricia Edgeware who put up the greatest fight.

'You're not taking us off this plane!' she screamed, as though three-quarters of her family were not already halfway down the gangplank. 'Let go of me! Let go of me!'

She hung on to the seats as Jasmine and two women detective constables attempted to prise her loose.

'Oh God!' she said, becoming hysterical. 'Help us. Tell me this isn't happening. Let me go! Let me go! This is a family holiday, that's all it is, a family holiday! What kind of man are you?'

'A bad sport,' Madden answered.

They practically had to carry her off. It then took another half hour for the baggage handlers to remove the Edgewares' luggage from the hold. An hour later, they were back in Brighton. It wasn't St Lucia, and the accommodation wasn't exactly first class, Madden told himself, but the tea was good, though not perhaps as nice as the copious amounts of champagne the Edgewares would otherwise have been sipping.

'The Flying Squad want to talk to Ronnie Edgeware,' said Millington, who had been involved in a series of phonecalls while they had been up the motorway.

'They can wait, sir,' said Madden.

'They're on their way down here now.'

'With our medals?'

'Don't get pompous,' Millington warned him. 'You haven't got anything out of Edgeware yet, and you didn't the last time.'

'I didn't have him in custody last time. Besides, it's not Ronnie Edgeware whose going to do the talking, it's his wife Patricia. She's the weakest link.'

'What about the daughters? What do you think they know?'

'The daughters are going to be my lever,' Madden explained to him.

'Edgeware's a big fish,' Millington warned him. 'And you could be swimming in shark-infested waters. He's got off before and if he escapes the rap this time – I'm just cautioning you, Steve.'

'You're telling me we ought to be afraid of him.'

'Get real,' Millington said. 'One of his brothers blew the head off a policeman.'

'Let's hope it doesn't run in the family.'

'You're going to try and get evidence out of his family and possibly incriminate them, in Ronnie Edgeware's circles that's probably tantamount to breaking a Mafia code of honour. He could hold a very powerful grudge.'

'Three people are dead, sir. Have you forgotten that?'

'No. I just don't want another corpse on my hands. That's all.' Millington stared at him. 'Make sure you're damn right about this.'

Patricia Edgeware was inspecting her nails. They were long and pillar-box red. She looked up with carefully contrived indifference as Madden and Jasmine stepped into the interview room, and then returned her gaze to her talons. They sat down across from her.

'Nice and cosy,' said Madden.

'Where are Claire and Clementine?' Patricia asked.

'They're with a responsible adult,' said Madden. 'They won't be questioned without one present, in light of the fact a parent can't be there. Then, I suppose it's debatable in the present circumstances whether a parent might be classed a responsible adult.'

'I don't know what you mean,' she said, without looking at him.

Madden reasoned that as the news about the heist was just breaking while Ronnie and Patricia were boarding the plane, there was every chance that neither of them knew the outcome. Unless Ronnie was taking calls on his mobile right up to the last minute, the success or failure of the venture was probably still a mystery to them. And almost certainly to Patricia, even if she did know about it in advance. Madden decided to play that card.

'It failed,' he said.

'What failed?'

'The job.'

'I don't know about any job.'

'The one Ronnie set up. The Flying Squad are on their way

down here now to interview him. They'll probably take him up to London and that's the last you'll see of him for a while.'

'I don't know what job you're talking about,' she said, staying cool.

'He didn't tell you?'

'He doesn't tell me anything about his business,' Patricia explained.

'Don't you ever ask?'

'It's not my place.'

'Aren't you worried?'

'Worried about what?'

'They've got people who are going to talk, Patricia. Who are going to put the finger on Ronnie. They don't exactly use rubber hoses up there, but they have a way of getting at the truth. They let Ronnie slip through the net the last time he pulled a big job, but this time it'll be different. I hope he's made provision for you.'

She swallowed. It was a good sign.

'I told you, I don't know anything about Ronnie's business.'

'It was just pure coincidence you were taking off for the Caribbean on the very morning it was taking place?'

'What was taking place?' She blinked her eyes. It was a good performance.

'Ronnie must have picked a good team. Reliable. Trustworthy. People that would make sure his share went somewhere safe, out of the country. Tell me, Patricia, I don't live that kind of lifestyle, but how much cash does one need to live in relative comfort and send one's daughters to a good school and give them cello lessons?'

She shrugged.

'I've no idea,' she said.

'Five million? Ten million? Twenty million? Let's try eighteen million.'

'You really are talking about things I don't know anything about.'

'All right, well let's talk about somebody you do know about. Michael Bird.'

She swallowed again. A restlessness came over her. She tried to control it, but Madden knew the subject was uncomfortable for her.

'Not that again,' she said. 'I've told you everything I know.'

'He's been seen,' said Madden.

She acted as though she didn't believe it.

'Really?'

'Yes. Really. I want to know who's hiding him.'

'I don't know who's hiding him.'

He decided on a passionate approach. He leant forward, earnestly.

'Mrs Edgeware, a child was murdered. An innocent child. Bird was seen near where it happened. We know that had nothing to do with you but if you don't help us and tell the truth, he might kill another one. Would you want that?'

'No,' she said. 'I wouldn't.'

'Then please tell us.'

'I've told you. I've told you till I'm blue in the face telling you, he went to bed and in the morning he was gone.'

'My colleague was watching the house, Mrs Edgeware. He never left. At least not by the front door. If you or either of your daughters helped him sneak out in the dark, then just tell us.'

'Our daughters had nothing to do with it,' she snapped. 'Leave them out of it.'

'You realise that if they did,' Madden cushioned the threat for the moment, 'or if one of them did, and she knows where he's hiding, she could be charged with assisting an offender?'

'They went to bed. I went to bed. Ronnie went to bed. And Michael Bird went to bed. And in the morning he was gone.'

And in the morning, thought Madden, someone had eaten mummy bear's porridge.

'He was part of the job, wasn't he?'

'Which job?'

She was beginning to irritate Madden.

'That's why Ronnie met him, befriended him after prison. Fixed up a meeting with him in Ratty's Bar. Let's forget all this crap about about Ronnie offering him a job in a repair workshop, he was to be one of the gang, wasn't he? Only something went wrong. He was superstitious. He did what he'd done before, he went to half a dozen or more clairvoyants to find out how it would all work out. Then we arrested him for another crime, and that threw Ronnie into a panic.'

She fidgeted nervously as she listened to him and tried desperately not to look him in the eyes. He could tell she was scared, that he had stripped away a few layers to reveal the kernel of truth.

'The biggest job of his career, the culminating one, Patricia. The job that was going to set you up for life and probably for the next one as well. Ronnie's pension. All that was threatened. I'll bet Ronnie was terrified Bird was going to spill all the beans and needed to spirit him away somewhere.'

'Oh God,' she said.

'Is that the truth? Is that why you or Ronnie helped him escape? Arranged for him to go to a place where we would never find him until the job was done? The only question is – did he take part in that job?'

She didn't answer. She just bit her lip and shook her head.

'Where is he, Patricia?' Madden asked outright once again.

Once again, she said, but this time in a cracked, nervous voice, 'I don't know.'

He decided to give her a little time to think about it. Upstairs, Jasmine was going through the Edgewares' luggage. He told her what he reckoned.

'Edgeware must have been petrified at the prospect of us re-arresting Bird, in case he dropped us a clue to that job. Think of all those months of planning, gone out of the window.'

Madden picked a leopard-skin bikini out of Patricia's suitcase and dangled it from his finger.

'Pretty tasteless,' he said.

'You should see what's in his. What is it about men over forty that they think they look great in floral shorts?'

'Shall we pass on that? Found anything?'

She showed him a receipt from a credit card transaction. She had found it in Patricia Edgeware's handbag.

'They bought petrol – or at least she did – in Tillingham in Essex on the day after Bird turned up at their house. At one forty-five in the afternoon.'

'Tillingham in Essex? You think they rendezvoused with Bird there?'

'It's possible. It's quite remote. Right on the Essex marshes. If they'd wanted to hide him away in a house somewhere, that would be the place to do it.'

'How would he get up there? In the middle of the night? Without a car?'

'Maybe,' said Jasmine, 'they arranged to meet him somewhere. He sneaked out of the back of the house when it was dark with Ronnie Edgeware's help and laid low somewhere until morning. I was watching the house. They took the girls to school at half past eight in the morning and brought them back at half past four in the afternoon. That gave them eight hours to pick up Bird, drive him up to Essex, put him somewhere safe, and get back in time to collect the girls from school.'

'It makes her complicit,' said Madden, with a satisfied gleam.

'You doubted that?'

'No. It's just reassuring to know your instincts are right. Besides, there's something sexy about rich, guilty women.'

'I'll remember that,' she smiled.

'Are we sure they *did* take the girls to school?'

'They were in their school uniforms and they had their cellos with them,' said Jasmine.

'Better get on to the school just to make sure. It might have been a ruse.'

'Surely he wouldn't involve his daughters?'

'He involved his wife. Maybe this was one big family awayday.'

He drew breath for a moment. There hadn't been much time. A second child was dead, a second mother had been assaulted, Bird was still free, and as if that wasn't enough, there was something else bothering Madden. It concerned Jack Fieldhouse. The man was dead and couldn't defend himself, but the truth, uncomfortable and unpalatable as it was, had to be faced.

'I believe Jack Fieldhouse knew about the job this morning,' he said.

'You think Bird told him?'

'All that nonsense about hoping Bird would turn informer. Jack had already got all the information out of Bird he'd ever wanted. Bird tipped him off and Jack thought he would keep it to himself and get some of the spoils. He was in on this with Bird, Jaz. This was going to be Jack Fieldhouse's pension as well.'

'Are you going to tell Millington, or am I?'

'Am I hell. Let's keep it to ourselves. For the moment.'

The truth was, Madden felt too tired and too sick to go down that road right now.

42

Jasmine had been on to St Catherine's School. It was twenty minutes later. Madden was still getting nowhere with Patricia Edgeware. He had put the words *Essex* and *Tillingham* to her but all she would say was that it was where her father used to run a pub and where she and Ronnie used to live and they had decided to go back out of nostalgia. Madden thought it a likely story. Ronnie Edgeware was now entrenched with officers from the Flying Squad who had driven down from London at about the speed of light, or so it seemed. So far they hadn't shaken Madden by the hand or patted him on the back or invited him out for a decent meal and a drink. They were interested in the whereabouts of eighteen million pounds. Three corpses could go fly. That left the daughters.

And then Jasmine came off the phone.

'It's odd,' she said. 'Really odd.'

'What is?'

'Claire and Clementine did go to school that day. But the strange thing is – their music teacher told me, they didn't take part in the orchestral practice.'

'Why's that peculiar?'

'Because they said their cellos were being revarnished.'

That sounded the second unlikely story in less than half an hour.

'Hang on. I thought you said – they took their cellos with them that day.'

'They did. That's the odd thing. I saw their parents put the cello cases in the back of the Range Rover in the morning and when they brought the girls back from school they had their cello cases with them.'

'Maybe they dropped the cellos off at the revarnisher's on the way and picked them up again on the way home.'

Jasmine made a long humming sound.

'Yes, I agree,' Madden said. 'On the same day that they squirrel Bird away somewhere in deepest Essex, it hardly seems a pressing priority. You could say it strikes a wrong chord.'

They exchanged a quick look.

'Which daughter do you suggest?' Jasmine asked.

'Clementine. Claire's a bit feisty.'

They sat down with Clementine. Madden assumed the social worker who was present was a responsible adult, whatever that meant. He was having his doubts, though. Not without some justification. She looked somewhat prim, not the sort of woman who would take kindly to the merciless bullying of fifteen-year-old schoolgirls. Madden didn't think it would come to that.

'Sorry about your holiday,' he chucked in for openers.

'I didn't want to go anyway,' said Clementine.

'Why not?'

'Just didn't.'

'Boyfriend?'

She shrugged and swept back her hair. There was a boyfriend. Madden felt for her. To be dragged away by your parents on a long foreign holiday when all you wanted to do was snog with your first love was like being put in prison. The Caribbean was one hell of a long way from Brighton.

'Thought your first love might be music,' he brought her on side.

'Not necessarily,' she said.

'Get the old cello revarnished?'

She stuck her tongue in her mouth and worked it around. She stared at him while she was doing it.

'No,' she said.

'I think you know the day we're talking about?'

'I think so,' she said.

'You know what I think, Clementine. The sooner you tell me

the truth, the sooner you and your sister can walk out of here. What's your boyfriend's name?'

'Ethan,' said Clementine.

'What does he do?'

'He's at school,' she said. 'Will Mum and Dad walk out too?'

'That depends. They're hiding somebody I'm looking for. Now, that's a serious crime and they could get into trouble. You wouldn't want that, would you?'

'No,' she said.

'So honesty could help them. Your honesty.'

She twisted her head to one side and looked at Jasmine. She wasn't fooled. But she was prepared to play the game.

'Dad told us to tell that story,' she said. 'He said that he had something to move out of the house but he couldn't do it because you were watching.'

'Something to move out? Did he say what?'

'Claire and I discussed it and thought it was money.'

'Money? In *two* cello cases?'

'Dad has lots of money,' she boasted.

Madden had to smile at that. The social worker clicked her teeth at the thought of two cello cases filled with cash.

'You didn't see him put the money in the cello cases?'

'Claire and I were sent to bed that night,' she said. 'In the morning he told us not to go near them. Has he done anything illegal?'

'I couldn't tell you,' Madden said.

'He hates Ethan,' she volunteered.

'Well, that's fathers for you, Clementine. They never think any boy is good enough for their daughter. Just one more question. Did you meet a man called Michael Bird who visited your parents the night before?'

'He was one of Dad's associates. We're not allowed to meet them.'

'But did you?'

'He was cool,' she grinned.

'Cool? I thought you said you didn't meet him?'

'He put his head round our bedroom door. Said hello. We said hello.'

'That's enough time to gauge that someone's cool?'

'You're pretty cool,' she said.

'I've been called a lot of things, Clementine. Cool isn't one of them.'

'You never arrested the right people then,' she said smartly.

Madden was still smiling at the compliment as he and Jasmine drove back to High Hedges. He wanted to take another look at that outhouse. Something hadn't seemed right to him on the first visit. Now, as they stood by the pile of logs and smelt the sweet lemony air-freshener all around and looked at the concrete floor, he looked gloomy, almost despairing. Because if what he was thinking was true, it blew his theory right out of the water. The floor had been washed and scrubbed thoroughly. Although the chainsaw must recently have been used to cut up logs, the blades were clean, wiped of any vestige of splintered wood. He looked again at the mattress, then went back upstairs and opened up one of the cello cases.

'Jaz,' he said, 'the morning you watched the house, who carried the cello cases when they came out?'

'Ronnie and Patricia,' she said. Then, 'Steve, you don't think—'

'I do think.'

He removed one of the cellos. It made a deep reverberating note as he laid it down on the carpet. They took out the other one. At the very bottom of one of the cases, just underneath the soft lining, Madden saw what he thought was a tiny blood stain that someone had scrubbed and attempted to get rid of.

'Bird must have weighed about nine stone,' Jasmine said.

'Divide that in two.'

'Edgeware *dismembered* him? While I was watching the house? Is that what you're suggesting?'

'You didn't hear a chainsaw?'

'I was too far away,' she said. 'The outhouse is at the back. But if Bird is dead—'

Madden was thinking the same thing.

'It was Bird's body they got out of the house. Right under your nose. Ronnie killed him that night because he couldn't risk us taking him in and interrogating him again. Do these cellos look revarnished to you?'

'Then who was at the bonfire? Who did Paula see?' asked Jasmine.

Madden had felt as though he was chasing a phantom. Now it seemed he'd been doing just that. They went back to the police station and put a host of new questions to Patricia. When they mentioned cello cases, the blood drained from her face.

'Oh God,' she said.

'Where is he?' asked Madden.

'A solicitor,' she said. 'I must have a solicitor.'

'For your daughters? You've involved them in this. What did they know?'

'They knew nothing.'

'Convince me.'

'It was an accident,' she said.

'Where is he?' Madden repeated.

'It was an accident. The girls had nothing to do with it. They were in bed.'

'Where is he?'

'I want you to know – I didn't want to have anything to do with it. Ronnie – got into this fight with him over – I don't know what it was over – anyway, he needed my help and I – I think Ronnie said he fell against the mantelpiece or something like that. It's solid marble.'

'Where is he?'

Patricia Edgeware was slowly fracturing.

'All I did was help him dispose of the body,' she wept. Her mascara stained her cheeks. All the jewellery in the world couldn't make Patricia Edgeware look a lady again. 'He's my husband, I was the only person he could turn to for help. And now I'm turning to you for help, Mr Madden. If I tell you the truth, will I be free to go? Because Claire and Clementine need me. I need to be with them. Please help me. I'll do all I can to help you. Only – I need to be with my little girls.'

She stretched her hand out across the table as though to try and touch him and bond with him. He had never seen a woman look so desperate in her life. He almost felt sorry for her. Within the space of a few minutes she had guessed the game was up, betrayed her husband and thrown away the kind of life that only a few million extra pounds could buy. It was a supreme sacrifice. What it would gain her was out of his hands.

He leant back in his chair and folded his arms and looked away.

'Where is he?' he asked gently.

43

Michael Bird was dead and he wasn't coming back. Neither had he been anywhere since Ronnie Edgeware and his wife Patricia had dumped his body – that was the word for it, not placed – in a shallow grave of saturated bog at the end of a muddy track in deepest Essex. The corpse was naked and cut in two halves, severed through the waist by a chainsaw. Each half was tightly packed in a large polythene bag of the type mattresses came wrapped in, and the ends sealed with tape. The tribal head on the skin of the back, visible through the plastic, was all Madden needed in the way of identification. The insides of the bags were splashed with blood to which shreds of torn flesh adhered. Michael Bird might have been weird but he wasn't a zombie. He had been dead over a week. He hadn't climbed out and put himself together and walked back to Brighton and killed two kids and cut the heart out of one of them.

DI Bob Quinn was the man in charge. He didn't like bodies being dumped on his patch. He spoke pure Estuary. The body in the bags was a geyser. Everything he said was suffixed with 'know what I mean' and a sniff. He was also a keen bird watcher. While the pathologist was doing his stuff, Quinn watched some geese flying in V formation out to sea.

'Greylag geese,' he said. 'Been breeding here. Going south for the winter.'

It was thirty-six hours later. Madden had caught up on some sleep but the dreams bothered him. In one, Jason had appeared. He'd felt as real as in life and Madden had woken up sweating, believing that the last year of his life hadn't happened after all and that Jason was still alive. Then the truth had slowly edged into his consciousness. Patricia Edgeware had given them a pretty precise location and at that moment the Essex police were digging holes. He dressed, got into Jasmine's car, and they drove up in time to witness the unearthing and smell the appalling putrefaction as the end of one of the bags burst open and Bird's decomposing legs slid out.

'Want to take it back with you?' Quinn jested. 'We have enough corpses in Essex without you lot on the south coast sending us more.'

More geese flew over, presumably on their way to sunnier climes. Madden reckoned it was time he and Jasmine hit Brighton again.

'No thanks,' he said. 'You can have this one with our compliments.'

They drove back. Madden had never liked Essex. He hated its flatness, its seemingly endless miles of watery wilderness dotted with houses that were either plain drab or dressed up in pretty shades of pink and yellow, like children going to a party. He hated the empty sky, empty except when birds were leaving the place. Something about Essex always reminded him of winter. It was a cold bleak day, to match his mood. Well before they got to the Dartford Bridge that straddled the Thames, they pulled into a lay-by to buy two coffees from a caravan. The woman who poured them had huge fleshy forearms and a skin complaint and coughed over them as she squeezed on the plastic lids. Madden poured his away. It made a little crater in the mud in the lay-by. Madden imagined satellites picking it up and the next Ordnance Survey map of the area marked with a new feature. Where Madden Threw His Coffee Away In Despair In Essex.

He sat in the car and watched rain spattering on the windscreen.

His phone rang. It was Dr Colly. She thought he would want to know that the autopsy on Jacqueline Needham had proved conclusively that she was drowned. The County Hospital had established it was fresh water and not river water in her lungs. There was no sign of sexual abuse. But the fibres were back.

'The same fibres?'

'The same fibres, m'duck. A lot more of them in the lungs this time. Consistent with her having a towel or some such cloth placed over her mouth and nostrils while she was struggling to breathe.'

'Thanks, Colleen.'

'How was Essex?'

'Grim. We didn't stay for that party either.'

'You reckon it was an accident?'

She was well informed.

'Yes. Every day you get villains that push each other against marble fireplaces and accidentally kill them and then cut them in two with a chainsaw and smuggle them out of the house and bury them in Essex.' He paused for breath. 'This was premeditated and well planned. Trouble is, I just lost my chief suspect.'

'Again,' she said.

'Again,' he reflected caustically.

'Sawn-up torso in cello cases. Nice one. Not even Sarah Mahoney's had that one.'

'Tell your partner she can use it. I want fifty per cent.'

Madden switched the phone off. So Jacqueline Needham's murder was forensically linked to that of the Albanian boy, which was forensically linked with that of Lavinia Roberts. Which meant that the same person had to be involved in all three. Michael Bird had died after Murder One. He couldn't have been responsible for Murders Two and Three. The likelihood was therefore that he hadn't been responsible for Murder One. You didn't need to be brilliant to work that one out. Just stupid would do.

'Didn't it even cross your mind? When you saw those cello cases?' he said to Jaz, guessing her reaction.

''Course it did. Every time I see cello cases I think there's a sawn-up body inside. Especially with the two daughters walking alongside.'

'Sorry,' he smiled. 'I just so wanted to believe Lavinia Roberts. That's why I went after Bird.'

'Is *that* what this is about, Steve?'

He looked at her ruefully.

'I don't believe in clairvoyance, never did. That's the funny thing. But so much of what she said seemed to come true. And she was right about the Devil's Dyke case. Somehow she did accurately pinpoint the place where Millington found Shauna Lewis. Maybe she did have some talent that we can't explain. Like magic is only a branch of science we haven't discovered yet. And I didn't and still don't believe in spiritualism.'

'What has that got to do—'

She broke off. The rain was hammering on the car roof now and streaming down the windows. She put on the wipers. She was clearly finding it hard to believe what Madden was telling her. But before he even uttered the boy's name, she knew.

'I thought if she was right about everything else, she just might have been right about Jason. That's all,' he said.

'This was all about *Jason*? You talked yourself into a mindset over Bird *all because of Jason*? When by your own admission you don't even believe in such things?'

She leant back in the driving seat and drummed the wheel impatiently with her fingers.

'The dead don't leave messages, Steve,' she said.

'I know they don't. That's the thing, Jaz. But it would be comfortable to believe, wouldn't it? Reassuring to know that there's just that tiny chance it might be true? We had strong grounds for suspecting Bird. He'd visited six clairvoyants and Lavinia looked the next on his list and he'd lied about it. He tried to run away when I apprehended him. He had a record for violence. He had an unhealthy interest in black magic. We thought he'd done a runner after we released him. And then Paula was convinced she saw him at Lewes, convinced he was her attacker.'

'Which he wasn't and couldn't have been. Maybe she was trying to help you, Steve?'

'Help *me*?'

'You told her who you were looking for. You were convinced he was going to be there. She saw somebody who resembled him and her imagination did the rest. You passed your own mindset on to her.'

'She'd spoken to the guy, met him. She'd had him in her treatment room, given him an Indian head massage. She knew what he looked like. I don't know how she could make a mistake like that.'

'He didn't come back from the dead, Steve. And neither did Jason. The dead don't come back. In your religion, you join them, they don't join you.'

They drove back to Brighton and went straight to Hubble Bubble. The shop was closed. Ray Millington was coming down the stairs from the flat above where he had just spent an informative hour talking to Paula and Jeff Walker. He frowned when he saw Madden. Madden looked up at the sky and then down at the pavement.

'Six bloody days searching for a dead man!' he fired off. Millington was clearly in no mood for mincing words. 'Six bloody days wasted. Congratulations, Steve, on one thing. You got the right person but for the wrong crime!'

'Praise where it's due, sir,' said Madden.

'She maintains you told her Bird would be there. She spent an hour searching for him. She still maintains she saw him there. In the dark, among thousands of people, with his back to her.'

'She didn't tell me, sir, that he had his back to her.'

'Did you never learn, Steve, that sometimes witnesses tell you what you want to hear?'

Jasmine looked uncomfortable.

'Shall I—'

'Yes, I think you'd better,' said Madden.

She carried on upstairs to the flat. Madden went and sat in Millington's car. Millington had learnt more. What he had discovered rankled.

'I hear you were to have been Jacqueline's godfather,' he said.

'I didn't think it important enough to mention,' Madden responded.

'You didn't think? After what happened to Jason, you didn't

think that might cloud your judgement, make you emotionally involved? Good police work requires us to be detached, Steve. At all times.'

'Detached?' Madden threw at him. 'When did murder ever make you feel detached? You see a kid with his heart cut out, do *you* feel detached. You see a four-year-old girl drowned, lying on her back next to a railway bridge, you look at her, are you supposed to feel *detached*? When did you ever feel detached, sir?'

'I get your point.'

'Good.'

'No one does. But there's a difference between that and what you're doing. This was a personal vendetta of yours against Bird for reasons I'm not going to go into now.'

Just as well, Madden thought.

'Let me just say that I know how you felt about Lavinia Roberts. Word gets around.'

'Oh, come on, sir. I was twelve years old!'

'I'm not talking about that. I'm talking about what she told you. How that has coloured every single thing you've done. If we credited and acted on every psychic, we'd be laughing stocks.'

'Hasn't it struck you, sir, that some of the stuff she said has come true? What about the Devil's Dyke case? Where would you have got with that if it hadn't been for her?'

'That was a last resort,' said Millington. 'A very last resort. And maybe, who knows, she just got lucky. And so did I.'

'Luckier than Jack Fieldhouse,' said Madden.

He had touched a raw nerve and he knew it.

'Jack is dead and can't defend himself.' Millington all but closed the matter. 'I don't want any rumours spreading about Jack. It's not going to do any of us any good.'

'He knew what Bird was involved in, he knew what Edgeware was planning. He could have told us from the outset why Bird went to six clairvoyants in one day. He could have prevented an eighteen-million-pound robbery, averted the injuring of two security guards, he could have blown our case against Bird out of the water from day one, but he didn't. And for what? His own greed. Part of Michael Bird's cut. Enough to retire on and more. What are we supposed to pin on him for that? A posthumous medal?'

'Go home and rest.' Millington gave every impression of wanting to move on from that.

'Oh, I get it, sir. It's protect-the-force time again, is it?'

'It's protect the force against innuendo and allegations that you can't prove and nobody will ever prove. I'm ordering you, Steve. Go home and take some rest. And that's not an order to disobey.'

'Are you saying I'm off the case?'

'I don't like doing it. But look at you. You look like you haven't slept properly in three days, and you have to rest that shoulder.'

'It feels better, sir,' said Madden, lying.

'I have plenty of other officers, and right now a few new leads. We've got a gang of psychic vampires – or Goths as they want to call themselves – they were near the Rottingdean path at Hallowe'en. We've got two student Satanists at Sussex University into blood drinking, and any number of weirdos between here and Eastbourne, not to mention three witches' covens.'

'The killer was a customer of Hubble Bubble, sir,' Madden said, looking in at the darkened shop. 'Someone who knew Lavinia Roberts, maybe when she worked there, someone who'd met Paula and seen Jacqueline. The connection between them is no coincidence.'

'Don't you think,' said Millington, 'I'm well aware of that?'

Madden climbed out of the car. He stood on the pavement for a few moments while Millington seemed reluctant to drive off.

'Let me give you a lift home,' he said.

'No thanks, sir. I'll walk.'

'I hate doing this, Steve. But you're not thinking clearly. I can't risk that.' He added by way of a sweetener, 'The Flying Squad expressed their gratitude.'

'At least somebody has,' said Madden.

'They've picked up most of those they believe were involved, and a few are squealing. Including two garage mechanics who acted as drivers and were to be paid fifty thousand pounds each. They found two red devil masks with horns and a pair of pliers in the home of one of them, guy called Vince Lake. Bit of a record as an enforcer. Hadn't even washed the blood off the pliers.'

'I'm sure Lucky Maynard will be pleased to know that,' said Madden.

Millington drove off. Madden wondered how many brain cells went to make up the average villain. Ronnie Edgeware had gambled on the big one and lost. It happened in casinos all over the world and it happened in life. Human greed was omnipresent. There was never enough in the pot.

He went up the stairs to Paula Needham's flat. The door was open and he let himself in. Jasmine was sitting having tea with them. Paula was still in a deeply distressed condition. Jeff had been given compassionate leave from his training to look after her. She had recovered from her own physical ordeal only to come home and face the lingering pain of an emotional loss.

'I hear you found Bird,' said Jeff, who seemed to have heeded Madden's advice. He was sitting squeezing Paula's hand. Madden was pleased he had done some good.

'We found him,' said Madden. 'Cut in two and in an Essex bog. He'd been dead over a week. Which means he wasn't the person you saw at the bonfire, Paula.'

'It was him! I'm sure it was,' she assured him.

'Not unless he came back from the dead or has a twin brother,' said Madden. 'How long were you looking at him for?'

'At least fifteen minutes,' she said.

'She wouldn't have called you if she hadn't been certain,' Jeff came angrily to her defence. 'Are you trying to say she's lying?'

'No. Just mistaken,' Jasmine said.

'I wanted to help you.' Her face screwed up tightly. 'From that day you took me around the tattoo parlours and I picked out his picture, I wanted to – to help you.'

In her other hand, she was holding a framed photograph of

Jacqueline. She started to sob over it. She clutched it to her mouth as though trying to breathe life back into the child through the medium of a piece of glass and plastic and the image on a three-inch-square piece of card. Then she let out a sound that Madden hoped and prayed he would never have to listen to again. It was the agonising lament of a mother for her lost child, a wail of hopelessness, a cry of utter despair. Jeff turned to her and took her in his arms and pulled her close, and she fell towards him, still weeping, still grasping the photograph.

'I know,' said Madden.

'Then who was it? Who was it I saw?'

'A complete stranger,' said Madden. 'But somebody at the bonfire wasn't. I need you to think back, Paula. When you were attacked, were you aware of anything else?'

'I – I don't know what you mean,' Paula said, looking at Jeff.

'Were you aware of anyone else? Other than the person who attacked you?'

'I – I don't know,' she said.

Madden was trying not to lead her. He had done that once, it seemed. But he had no choice.

'Were you aware there might have been a woman present?'

'I don't know,' she said. 'I was hit on the head and knocked unconscious and it was a man who hit me in the face and put the tape round me, I know it was. But I didn't see anybody else.'

'You see, Paula, whoever attacked you and took Jacqueline came prepared and equipped. The rope, the tennis ball, the duct tape. They were hardly going to attack you in the crowd. You were to be tied up exactly like Delina Vllasi, the mother of the Albanian boy. The original plan was to lure you into that wood, to give them time to escape. A man couldn't have done that but a woman might have done. You see what I'm getting at?'

'I think so,' said Paula.

'A woman might have asked you to help her look for something she'd lost, or a child,' said Jasmine.

'You're saying *two* people took Jacqueline?' Jeff stared in horror.

'It's only a theory,' Madden said. 'That's why I need you to think back over every one of your clients, everyone you've ever given Reiki to, head massages, whatever.'

'DCS Millington already asked her,' said Jeff. 'She went down and got her appointments book and gave it to him. All it has is names, though.'

'I want you to do more than that,' said Madden. 'I want you to remember anyone who met Jacqueline, played with her. The Albanian boy wasn't taken at random. We believe the killer went to his mother, who was a prostitute, as a client, saw the boy, stalked her and got to know her routine. In the same way, it's possible you had a client who saw Jacqueline, did the same to you. When we first met, Jacqueline was at the shop.'

'That's right,' Paula said.

'You told me you'd brought her from the creche because a client who liked children wanted to see her?'

'Yes, I remember that.'

'Who was that client, Paula?'

'She's called Ella. She comes every two weeks for Reiki.'

'Do you know her second name? Where she comes from? Anything about her?'

'I don't know her second name. Only that she's about forty, a bit fat. She told me she was a doctor.'

'Physician heal thyself,' said Madden.

Jasmine was writing it down. Madden remained standing, watching her.

'Could you look into that, Jaz?' he asked her. 'I'm off the case. Officially. As from now. Millington's orders.'

Jasmine looked up, as startled as Paula and Jeff were.

'I don't want that,' said Jeff.

'Neither do I,' said Madden. 'But it's what happens. Sometimes.'

'Did he give you reasons?' Jasmine asked.

'Want the list? One, I screwed up. Two, I trusted in a psychic. Three—'

He glanced down at the photo of Jacqueline, still in Paula's hand.

'Three, I got too involved.'

'I don't *want* that, Steve,' Jeff was even more adamant. 'You were in on this from the beginning, they can't just take you off, not just like that.'

'They can and they do.'

Madden put his hand to his shoulder. The pain wasn't so bad now but it had drained him of energy. Maybe Millington was right. And Jasmine too. His judgement had become clouded and he needed to rest. Perhaps, after some undisturbed sleep, the picture would become clearer.

'I'm sorry,' he said. 'I really am.'

44

Madden wasn't sure what took him back via Southover Street. Perhaps it was something to do with passing the end of the road where he was born. Or because he wanted to delay going home to an empty house. Or maybe he just needed a drink, and the quietest pubs known only to locals and a handful of visitors were in Hanover. He had a pint of Guinness with a shamrock carved into the froth at The Geese Have Flown Over The Water, the name of which derived from the fact that the pub sign painter couldn't paint geese and had painted an expanse of water instead. An Irish musician with a guitar and an ill-fitting toupee and a soft, melodic voice was singing sweetly about going home. It made Madden drink up and think of going finally to his.

As he reached the top of Southover Street, he had the feeling of coming full circle. He had come back to where it all began. Not just two weeks ago. But much further back in time, when he was that twelve-year-old kid, climbing nervously up the steep hill, pubescent urges simmering. In the musky autumn darkness, with the chill of impending winter in the wind that suddenly blew in his face, Madden stood outside Lavinia Roberts' house. The lights were on. He smelt burning wood.

All of a sudden, he couldn't pass by. It was as though providence had taken him there. He rang the bell. Natalie answered. As she stood in the doorway, she seemed even more the image of her mother. A bit more worn now and troubled than the first time he had seen her, but she looked every bit as magical, so alike that she almost took Madden's breath away. It was as though once again the clock had turned back nearly forty years and he was standing there, asking to be let in. Lavinia Roberts' daughter did not disappoint him.

'It's nice to see you,' she said.

'It's nice when people say it's nice to see you. That doesn't happen often in my job.'

He stepped into the parlour. She was burning logs in the grate. They crackled and spat and the flames roared up the chimney. She was also burning candles on the mantelpiece.

'Candles purify a place,' said Natalie. 'Richard always hated me burning them but now I'm free to do as I like. I've moved back here. Until I decide what I want to do.'

'I'm sorry,' said Madden. 'First your mother's death, now your marriage.'

'We get over these things,' she said.

In some ways, Madden thought, the room was a shrine. To her mother.

'Did I tell you?' she said breezily. 'I got an e-mail from that company in Chicago. The one that creates diamonds out of people's ashes.'

'No you didn't,' said Madden.

'I'm going to send them Mum's ashes and have a diamond made that I can wear round my neck.'

'Good. I'm pleased you're going ahead.' Madden could think of no other way to put it. Not right then.

'Yes, isn't it. Pioneering. So you never have to say goodbye to someone you love.'

She hit a plateau, and then descended from it, her mood swinging between ebullience and anger.

'I feel so sorry for Paula,' she told him. 'I can't feel any bitterness towards her. Not now. She might have deceived me, and Richard too, but what I'm going through is nothing compared to what she's feeling.'

'Very noble of you,' said Madden. 'Very understanding.'

'What makes it so difficult is that I was very jealous of her.'

Natalie pulled some more candles out of a box, was about to

light them, changed her mind. Maybe it wasn't just the house Natalie was purifying.

'How jealous?' Madden sat down, watched her.

'Bitterly so. As I told you, you had nineteen years to enjoy your son, I had all of six minutes. You don't know what that's like. What Richard said brought it all back to me.'

'Did he mean it?'

'He said if I had looked after myself I wouldn't have miscarried. It was a cruel, horrible thing to say, Mr Madden. Just because you want to live your life a certain way, don't eat meat or dairy products, it doesn't mean you're unfit to become a mother. I don't know why I miscarried, it just happened, but Richard always blamed me because I was so thin, and never forgave me. And for years afterwards if I saw another child I wanted to cry. I even hated their mothers for being lucky enough to—'

She broke off. The blaze of logs spat and a glowing ember landed on the carpet. Madden leant forward, and flicked it back into the grate. All the time, he watched her. Her fingers were black from lighting the fire.

'You said you were jealous of Paula and Jacqueline.'

'When she came to work at the shop and Richard gave her the flat above, I thought, that could have been me. To watch a child grow up and to see Richard – to see Richard making a fuss of it, adoring it. I didn't know – I didn't know it was *his*!'

She sat down next to him on the sofa, one of the unlit candles in her hand. Madden gently prised it loose and put it to one side. He held her hand. He looked at the glow of the firelight on her bare knees. She was wearing her vegetarian sandals. Her feet looked bony and delicate.

'That, Mr Madden,' she said, 'is the hardest thing of all to bear. Knowing that he gave to her what I couldn't have.'

She looked up at him. She seemed to sense a kindred spirit.

'And how,' she asked, 'are you?'

'Off the case,' said Madden simply.

'Why?'

'Too long to go into. Let's just say I wasted too much time chasing the wrong person.'

'How do you know he was the wrong person?'

'Because he's dead. Dead men don't commit crimes.'

'Maybe,' she said, 'I should give you a reading.'

'Oh no,' said Madden, conjuring a smile. 'I've had enough of that. Another tarot card reading is what I *don't* need right now.'

'What have you got to lose?' Natalie urged him.

'What remains of my credibility, that's all.'

'No one will know. Just you and me. And maybe the cards will show the way to go. Let me help. Please?'

'Not tonight.'

'You look as though you need to know which direction you're heading in. Me too,' said Natalie.

Madden decided that resisting the entreaties of Natalie Blance was hopeless. He finally agreed, went through into the kitchen with her and walked round the table while she dropped into the little chair her mother had been found dead in. Madden pulled up a stool on the other side. The cloth on the table was brand new, a bright, canary yellow. The telephone cable had been replaced. Apart from that, the room was the same. The window had been repaired. The ghosts were vanquished. He would hear what she had to say, and go. There was a single candle burning in the kitchen too. He stood up and closed the curtains.

Natalie took her own set of tarot cards out of her bag. They were wrapped in a square of blue silk, just as her mother's had been wrapped in a scarlet piece.

'Shuffle the cards and divide them into three piles,' said Natalie.

Madden shuffled them. He made a mess of it. He was finding it hard to believe he was actually doing this. He tried to concentrate as Natalie lifted the three piles he had laid out.

'That's funny,' he said.

'What?'

'You didn't do what your mother did. She asked me my birthday and put out some card – she said it was a significant or something like that.'

'Significator,' said Natalie. 'It's very old-fashioned, I don't know of anyone who does that any more. Except Mum.'

It was odd to hear Natalie talk of her mother in the present tense, as though she was still alive. Madden felt, sitting in that little kitchen again, as though she wasn't very far away.

'What does it represent? This significator?'

'You,' she said.

'How? In what way?'

'Court cards – Kings, Queens, Knights and Pages – used as significators represent the querant, the physical features and the age and the zodiac sign, but like I said—'

'She picked out the King of Swords,' said Madden. 'To represent me. Why?'

Natalie looked at him. She shrugged.

'I don't know,' she said. 'Probably because you have dark hair or something.'

'Just a minute—' Madden entertained a sudden, startling thought. 'Are you telling me that these significators *describe* people?'

'I never use them. It's old hat.'

She seemed anxious to get on with the reading. Madden had become diverted. Something started to become clear to him. Something that hadn't made any sense initially. He had a vivid picture of the crime scene. He couldn't forget it. Lavinia Roberts slumped over the table, cards spread out, two of them in her hand. The ones on the table – *Death, the Devil, the Magician.* The telephone cable cut. The broken window in front of her. The blood splashes on the wall above her. The impression that she had been sitting, reading the cards, looking at her assailant as he broke in.

It hadn't happened like that. It hadn't happened like that at all.

'But your mother did. Use significators,' said Madden.

'She was of that generation. Nowadays people change the colour of their hair, wear contact lenses. Picking a card to represent them just isn't useful or practical. The tarot's more of an instinctive thing.'

Madden took out his phone, rang Jasmine. She was at the station. She was in the process of tracking down a general practitioner by the name of Dr Ella Jones who put her own faith not in modern medicine but in universal energy. There was hope for the world yet.

'Forget that,' said Madden.

'I thought you were off the case, Steve.'

'Forget that too. Look at the crime scene photographs. Tell me what the two cards were that Lavinia Roberts had in her hand when she died.'

'That's important?'

'Blindingly important, Jaz.'

She went away. A couple of minutes later she returned.

'The Knight of Wands and the Page of Wands,' she said.

Madden turned to Natalie.

'What do the Knight of Wands and the Page of Wands represent? What kind of people?'

Natalie shrugged, slightly annoyed that he had disturbed the reading.

'I don't know,' she said. 'Like I said, I never do that stuff.'

'Maybe,' said Madden, 'your mother has a book somewhere that will tell us.'

'I can have a look,' said Natalie.

Madden pressed the phone back to his ear.

'You still there, Jaz?'

'Where have I got to go?' she asked.

'Come to Southover Street. And don't waste a minute. We read the crime scene wrong. Lavinia Roberts was trying to tell us something. We missed it.'

45

Natalie was still upstairs searching when, ten minutes later, Jasmine arrived. Madden closed the door to the parlour. He had asked Natalie to stay up there. He didn't want her upset further by what they had to discuss.

'Millington will go ballistic,' she said.

'Fine by me. We got what happened here completely wrong, Jaz. Lavinia didn't watch her intruder coming in, she wasn't reading cards in the middle of the night, she was in bed asleep. And she woke up when she heard the break-in. It's my guess that's when they cut the cable.'

'They?'

It was the first time she had heard him use the word so positively, as if there was no doubt in his mind. There wasn't any more. Lavinia had removed that doubt.

'There were two people involved, Jaz. One cut the cable, just in case Lavinia might have a chance to phone out.'

He opened the door to the parlour just a little, checked Natalie wasn't listening, and asked Jasmine to step through to the other side.

'Now come in,' he said. 'And remember you're elderly and frail and surprised. Don't put up too much of a struggle.'

Jasmine came back in. Madden hooked her by the neck with his arm. Her head went down, angled towards the kitchen door. She was right above the little card table with its bright, canary yellow cloth.

'You're hurting,' she said.

'This is how and why she was first hit. From in front.'

Jasmine's legs knocked against the table. Madden forced her

down and she ended up sitting in the chair Natalie had sat on just a few minutes before. She was positioned awkwardly, but it was one which Madden knew, Lavinia had never risen from.

'That's how it happened,' said Madden. 'One grabbed her and forced her down while the other hit her with the hammer. She dropped onto the chair and then they went on hitting her, maybe taking turns. All the blood splashes were consistent with her head being just above the table when she was struck. There were two different kinds of injury to her head. Compressed fractures delivered with some force, and a number of weaker ones, tentative ones. Almost as though one of the parties didn't want to be doing it. A serial killer in embryo, you might say.'

'Who are we talking about here, Steve?' she asked.

Madden flopped down into the chair opposite her. He looked at the tarot cards spread out in front of him. Had Natalie not persuaded him to sit for a reading, he would have missed it entirely. He flicked through the cards until he found the Knight and the Page of Wands.

'I'm talking about them,' he said.

Jasmine blinked at him, uncomprehending.

'They're called significators. They're always court cards – Kings, Queens, Knights and Pages. Cards that represent a querant. His or her colour of hair, eyes, age. Those kinds of details. Lavinia picked one out for me. To represent me. She did that sort of thing.'

'You really are into this, aren't you?' Jasmine was still not getting the point.

'The thing we could never fathom, Jaz – why Lavinia died with two cards in her hand. Why, with one hand, she lifted the phone to call for help and found it dead but in her other hand held onto these two cards. It didn't happen that way. They left Lavinia for dead but she had enough strength to reach for the telephone. When she realised it was dead, she did the only thing she could. With the cards in front of her, just before she lost consciousness, she picked those out.'

Madden stared for a few moments at the cards in his hand.

The mediaeval figures they depicted seemed oddly at variance with the contemporary horrors Madden had witnessed.

'You mean she was describing her killers?'

'Natalie's upstairs now, trying to find a book that gives the categories of people these cards represent. She never uses them herself. They're old hat. But Lavinia did. That's the point. She hoped we'd get it. She wasn't doing a reading, not in her nightdress, not at that time of the morning.'

'What about the three cards laid out on the table.'

'Death, the Devil, the Magician. Her killer laid those before he left. Every serial killer has his signature. This was more obvious than most. That's how he sees himself, Jaz. As all three. The man with the power who sends me a bottle with my name inside, who wants me to have the case.'

Madden was remembering Jeff's words to him only an hour earlier.

I don't want that, Steve. You were in on this from the beginning, they can't just take you off, not just like that.

'Who are we talking about, Steve?' she asked him again.

Madden rose, stared out of the little kitchen window into the dark courtyard garden.

It's a way of him telling you that he has control over you . . .

He passed the palm of his hand over the candle flame. It was strange how you could hold it there for a second without it hurting. He did so until it burnt, but even then he didn't pull his hand away immediately. Madden knew all about pain. What he was experiencing inside at this moment was far more acute than just the sharp stinging sensation of a burning wick on skin. He drew his hand away slowly and looked at the little black sooty mark in the centre.

. . . over your life, your emotions.

He didn't want to believe it could be true. But he had faced worse horrors, and knew what twisted love could do. As he gazed out into the garden, he put it to Jasmine.

'Why do you think Paula was so adamant she saw Bird there?'

'She wanted to help you.'

Madden shook his head.

'I didn't pass any mindset onto her. She lied. She knew we were searching for Bird and that the story would grab our attention. Unfortunately, she didn't know Bird was dead.'

He turned round, saw her reaction. It was entirely expected. Jasmine wasn't a mother, but she was a woman. What Madden was suggesting went against every fibre of motherhood.

'She's a good little liar. She proved it. She managed to convince Jeff she'd been raped by four guys when Jacqueline was Richard Blance's daughter. Why four? Why not one? A case of over-inventiveness if ever there was one. She had no qualms about living upstairs with Richard's child and being employed by his wife. One wonders if she'd ever have told the truth if Richard hadn't broken down and revealed it.'

'Why?' Jasmine put the question Madden himself was asking.

'Let me put another question to you, Jaz. Who else but a mother would wrap a towel round the face of a child she was drowning? Especially her own child?'

She stood up, confronted him across the little kitchen.

'Are you saying he—' she broke off. 'For goodness sake, Steve, they asked you to be Jacqueline's godfather.'

'Jeff did.'

Madden thought back to the moment it happened.

'I asked him why he hadn't reported the break-in at Hubble Bubble, even criticised him for it. It was then that he popped the question. As though I was getting too close, as though he had to keep the upper hand. Caught me off guard.'

Little things crept into his mind, little things that hadn't seemed important but were. Like Hallowe'en night. It had seemed such a harmless, insignificant question at the time, perfectly in its place, one that he never gave a thought too. Until now. The same night he had taken Jeff Walker into his house, drunk beer with him, allowed him to call him by his first name, talked about his son, taken him upstairs to Jason's room, discussed the case with him. Suggested he might stay the night. Shown him Jason's red football scarf. Introduced him to Clara. One copper who didn't like spending nights in an otherwise empty house and a kid that probably guessed that. Even at this stage Madden was prepared to believe he could be wrong, if only because being right was such a stab in the heart.

'On Hallowe'en night before you showed up, I had Jeff in my house,' he told her. 'I showed him the crime-scene video. Thought it would be good experience for him. Good training. He even sat there and gave me his own theory of the crime and it was a very good one. Well thought out. Then he asked me a strange question. He asked me why she was holding two cards in her hand. It didn't seem that strange at the time, but look at it in the light of what we know now. It was the only thing, Jaz, that was different from the scene the killer left behind. The only thing that didn't make sense to him.'

'Paula is a Reiki therapist, Steve. She heals,' said Jasmine bluntly.

'I think we'll find,' he said, 'that these were crimes of passion of some sort you and I don't even want to imagine right now.'

The phone in the kitchen rang. Madden called upstairs to Natalie to see if she wanted to answer it. There was no reply. He ran upstairs to look for her. She wasn't there.

Jasmine picked up the phone.

'Hello,' she said.

It was Natalie.

'Where are you?' Jasmine asked.

'At the shop,' she said. 'Jeff's with me. I couldn't find anything upstairs so I came down to look for the book you asked me for. We found one. I told him why you were interested.'

'Natalie, don't say anything. Just bring it.'

'But I found what you're looking for.'

'Natalie, listen to me. Say nothing to anyone, just get back here.'

Madden came back into the kitchen. She looked at him.

'She's at the shop. Jeff is with her. She's told him.'

Madden snatched the phone.

'The Knight and Page of Wands signify a young man and woman with blond hair and blue eyes,' he heard Natalie say.

And then silence.

46

When they arrived at Hubble Bubble a few minutes later, the ground floor of the shop was in flames. Jasmine pulled up and they leapt out. A small crowd of people had already gathered and one had just phoned the emergency services. Madden wasn't waiting. He looked through the window for any sign of Natalie. He knew enough about fires to be aware that they could engulf a building in under two minutes. There was one hell of a lot of glass at the front of the shop. If that shattered, the rush of oxygen would act like a huge fan. Even opening the front door or kicking it in if it was locked would worsen the situation.

They ran round the back. The service area door was shut, and it was locked. Madden put the back of his hand to the metal handle. It was still cool. That meant the heat hadn't built up on the other side of the door. He began kicking it with his foot until the jamb splintered and it burst open.

'Stay out!' he told Jasmine.

'You're not risking your life on your own,' she said.

'Thanks.'

She shut the door just as there was an eruption of fire and a loud crash in the main shop. The candle display had collapsed and melting wax was fuelling the flames. Acrid smoke billowed against the ceiling dropping down like some malevolent poisonous cloud, the fumes already catching at their throats.

He shouted out Natalie's name but there was no answer. The smoke was piling up the staircase. Madden had heard fire described as a living creature, but he had never witnessed it at first hand before. The black smoke was like an exploring worm of huge proportions as it coiled and moved and probed, seeking out the rooms above. Madden and Jasmine kept low, crawling on all fours. The treatment rooms above were already dense and filled with fumes. They grabbed towels in one, dampened them from the sink and held them over their mouths and noses.

Madden scarcely had time to register that it was the room in which Paula Needham had placed her healing hands upon his tired and worn body only forty-eight hours previously.

'Natalie!' he shouted.

He heard a muffled cry, more of a scream, from the floor above. At the same time, there was a loud splintering of glass and what sounded like an explosion. He knew what it was. The shopfront had shattered in the heat. Now the flames were licking up the stairs, blocking off their escape.

Jasmine ran after him to the top floor where the flotation tank stood. Natalie was lying on the floor by the tank. She looked unconscious and there was a large red mark on the back of her neck that oozed with blood, where she had been hit with something heavy. Her clothes were rucked up, indicating she had been dragged up the stairs. Madden leant forward and tried to remember how to perform a fireman's lift. He was pulling Natalie across his back and shoulders when Jasmine pointed to the thick dark pungent smoke pouring in through the door, hugging the ceiling as it spread around the room.

'Keep low!' she shouted.

He lowered Natalie back on to the floor and they started to drag her out. Madden pulled a towel off a rail and wound it around Natalie's face. He noticed a gold chain hanging beside it with a heart-shaped pendant containing Jeff Walker's picture. Natalie started to regain consciousness. And then they heard the scream again. It wasn't Natalie. It was coming from inside the tank.

'Paula's in there!' said Madden.

He let go of Natalie and tried to open the enormous lid of the tank but it didn't open manually. He searched for controls but there were none. She was now thumping frantically from the inside.

'How do you open these things?'

Jasmine bent down close to Natalie. The fumes were starting to irritate Madden's throat. If they had seconds to get out of there, they were lucky.

'Natalie, the tank. How does it open?' Jasmine shook her.

Natalie opened her eyes and started to fight. Then she began screaming. Jasmine held her.

'The tank. Paula's in there. How do we open it?'

There was a low ominous rumble from under the floor. The fire had clearly taken hold below. There was a small window in the flotation tank room but they were two floors up. Natalie took a few moments to come to her senses and to realise where she was and the predicament they were in.

'Downstairs,' she said. 'Panic button – control in the treatment room—'

Madden suddenly remembered seeing some kind of a button. He tried to get downstairs but the flames and the smoke worked together like some evil serpent to push him back. They were trapped. The screams from the tank became more desperate, the fists hammering on the lid more frantic.

Madden covered his face with the towel and keeping as low to the stairs as posible threw himself down them. He heard the sound of fire engines and police sirens. His eyes stung and his mouth tasted of something foul but he pressed on. He crawled into the treatment room. Black smoke obscured almost everything, but in the deadly gloom he saw a red bulb flashing. He propelled himself towards it and threw a switch. He hoped it was the right switch, because once he was up these stairs again there was no coming back. It wouldn't strike him until much later that he had risked his life to save a woman who had murdered her own child. He snaked out of the room, keeping below the poisonous thickening fug, and slithered up to the top floor on two knees and one elbow and with his free hand pressing the damp towel across his mouth which he kept only inches from the ground. The other thing he knew about fires was that in most cases the smoke and the fumes killed you before the flames got anywhere near.

As he got back into the flotation room, he was relieved to see the lid opening slowly like one half of a large scallop shell. The girl within didn't rise like Venus this time. She burst out in a state of shock and panic. Paula Needham was naked. She collapsed to her chubby pink knees on the floor, completely disorientated, and screamed as she realised the building was on fire. Jasmine threw a large bath towel over her. Madden shut the door, bolted it from the inside and threw open the window. The fire brigade were in the service yard at the back of the shop.

'There are four of us!' Madden shouted down.

There was a low roof below them, then a ladder. Madden leapt first, then caught Natalie as she jumped. Jasmine held on to Paula as they sprang together. Fire exploded into the flotation tank room behind them. It was too late to look for anyone else. If Jeff Walker was anywhere in the building, he was beyond help.

Down in the service area, Paula stood shivering with the large bath towel wrapped around her and her body still dripping. Madden cautioned her. It was the first time in his life he had ever cautioned a naked woman in a public place, he thought to himself. She appeared stunned, but said nothing, and when they put her in a police car she just sat quietly, as though being arrested was an everyday occurence among New-Age therapy folk. Suddenly, her hands flew up to her neck, and she looked up at the burning building, remembering the pendant she had left hanging there on the towel rail.

It was the tiniest of details, but it was the image that would stay with Madden long after the embers were cold. She had nearly died and it was increasingly likely that her lover had tried to kill her, but for a brief, unchecked moment it was clear that she cherished that article above all else. Then, as she was driven away, Madden watched as she sank into the seat and did not look back, but just stared straight ahead, her thoughts at that moment beyond his comprehension.

47

Paula Needham sat motionless within the stark confines of the interview room, her piercing blue eyes fixed upon a spot on the wall directly in front of her, her blonde hair towelled dry but bedraggled. She was little more than a teenager in looks. Madden found it difficult to take his eyes off her hands. These were hands that healed, he told himself. Where was the universal energy now?

At first it seemed she was reluctant to talk. No amount of coaxing would get her to open her mouth. Even her hands remained tightly clenched. Madden and Jasmine faced her in the time-honoured fashion of accusers who had all the time in the world because they knew that everybody who had a story to tell sooner or later wanted to tell it.

'If you're thinking about protecting him,' Madden said, 'consider this. It was Jeff's intention to burn the shop down and you with it so you couldn't betray him. He had no scruples about killing Natalie either. So why not just think of yourself, Paula, and not him.'

Natalie hadn't seen what Jeff hit her with. From the fragments that had become embedded in the back of her head, it appeared to be a glass shelf. Jeff Walker was still missing. He wouldn't get far, of that Madden was certain.

Paula turned her gaze to him. She looked forlorn, a sad creature lost in a horrific maze of her own creation, one out of which there were only two exits. To lie or tell the truth. To keep the nightmare locked in or to unburden herself. Madden was in no doubt which exit she wanted to take. Coaxing her towards the right one was only a matter of patience.

Millington's visit and theirs had made her panic. Her story about seeing Bird at the bonfire had fallen to pieces. Like Humpty Dumpty it could not be put back together again. She knew that her lies had caught them out. There was no question in Madden's mind as to who had suggested she lie down in the flotation tank to calm down. Paula was always the weaker of the two links and Jeff knew it. Murder was always a tricky situation for one to control, but when two were involved it became even more difficult.

She was eerily calm as she unburdened herself. So willing to talk was she that Madden felt almost overhelmed as well as appalled by the evil that issued forth from these sweet lips. Occasionally she would lift her hands to her throat as though to feel for the heart-shaped pendant containing Jeff's picture and, realising it wasn't there, would carry on as if she had been freed of some terrible curse.

'He put a spell on me, you know.'

'This is the twenty-first century, Paula. People don't put spells on others.'

'But he did,' she said. 'He did.'

Madden recalled Holly Elder telling him that mankind didn't need Satan for evil to flow out into the world, that human beings were perfectly capable of being their own Satans.

'I loved him. I don't know why I did the things he asked me to. It was like – there was somebody else inside me doing the things he asked me to do, that it wasn't me. I know it was me, but – it just didn't seem that way. I want to explain it. I think maybe I loved him too much.'

If this was a defence of schizophrenia, it didn't wash. Nevertheless those words would stay with Madden a long time. It was a look down a long tunnel into a dark soul.

'Who killed Lavinia Roberts?' he asked her.

'He did. And I suppose I did.'

'You suppose?'

'Jeff said it was a test of our love. That was how he put it. He said he didn't want us just to be an ordinary couple, that we had to be an extraordinary couple. That was how he put it. An extraordinary couple had to be united in blood and that meant committing murder together.'

Madden observed Jasmine shifting uncomfortably in her seat. Paula spoke in such a cold-blooded matter-of-fact way and with a nervous smile playing on the contours of her mouth that it almost *did* seem to be someone else doing the explaining for her.

'We spoke about it after his attestation evening, when he took the oath,' she said. 'I was so proud of him, so in love with him I would have gone to the ends of the earth for him if he'd asked me to. I know that was wrong but he just seemed – so sure. So certain. He said there had to be proofs of love, that to love somebody wasn't enough. That love demanded sacrifices. That it wasn't enough for me just to love him, I had to prove that I loved him. He said he would marry me but I had to meet certain conditions.'

She wiped her hand across her eyes. It was difficult to tell if she was seeing the light or still in the darkness. Conditions? Sacrifices? Proofs of love? What kind of love was this, Madden wondered. Not the kind you got on Valentine cards. Jasmine remained poker-faced, sometimes shifting her weight to one side, sometimes to the other, sitting on her hands lest she was tempted to use them.

'You went along with that?' Jasmine asked, incredulous.

'I know how crazy it seems,' she said. 'Have you never loved anyone so much you would do anything for them? Anything to keep them? Jeff said he had all these previous girlfriends, a whole string of them, he used to torture me by telling me about them. I didn't want to know and yet I *did*, if you know what I mean. He said if I didn't do what he asked he would go back and sleep with one of them. I couldn't stand that. I really couldn't.'

Her face screwed up and she started to sob.

'Are you crying for the people you killed or for yourself?' Jasmine asked.

'Both,' Paula lied.

'We don't believe you.'

'I thought it would stop – I thought it would stop with one.' She pleaded for them to understand. 'Oh God, I'm sorry. I'm so sorry. If I'd never met him, I wouldn't be here. I wish I'd never met him.'

'You met him and you are here, Paula,' said Madden. 'Just tell us about Lavinia.'

They sent out for a cup of tea for her. She held it with two hands as she drank, shaking as she spoke.

'I'd told him about Mrs Roberts, that she used to do readings in the shop and how she got drunk and had been barred from coming there. Jeff said – said she was a useless person, old and washed up, that she should be our victim. That no one would miss her when she was gone.'

'Je-sus,' muttered Madden, tempted to interject. He wanted to tell her how much Lavinia Roberts meant to him, but now that they had prised open the oyster they weren't going to risk it clamming shut.

'Jeff went for a crystal ball reading from her to suss out the place and told me we should break in one night and kill her with a hammer and that would unite us. I didn't want to do it and I told him so, but he kept threatening to leave me and said if I didn't do it he would marry another girl, one of the previous girlfriends who were all still mad on him. I don't know what made me do it, and I felt physically sick afterwards. We broke in and she came downstairs. Jeff grabbed her and made me hit her with a hammer. I didn't hit her hard enough to kill her, I just – couldn't. I wanted to leave but by then it was too late. We had to go through with it. Jeff grabbed the hammer from me and kept hitting her. He was the one who killed her. I turned away, I couldn't watch.'

'You could have walked away from it much sooner,' said Madden. 'You could have walked away from it the moment Jeff suggested his sick crazy plan.'

'I know.'

'Why didn't you?'

'I couldn't. I wanted to but I couldn't. He made me.'

'Nobody makes anybody do anything.'

'He said—'

She broke off briefly and looked at Madden as though begging for his understanding.

'He said that if I did it it would prove how much I loved him and that we'd get engaged that night.'

She paused and looked long and hard at the ring on her finger, and finally tugged it off. She put it on the table in front of her. She stared at it bleakly. Its removal seemed to sever a tie. Or perhaps break a spell.

'We wore plastic hairnets,' she said, with a vestige of sick pride. 'Jeff said that fragments of hair could be left at a crime scene and that DNA could be extracted from roots. We wore plastic washing-up gloves, too. When you asked me to go round and visit the various tattoo studios with you, for the man you said you were looking for, I was pleased because I thought it would divert attention from us.'

Madden could no longer help himself. He had to say it. He leant on the table so hard that he felt the blood coursing through his hands.

'You killed a woman *I* liked!' he said to her. 'A woman I admired. A woman I knew when she was a girl, a woman who helped people, who comforted people, a person who was kind and compassionate and gentle. That was the woman you killed, Paula. The woman you battered to death with a hammer because your boyfriend threatened to sleep around or leave you if you didn't, the woman *you* might have saved if you'd said no. The woman who would still be alive today if you weren't so—'

He tried to think of the word to describe her. But it didn't exist.

'Pitiful,' he said with barely disguised anger.

Jasmine put a restraining hand on his arm. Madden wasn't sure how or where he was going to stop. He felt mad, so mad he could have struck her. The job got you like that sometimes. But you had to be better than the criminals, better than the people who sat in front of you and admitted deeds that were beyond imagining.

Paula retreated briefly. He didn't want her to do that. As fervently as he wanted to leave the taking of this statement to someone else, he needed her to carry on. He had come across psychologically destructive relationships aplenty but this one plumbed depths beyond his wildest dreams.

'Tell us about the Albanian boy,' asked Jasmine, her voice cold as ice.

'Dana Vllasi.' Madden gave the child a name.

'I didn't know his name,' said Paula. 'I didn't want to know. I didn't have anything to do with his death.'

It was a lie. Madden knew it, Jasmine knew it, and Paula knew it too, even though she was trying to block it out, to apportion blame.

'I think you did it, Paula,' said Madden. 'I think the second test of your love had to be more challenging than the first. Don't you see?'

'No, no!' she said, scared.

'Were you in the room when Jeff did it?'

'Jeff had already planned it, another murder, to make our love "special" as he called it,' she blurted out incautiously. 'He said it was a test, that I had to prove how much I loved him by committing a murder on my own, that he wouldn't help and guide me. I said I couldn't, not a child, but he threatened to leave me again and told me there was an old girlfriend who wanted to sleep with him, and that if I didn't do what he wanted, he would sleep with her and make love to her and that he would punish me by telling me everything about it. I couldn't bear it and agreed. And anyway he said I'd been involved in one murder and that if I didn't go along with it he'd make sure I got into trouble.'

'And you call that love?' Jasmine said stonily.

'I did then.'

'Then was only a few days ago, Paula. Not a lifetime ago.'

'He said he'd been with this Albanian prostitute. I was angry, furious. He said that she had a son, that she was an illegal immigrant, and that it would never be reported. He came back one evening after the shop was shut and I let him in the back entrance.

He had the boy. He told me I had to drown him, but I told him I couldn't. I left the flat and I don't know what happened after that. I wanted to run away, I really did. From Jeff, from everything.'

'What stopped you?' asked Madden. 'You had two legs and a brain, Paula.'

'It was too late,' she said. 'Too late.'

'Too late to do what? Leave him? Turn him in? Tell him enough was enough? Walk into the police station and confess? You had a lot of choices, Paula.'

'I know,' she said.

'Go on.'

'That's all,' she said.

'No, I don't think it is all,' said Madden. 'I think you stayed in the flat and that you did it in front of Jeff.'

'I didn't!' she cried. 'I didn't!'

'We know that you put a towel over the boy's face because you didn't want to have to look at his face.'

'I didn't,' she said. 'I wasn't in the flat. I left it.'

'So who did?'

'Jeff did,' she said.

'How do you know if you weren't there?'

'It must have been him.'

'You think Jeff cared that much? I don't see Jeff doing it, frankly. But I see you doing it, Paula. I see you not wanting to do what Jeff asked you to do and covering Dana's face. That was your test. Isn't that how it was?'

'No,' she wept, shaking her head.

'Like you did with your own daughter, Jacqueline.'

Paula let out a scream and covered her own face with her hands. She shook her head back and forth repeatedly.

'You're an accomplished liar,' Madden told her. 'This is just another one, isn't it? To lessen your role. To shift the blame on to Jeff. You took that child's life while he stood over you and watched, isn't that how it was, Paula?'

The head-shaking went on, even when eventually she removed

her hands after a period of five minutes. Five minutes during which she couldn't even look at them. She had covered her own face as surely as she had covered Dana's, Madden thought.

'You're going to prison, Paula. For a very, very long time for what you've done. What might help just a little is if you face up to what you've done now, to be completely honest. Start burying the truth now and in years to come you might not even be able to find it, no matter how deep down inside your soul you dig. You'll just rot for the rest of your life in limbo, your conscience never clear. Don't you want to do that now? Clear your conscience?'

After a long silent period of contemplation, she looked at him and nodded.

'Good,' said Madden.

'It's difficult – to talk about,' she said.

'You did it, you can talk about it,' he told her. 'Did you have anything to do with what Jeff did to the body afterwards?'

'No,' she answered quickly, and probably truthfully, he thought. 'I only found out about that later, when it was in the paper.'

'You're sure you knew nothing about that?'

She turned away as she spoke, stared at the wall again.

'Jeff said that he was an illegal immigrant's child, that he was worthless, and that I had to do it. He said it was too late to go back, that if I didn't he would have to let the boy go and we would both probably be arrested. So I – I put a towel round the boy's head and drowned him in the sink in the treatment room so that I didn't have to look at his face. Jeff took the body. I don't know what he did with it. I had nothing to do with – what he did afterwards. I swear that.'

'You know what was done? What your lover did?'

She nodded, tight-lipped.

Madden took a deep breath and said, 'Yet you stayed with him even after that? After you'd discovered he cut out that kid's heart with a knife.'

'How could I leave?' she begged him to understand. 'How could I leave then?'

Yes, how could she have left? Two murders into a relationship forged in the bowels of hell and they were chained to each other for ever, conjoined twins of evil, linked by guilt, blood and – it had to be given its name – human sacrifice.

'I was horrified that he could have done such a thing,' she said. 'He told me he staged a break-in at the shop and stole some things which included a ceremonial dagger because it made him feel powerful, but that's all he said he wanted it for. He believed that because he was training to be a policeman, he would never be caught. He used to say that he was protected. I don't know what he meant by that. He didn't like it when I asked him too many questions.'

Jasmine got up and left the interview room. Madden switched off the tape. He went out into the corridor after her. He found her crying. It was the first time he had ever seen Jasmine weep. Properly weep, that is.

'She's a mother,' Jasmine said. 'It just got to me. Listening to her. That's all.'

'I know. And we're police officers, Jaz, and we can't get emotional at a time like this. We have a job to do.'

'I don't know that I can finish this one,' she said.

'You want to be relieved?'

She took a few moments to compose herself.

'I got angry too,' said Madden. 'I said more than I should have done. We're only human. You'll hear a lot worse in your career. Where's that steely girl I used to work with?'

'Metal fatigue,' she quipped.

'I want you to finish it with me. If you can. When we find Jeff Walker, we've got to listen to it all again.'

'I don't mind that,' she said. 'I can cope with that. But a mother who—'

'Who kills a child? Mothers have killed children from time immemorial, Jaz. So have fathers. In my culture, in your culture, in every culture. Sometimes in this job you just have to suspend your horror. At least for a little while. You can let it all out later but right now we're doing fine.'

She dried her eyes. He patted her on the back.

They went back into the interview room. Paula was sweeping back her hair with her hands, as though conscious of her appearance. She stared at them as they sat down. She knew the worst was to come and she was ready for it. Ready to sit down and explain why and how a young mother could kill her own offspring for the man she loved. If she had intended blaming Jacqueline's death on her lover, that intention had long been swept away. This girl, Madden reminded himself, had not only killed her daughter but she had covered it up, lied about it, and God knew what else. If Jeff Walker was looking for tests of love, she had passed with flying colours.

Madden sat down with Jasmine just two feet away from him, and as he did so he cupped a comforting, reassuring hand over that of his colleague. Jasmine, he could tell, was grateful. This interview wasn't easy for either of them. Paula wasn't the only one going through purgatory. At the end of the day, they would have to bear it too. And for as long. The images of these bodies implanted on their minds, remembered smells, the cold words and the tortured reasoning, three lives reduced to paperwork for use at a trial, the inevitable acres of newsprint searching for the psyche behind the psychotic. And then filed away at the end of it all, as though you could file away horror in your head. All done and dusted, the expression went. Murder never was, and this one especially could never be. This was for reliving, in the coldest, darkest hours of the bleakest dawn.

'Tell us about Jacqueline,' Madden said.

He told me that there was one ultimate sacrifice I had to make to prove my love for him, and that he would not marry me unless I made it. Her statement went on. *He said I had to kill my own daughter. I pleaded with him not to ask me that, but he made similar threats to before. He also said I would be charged with murder if I did not obey him. He told me that as Jacqueline was a child of rape he had no love for her and had no desire to bring her up, and that we would have children of our own. He promised me that, that if I killed Jacqueline he would give me three children. I could not tell him that I had lied, that Jacqueline was not a child of rape but my employer Richard Blance's daughter. I was scared of what he would do. I drowned Jacqueline and wrapped a towel round her head so I did not have to see her face. I would like to say that I did not feel it was me doing this thing. It was as though somebody else inside me was doing it. We put her in the boot of the car and I made Jeff promise he would not harm her body. He said he would not as she was 'special', and that he did not want to upset me. He beat me and tied me to a tree at Lewes. He said it was what he had done to the other mother. It was his idea I should call DI Madden and tell him I had seen Michael Bird there, the tattooed man who was a suspect. We did not know he was already dead. Jeff drove back to Brighton and I was to say he had remained at home studying. He told me that on the way he had put Jacqueline's body under a bridge. I have been asked why I did all these things and I can only say that I am deeply sorry, that it seemed to be someone else inside of me doing these things. Jeff had a hold over me. I would like to explain it but I can't. I think that I loved him too much. Signed, Paula Needham. 6 November.*

Madden read and reread that last section many times. It took only a minute but that minute took no account of the tears and the emotional wrangling which had accompanied the taking of it. He remembered an adage about gods and monsters, that the same qualities which went to make one also made the other.

Enough, thought Madden. He had travelled a river of poison. It was time to set foot on the shore. He put the statement away in his desk until morning.

There was a message for him. Clara was working late at the gallery and had heard on the news about the fire and the arrest and wanted to know what had happened. He called her.

'We just had an art show,' she said. 'I'm still here. I thought if you had the time maybe we could meet for a drink. There are things we have to talk about.'

'I could do with a drink,' he told her. 'I'm not sure I could handle any heavy stuff.'

'You sound drained.'

'I am.'

'Okay, a drink and we'll handle the heavy stuff another time?'

'That sounds good.'

He put the phone down. Jasmine was with him. Millington was waiting to see them. There was a loose end and it was called Jeff Walker but as every police force in the country was now on the lookout for him, Madden reckoned he could afford a little relaxation. He'd earned it. It wasn't every day you rescued two people from a burning building, got a confession that helped your career, and proved to your super that he was wrong to suspend you. That merited a drink. It wasn't every day either that you brushed up against something you could properly call human evil, and he needed to wash it out of his system.

'You're going to see her?' Jasmine asked.

'She wants to meet. To talk. That's all.'

'I thought after all we'd been through tonight, Steve, we might spend the rest of it together? Find some way to celebrate?'

'That's what I want.'

'That's what I want too,' she said.

'What Clara and I have to discuss is important,' said Madden.

'All right then,' Jasmine was planning it out, 'so after you've been round to see Clara and talked about whatever it is you have to talk about, maybe we could meet up and have a drink together and go back to your place?'

'Complex lives,' Madden said.

'Whose?'

'I was just thinking about what we've listened to. What happens when people's emotions get out of control.'

'Are you suggesting that we don't have things under control?'

'No. But then when Paula met Jeff, I don't imagine she ever dreamt that two years down the line she would commit murder. Maybe there's something in all of us, Jaz, a potential for evil. To make our own devil. Like the one Lavinia felt when she met Jeff Walker.'

His mind went back to the last time he had seen her alive.

There had been warmth and comfort in that small house at the top of Southover Street, an aura of altruism around Lavinia Roberts. It was a house from which evil fled, and evil had indeed fled after her murder. It was a place where, if you tried hard enough, you could still believe in childhood innocence, in dreams. In magic. Like a womb, it was the sort of house in which you felt protected, inviolate even. Unfortunately, whatever unconscious spell Lavinia Roberts cast on the house over the span of her life was not strong enough to ward off the horror that eventually came.

When the Devil walked up Southover Street, all the love she had shown in her life was not strong enough to fight it.

'She was,' said Madden, 'the most remarkable woman I ever met.'

48

He found Clara at the gallery. There had been a party. Crumb-covered plates and unwashed glasses littered the place. The occasion had been the promotion of a new artist, whose work adorned the walls. Madden didn't profess to understand it. The party had moved on, and Clara was left to clean up the mess. She was doing that by sitting on her own at the desk with a glass of white wine in front of her, her umpteenth it seemed from her manner.

'Can anyone join in?' he asked her.

'Pull up a chair,' she said.

'Good night?'

'Great night. And yours?'

He told her about the escape from Hubble Bubble, how they were still searching for Jeff Walker, how Lavinia Roberts had been right after all, and how he was the greatest detective in Brighton. She put out a hand and gently stroked his cheek.

'You need a drink,' she said.

'Warm white wine?'

'Yes, pretty ghastly, isn't it? Shall we go to the Basketmakers?'

He helped her pile the dishes and glasses into the sink in the back kitchen of the gallery, she locked up, and they went round the corner to the pub. Washing up, she said, was no way of celebrating anything. He had a pint, she had a fruit juice.

'Celebrations are a bit premature. Walker's still on the run but he can't get far.'

'To think I met him. He seemed such a pleasant boy. Who would think.'

'Yes. Who would think.'

'How did he ever get into the police force?'

'We'll take anybody these days.' Madden made light of it.

'What did I tell you? Trust your instincts. Lavinia was more talented than any of you thought, If you made one mistake, Steve, it was to not have *enough* faith in her.'

She wouldn't stop at that. When she was drunk, she was lovely.

'You saw the obvious, a person with shaven head and tattoos and evil eyes, but she saw through somebody with blond hair and blue eyes and a nice smile, she saw deep, Steve, deeper than any of you did. She was clever.'

Madden got her point.

'If I made one mistake, Clara, it was to want to believe in her too much. What she said about Jason – if she was right about the other, she might just have been right about him.'

'She might have been a gifted clairvoyant, Steve. But that doesn't mean she was a good spiritualist. They're totally different things. Spiritualism relies on there being life after death.'

'I know.'

He stared down into his beer.

'All the same, it's comforting to think about, isn't it.'

'Yes. Shame somebody can't find incontravert – incontroverse – what am I saying?'

'I think you're a drunk woman trying to say incontrovertible evidence.'

'Proof,' she said.

'You're probably right,' he admitted. 'Lavinia gave me comfort, or tried to give me comfort. All the same, Clara, there's nothing I wouldn't give to have Jason back again. If just for an hour. Just to talk to him.'

'Oh stop it,' she said, squeezing his hand gently. 'Don't you think I feel the same?'

There was a topic they hadn't discussed yet. It was only a matter of time. She brought it up.

'I'm sorry about Clive.'

'He told you?'

'We had a huge row. I told him he shouldn't have gone to the police station and embarrassed you like that.'

'I can take it on the chin,' he said. 'In fact, I nearly did.'

'It wasn't right, Steve.'

'He was only a husband protecting his interests. I'd have done the same if I'd been in his position.'

'I'm not his *interests*, Steve. I'm a woman, with my own life, I can make my own decisions.'

'Like you did to leave me for him?'

'Yes.' She qualified that. 'After all, I only came round because you'd been shot in the shoulder and I was concerned about you. How is the shoulder by the way?'

'Great agony,' he lied.

'Good. It serves you right for being reckless and putting yourself in these situations.'

'Like the one we nearly put ourselves in?'

'What do you mean?'

'That night we found the boy. You and I were ready to go to bed together. Let's not fool ourselves, Clara. It probably would have happened the other night too if Jasmine hadn't interrupted us again.'

'Yes, she is rather good at that, isn't she,' said Clara. 'I think she must have very highly developed antennae.'

'In a way, I feel I did wrong.' Madden expressed some contrition. 'I can't help feeling I manipulated you a bit.'

'You didn't manipulate me.'

'I manipulated your affections then.'

'My effations are incaptible of being manipulated.'

'How's the fruit juice?'

'Sobering,' she said. 'Seriously, Steve, do you really think if I hadn't wanted to, I wouldn't have suggested it either?'

'I just don't want to create problems for you, Clara. Or for me. Though I care more about you. You made your choice. Maybe it would be better if we didn't see each other at least quite so often.'

'Is that your way of telling me to be a good wife?' she said somewhat acerbically. 'Good little wife has to go back to her new home, behave herself, and minister to the needs of her sexually-challenged husband?'

Her smile could have grated cheese as she said it. He wanted to kiss that mouth, to take away the anger. To return her to the soft, non-bitter, caring, gentle Clara he knew.

'Is that how you see him? Sexually challenged?'

'Don't get me wrong. I love him, but he's one of these men who thinks that when a woman's over forty she isn't interested in sex any more.'

'How bad can things get?'

'Let's talk,' she said, 'about how *good* they could get?'

Madden looked at the pub clock. Jasmine would be waiting for him outside his house. He had promised her it would only be a quick chat with Clara. She had patience, but it wasn't infinite.

'Let's go for a walk on the beach,' she said.

'It's cold.'

'We can keep each other warm.'

They drank up and strolled down towards the beach. Madden wondered where Jeff Walker was. His mobile was switched off. He couldn't go far. He didn't have his car. On foot he could hide out in a deserted house somewhere, or make it out into the countryside and squirrel himself away in a barn until dawn, or hitch-hike somewhere further afield. Maybe at this moment he was dying his hair black somewhere. Madden doubted he could stay undiscovered for long. Lord Lucan was the exception, not the rule. His fear was that Walker could kill again. His hope was that without his willing apprentice, the boy was nothing. The French had an expression for it. *Folie à deux*.

Clara took his arm and snuggled up close to him. There was a bitingly cold wind coming in off the Channel and it blew her tousled hair across the bridge of her nose.

'I didn't tell you,' she said. 'Clive is away on business. A conference in Paris. Company accounting for the new century or something boring like that.'

'He trusts you? On your own?'

'Why shouldn't he?'

'What did you tell him? About us?'

'I told him that as we both lived and worked in the same town it was impossible not to meet occasionally, that I wasn't going to be dictated to by him, that we occasionally would want to meet to visit Jason's grave together, and that if he didn't trust me there wasn't any point in being married. So there.'

'How did he react to that?'

'I also said to him that if he ever threatened you again, I would leave him.'

'Wow.'

She turned to face him, swept her hair back from in front of her eyes and looked straight into his. They kissed, and all that old familiar electricity ran through them, as though their bodies were too dusty old implements freshly charged. He hugged her. She was his Clara. Nobody could ever take her away from him. This wasn't the time to stop and think what he was getting into. This was simply the time to remember what they had lost. A part of it would always be irretrievable. Madden wasn't stupid enough to think that it could return to being the same. It couldn't. But just for a moment, on Brighton beach, in the dark, the illicit bonding felt good.

He was feeling guilty about Jasmine, but he couldn't tell Clara that. It would have ruined everything. Maybe her antennae had detected this happening.

'Are you going to invite me back?' she asked.

'I can't tonight. I've still got a job to do. There's a psychopath out here on the loose, remember?'

He felt horrible about lying. Especially to her.

'There's only one detective who can possibly catch him, is that what you're saying?'

'If he's found tonight, I'm going to get called out, and I don't want that to spoil a great evening.'

'Tomorrow night, then? Clive doesn't get back until Friday.'

'Okay. Tomorrow night.'

'Jasmine-free?'

'It'll be like old times,' he said.

He drove her back to the Marina, they kissed again in the car.

He felt like a teenager. Then she bounced out, waved to him, and disappeared into the concrete jungle. He tried to get Jasmine on the phone to apologise for being late but she had switched it off, irresponsibly he thought.

He was driving home when his phone rang. He thought it might be her. He pulled in and answered it.

'Jaz?' he said.

'Hello, Steve.'

Madden recognised the voice straight away. He looked at the number on the screen. Jeff was calling on his mobile.

'Jeff. Where are you?'

'You don't expect me to tell you that, do you? Anyway, just as soon as you finish this call, you'll get onto the phone company and trace it and pinpoint me to the nearest few square yards. By that time I'll be far away.'

'Look, I don't need to do that,' Madden said.

'No. Is there an alternative?'

'Yes. We could meet and chat. Just you and me.'

Jeff gave a derisory laugh.

'Oh, come on, Steve,' he said. 'You're more intelligent than that.'

'So why are you ringing me?'

'To chat.'

'Okay, let's chat.'

'What shall we chat about?'

'I don't know,' said Madden. 'What do you want to chat about?'

'How lonely it feels,' said Jeff.

'It doesn't have to feel that way,' said Madden.

'Remember how I told you my father never spoke to me. About the day I came back from school after being bullied. I want to say – I want to say, Steve, that I wish I'd had a father like you.'

Jeff's voice faltered. Madden tried to keep his direct.

'Why do you say that, Jeff?'

'I might not have turned out the way I am. Having control over people is a real sexual turn-on you know, did I ever tell you that?'

'No. I don't think the subject ever came up.'

'I never had any as a child. Any real power. That's why I joined the police force. I don't suppose what's happened is going to look very good in my PDP.'

'No, Jeff, I don't think it is.'

'Oh well, that's one bad apple weeded out. Sorry to mix metaphors.'

'That's okay, Jeff. You mix metaphors all you like.'

'Don't patronise me.'

'I wasn't. I was just trying to think of things to say. It would be much better, you know, if we could meet face to face. Have a real chat.'

'You mean like father and son?'

'I wasn't thinking that.'

'I was,' said Jeff. 'Hey, she was right, that old bird, wasn't she? About me. Means she might have been right about your son too.'

'Let's not talk about that,' said Madden.

'What are we going to talk about, then?'

'I don't know.' Madden felt that they had gone full circle. 'What do you want to talk about?'

'I think I'm going to go soon,' said Jeff.

'Why? Just when it seemed we were getting along.'

'I'll see you around,' said Jeff.

'Why go?'

'Thank you for being a friend, Steve,' said Jeff. 'I never had any, you know.'

And then he hung up.

Madden called Millington straight away.

'I just had Jeff Walker phone me up from his mobile, sir,' he told him. 'You'll be able to trace where it came from. If you find him, call me. If not, don't bother me till morning. Frankly, one sick bastard is enough for a night.'

He arrived home only to find a note put through his letter box. It said, *Got fed up. Didn't we have a great night? Can't wait for the next time we do heroics together. If Walker is found tonight and we get called out of our beds and see the dawn, how about an early breakfast together?*

Madden crumpled up the note in annoyance. He tried Jasmine again but her phone was still switched off. How did she expect to be called out if she switched her phone off? He tried her home number but clearly she wasn't back yet.

How had he got into this? He poured himself a glass of beer and nursed it while sitting alone in his living room. He thought of ringing Clara, but it seemed cheap. He thought more of both Clara and Jasmine than to resort to such desperation. If there was any night he didn't want to be alone, it was this one. Maybe, he thought, he wouldn't have to be alone. The phone would ring and he would spend the small dark hours face to face with a blond killer who had a sunny smile and looked as though he hadn't started shaving, yet one who was responsible for the deaths of three people and the attempted murders of two more. And before he had even reached the age of twenty-four. Madden wasn't sure what made him feel sadder. The fact he had been so completely taken in by the youth, or the fact that he was secretly praying for work to drag him away from that empty house.

He sank the beer and poured himself another. He watched a bit of television but it went over his head. The adrenalin surge that had kept him going for much of the day was still in his veins but it had nowhere to go. That was how the job got you sometimes. You wanted to talk about it, to talk the horror out of your system, to try and rationalise the awful words you had been forced to listen to.

. . . we should be an extraordinary couple, which meant being united by blood. He said that love wasn't enough between two people, that it had to be proved in some way. That there had to be proof of love, that it demanded sacrifices.

You had to come home to the awful banality of your home life with sentiments like that ringing in your ears.

He switched off the lights and turned up the heating because it felt cold, and went to bed. He thought of reading but he just wanted to shut himself off from the world. At least until that phone rang. Two or three hours, he thought, give me two or three hours. He reckoned he would be fresher then.

He woke up half an hour later, feeling cold still. There was a draught. It wasn't coming from his bedroom window, it was coming from another room in the house. Wearing just his boxers, he stepped out onto the landing and saw that the door to Jason's room was ajar and moving slightly. A chill ran down his spine. He pushed it open.

It was as though everything inside of him drained out. His heart beat fast until it felt as though it was going to burst. Reason fled. For the boy was standing there, in the corner, against the window, the red football scarf around his neck, and he was looking – or so it seemed – straight at Madden. And he seemed to be smiling.

Madden found himself locked to the spot, could not move for what seemed an eternity. He thought he might be dreaming.

'Jason?' he said.

He would never know why he said it. He didn't believe in ghosts. He didn't believe in the dead coming back. That was the trouble. He wanted to believe, and in that eerie, frozen and unreal moment it was that need which almost drove him to accept the impossible.

Then he turned on the light.

He crumpled to his knees, suffused with repugnance and feeling nauseous.

'Oh God, no!' he cried.

Madden almost fell down the stairs. He punched out Jasmine's home number on the phone. This time she answered.

'Jaz, get over here,' he wept.

'What's wrong, Steve?'

'Just get over here.'

He put the receiver down and waited for her. She arrived twenty minutes later. He let her in. She saw the state of shock he was in.

'I thought – for one stupid, horrible moment, Jaz, that it was – that it was him.'

'Who are you talking about, Steve?'

'I thought it was him. Oh Jesus, Jaz, I thought it was him.'

Jasmine ran upstairs. She didn't scream. Jasmine wasn't that sort. It would, anyway, have been very unprofessional. She just came back downstairs, kissed him, gave him a great big hug, and then did the necessary phoning.

Madden never went back upstairs that night, throughout it all. He didn't need to. He knew what he had seen. There was a metal clothes hook fixed to the wall by the open window. One end of Jason's red football scarf had been tied tightly round it, the other end knotted and wound around Jeff Walker's neck. Jeff was still upright though his legs were somewhat crumpled and twisted beneath his suspended body. One set of fingers was locked into the folds of the scarf as though he had tried in the last seconds of his life to ease the agony of the restriction. The other arm hung limp by his side. His head lolled obscenely to the side, the skin purple, the tongue protruding.

It was the angle of the protruding tongue that Madden had mistaken for a smile.

Holly Elder had said that the killer was signalling his desire to have control over him, his life and his emotions.

Jeff Walker had done just that, right up until the moment he drew his final, choking breath. The Magician had played his last trick.

49

Madden was sitting at the boardwalk café a few weeks later. It was a surprisingly mild December day. There was no wind to speak of and the sea appeared unruffled. A seagull swooped overhead and narrowly missed defecating in his lager. It was that kind of day, when you praised small mercies.

Things were good. Too good. They shouldn't have been, but then if he didn't count his blessings nobody else was going to come along and do it for him. He had enjoyed Clara's company a few times since. Neither of them had felt guilty. So far he had not been accosted by a bald man wearing a Rolex watch, as a clairvoyant might have predicted. Clive didn't know. What he didn't know, didn't hurt. They were careful. Not so careful as to make the situation tense and unbearable, because there always had to be a little bit of risk to make it exciting. At least they had started to play by a set of rules. That was how order was kept. How society functioned. Responsible adults, he thought to himself in a rare philosophical moment, enjoying the fruits of irresponsibility. It was when you lost the rule book and crossed the line that life became chaotic and unpredictable.

Jasmine asked nothing. Questioned nothing. In fact, for the last few weeks she hadn't brought up Clara's name once. And she had slept with him, and it had been good. She still didn't do romance and neither did he, and that was the way he was determined to keep it. He wasn't sure how long it would all last. Like the south-coast weather, all things were subject to change. But while it lasted, he was going to enjoy life. You didn't get a second shot at it. When you were dead, you couldn't come back.

Since that night, he had not been able to set foot in Jason's room. He kept the door shut. It had been defiled. He had no doubt he would get over it. Clara had helped him. So had Jasmine. To have two understanding women in your life was a blessing not bestowed on many, he thought. Maybe they were two more than he deserved.

So he shouldn't really have had the need to look at another woman. But this time he couldn't help it. The two lithe young ladies stepping across the shingle as they made their way towards the pier were followed rather incongruously by a tall, stout and bluff gentleman in a sports jacket and flannels and carrying an umbrella. He called over to them.

'Natalie? Holly?'

They came over and said hello. Professor Grimaldi shook his hand.

'Perfect weather,' he said. 'For doing no police work.'

'No doubt down to a bit of witchcraft,' Madden quipped.

'High pressure,' said Holly. 'Sorry to disappoint you.'

'I didn't know you two knew each other?' he said to Natalie.

And then he noticed it. She was wearing a diamond round her neck on a chain. It was large and round and seemed to catch the turquoise of the sea. He was almost afraid to ask. But he did.

'I just got her back yesterday,' Natalie told him. 'What do you think? Isn't it *beautiful*?'

Madden touched it.

'Look after it.'

Sadly, it was all he could think of to say. It seemed woefully inadequate.

'She will never leave me,' said Natalie. 'Never. Mum will always be with me, Mr Madden. Catching the light. Isn't that a wonderful way of staying close to somebody you love?'

'Yes. Quite wonderful, Natalie. I didn't think you and Holly and the Professor knew each other.'

'Just recently,' she said. 'Guess what? I decided not to become a Hindu. I've joined the Coven of the Celtic Moon. I'm becoming a witch.'

'That's nice,' said Madden.

'Thank you for that recommendation about Ratty's Bar,' Professor Grimaldi said. 'We're holding an open coven meeting there tonight, in one of the back archways.'

'Why don't you come along?' Holly asked him.

'No thanks. I've had enough New-Age stuff. I think I'm going to have an old-age kind of a day,' he said. 'You know, maybe have a quiet pint somewhere, go home, put my feet up. Why don't you all join me for a drink, though?'

'We'd love to,' said Natalie.

'But we've got to go and set things up at Ratty's,' Holly explained. 'For tonight. Are you sure you won't come?'

'Quite sure. But thanks for the invite.' He turned to Natalie. She was fondling the diamond with her fingers. He hoped that chain was strong. You couldn't replace a stone like that. 'How's Richard?'

She shrugged.

'All over,' she said. 'We're getting a divorce.'

'I'm sorry to hear that.'

'Life's about that,' said Natalie. 'Renewal.'

'Sometime's life is about forgiveness.'

'Sometimes you can't,' she said. 'You have to move on. You can't stand still, Mr Madden.'

'It's funny. That's what your mother said to me.'

'We're very alike.'

'Yes,' said Madden. 'You are. Well, don't let me keep you.'

The three of them walked off in the direction of Ratty's Bar as though blown by some mysterious breeze that only they could feel behind them. Madden stood up and wondered if the same breeze could propel him in a different direction. He *was* moving on, letting go of the past. Slowly, in his own time. He picked up a pebble and threw it as far as he could. It made a soft splash in the sea. He turned and realised that Jason could never forgive him because Jason had moved on too.

It was time he accepted that.